continued . . .

continued . . .

Much Ado in the Moonlight

"A consummate storyteller . . . Will keep the reader on the edge of their seat, unable to put the book down until the very last word."

—ParaNormal Romance Reviews

Dreams of Stardust

"Kurland weaves another fabulous read with just the right amounts of laughter, romance, and fantasy."

—Affaire de Coeur

A Garden in the Rain

"Kurland . . . consistently delivers the kind of stories readers dream about. Don't miss this one."

—The Oakland (MI) Press

From This Moment On

"A disarming blend of romance, suspense, and heartwarming humor, this book is romantic comedy at its best."

—Publishers Weekly

Titles by Lynn Kurland

STARDUST OF YESTERDAY

A DANCE THROUGH TIME

THIS IS ALL I ASK

THE VERY THOUGHT OF YOU

ANOTHER CHANCE TO DREAM

THE MORE I SEE YOU

IF I HAD YOU

MY HEART STOOD STILL

FROM THIS MOMENT ON

A GARDEN IN THE RAIN

DREAMS OF STARDUST

MUCH ADO IN THE MOONLIGHT

WHEN I FALL IN LOVE

WITH EVERY BREATH

TILL THERE WAS YOU

ONE ENCHANTED EVENING

ONE MAGIC MOMENT

ALL FOR YOU

ROSES IN MOONLIGHT

The Novels of the Nine Kingdoms

STAR OF THE MORNING

THE MAGE'S DAUGHTER

PRINCESS OF THE SWORD

A TAPESTRY OF SPELLS

SPELLWEAVER

GIFT OF MAGIC

DREAMSPINNER

RIVER OF DREAMS

Anthologies

THE CHRISTMAS CAT
(with Julie Beard, Barbara Bretton, and Jo Beverley)

CHRISTMAS SPIRITS
(with Casey Claybourne, Elizabeth Bevarly, and Jenny Lykins)

VEILS OF TIME
(with Maggie Shayne, Angie Ray, and Ingrid Weaver)

OPPOSITES ATTRACT
(with Elizabeth Bevarly, Emily Carmichael, and Elda Minger)

LOVE CAME JUST IN TIME

A KNIGHT'S VOW
(with Patricia Potter, Deborah Simmons, and Glynnis Campbell)

TAPESTRY
(with Madeline Hunter, Sherrilyn Kenyon, and Karen Marie Moning)

TO WEAVE A WEB OF MAGIC
(with Patricia A. McKillip, Sharon Shinn, and Claire Delacroix)

THE QUEEN IN WINTER
(with Sharon Shinn, Claire Delacroix, and Sarah Monette)

A TIME FOR LOVE

Specials

TO KISS IN THE SHADOWS

Lynn Kurland

River of Dreams

BERKLEY SENSATION, NEW YORK

THE BERKLEY PUBLISHING GROUP
Published by the Penguin Group
Penguin Group (USA) LLC
375 Hudson Street, New York, New York 10014

USA • Canada • UK • Ireland • Australia • New Zealand • India • South Africa • China

penguin.com

A Penguin Random House Company

RIVER OF DREAMS

This book is an original publication of The Berkley Publishing Group.

Berkley Sensation trade paperback ISBN: 978-0-425-26282-5

An application to register this book for cataloging has been submitted to the Library of Congress.

PUBLISHING HISTORY
Berkley Sensation trade paperback edition / January 2014

PRINTED IN THE UNITED STATES OF AMERICA

10 9 8 7 6 5 4 3 2 1

Cover art by Dan Craig.
Cover design by George Long.
Map illustration copyright © 2012 by Tara Larsen Chang.

The Nine Kingdoms

Aigeann Sea

Riamh

Jor Neroche

Diarmailt

Penrhyn

× Well

NEROCHE

Chagailt   Gilean

AIM

Gobhann

Bère

Angesand

Lismòr

Melksham Island

Istaur

M. I.

Bay of Sonasach

Sonasach

Diore

MEITH

Shettlestoune

WICHWEALD

One

There were only five great libraries of note in the Nine Kingdoms. Tor Neroche boasted one, especially when its noble collections were augmented by those at the palace of Chagailt. The
library of Buidseachd found itself firmly on that list, of course,
due simply to the number and variety of the tomes to be found in
the bowels of the magic-slathered castle in Beinn òrain.

Faodail in Gairn required an arduous trek in order to reach its
well-tended and jealously guarded shelves, but scholars through
the ages had found the journey to be a fair price to pay for the
opportunity to linger in a place of such seclusion where they might
read in peace. The library at the university at Lismòr contained,
arguably, a collection of the finest and most extensive scholarly
works available.

But the greatest of them all was the library of Eòlas, in Diarmailt.

The sheer number of books housed there was staggering, as was the depth and breadth of the topics those books contained. A small army of librarians patrolled the hallways and supervised the reading chambers to keep those granted entrance not only supplied with what they had come seeking but to keep the more obstreperous consumers of words on their best behavior.

Most only saw the lower floors where the lesser tomes were housed for perusal by the unwashed masses. The collections became more exclusive—and progressively more hazardous—as the stairs wound upward, until the discriminating peruser of fine manuscripts would find himself on the most exclusive floor of all.

In Perilous Collections.

Aisling of Bruadair stood with her back against the exquisite wooden paneling on that uppermost floor in the great library of Eòlas, looked at the dozen soldiers standing there with arrows and swords pointed her way, and wondered just how in the world she had managed to get herself in her current straits.

Finding herself completely out of her depth had become a terrible habit. That sort of thing had begun almost three fortnights ago when she had been plucked out of her uncomfortable life as an unwilling weaver, dressed as a lad, and then shoved into a carriage that had carried her off to places she had never dreamed she might see for herself. Her task had been straightforward: find a mercenary to save her country from an evil usurper. With the added incentive of a death sentence awaiting her if she didn't find a lad to hoist a sword in Bruadair's defense within a certain amount of time, she had continued her quest with all due haste through the western half of the Nine Kingdoms. Her companion for the most of that time had been the man currently standing next to her, trying to look harmless.

In truth, he had no reason to look guilty. They had arrived outside the walls of Eòlas at dawn, hidden their steed, then walked through the gates as nothing more than simple travelers seeking enlightenment, which they were. They had gotten inside the library, she had gawked briefly at the seemingly infinite number of books, then they had set about their business of looking for things to aid them.

Or, rather, things to aid her. The truth was, she had recently come to believe that everything she had been told about her home-land was absolute rubbish. She had to know the truth, because she had the feeling her life depended on it.

Unfortunately, they hadn't been inside the library an hour before they realized that they had attracted the attention of a few well-garbed library officials. Then, as seemed to be her wont of late, Aisling had found herself thrown from one piece of peril directly into the jaws of another.

Because there was apparently nothing quite as dangerous in the country of Diarmailt as a feisty librarian.

The librarian standing in front of them presently, the head librarian as he had identified himself pointedly, was proof enough of that. The man had appeared suddenly at their table and insisted that they come away from where they'd been calmly and methodi-cally looking through things that found themselves on the first floor whilst discarding as useless tomes that hadn't offered them what they'd been looking for.

Well, perhaps that wasn't entirely accurate. Her companion had been thumbing calmly through whatever caught his eye; she, on the other hand, had been frantically searching for something to disprove what she'd grown to womanhood believing about curses and the certainty of them falling upon whomever dared set foot beyond Bruadair's thorny border. It was possible that she had been giving vent to exclamations of increasing dismay as she'd failed.

The librarian had backed up his request with several swords carried by lads who looked as if they meant business with those blades. She and her reading companion had been marched up several flights of stairs until they had wound up in the inner sanctum of the library itself. The assortment of glass cases containing what she could only imagine were priceless treasures of the written word stretched as far as the eye could see. The man standing next to her had begun to purr. Then again, he had a fondness for libraries . . .

"Now," the head librarian said suddenly, looking at them both as if their sole purpose in his domain were to steal his most valuable personal treasures, "I believe we'll have a bit of information from you two ruffians."

"Are things so changed in Diarmailt," the man standing next to her asked mildly, "that two simple travelers having sacrificed much to enter these doors are greeted with this sort of ridiculous and unnecessary suspicion?"

The head librarian, a Master Laibridh by name, drew himself up indignantly. "You are hardly simple travelers."

"And what makes you say that?"

"Because of what you have," the other said shortly.

Aisling frantically struggled to recall everything she had with her, but considering that consisted of two books in a leather satchel slung over her shoulders, she didn't suppose that was what had gotten them into trouble. Then again, it was possible that just the sight of those books might send everyone in the area into a hearty case of the vapors.

"What do we have?" her companion asked.

The librarian looked at them shrewdly. "Magic, and don't spare the breath to deny it."

"But I don't have any magic," Aisling said in surprise.

The librarian frowned at her. "I wasn't talking about you, though I might have you examined later. I was talking about the man standing next to you."

That man standing next to her happened to be the second son of the most infamous black mage in the history of the Nine Kingdoms, but Aisling thought it was perhaps prudent not to mention that.

That second son shrugged casually. "I have no magic."

Aisling looked at Rùnach of Ceangail, son of that black mage and grandson of an elven king—an elven king she imagined was full of some fairly mighty magic himself—and wished she didn't know he spoke the truth. Unfortunately, Rùnach did indeed have no magic, because his father had taken it all for himself.

Then again, perhaps Rùnach had set alarms to ringing just by virtue of whom he was related to.

"We shall see," Master Laibridh said shortly.

Rùnach leaned back against the wall and folded his arms over his chest. He might have sighed as well, but Aisling couldn't be certain of that because all she could hear was the blood pounding in her ears. She supposed she had no reason to be nervous, but then again not only had she almost been killed by one of Rùnach's bastard brothers the day before, but she only had three days left before she either had to complete her quest or die. The last thing she had time for at the moment was to find herself lingering in a dungeon thanks to the overzealousness of self-important keepers of books.

A beefy-looking man parted the swordsmen and came to a halt next to Master Laibridh. He had large, protruding eyes that matched perfectly his large, protruding nose. Whatever he sniffed likely found itself unable to hide.

"This is Fàileadh," the librarian said coldly, "and he can smell magic from a league away."

Aisling felt Rùnach hesitate, then sigh.

"Damn."

She looked at him in surprise. "What do you mean *damn*?"

"You'll see," he muttered. He reached down and pulled a dagger from his boot and held it out. "I forgot about this."

Fàileadh leapt forward and took the knife, looking at it with a strange, unsettling sort of reverence.

"The runes of Tòrr Dòrainn," he breathed.

The librarian's mouth fell open. "Impossible."

"He wears them on his hands as well," Fàileadh said. He considered, then gestured toward Rùnach's face. "And somewhere on his brow."

Swords whispered as they came from sheaths, and arrows made particularly birdlike noises as they came from quivers. Master Laibridh looked at Rùnach narrowly.

"Reveal yourself," he demanded.

Rùnach remained motionless for a moment or two, then sighed lightly as he lifted his hood back from his face. He shot the librarian a look of irritation. "Satisfied?"

There were gasps, mostly of horror. Aisling understood. Her first sight of Rùnach's face had left her gasping as well, but then again she'd been looking at the unscarred half, which was almost too difficult to look at thanks to its perfection. The other half was almost too difficult to look at as well, but that came from the web of scars that stretched from his mouth to the corner of his eye to his ear, covering the whole of his cheek.

Fàileadh murmured appreciatively.

Rùnach shot him a look that Aisling suspected had brought more than one courtier to his knees, wondering which words might most quickly restore him to an elven prince's good graces. Fàileadh remained unmoved.

"Impossible," Master Laibridh repeated faintly. "'Tis common knowledge that all Prince Gair's children were slain at Ruamharaiche's well."

"Apparently common knowledge is mistaken," Rùnach said evenly.

"But surely you would have been found long before now, Prince Rùnach. And to have you here—"

"Being treated with such discourtesy," Rùnach said smoothly. "Appalling, isn't it?"

Master Laibridh seemed to realize quite suddenly that his guardsmen were still brandishing their swords. He waved them away impatiently. "No need for that, of course." He put his shoulders back and seemed to pull himself together. "The king will want to know about such an august visitor to the library."

Aisling didn't have to look at Rùnach to know that was the last thing he wanted. Their goal had been to get in and out of the library without garnering any notice. She was in haste, and Rùnach had his own reasons for wanting to lose himself in a crowd for a bit. After the previous fortnight they'd had, she couldn't blame him.

"Don't go far," Master Laibridh added to his men, half under his breath. "In case you're needed."

"By all means," Rùnach said caustically, "have your men escort my companion and me as we investigate your priceless treasures." He reached out and took his knife back, then slid it down the side of his boot. "Unless you worry that the grandson of Sìle of Tòrr Dòrainn would stoop to something as pedestrian as theft."

"Of course not," Master Laibridh said quickly. "I never would have considered that. It was just the magic, you see, which set off alarms—"

"Since when is having magic a crime in Diarmailt?" Rùnach asked.

Master Laibridh considered, then shooed his guardsmen farther away. He sent the man with the nose off to sniff other patrons before he stepped closer to Rùnach. "I don't like to tell tales," he said a low voice, "but 'tis naught that you won't hear from the king himself, I daresay." He looked about him carefully, then back at Rùnach. "The king's magic is . . . lessened."

"Is that so?" Rùnach asked, looking rather surprised. "I heard something different quite recently, but perhaps things have changed since *my cousin* has misplaced his crown."

Master Laibridh flushed. "Forgive me, Your Highness. I forget to whom I'm speaking."

Aisling found herself flushing a bit as well. She had grown rather accustomed to thinking of Rùnach as simply, well, Rùnach. In her defense, it had only been recently that she'd realized he was not at all who he was pretending to be.

"This untoward lessening did indeed happen after the loss of his crown, Your Highness," Master Laibridh continued uneasily. "I have no important magic myself save a rudimentary ability to invoke the odd spell of finding if I've lost a treasured book, so my opinions on the matter are perhaps less valuable than another's might be, but I will say that while there are court mages to keep our spells of defense intact, the king, ah, himself . . ."

Rùnach did the man the favor of rescuing him from what was obviously a delicate subject.

"I understand," he said quietly. "There are many ways to lose one's power. Not even kings are immune, I daresay."

The head librarian nodded slowly. "So they aren't, Prince Rùnach. But the king assures us happier days are ahead thanks to his cleverness, so we soldier on as best we can. But perhaps now you can understand why we are careful about who we let inside our gates and our library."

"I can," Rùnach agreed.

"I'm sure the king will send a proper carriage for you, but perhaps you would care to take your ease in my chambers until that happy time arrives?"

"Actually, it would indeed be a pleasure to peruse your perilous tomes here," Rùnach said. "If that wouldn't be an imposition. After all, it isn't as if we're here to steal anything, is it?"

"Of course not, Your Highness," the librarian said quickly. "Please feel free. We're unable to open the cases any longer thanks to, ah, the lack of proper, ah, kingly abilities—"

"Say no more," Rùnach said with a nod. "We'll be happy just to look, I assure you."

Aisling listened to them exchange another handful of pleasantries before Master Laibridh was apparently satisfied that he had redeemed himself from his display of bad manners. Rùnach started to walk away, then paused and looked at the master of the books.

"Why does the king think happier days are ahead?"

Master Laibridh shrugged. "Perhaps he's found a new source of magic. Heaven knows we could use it." He made Rùnach a low bow, then hastened away.

Aisling watched Rùnach stare after him thoughtfully for a moment or two, then reach for her hand and pull her with him toward the long gallery full of finely wrought cases. She waited until she was sure they were out of earshot before she looked up at him.

"That was interesting."

"Wasn't it, though," he said thoughtfully.

"Are we going to see the king?"

"I'm not sure how we can avoid it now, though I'm less than thrilled by the prospect. Not only is Simeon an insufferable prig, he also sets an inedible supper."

She managed a smile. "We all have our flaws."

"He has more than his share, trust me." He sighed, then nodded toward the cases. "We might as well avail ourselves of these lovelies whilst we have the chance. I think I can safely say we will never see anything like them anywhere else in the world."

"How did the king come by them, do you suppose?"

"I believe it was the previous king, Nicholas, who is responsible for the bulk of the collection."

She looked at him in surprise. "Nicholas? As in—"

"The former wizard king of Diarmailt?" he finished for her with a smile. "Aye, that's the one."

She put her hand over her satchel almost without thinking. Nicholas, that erstwhile king of Diarmailt who was now the head of the university at Lismòr, had given her one of the books she carried constantly on her person. She hadn't had much of a chance to look at its innards yet, but there was no denying the outside was certainly fit to keep company with the books she could already see in the cases ahead of her. "Do you think my book came from this collection?"

"It wouldn't surprise me in the least. In fact, if we look hard enough, I suppose we'll see the place where it once resided."

She leaned closer. "You mean he stole it?"

"So much nuance to the word *stole*," he said with a smile, "given that he no doubt acquired your book in the first place. I also wouldn't be surprised to learn that he had foreseen your need for it."

"And I haven't taken the time to read it."

"We'll find you privacy for that as soon as we can. For now, let's see what sort of collection my discriminating uncle amassed during his tenure on Diarmailt's throne."

She nodded and trailed after him as he moved from glass case to glass case, peering intently at the books inside. She supposed she would have been more interested in what she was seeing if she hadn't felt such urgency about discovering the truth about Brua-dair. She had spent so many years—all of her life that she could remember, actually—believing certain things only to have doubt cast on them . . . well, she wasn't sure what to believe any longer.

She had been told that leaving the Guild meant death, that crossing Bruadair's border meant death, that speaking of Bruadair to *anyone* meant instant death. The first she had shown to be not true because she had indeed left the Guild and was still breathing. She had also crossed the border, though she wasn't entirely sure that that curse wouldn't fall upon her at some point in the future.

The last one she hadn't dared attempt because she wasn't at all sure that there wasn't some veracity to that rumor, and the sad truth was, she didn't think she had the courage to test it.

She had decided, thanks to several timely suggestions, that seeking the truth might be best accomplished in the library where she currently stood. Rùnach had agreed to accompany her there, partly because he was that chivalrous sort of lad but perhaps mostly because he wanted to be out of the open for a bit. She understood that perfectly because she had no more interest in encountering his bastard brothers than he did.

She watched him for a minute or two, then realized there were underlibrarians standing a discreet distance away, gaping at him as he looked as if he were nigh onto putting his elbow through the glass to liberate a priceless book or two. Actually, he looked as if he might be considering it. She glanced at the books in the case, then looked at him.

"What's so interesting?" she whispered.

He pulled back and shook his head. "Nothing."

"Nothing?"

He started to speak, then shook his head again, as if there was something he just couldn't fathom. "I need to sit, I believe," he said absently. "Let's go find something interesting to read whilst we wait, shall we?"

And with that, he walked over to the librarians standing there and introduced himself. Aisling had another look at what was in the case and wondered which book it was that had caught his attention so thoroughly. There were several quite lovely things there, displayed on stands of intricately wrought gold. The books themselves were spectacular, either obviously terribly old or boasting covers that sported gems and fine silkwork.

Well, save one of them.

It looked rather out of place, that particular book. The cover was nothing more than simple leather, though it had been tooled with all manner of intricate shapes that left her feeling that what lay inside would not only be magical but a magic full of might and elegance. But there were no precious gems or heavy stitching or guilding on the pages. It looked most definitely out of place compared to the other books there.

She frowned thoughtfully as she walked away from the case and stopped next to Rùnach in time to hear him give the lads standing there a list of things to look for.

"An atlas," he was saying, "a selection of histories of the world, a wide variety of books on myths of the Nine Kingdoms, and finally a volume or two on the shearing of sheep and the dyeing of their wool. If that wouldn't be too much trouble."

The three men standing there gulped as one, then bowed to him before they turned and hastened off. Aisling considered, then looked up at Rùnach.

"The dyeing of wool?"

He merely lifted his eyebrows briefly and smiled before he led her over to an enormous table set under an equally large glass dome set in the ceiling above them. It was, she had to admit, the perfect light for reading, and the chairs surrounding the table looked very luxurious. She sat, then helped herself to a book on sheep when it was set down next to her. She glanced over after a moment or two to see what Rùnach was reading, though she supposed the nature of the subject didn't particularly matter given that he was turning pages without seeing what was written there. Perhaps that might not have been obvious to anyone else, but she had seen him pore over books before.

She would have asked him what was amiss, but it was at that moment that Master Laibridh and another man came rushing toward them. The man who skidded to a halt a respectful distance away from Rùnach wore velvet robes, an important-looking hat, and appeared thoroughly out of breath. He bowed deeply.

"Your Highness."

Rùnach looked at him politely. "You must be one of Simeon's ministers. How is the king these days?"

"Very well, thank you for your solicitous words," the man said automatically. He looked at Rùnach again and flinched a bit. "He sends his most heartfelt greetings, Prince Rùnach."

"How lovely of him."

Aisling listened to them continue to spew out all manner of pleasantries she supposed were necessary for the moment. She sat back in her chair and watched Rùnach, marveling at the change in him. She knew him as an ordinary sort of lad who seemed more inclined to laugh at himself than take himself too seriously. At the moment, though, he looked nothing less than what he was: an elven prince with generations of mythical beings lurking in his family tree. She wondered absently how she could have ever mistaken him for anything else.

"The king sends his most humble request that you and your companion join him for luncheon."

"It would be our most profound pleasure to accept."

The man paused, then cleared his throat. "His Majesty was also curious about what you were researching. If that isn't too impertinent a question, Your Highness."

"Oh, this and that," Rùnach said dismissively. "Surely nothing worth wasting the breath to report."

She wasn't sure the man was satisfied with that answer, but she knew Rùnach wouldn't provide him with a better. If there was one thing that could be said about their activities over the past month, it was that secrecy had been paramount. Rùnach had been unwilling at first to tell her who he was, but now that his identity had been revealed, he had chosen other things to remain silent on, namely who he thought was trailing along behind him or what that someone might want from him. Add to that her own reasons for secrecy and it was a wonder they had anything to talk about.

She followed Rùnach, who was following their escort, and watched the possibility of solving her dilemma slip through her fingers. She could only hope they could escape the king's hospitality long enough to get back to the library, preferably without guardsmen in tow.

They walked out into the morning sunshine, and Aisling

couldn't help but catch her breath a little. Perhaps the king had lost his crown and things weren't as perfect as they had been in the past, but there was no denying that the city of Eòlas was spectacular and the library its crowning jewel. Even the courtyard in front of them was like nothing she'd ever seen before. Trees were beginning to bloom, fountains leapt up into the air with abandon, and peaceful-looking scholars either paced about or sat on benches, no doubt thinking deep, scholarly thoughts.

It was a far cry from Beul where everyone dressed in grey and shuffled along from one endless day to the next.

"What was that, sorry?"

She heard something in Rùnach's voice that sent a chill down her spine. She looked at him in surprise but found him wearing a neutral expression on his face. She frowned, then looked at the king's emissary.

"One of your brothers is here," the man said. He cleared his throat uncomfortably. "Of course we have seen your father's bastard—er, *natural* sons quite often."

Aisling felt the world slow to a halt. She and Rùnach had encountered one of Gair's natural sons just the day before and almost lost their lives at his hands. It was one of the reasons they had come to Diarmailt, to escape undue scrutiny from any of Rùnach's unpleasant relatives who might want them dead.

"In fact, I believe he was only a few moments behind me, having been at the palace to speak with the king—"

"And, of course, I'll be thrilled to see him," Rùnach said, "so perhaps we might—oh, did you forget something, Aisling?"

Aisling looked at him quickly. "Ah—"

"Your gloves, of course." Rùnach looked at the secretary. "Gifted to her by her father, as it happens. Very dear to her. I couldn't in good conscience leave them behind."

"I'll send someone back for them."

"No need for that," Rùnach said firmly. "Is there, Aisling?"

Aisling shook her head, because she had the feeling she knew what Rùnach was getting at. "I don't remember exactly where I left them, so I'll have to retrace my steps. I wouldn't want to put anyone to any trouble."

"She wouldn't want to put anyone to any trouble," Rùnach said in a tone that said very clearly that the topic was no longer open for discussion. "I'll help her retrace her steps."

"But, I can see Master Gàrlach's escort from here," the secretary protested.

"And I would wave, but we're hidden by this rather large topiary that seems to have sprung up just now to shield us from the morning sun," Rùnach said. "We'll meet you back here in a quarter hour, Secretary Rùnaire. Please let my half brother know how much I'm looking forward to breaking bread with him in King Simeon's luxurious great hall."

And with that, he took Aisling by the arm and pulled her back inside the library. She didn't dare look over her shoulder to see if they were being followed, not that it would have made any difference, because Rùnach quickly pulled her into an alcove with him.

"What are you doing?" she managed.

"Hiding. And with any luck, we won't have to for long, because I'm going to use Miach's spell to render us perfectly invisible as we trot back upstairs."

She felt her mouth fall open. "We're going back upstairs? Why?"

"Because we're going to save our sweet necks," he said. "And steal a book."

She supposed she might have wanted to sit down sooner rather than later, but Rùnach didn't give her a chance. She saw Miach's spell of un-noticing fall over them, then hardly had the chance to take note of the fact that she was able to see something she wouldn't have believed could exist three months ago before Rùnach had taken her hand and was pulling her up the stairs after him.

He stopped suddenly and flattened them both back against the wall in the stairwell. Aisling held her breath as a pair of scholars climbed the stairs past them. She waited until they were out of sight before she attempted even a whisper.

"They didn't see us."

"Miach's spell of un-noticing is a very good one," Rùnach murmured. "Thankfully."

She let out a shaky breath, then looked up at him. "Gàrlach is here?"

"Apparently so," Rùnach said. "I'm surprised he's already recovered from his recent encounter with his own spells, but he's a resilient lad. Not to worry, though. He's no one of consequence."

"Which is why we dove behind that bush."

"I believe it was actually a horse-shaped topiary."

"I think it was Iteach."

He smiled. "I think so too." He looked up and down the stairs, then nodded. "Let's hurry."

She was more than happy to oblige him, though she soon realized that keeping up with him was leaving her in a flat-out sprint. When he finally stopped, she leaned over and gasped for breath.

"Short of smashing the glass, I'm not sure I can get at what I want here."

She heaved herself upright and saw that he was looking far too interested in the contents of the case in front of them. She started to tell him that when one encountered that sort of resistance, it likely meant one *shouldn't* be getting into what lay before him, but before she could blurt the words out, he had shrugged out of his pack and was rummaging about inside it.

"What are you doing?" she wheezed.

"Looking for lock-picking tools."

She felt something sweep through her that she was fairly confident was terror. "You can't be serious."

"Can you see if there's a spell laid over this case?"

"A better question is, 'Do I want to look?' And the answer is, 'Nay, I do not.'"

He paused with a small leather case in his hand, then looked at her with a small smile. "I'll answer three questions for you without demanding anything in return."

"Ten."

"Six."

She pursed her lips. "I don't like this bargain."

"Ah, but think of the things you will learn. I know many secrets."

She imagined he did, and she wasn't at all sure she wanted to know any of them. But she looked at the case just the same.

It was covered by several spells; that she could see easily. She patted herself for something to use in moving them aside, then found herself holding on to Rùnach's knife.

"Will that suit?" he said. "'Tis a gift from my grandfather. I imagine it's enspelled."

"It is," she agreed. The echo of the runes engraved on the hilt ran up her arm, not revealing themselves in their entirety but giving her a very good idea of what they were capable of. She imagined Rùnach could cut through solid rock with that knife.

She faced the glass case, then lifted up the bulk of the spells to reveal a lock on the case.

"Well done—"

She stopped him before he reached out with his tools. "There's another spell there."

"An alarm?"

"I think so. Let me see if I can get the knife under that as well."

She could hardly believe she'd said as much, but it had been that sort of spring so far. As she lifted the spell up, she supposed it wasn't a good thing that she managed it. Unfortunately, Rùnach opened the lock before she could come up with anything stern to say about his abilities. Obviously he'd done this sort of thing before, though she had absolutely no desire to ask him where or for what purpose.

He reached in and pulled out the book she'd noticed before, the one with the beautifully tooled leather cover. She would have asked him why he wanted that one, but she didn't have the breath for it. All she could do was stand there and panic over the reality of their situation.

They were, it had to be said, trapped in a library, un-noticed for the moment, with one of his bastard brothers wandering around outside wanting to kill them and what would no doubt be very angry librarians inside soon wanting to hunt them down and punish them for assaulting their domain.

"I'm hurrying," he said.

And indeed he was. That was quite possibly why the edge of the book he was filching caught the knife she was still using to hold the spells away from the case. Before she could compensate, the knife had gone through the spell of alarm, and bells started ringing wildly.

Rùnach shoved the book and his tools into his pack, took his knife back and slid it down into his boot, then took her hand.

"Let's go."

"Let's go," she repeated incredulously. "Go where? We're finished!"

"Not quite yet, I don't think."

"But—"

"Let's go up, shall we? That seems like a useful direction."

"You're daft!"

"Probably," he agreed with a smile as he pulled her along toward the nearest window, "but let's give this a go just the same."

"Are we jumping?" Aisling asked in disbelief. "From this height?"

"Hopefully not. Ah, look you there at our pony, ready and conveniently wearing dragonshape in order to help us make our escape."

She took a deep breath. "It looks very locked."

"I think Iteach intends to melt the glass. Stand back and let's see what he can do."

Aisling stood back and waited, but the window didn't melt. Rùnach frowned at it, but that didn't accomplish anything either.

"Is there a latch?" Aisling ventured.

"I believe there is," he said, reaching for it. He touched it only briefly before he cursed, then sucked on his finger. He used his knife to unlatch the window, then used it again to push the window outward. "That will have to do, I suppose. Mind the gap between library and dragon."

She hesitated, partly because she could feel the window's heat from where she stood, but mostly because she didn't like heights. "I think he likes this shape—"

"I think he loves this shape," Rùnach said dryly, "and you're stalling. Off you go."

Aisling leapt because Runach had boosted her up onto the windowsill and given her a wee nudge. He followed her immediately, which almost sent her spilling out of the saddle off the far side. He steadied her, then gave Iteach a friendly pat before suggesting a hasty exit upward.

It was not a pleasant ascent, but she supposed she couldn't have asked for anything else. It occurred to her that she was neither fainting nor shrieking, which likely said more than she cared for about her methods of travel over the past fortnight. She was fairly sure Iteach had spent far more time ferrying them about in the air than he had trotting with them on the ground.

She waited until he had stopped clawing at the air to carry them skywards and was merely flapping off into the distance in a measured sort of way before she looked over her shoulder at Rùnach.

"What now?" she managed.

"How do you feel about a journey into the mists of legend and myth?"

It took her a moment or two before she realized where he was talking about. "Tòrr Dòrainn?" she asked, feeling a little breathless at the thought.

He smiled. "I can think of worse ideas. Are you interested?"

"Slightly."

He laughed. "I imagine that's exactly true." He nodded back behind them. "I apologize for leading us into a hornet's nest. It didn't occur to me that things would be so changed. I don't believe Diarmailt has always been as unfriendly as it seems to be now."

"How were you to know?" she asked.

"Well, the first indication might have been that the king was stupid enough to lose his uncle's crown." He glanced over his shoulder, then swore. "I was afraid we wouldn't leave without attracting some sort of notice."

Aisling looked behind them to see another dragon there, flapping fiercely. She clutched the pommel of the saddle. "Who is that? Gàrlach?"

"I imagine so." He had another look, then shook his head. "He won't see us, of course, but it's possible that he might sense a shadow of our passing."

"Then what are we going to do?" Her voice was more a squeak that was carried away almost immediately on the rushing wind, which she supposed was just as well. "Rùnach, he's spewing something out at us. Well, not exactly at us, but more in all directions, I daresay. I think it's a spell—"

"Hold on."

She whipped her head around to look at him so quickly, it pained her. "What are you talking about?"

"Whatever you do, don't let go. Iteach is going to change shape."

"Well, a larger dragon would be faster—"

"Not a larger dragon."

She felt something curl in her stomach, and it wasn't the breakfast she hadn't had a chance to eat that morning. "What?"

"Ah—"

Iteach disappeared.

And that was the last thing she remembered as she slid happily
into a faint.

Two

Rùnach clung to nothing he could see and reminded himself of all the years he had shapechanged. He had enjoyed it in the past. He was not enjoying it at present. To keep himself from making any sort of unmanly noises of distress, he distracted himself with a few pertinent memories.

He could safely say that he had at first changed his shape as an act of rebellion. If he'd had a piece of gold for every time his grandfather Sìle had bellowed, *Elves do not shapechange!* he would be a rich man indeed. His paternal grandfather had been less fastidious about it, admittedly, though Sgath generally preferred to overwhelm and astonish with unmistakable elven heritage alone when such a thing was called for.

His father had never been a shapechanger. It wasn't that he couldn't; he simply wouldn't. Perhaps he had feared that if he wore a shape not his own, someone might fail to recognize him for who he was and thereby miss out on an opportunity to offer the requisite, effusive praise.

Rùnach's mother Sarait had refrained simply out of respect for her father—at least in his presence. Of course she hadn't been above suggesting a shape or two to her lads whilst sending them out to work off a bit of restless energy. If she had also whispered the appropriate spells to them on their way out the door, so much the better.

He had loved his mother terribly and missed her just as much.

He supposed that thinking on either would render him unfit for anything useful, so perhaps it was a good thing he was clinging to Aisling, grateful that his daypack was at least still on his back, and trying to convince himself that the breath of wind that was keeping them aloft was actually his damned horse.

Aisling had fainted when Iteach had changed his shape and Rùnach hadn't blamed her a bit. If he hadn't been so familiar with various shapes, visible or not, he might have joined her in oblivion. As it was, he'd managed to gasp out a fairly breathless *Head south* before he'd simply had to concentrate on taking his mind off their mode of travel.

It was an absolutely shattering journey.

The only thing he supposed he could say for it was that at some point in the past hour, he had stopped seeing even a hint of whoever had been following them. He hoped it had been Gàrlach.

He didn't want to believe it had been the most powerful of his bastard brothers.

He allowed himself a brief moment of regret over lost anonymity. He had gone with Aisling to Diarmailt, hoping to blend in with the locals there. It was something he was accustomed to, having spent twenty years of his life hiding in plain sight as the servant of the most dangerous master at the schools of wizardry at Buidseachd. A false move, the pulling back of the hood at an inopportune moment, a slip of the tongue at any time during that score of years would have spelled death for him, yet somehow he had managed to move about in at least a healthy semblance of security and peace.

He had left that place of safety to attend the nuptials of two of his siblings, not unhappy for the opportunity to perhaps choose a different direction for his life. He'd been considering the like for quite a while, for a man of action and purpose could only remain stationary for so long.

Of course it had helped that a pair of his relatives had given him the miracle of two hands that worked where gnarled claws had existed before. He'd been able to hold a sword, which had been a great improvement over merely being able to drop glasses of wine. That had perhaps been what had finally given him the impetus necessary to take a step into the darkness, a step he had intended to be the first toward a new life as a serviceable but unimportant guardsman in the garrison of an equally unimportant lord.

Only somewhere along that road to obscurity he had met a woman with eyes whose color still escaped him, a woman who came from a land she refused to name, a woman saddled with a quest she refused to fully divulge.

Add to that the annoyance of having the most powerful of his bastard brothers hunting him whilst he himself had not a shred of magic in his hands, and he supposed his finely laid plans were perilously close to coming completely unraveled.

He and Aisling had gone to Eòlas because she had needed truth and he had been happy to help her search for it whilst he tried to determine why his entrance back into the world had been noticed by those he'd never had any intention of encountering again. His plan had been to simply slip into the library as an unremarkable scholar accompanied by his faithful aide, find what they both needed, then perhaps spend a se'nnight holed up in one of the more eclectic districts of Eòlas enjoying decent food and music whilst the world rolled on without them, hopefully to the point where certain hunters lost interest and moved on to seek other quarry.

He had assumed that he would, at some point, tell Aisling that he knew where she was from whilst assuring her that saying the word aloud wouldn't bring instant death, but he supposed that if twenty years in the company of Soilléir of Cothromaiche had taught him anything, it was to keep his mouth shut and allow others to walk their own path as they needed to. Aisling needed to find out for herself that her country was nothing out of the ordinary, or she would never believe that the cheek to cross the border hadn't earned her a death sentence.

For himself, he had been content with the idea of nosing about in a spectacular library and keeping himself busy with this and that.

Or at least he had been until he'd had the questionable pleasure of wandering through Perilous Collections where he'd seen a book housed there that had rendered him almost speechless with surprise. He thought he could say with a bit of authority that it hadn't belonged there, but that might have been because he had been the one to hand tool the cover and fill the pages with his own spells.

He had, before he had gone with his mother and brothers to the well, given it to the witchwoman of Fàs for safekeeping. An odd choice, perhaps, but he'd been convinced that she wouldn't have simply tossed it in the pile of donations for the local orphans' home.

Who had then liberated it from her gnarled fingers and why had they chosen Diarmailt as a safe place to hide it?

The wind stopped suddenly. Rùnach was frankly amazed that as Iteach resumed his proper shape as a pegasus, that blessed pony managed to make it so Rùnach was in the saddle and could haul Aisling in front of him. His pack was still on his back, her satchel was still over her head, but their bows and quivers of arrows were gone.

Ssssssile has betterrrrrr.

Rùnach didn't want to know how his horse had come to be on a first name basis with the king of Tòrr Dòrainn or how he knew anything about the quality of weapons to be found in that king's realm, so he merely agreed silently. His grandfather's guardsmen were excellent swordsmen, true, but there was nothing like a bow made from elvish wood that had agreed to the cutting and honing that produced such a weapon. Elegant and deadly were not only the weapons but also the archers who wielded them. If he and Aisling managed to get to Seanagarra, she would find much there to delight her. At least his sword was still attached to the saddle, but he had to admit he had done a much better job of securing that than he had their bows. Perhaps Iteach's ability to reshape things out of thin air extended only to things that were well-fixed.

Aisling regained her senses suddenly and with a squeak. She patted herself, patted Iteach, then sagged back against his chest.

"Not dead."

"Not yet," Rùnach said with feeling.

"Where are we?" she asked uneasily.

"South."

"Regular south or mythical south?"

He managed a smile in spite of the fact that he was fairly sure his face was frozen in a grimace. "The latter, or so I dare hope. We're obviously close to safety, else Iteach wouldn't have resumed a more equine shape."

"Oh, please don't remind me of that."

He squeezed her hands, which he was covering with his own, then turned his mind to more pedestrian matters. He glanced up at the canopy of stars above, then considered the horizon to the east. Dawn was close, thankfully. He studied the landscape beneath him until he realized with a great sense of relief that they were much farther south than he'd suspected earlier.

"We're near the western border of Tòrr Dòrainn, actually," he said, having to shout a bit over the wind. "We'll be safe once we land inside my grandfather's spells."

Aisling nodded but said nothing. Rùnach gave Iteach a mental picture of where he wanted to come to earth, then closed his eyes against the wind. He wasn't entirely sure that Iteach wasn't conjuring up a bit more loft and speed than might normally have been available, but he wasn't going to question it. His only thought at the moment was to get Aisling to safety. He supposed he would indulge in a fair amount of berating himself for not being able to protect her after the fact.

Iteach landed with as much grace and gentleness as Rùnach could have wished. He slid off the saddle and landed on the ground with substantially less of both. He let go of the breath he felt as if he'd been holding for hours. He'd expected to feel some bastard brother's claws in his back every moment of that horrendous journey during which he'd cursed himself so often and so thoroughly for not having any magic, he was sure he'd used up an elven lifetime's share of curses.

He felt Aisling's hand on his arm. He hadn't heard her dismount, but he supposed that wasn't a surprise. He was definitely not at his best.

"Rùnach?"

He was too weary to even open his eyes, much less lift his head from where it rested against Iteach's withers. He felt for Aisling's arm and pulled her closer to him that she might lean on him if she felt the need. "Aye?"

"There are elves over there."

Thank heavens. "How do you know they're elves?" he asked wearily.

She considered for a moment or two. "They hurt to look at."

Well, that would do it, he supposed.

"You know, they're also pointing arrows at us. A dozen of them, as it happens."

Obviously there were a few lads from a lesser elven realm out that morning for a bit of sport. He sighed. "Hell."

"Gauche," said someone from behind him in tones so chilly, it was tempting to shiver, "but what can you expect from our rustic neighbors to the east?"

He frowned. He was standing in Tòrr Dòrainn. Elves were particular about their borders, true, but why would elves from Ainneamh have arrows trained on him given that he was in his own country?

"Are we in the right place?" she asked. "There is a very thin blue line over there to our right. A rather crooked thing, actually—"

"The line is straight and true," came the angry retort. "And you are on *our* side of it."

Rùnach lifted his head quickly to look over Aisling's shoulder to find that there was indeed a rather wobbly blue line about ten paces from where they stood. Unfortunately, they were standing to the west of it, which most definitely put them on the wrong side of the border. He pulled back so he could glare at Iteach. And damned if that pony didn't simply shrug.

Rùnach sighed, reached up to push his hood back from his face only to realize his head was bare. He muttered another strengthening curse or two before he resigned himself to the reaction he was absolutely sure his face would inspire. He smiled very briefly at Aisling, then turned around to face the arrows and those holding them.

Elves fell back, dropping their arrows and shielding their eyes while giving vent to artistically executed gasps of horror.

"Please spare me," Rùnach said coolly. "I'm sure you've all seen worse. Surdail, inform your lads they can dispense with the histrionics."

Surdail of Ainneamh, captain of King Ehrne's guards, considered, then waved off his men, who left off with their howling and picked up their arrows. They didn't, however, put those arrows back in the quivers where they belonged; they nocked them. Rùnach folded his arms over his chest and glared at his cousin's captain.

"Tell them to lower their weapons."

"I think not," Surdail said smoothly. "It isn't often, Prince Rùn-ach, that we have a guest of your breeding and beauty to adorn our dungeons. I can hardly let that opportunity pass me by." He waved toward his men. "Take him and the woman."

Rùnach blinked. "You can't be serious."

"I'm always serious about rabble found wandering inside our borders without permission."

"You forget who my mother was," Rùnach said.

"Perhaps," Surdail said, inclining his head, "but I haven't for-gotten who your father was."

"*His* father is your king's uncle!"

Surdail shrugged. "I can't help that."

"This is preposterous," Rùnach said with as much hauteur as he could muster, which, given the events of the past few days, wasn't all that much. "We've had a spot of trouble and merely landed inconveniently. We'll be going—"

"Halt," Surdail commanded. "The only thing that saves you being slain on the spot, Your Highness, is the fact that you obvi-ously have no magic."

Rùnach froze, then turned back around and looked at him in surprise. "What did you say?"

Surdail looked down his nose. "You rustics in Tòrr Dòrainn may not be able to see past the length of your arms, but here in Ainneamh, we enjoy a finer vision. It is perfectly obvious that you have no magic. I can only speculate on where it is you might have lost it."

"I'm not sure I would bother," Rùnach said shortly.

Surdail shrugged. "Agreed. Now, come along quietly and it will go well for you."

Rùnach wished he could say he couldn't believe his ears, but unfortunately he could. The political machinations between his grandfather's kingdom and the kingdom of Ainneamh were too tedious and long-standing to contemplate at present, though he supposed if he wound up in Ehrne's dungeon—if such a thing even existed—he would have time enough to reflect on their twists and turns.

"On second thought, I don't like the look of the woman," Surdail said with a deep frown. He waved to one of his archers. "Kill her now."

Rùnach pulled Aisling behind him before she could gasp, though she indulged in a good bit of raspy breathing once she was out of sight. "You harm her at your peril."

Surdail frowned. "Better that than have her loose in our land. She has an odd magic I don't care for."

"I don't have any magic," Aisling protested.

"She doesn't have any magic," Rùnach agreed, though he had to admit he was beginning to find it very curious indeed that so many people seemed to be convinced she did.

Perhaps it had something to do with Nicholas's book she kept in her satchel, though if that were the case, he was fairly sure he would have seen the book's magic. He looked at his cousin's guardsmen and wondered things he hadn't had time to before.

Were they seeing magic of another sort in her that he couldn't?

He shook aside the thought because it surely wasn't possible, conceded that the subject might warrant a decent think when he wasn't worried about finding himself in chains in Ainneamh's dungeon, then glanced over his shoulder to see what condition Aisling found herself in. She was pale, but he had expected that. What he hadn't expected to see was what hovered in the air near her hand.

The hint of a spinning wheel.

It struck him suddenly as very odd, the sight of that, even though it wasn't the first time he'd seen her make flywheels of various things, including water, air, and fire. He'd then watched her spin onto them water, fire, and spells—

That was curious enough, wasn't it?

He dragged his thoughts away from that tantalizing mystery and focused on what was before him. He wasn't sure exactly what she intended to do with that flywheel, so he thought it wouldn't be inappropriate to ask her.

"What are you planning?" he murmured.

"I'm not sure yet."

He smiled. "I can scarce wait to see what you decide."

She looked as if she might soon be ill. "Will they kill me, do you think?"

"I'm not sure they know how to use their bows, hailing as they do from a country full of lesser beings. Besides, to get to you, they will have to go through me."

"And you do make a rather handy bulwark to hide behind."

"See?" he said cheerfully. "Nothing to worry about. Go ahead with what you were doing. I'll keep the rabble at bay for another moment or two."

She smiled then, a bit less sickly than before. He winked at her, then turned back to try to negotiate something sensible with the stubborn fools in front of him—to buy Aisling a bit of time, if nothing else. That might take his mind off the fact that he was being forced yet again to allow Aisling to save his sorry arse. He would find a way to keep her safe even if it meant casting aside what was left of his pride to beg spells from those with the power to gift them to him so they would work without any input from him.

He turned back to the problem at hand and tried to maintain a neutral expression instead of snarling at the lads in front of him. He had to admit—grudgingly—that he had forgotten in all his years at the schools of wizardry just how terrible those elves from Ainneamh were to look at. His kinsfolk in Tòrr Dòrainn were likewise handsome, but those lads from Ainneamh were the stuff of legends and rightfully so. Still, that was no reason to humor them any more than necessary.

Rùnach gritted his teeth. "You can't be under any illusions

about what King Sìle will say when he finds out what you've done with us."

"We are not frightened by the lesser magic and provincial stylings of an old elf who cannot possibly compare—"

Surdail fell abruptly silent.

Rùnach supposed he had reason. He found that he preferred to have his mouth open, because that made it easier to gape at what was going on around him.

The world was shrieking.

Actually, that was just the border shrieking because Aisling had somehow managed to get a part of it up onto a bobbin she had apparently created out of thin air. He clapped his hands over his ears, because he simply couldn't listen to the sound any longer.

And then a hand came out of nowhere and stopped the wheel of air from spinning. Rùnach looked and saw that the hand was attached to his grandfather, who had apparently not quite finished his toilette for the morning. His hair was rumpled, his eyes were wide with shock, but at least he was dressed.

"Oh," Aisling said, drawing her hand back. "Sorry."

Rùnach bowed his head and laughed. He simply couldn't help it. He glanced over to his left to see what, if anything, was left of Surdail and his lads. He wasn't terribly surprised to find that they had been joined by Ehrne, king of Ainneamh, who looked every bit as startled as Sìle of Tòrr Dòrainn, though perhaps that was because he had obviously had his slumber interrupted.

"Lovely nightcap," Rùnach said, then winced as his grandfather reached over and flicked him sharply on the ear. He would protest that later, when he was certain the world wasn't about to split in two.

For the moment, though, he supposed there was no time like the present to get on the right side of things. He clicked at Iteach who wasted no time hopping elegantly over the border hanging there in the air, caught as it was on Aisling's bobbin made of nothing. Rùnach leapt over it as well, then reached under it and pulled Aisling over onto the proper side of things. No one noticed, he supposed, given that most of the attention was focused on the two mighty elves standing there glaring at each other.

Aisling eased closer to him. "I wonder," she began slowly, "if perhaps that was a mistake."

"Oh, I don't know," he said dryly. "There's nothing like ripping apart kingdoms that have stood for millennia to get a morning off to a rousing start."

"I could fix it," she whispered. "I think."

He shook his head. "Let's wait a bit and see how the game progresses. I don't think anything will be solved either soon or easily, but when it comes to relations between these two kingdoms, I'm cynical."

She looked up at him. "Who are these people?"

"Well, that is my grandfather Sìle standing nearest us, holding onto your flywheel. The rumpled-looking curmudgeon over there in the striped headwear is my paternal grandfather Sgath's nephew Ehrne."

"Your cousin?"

"To his continued disgust, aye."

She considered a bit longer. "Are those elves standing with him still going to shoot us?"

"I would imagine not," Rùnach said. "Not given that we have our own set of lads interested in a good brawl."

Aisling looked over her shoulder and jumped a little. "I didn't notice them."

"Not to worry, my lady," said a voice from behind them. "This hardly merits us bringing weapons. A few fierce frowns will send those cowards there scampering homeward."

Rùnach looked over his shoulder at his grandfather's guard captain and smiled. "And so it would, Dionadair." He turned back to the arguing going on in front of him and wondered how it would all work itself out. Ehrne's elves had put up their arrows, which Rùnach appreciated, but he didn't imagine the border dispute was going to be so easily attended to.

"They seem to know you here, Prince Rùnach."

He smiled slightly because Aisling had said it so gently. "Well," he said slowly, "I suppose they might. Mythical creatures that they are."

She pursed her lips. "I'll allow that there are quite a few things that exist in the world that I hadn't imagined before." She looked at his grandfather for several minutes in silence. "And that is the king of the elves."

"Of Tòrr Dòrainn," Ehrne put in loudly. "As if that is something to boast about. *I* am the king of the elves of Ainneamh, which is the only land in existence worth claiming. Ehrne is my name, though I suggest you don't use it."

"Oh, I don't know that I ever would have anyway," Aisling said.

Rùnach rubbed his hand over his mouth to keep from laughing. He knew that Aisling hadn't meant any offense, but obviously for the king yonder, the thought of anyone not waiting breathlessly for any opportunity to speak his name was simply not to be believed. Rùnach supposed he shouldn't have enjoyed the huffing and puffing that ensued from across the border, but he did. Ehrne drew himself up and so stiffly, Rùnach was half surprised he didn't hurt himself.

"I wouldn't have given you permission anyway—"

"Ehrne, you are an ass," Sìle said shortly. "Do be quiet and let me see to this." He moved to stand on Aisling's far side where he proceeded to study his border caught up in her spinning. "We seem to have ourselves a bit of a situation here, my gel."

"A situation?" Ehrne bellowed. "She used whatever vile magic she possesses to destroy my rights!"

"And attempt to steal your land, Your Majesty," Surdail added. "A capital offense, that one."

Rùnach found that Aisling was looking at him as if he were all that stood between her and the jaws of hell. He sent her his most encouraging smile, then clasped his hands behind his back so he wouldn't be tempted to walk across the border and bloody Surdail of Ainneamh's nose. He had spent a fair amount of time in his cousin's kingdom—to the disgust of his grandfather Sìle—in his eternal quest to find things to stop his sire, so perhaps he had had more opportunities to become annoyed by Ehrne's captain than he might have otherwise.

Aisling cleared her throat with apparent difficulty, then looked at Sìle. "A situation, Your Majesty?"

"Well"—Sìle gestured toward the border—"it would seem that you've taken a bit of my border with that wasteland to the west and spun it up onto, ah, whatever you've spun it onto."

Aisling took a deep breath. "I didn't know what else to do, Your Majesty. Those men were threatening to throw Rùnach in prison and let him rot there."

Sìle shot Ehrne a look of undisguised loathing. "Aye, well, they could have attempted it, I suppose."

"And succeeded," Ehrne said imperiously. "Unwind my border, you silly peasant, before—"

Rùnach stepped forward into his grandfather's hand, realizing only then that Sìle had stepped in front of him and Aisling both. Sìle didn't bother to look at Rùnach, which he supposed was just as well. He took a careful breath and stepped back, conceding the fighting of the battle to his grandfather.

"Insulting my guest is no way to get what you want, whelp," Sìle said crisply. "Why don't you toddle backward a few steps into that swamp you call home and let me see to this. Or perhaps I can simply allow this lovely girl to continue to rip up your border and set it back down where she cares to."

"So you can increase your holdings at my expense?" Ehrne demanded.

"I wouldn't have any of your paltry bits of soil if you fell on your knees and begged me to take them."

"You arrogant old fool!"

"You uncouth young cretin!"

The insults continued to fly. Sgath had often told Rùnach that in his youth, Ehrne had been a fairly pleasant sort, but perhaps the crown had gone to his head over the centuries. There was obviously a reason Sgath preferred Lake Cladach to his boyhood home.

Aisling stepped past Sìle to stand next to Rùnach. "Is that truly the king of the elves—"

"Of Ainneamh," Ehrne said loudly. "Which is, again, all you need to know about the only elves worth discussing. Or not, as we prefer."

Aisling frowned. "I'm not sure I like him."

"I don't care who you like," Ehrne snapped. "Just repair my damned border!"

Sìle ignored Ehrne and looked at Aisling instead. "I wouldn't bother with him," he said seriously, "but you could do this for me, if you would. Keeps the undesirables out, you see."

Rùnach watched Aisling look at his grandfather, then turn to consider her work. She took a deep breath, then carefully unwound what she had caught up. Her wheel disappeared. The border fell back to the ground readily enough, but that was when the true trouble began.

"That's too far into my side," Ehrne insisted.

"Now, now, Ehrne, my lad, I realize you were but a sapling when we finally resolved the border dispute—"

"I'm as old as you are, you fool!"

Sìle drew himself up. "I am a full three hundred years your senior, you ridiculous boy, and you will accord me the respect due me!"

Rùnach took Aisling by the arm to pull her behind his grandfather's guards. He supposed they could have continued on for quite a distance and still heard the two monarchs exchanging slurs, but it was a long walk to Seanagarra and he held out hope that his grandfather might provide a carriage or something else useful if he didn't get too far out of reach.

The negotiations came to an abrupt end after a final volley of disparagements, then Sìle himself parted his guards and strode over to Rùnach and Aisling.

"Let's be off," he said briskly. "He'll go back to his hovel and we'll make for luxury. Come along, children."

Rùnach left Iteach in the care of his grandfather's guardsmen, who seemed properly impressed with his spectacular self, then offered Aisling his arm. Or he would have if his grandfather hadn't beaten him to the courtesy. He found himself walking behind the pair as Sìle made his way toward a path that opened up suddenly in front of him, wide enough for three to walk comfortably together. Rùnach remained behind, however, because it was easier that way to catch glimpses of Aisling's face as she stole looks at the king.

He suspected he knew what she was thinking. She had made it very clear whilst they had been at Gobhann together a pair of fortnights earlier that she fully believed that elves, dwarves, and other legendary figures were simply myths. Watching her discover that the world was full of more things than she had considered before had been less amusing than it had been rather heartbreaking. That she should have passed the bulk of her life in what she had described as an unrelentingly grey, unpleasant, and surely unmagical weaver's guild whilst he himself had grown to manhood for the most part in the absolutely glorious palace of Seanagarra . . .

She shot him a look over her shoulder as his grandfather gave instructions to his guardsmen, a look Rùnach had no difficulty interpreting.

She was going to have to sit and think, sooner rather than later. He smiled to himself and continued on behind them, listening to his grandfather make polite small talk with her with an effort Rùnach had never seen his grandfather use even with ambassadors from countries he actually liked. Aisling watched him as if she simply couldn't believe he was real.

"Is something amiss, Mistress Aisling?" Sìle asked finally.

"How did you know my name, Your Majesty?"

Sìle scratched his head. "Didn't Rùnach tell me?"

"I don't believe so, Your Majesty."

"Then perhaps 'twas the border that said as much." He looked at her thoughtfully. "Does something trouble you?"

"No indeed, Your Majesty, save that 'tis difficult to look at you, if you'll forgive my saying so."

"I don't think I had time to comb my hair," he admitted, smoothing down his snowy crown that was indeed standing up in quite a few places. "But it was worth it to see Ehrne in his nightshirt."

"It isn't that, Your Majesty," Aisling said seriously, "'tis your runes. So many layers upon layers of them. You didn't put them on yourself, though, did you?"

Rùnach almost ran into his grandfather who had stumbled to a halt and was looking at Aisling in astonishment, apparently unable to find a single thing to say.

Aisling looked at Rùnach quickly. "Should I not have said that?"

"Oh, you definitely should have," Rùnach said, trying to suppress a smile. "Not many people manage to leave him speechless. It's good for him."

Sìle frowned at him, then turned a softer look on Aisling. "What do you mean, missy?"

"Well," she said hesitantly, "there are runes around your wrist, of course, but they claim your father put them there."

"He did," Sìle said faintly. "As it happens."

"The rest I think have come from the land somehow." She paused. "I think it loves you and is grateful for your care of it."

Rùnach wasn't sure who would weep first, he himself or his

grandfather. Sìle was standing there, as winded as if Iteach had casually kicked him full in the belly.

"Miach doesn't wear his kingship in that same way, though," she said thoughtfully. "It's less visible."

"Well," Sìle said finally, "that's a bit of a surprise, isn't it, given how those lads from Neroche feel the endless need to show off. Now, let's speak of our journey home this morning. It is a long walk to my house, and I imagine you both have been traveling for quite some time. Is that so, Rùnach?"

Rùnach nodded. "Since yesterday morning."

Sìle harrumphed. "I'll talk to you about the care of this sweet girl later, when we've a hot fire in front of us and breakfast inside us. For now, I believe we'll see if there might be a less tedious means of travel save our feet."

Rùnach watched his grandfather go confer with his guards and assumed that *less tedious* meant something besides the shapechanging his grandfather had obviously done to get to the border so quickly. He looked at Aisling and was slightly surprised to find she didn't look nearly as relaxed as he felt.

"What is it?"

She looked up at him with her fathomless eyes. "Two more days."

He knew exactly what she meant. "We'll find the answers here."

She didn't look convinced, but he knew things she didn't. The only thing that remained was finding the proper time to give them to her.

His grandfather finished with his business and returned to stand in front of them. Rùnach supposed he would be wise not to remark on the fact that Sìle had found a comb and acquired a cloak from some no-doubt-magical source. His grandfather held out a wrap for Aisling that he had likely procured from the same source, namely his own imagination.

"I believe, Mistress Aisling, that we'll find our carriage awaiting us just beyond the break in the trees ahead. The snows have given way to more springlike conditions already, as you can see, which leaves the ground a bit soft. I think we might consider making the journey a bit off the ground, just to be safe."

Aisling took a deep breath. "As you wish, Your Majesty."

"You won't notice, my gel."

"I always notice, Your Majesty."

Rùnach smiled to himself because his grandfather was trotting out his best court manners and he knew Aisling was speaking the absolute truth. He did the honors of settling the cloak about Aisling's shoulders, then found himself invited to try to catch Iteach for his own ride east. He watched Aisling be handed into a very luxurious sleigh pulled by snowy white horses with golden wings on their feet. Trappings fit for royalty indeed.

"Don't dawdle, Rùnach," Sìle said, clambering into the sleigh himself.

Rùnach nodded, then faced off with his horse. He had the feeling things would go much less smoothly there. His horse started his demands with griffin-shape, but Rùnach negotiated him down to something with wings that Iteach claimed he had seen in a book of Eulasaid's. Just imagining how and why Eulasaid had felt the need to give a shapechanging horse any ideas, never mind provide him with illustrative instructions as well, was almost enough to leave Rùnach longing for a nap.

He climbed aboard the back of something mythical he didn't attempt to identify, refrained from complaining about the lack of saddle, and contented himself with knowing that for at least the next day or so, he had provided Aisling with a place of safety. He wouldn't be unhappy for the respite either, regardless of his earlier intentions of blending into a nameless garrison. It was obvious that sort of obscurity was not going to be in his future any time soon.

After he'd seen Aisling settled at Seanagarra and had taken a walk to clear his head, he would look at the book residing in his pack and turn his mind to the unsettling question of why it had found itself in the library at Eòlas.

And who had put it there.

Three

✿

Aisling sat in a sleigh apparently conjured up on the spot by the king of the elves, whose very existence she would have argued against until she ran out of breath if she'd been asked a sixmonth previous, and tried not to gape at the palace in front of her.

She would admit that she had been overwhelmed by her first sight of the palace of Chagailt with its soaring wings flung out from the main body, its lovely gardens stretching out as far as the eye could see, and all of it draped in a lushness that apparently only months on end of rain could provide. Tor Neroche, on the other hand, had been starkly imposing, sitting on a bluff as it did, and intimidating by its sheer size and location alone. She honestly couldn't bring to mind the particulars of the palace at Beul, mostly because she hadn't, even with all her years spent in the city, had much of a look at it.

But she was having a very good look at what lay before her, and the sight was leaving her without a single thing to say.

She couldn't say Seanagarra was enormous. It seemed to have only one level, though she could see from where she sat that there were parts of it that had to have ceilings that likely were so high, they were difficult to make out as one looked upward at them. It was clear that there were many wings built off the main building and many gardens surrounding those wings. She had never heard a tale about an elf that didn't involve some sort of garden, so obviously they wanted to have them at the ready. She wasn't much of a gardener herself. Then again, it wasn't as if she'd had the chance to do much gardening at the Guild.

She had to pause for a moment and think about that. She had few memories of her childhood, but she did remember a garden reached by a path that led from her family's kitchen. Beyond that garden had lain a forest, one she had often wished she'd had the chance to explore. Perhaps there were forests enough in Tòrr Dòrainn to satisfy even her longing to wander through them.

Nay, it wasn't the size of the palace that left her speechless or the king's glamour, which was draped over the entire place like a fine mist. It was that she was sitting in a sleigh so fine that not even any of the writers of the fables she'd read in her youth could have imagined it up, that the sleigh in question found itself currently in Tòrr Dòrainn—a mythical place if ever there were one—and that she was watching the elven king of that same realm hold out his hand to help her down from that sleigh as if she were a grand lady come to visit.

She'd made no secret to Rùnach of the fact that she was well acquainted with creatures that belonged only to the realm of myths, nor had she shied away from listing those same creatures even though she had supposed that disabusing him of any notions he might have had about their existence might cause him a loss of innocence. Painful perhaps, but necessary. Only the tables had been well and truly turned on her the longer she'd traveled with him. First had come flying horses, then magic and black mages, and then even more unusual things like elven princes and their grandfathers. She had definitely come to eat her words.

She considered the palace before her. It was easier to look on now that she was through the magic that guarded the king's palace itself, a protection that was different from what lay over the entire kingdom though no less serviceable or formidable. It took her a moment before she could lay her finger on exactly what struck her about the place, but when she hit upon it, she was surprised it hadn't occurred to her right away.

Seanagarra looked as if it belonged in a dream.

"Mistress Aisling?"

She looked at the king of the realm. She was a little surprised to find his hair white when those around him seemed to be eternally a score and ten, but she had the feeling that sorrow and trouble had given him that snowy crown. His eyes, eyes remarkably similar to Rùnach's, were less full of sorrow than they were an endlessly running stream of memory that stretched back through centuries of tending his soil and caring for his family.

A creature from myth, indeed.

She accepted his hand out of the sleigh, then smiled. "Thank you for the lovely ride, Your Majesty."

"The height didn't bother you too much, then?"

"It was the comfort of sitting on something solid, I think, that saved the day," she said. "Iteach brought us south as a rushing wind. Or at least I think he was wind. I spent most of the journey in a faint."

"I can't say that I blame you," Sìle said with a snort. "That pony has a wild streak in him that I'm not sure my grandson will ever root out of him, no matter the time spent at the task."

Time. Aisling found herself coming back to face the reality of her situation with a nasty jar. She had two days left. The sands of time were falling in a way that she couldn't stop, couldn't ignore, couldn't wish away, no matter how much she wished she could. She had failed to find the mercenary she'd been sent off to acquire. She was due to be at Taigh Hall in . . . she took a deep breath. She was due there in two days, mercenary in tow, which she obviously wasn't going to manage.

Unless the truth was indeed that everything she had been told was a lie. She had left the Guild and lived, crossed the border and lived, spun wool and lived. Who was to say that she couldn't walk away from the task she'd been given, against her will as it happened, and live as well?

Besides, even if she could find a man to take on the task, how would she get him where he was supposed to go in time? Worse still, who with any sense would want the burden of rescuing Bruadair from its all-powerful ruler when there was nothing to be gained but the promise of gold after the deed was done? The man would have to be mad.

"You look weary, my girl," Sìle said. "Perhaps you would care for a bit of a rest before we seek out something edible?"

She nodded, because it would have been rude to tell him that she was so nervous she wasn't sure if she could manage to down even something from what she was sure were his most remarkable kitchens.

Two days. How was she going to possibly save herself with only two days left?

She watched the king have a quiet word with one of his men, then turn to look at Rùnach. Iteach was standing there, pawing at the ground impatiently, as if he assumed he would have a decent meal as well but wondered why it was taking so long.

"So this one chose you," the king said. "Gifted from Sgath, I assume."

"Aye," Rùnach said. "Out of Geasan."

"It shows. And aye, Iteach, I know who you are. We met at Lake

Cladach, don't you remember? You may now stop scattering your name on the area around you like claps of thunder. Here comes a pair of lads to see to your comfort. I would suggest you remember which side of the border you are safest on, should you feel the need to roam."

Iteach tossed his head, then snorted at the king before he allowed himself to be escorted off to what Aisling was fairly sure would be kingly accommodations. She also suspected that Iteach didn't think borders applied to him, but she didn't dare say as much.

The king of the elves rubbed his hands together. "Very well, children, now that you're safely arrived, let us see to your comfort. Rùnach, your grandmother will no doubt be looking for the both of you to see you settled, so perhaps you can take this lovely gel here and walk in a garden until she arrives. I've the usual business to attend to, so I'll take my leave."

"Going to send a polite missive to Ehrne inquiring about his health?" Rùnach asked.

"Commenting on his nightclothes, rather. Mistress Aisling, it has been a pleasure."

Aisling shook hands with the king, then watched him deliver a fond slap or two on Rùnach's back before walking away. She watched him go, watched his guardsmen bow one by one to Rùnach before they followed him, then found herself quite alone with a man she had once thought was nothing more than an ordinary lad.

Well, that wasn't precisely true. She had always thought him more handsome than was good for feminine consumption, but perhaps that was beside the point. She had once imagined that his lordly qualities could be credited merely to a decent upbringing. She had learned a trio of days before that he was something far more than that, but she supposed she hadn't realized exactly what that meant until that moment when she had seen the locale where he'd spent his youth.

It was little wonder he'd kept that a bit of a secret.

She supposed there was no reason not to frown a little at him so he knew that hedging was bad. She pointedly ignored the fact that she had done nothing—up to and including the current moment—but hedge, but as she had once told him, she was less important than he was, so it didn't matter.

"You grew up here," she accused.

He smiled. "Part of the time, at least."

She blinked, then realization dawned. "Oh, I see. Not all the time, then?"

He shook his head. "Had to visit my father now and again."

"I'd forgotten."

"Thank you," he said. "I think."

She wasn't sure she wanted the details, but she supposed that since she'd begun the conversation, she couldn't play the coward and duck out of it. "Is your father's hall not so lovely, then?"

"It's a hellhole," he said easily, "and I pray you'll never have the pleasure of seeing it. Seanagarra more than made up for any time we spent there. After the wedding my father never returned here, so it made our time here that much more pleasant. I think some of it was that he was uncomfortable with the goodness of the souls here, but I wouldn't be surprised if most of it was because my grandfather's glamour kept him out."

She revised her opinion of the perfection of his youthful years. "I have a thought," she said.

"I cannot wait to hear it."

"Let's not talk about your father anymore."

He laughed a little and reached for her hand to tuck it into the crook of his elbow. "What a marvelous idea. What shall we talk about instead? All the answers you owe me to questions I've already asked, or shall we just dive right in and you reveal all the secrets you've been keeping from me?"

"Oh, look at those flowers over there."

"You can run, Aisling, but you can't hide," he said with a pointed look. "Not here. I know all the bolt-holes."

"I think I could hide quite a while," she said, "so instead why don't you tell me what it was like to grow up here? Or you can give me the six answers you owe me."

He smiled. "If you can procrastinate on difficult topics, then so can I, so I'll choose the first. As far as a childhood and youth spent here, I fear I didn't appreciate it as I ought to have."

She couldn't imagine that. If she had grown up in her current surroundings, she would have memorized every moment of every day to be held against a time when she might not be so fortunate. Perhaps Rùnach had never imagined he would live anywhere else.

Or perhaps he had been slightly preoccupied with how to help his mother save himself and his siblings from their father.

"Too busy shooting arrows into targets tacked to trees?" she managed.

He smiled. "How did you know?"

"One of the trees on the edge of what I'm assuming were your grandfather's lists said as much." She looked up at him. "I'm not sure I would walk past him in the dark if I were you. The tree, that is, not your grandfather."

"I'll keep that in mind." He smiled. "You would think they wouldn't hold grudges, wouldn't you?"

She smiled in return, because for some reason he just inspired it in her. "I think these trees have very long memories. I imagine you have the same."

"Honestly, I spent so much of my time either in the lists honing my sword skills or in the library looking for ways to kill my father, it seems as if I did little else, though I do remember the occasional ball in the grandest of audience chambers where I fruitlessly asked ladies of quality to dance and spent most of my time hovering uncomfortably against one wall or another."

"I don't believe it," she said. "I'm quite sure they were falling all over their hideously expensive gowns to throw themselves at your excessively charming self."

He raised an eyebrow. "Ah, now here is a topic about which I'm most interested in hearing more from you. Say on, woman, and tell me all about my charming self."

"I've already said too much," she muttered. "I refuse to flatter your enormous ego further. I'm sure there were lines of women vying for your attentions, something of which you couldn't help but have been aware."

"My lips are sealed."

She could only imagine how long those lines had been and just how charming Rùnach had been as a young man. She glanced at him. "How old were you . . . well, you know."

"Ten and eight," he said easily. "Still young enough to foolishly believe in my own immortality."

She could hardly believe he'd added a score of years to that, though perhaps he could credit his elven progenitors for that blessing. She'd already told him how old she would be later that summer, assuming she wasn't felled by any stray Bruadairian curses.

"Curses?"

"Was I muttering?" she asked uneasily.

"Something about curses," he said, "and surviving them so you can reach the advanced age of a score and eight."

"Is that it?"

"That's all I heard."

She sighed in relief. It was one thing to bluster about believing that curses were tales told to frighten children and that all the worry she'd suffered over the past several weeks was for naught. It was another thing to speak of Bruadair, even inadvertently. She wasn't entirely sure that the curse attached to that wasn't in full force for whatever hapless Bruadairian found himself outside the borders.

She looked up at Rùnach. "Perhaps I will survive to my next birthday after all."

"I would imagine so, though the passage of time won't, I imagine, touch you. Perhaps there is a bit of elven blood in your veins."

"I very much doubt it," she said with a sigh. "I have not your beauty."

"Aisling—"

She shook her head. "I have looked in a polished mirror, Rùnach. I have no illusions about the fairness of my face—or the lack thereof."

He stopped, turned her to him, and put his hands on her shoulders. She didn't want to look at him, but she supposed he would wait her out until she did, so she thought it best to get it over with as quickly as possible.

"What?" she said crossly.

He looked at her in silence for a moment or two, then shook his head. "I'm not sure *beautiful* is the word I would use for you, but not for the reason you think." He studied her for another eternal moment, his head tilted slightly to one side. "You are . . . ethereal."

"Is that a compliment?"

He only smiled, took her hand again, and pulled her along with him. "You need a rest. You're short-tempered."

"Death looming will do that to a woman."

"I think I can almost guarantee we'll find answers before you need face that."

She didn't dare hope for it, but then again, she was walking with an elven prince into his grandfather's palace and listening to that king's glamour whispering things she couldn't quite understand. She supposed if she'd had enough time, she might have been able to. A pity time was the one thing she didn't have.

Ethereal. And what was that supposed to mean? Worse still, why in the world did she care what he thought, that normal-eared, battle-scarred creature from myth who had dragged her from one piece of peril to another? She didn't care that he had put his own quest—whatever it might have been—aside to help her with hers. She didn't care that he was rubbing his thumb over the back of her hand as if he sought to soothe her.

She definitely didn't care what opinion he had about the lack of fairness of her face.

"Ethereal."

She scowled at him. "And just what does that mean, anyway?"

"Tell you later. Oh, look. Elves. Perhaps you'd like to examine their ears?"

She wanted to box his; that was for certain. She tried to hold on to that thought but realized that Rùnach hadn't been simply trying to distract her. She was indeed looking at several creatures from myth whose beauty was almost more than she could reasonably look at without wincing. They bowed respectfully to Rùnach, inclined their heads graciously toward her, then moved off as if they'd been slipping back into the dreams from whence they'd sprung. She wished she could do the same and avoid the very hard reality of her life.

She sighed. Perhaps it wasn't useful, but she couldn't help but wonder if she might have managed to fulfill her bargain—the one she didn't quite remember having made—to acquire a mercenary to rid Bruadair of its usurper if she had either stepped forward boldly or perhaps even chosen a different path. She wasn't quite ready to concede the latter, but she could certainly see where she could have been more successful at the former.

Having now been there, she wasn't sure she ever would have found a lad in Gobhann, but she surely could have asked Mansourah of Neroche to aid her, as Weger had advised, which might have left her currently and quite anonymously living in some discreet but obscure village where she might have made enough coin weaving to feed and house herself.

"Who?"

She looked at Rùnach as he paused alongside her. "Who—oh, I was thinking that perhaps I should have convined Mansourah of Neroche to take on my quest."

"It would have been an enormous mistake," Rùnach said without hesitation.

"Weger suggested him," she pointed out.

"Weger is merely impressed with Sourah's abilities with stick and string," Rùnach said dismissively, "which I will concede are unwholesome. But I can assure you that you wouldn't have wanted him for your quest. He wouldn't have lasted half an hour."

"Why is that?"

"Because he distracts easily."

"Do you know Prince Mansourah so well, then?"

"Unfortunately."

She smiled. "What did any of those Neroche men ever do to you?"

"They live and breathe," he said. "Our mothers were very close, as it happens, so perhaps 'tis nothing more than a bit of sibling rivalry."

"How did your mothers meet?"

"You're asking a terribly large number of questions."

"I'm trying to distract myself."

He smiled gravely. "I imagined so. Very well, I'll distract you as we walk along these lovely paths until we find a place where you can have a little rest before breakfast."

She nodded, because she was, when it came down to it, desperate for something to think about besides what she needed to be thinking about.

"I believe our mothers' first encounter was as they were reaching individually for the same spell they shouldn't have been trying to filch," he said thoughtfully. "Knowing them both as I do, that doesn't come as much of a surprise. Miach's mother, Desdhemar of Wrekin, came from a line of mighty mages full of insatiable curiosity. I believe she had a pair of sisters, though I can't bring their names to mind at present. Suffice it to say that Desdhemar was the most impetuous of the lot. As I said, she and my mother were apparently coveting the same spell, but being the politely raised gels they were, they poached it together, then repaired to the nearest tea house for a cup of something refreshing and a dividing of the spoils."

"In truth?"

"It is the absolute truth. Desdhemar went on to wed the king of Neroche and provide him with seven irritating sons." He took a deep breath. "My mother was already wed to my sire and had been mother to my brother for a handful of years at that point."

"Why did she marry your father—" She winced. "Forgive me. I shouldn't have asked that."

Rùnach shrugged. "Trust me, it isn't anything I haven't asked myself scores of times. My sire could be enormously charming, when it suited him. His reputation as a mage was the stuff of legends, and his collection of spells truly unmatched. But the truth is, there were few alive with power to match my mother's."

"Save Gair."

"Save Gair," he agreed. "I'm fairly sure he indulged her penchant for never having enough spells and wooed her long enough to acquire a legitimate posterity." He sighed. "In truth, I think their relationship was very complicated."

"I'm sorry, Rùnach."

He smiled. "As am I, though grateful for my siblings who are left. As for Miach, he is very much like his mother, though I would hope he will be a bit more sensible about the libraries he breaks into."

"Perhaps he will," she agreed. "His future son will no doubt appreciate it."

Rùnach stopped short. "What did you say?"

She paused alongside him, then looked up at him. "I speak too freely to you."

"Which is why I continue to hope you'll eventually spew out

something truly appalling," he said faintly. "Did Mhorghain tell you?"

"She said nothing," Aisling said slowly, "so perhaps she doesn't know yet."

He looked around himself, then shivered. "I would like nothing more than to sit down right now, but perhaps I would never manage to get back up. How in the world do you know, then, if she didn't say anything?"

Aisling took a deep breath. "I could hear his dreaming."

He bowed his head for a moment or two, then laughed. He finally looked at her and shook his head. "Aisling, I would wonder if there might ever come a time when you don't leave me gaping, but I have to admit even thinking that such a time might exist leaves me nervous." He took her hand again, tucked it under his arm, then nodded to the long sweep of pathway in front of them. "Now as we were discussing your birthplace—tell me again where that was?"

She shut her mouth before the word spilled out. She shot him a warning look. "I can't say, which you well know."

"Weren't we discussing that?"

"Nay, we were most certainly not."

He nodded down the path. "Then I'll leave this woman approaching us to pry it from you. That's my grandmother."

Aisling had to look twice before she realized what seemed so unusual about the elegant, lovely elven woman walking toward them with all the energy of a youth. "She looks a great deal like Mhorghain," she managed.

"So she does," Rùnach agreed. "I think you'll like her."

Aisling wasn't sure what to expect. Rùnach's grandmother was beautiful in the way she'd come to expect all elves to be beautiful, but there was something about her that made Aisling want to curl up next to her and tell her all the secrets she hadn't been able to tell anyone else.

She was obviously a very dangerous woman.

"Queen Brèagha," Rùnach said. "This is Aisling. Aisling, this is my grandmother, Brèagha."

Queen Brèagha leaned up and kissed Rùnach on his scarred cheek. "I'm happy to see you, love," she said, then she turned to Aisling. "And now you, Aisling. Given that you've arrived at this hour, I would say you had been traveling for at least part of the night. A chamber has been prepared for your comfort. After you've refreshed yourself, you may choose between a rest and breakfast. I suggest both, if you want my opinion. Then we'll turn our attentions to your future. I can sense that you are about some important business or other."

Aisling found herself walking with the queen without remembering exactly when she'd begun. She looked over her shoulder to find Rùnach simply leaning against a pillar, watching her with a smile. She waved uneasily. He waved back but didn't move.

"We'll catch him up later," Brèagha said. "Not to worry."

"Is that possible?" Aisling asked. "I mean, not to worry."

Brèagha looked at her gravely. "I believe it is. Your secrets weigh heavily on you, but perhaps you can lay them aside for a few days while you're here. You're perfectly safe, you know. Sìle's spells are impenetrable."

"And the land's."

Brèagha smiled. "And so they are. I would very much like to discuss with you the things you see, but perhaps later. For now, I'm most interested in where you met my grandson. Please don't tell me it was at that terrible keep of Weger's."

"It wasn't," Aisling said. "It was on a boat in Istaur. He paid my passage for me."

"Ah, chivalry. I'm pleased to see he hasn't lost it. So, what then?"

Aisling had to fight the temptation to tell Rùnach's grandmother more than she should. "I'm afraid I was off to Weger's tower. Rùnach tried to stop me, but it was there that I had been sent. He did look after me, though. As for the time after that . . . well, I have a quest, you see."

"And your errand is private."

"Aye, Your Majesty."

"And you are in haste."

"Aye, Your Majesty," Aisling said. "Very great haste."

Brèagha looked at her seriously. "Can you not tell me why at least?"

Aisling closed her eyes briefly. "I must find a mercenary to take on an unpleasant task. And soon."

"How soon?"

"There are two days left before—" She couldn't bring herself to finish. "Two days."

"Or something dire will happen?"

"So I've been told."

Brèagha stopped in front of a doorway, then turned to look at Aisling. "Whatever lies in wait for you outside our land, darling, will keep at least for another hour or two until you've rested from your journey. I'll send someone to fetch you for breakfast in a bit, shall I?"

Aisling supposed she shouldn't have been surprised by the queen's kindness, but she found herself surprised by many things of late. "I'm grateful, Your Majesty."

Brèagha only pressed Aisling's hand, then sent her off into the chamber they'd stopped in front of. Aisling went, partly because she didn't want to be impolite and partly because she was in truth very weary.

She stopped short at the sight of a servant. Aisling had no idea how old the girl was and didn't dare ask. At some point, she supposed she might grow accustomed to the startling beauty of the elves around her, but she couldn't dare hope she would be in Seanagarra that long.

"My lady?"

Aisling looked at the girl standing there. "Aye?"

"There is a bath awaiting your pleasure," the girl said. "Then you could rest, if you like, or I will help you dress. The queen is sending a lad to see you to the hall when you're ready."

Aisling attempted a smile, but she feared it hadn't been a very good one. Time was still running out, and she had no more answers than she'd had before she and Rùnach had made for Diarmailt. She put her hand over her heart, but it seemed to be beating as it should. As for anything else, she wasn't sure how to begin to assess the state of her poor self. Perhaps after she'd had something to eat.

She had a bath, then found herself offered a choice of several lovely gowns. She had no idea which was appropriate, so she'd left the selection up to the maid who had been assigned to attend her. The girl chose a pale blue gown that seemed to fit itself to her as if it had a mind of its own. The material spoke of who had first spun the silk, then woven the cloth. Over that were the musing of the dyer, then the happy song of the woman who had sewn the gown together.

She looked into the mirror in front of her. She couldn't look at herself, so she looked at the maid who was looking at what was left of Aisling's hair as if she genuinely mourned its loss.

"Someone cut it," Aisling said. "It had to be done, but it was admittedly done without care."

"Do you mind if I cut the uneven ends?" the girl asked. "I have not the art to make it grow again, unfortunately."

Aisling waved her on. "Do what you want to with it."

She felt the girl working on the ends, then supposed she was doing something to pin it up.

"Now you may look, my lady."

Well, she was certainly no lady, but she supposed there was no point in saying as much—

She looked at the woman in the mirror and wondered if she

were suddenly looking out a window instead of at someone who definitely wasn't her. The woman staring back at her was almost . . . pretty.

Elven magic at work, apparently.

The maid left Aisling alone, perhaps to give her time to adjust to seeing something unusual in the mirror. Beautiful she would never be, but perhaps interesting-looking might be possible. She might have admired herself a bit longer but she found she simply couldn't keep her eyes open. She wondered if anyone would notice if she took a moment or two to sit in the chair in front of the delicate fire in the hearth and close her eyes. Perhaps not, if she didn't fall asleep.

She rose, then felt something catch on the edge of the finely wrought bench where she'd been sitting. She frowned at the sight of a thread pulled from one of her sleeves. She paused, then carefully worked it out until she held a long, pale blue thread in her hand.

Something began to run under her feet. She looked at her hand and saw that the thread had gone from being a simple thread to being a waterfall that cascaded down to the floor and became a pool around her feet.

It was then that she realized she was beginning to understand the words the water was whispering to her.

It was Fadaire, the language of Tòrr Dòrainn.

She stood there, drenched thoroughly in the language and the magic and the beauty that was the birthright of the elves of Tòrr Dòrainn. She felt tears slipping down her cheeks, she who hadn't wept even when she'd realized that she would be spending the better part of her life in a weaver's guild, put there by her parents.

She had looked into the face of absolute beauty.

She stumbled across the room, sank down into the chair and leaned her head back against it, then closed her eyes.

She wasn't sure she would ever be the same.

Four

Rùnach strode toward his boyhood chamber, sparing a brief moment to think about how many times he had walked the same path in his youth. He supposed the fact that he still had a bed in his grandfather's palace said something about the nature of his grandmother's sight. He had never asked her if she'd saved any other chambers for siblings who might or might not have been alive. His older brother was definitely gone, and he wasn't sure he wanted to know with certainty the fate of his three younger brothers. There was simply no possible means for them to have escaped the devastation at the well.

He took a deep breath and continued on. The past was dead and gone, and the future was full of things he feared might cost people their lives if he didn't find answers sooner rather than later to questions that perplexed him.

Elves bowed to him as he passed them. They were servants for the most part, though there were a few of his younger cousins here and there who seemed to think he deserved the reverence. He tousled hair when appropriate and inclined his head politely when it wasn't. He was relieved to be where he was under different circumstances from the last time he'd been at Seanagarra some two months earlier. Then, he had spent most of his time trying not to scream as Miach and Ruith had rebuilt his hands.

He turned the corner, then almost ran bodily into his grandfather before realizing the hale and hearty elf was standing just outside Rùnach's bedchamber, waiting for him. He sighed silently, then put aside his own burning questions about the book that lay in his backpack. He would have to satisfy his grandfather's questions first, obviously, before he could see to his own. It was possible Sìle might also gloat. Rùnach wouldn't have been surprised.

He stopped in front of his grandfather to make him a bow. "Grandfather."

Sìle grunted. "That I am, my boy. I can only hope that you have finally brought to mind who you are. Your presence here indicates that you may have come to your senses."

"One could hope," Rùnach agreed.

"Have you given up the idea of wasting your life in some questionable garrison?"

Rùnach clasped his hands behind his back. "For the moment, I suppose."

Sìle only grunted, then gestured for Rùnach to proceed ahead of him. Rùnach walked into his bedchamber and stopped involuntarily. He had been there, of course, a pair of months earlier as he'd come home to attend Mhorghain's wedding to Miach of Neroche. For some reason, though, the sight of it hadn't affected him then as it did now. The truth was, everything was as he had left it the morning he and his family had left Seanagarra for the last time.

It was perhaps an unremarkable chamber in a glorious palace, but it was nonetheless startling to realize that he could have walked inside with his eyes closed and laid his hand on any number of things he'd owned in his youth. He knew what lay in the drawers in the small chest next to the bed, knew what clothes found themselves still in the wardrobe to his right. He supposed he wouldn't have been surprised to have sat in one of the chairs before the hearth, reached down the side of a cushion, and found pencils or ink pens or, heaven help them all, something he might have filched from the kitchens.

He took a deep breath and pushed those memories aside. Instead, he walked over to the hearth, dropped his pack onto the floor, and nudged it out of the way with his foot. No sense in giving his grandfather any opportunity to examine his belongings. He shrugged out of his cloak, then turned his back to the fire that some enterprising soul had obviously lit for his comfort. He sighed in pleasure before he could stop himself.

"You've been out of decent accommodations for too long," Sìle said with a snort, casting himself down into one of the chairs.

Rùnach looked at his grandfather steadily. "There is nothing like home, Your Grace, especially when home finds itself at your hall."

Sìle made a few gruff noises that Rùnach had no doubt were meant to cover his pleasure over the compliment. The king of Tòrr Dòrainn had a reputation for being impossible, but Rùnach knew better. That wasn't to say that his grandfather didn't have his opinions, which he tended to voice rather loudly, but when it came down to it, he loved his family more than his own life.

Rùnach could bring to mind several occasions during his youth when he'd compared his grandfathers to each other. Sgath was certainly as full of noble blood as anyone, but he preferred to wander about in as much obscurity as possible. Rùnach had passed many happy hours with him in a fishing boat on his lake, talking of simple things and, occasionally, less simple things.

Sìle, however, had always seemed a towering figure from legend, demanding, terribly proud of his heritage and his progeny. From him, Rùnach had acquired arrogance, true, but also a deep sense of responsibility to who he was and an abiding love for all things beautiful. Rùnach had admired them both for different reasons and been grateful for their love and care of those he loved.

"Again, 'tis good to see you've come to your senses," Sìle said with a knowing nod. "Don't see any mark over your brow."

Rùnach would have snorted if he'd had the energy. "And you had nothing to do with that, of course."

Sìle lifted an eyebrow. "Do you honestly believe I would allow my grandson to be marked by that foul-mouthed, half-witted—"

"Mhorghain wears his mark."

"Mhorghain was not under my care when she made that horrible decision to walk through Weger's gates," Sìle said briskly. "I never would have allowed it otherwise."

"Miach wears his mark as well."

"That young whelp from Neroche wears that mark because of his love for Mhorghain," Sìle said, "which does him credit. But you? Nay, there is no need for the paltry honors of men when you are who you are."

"Were," Rùnach corrected.

Sìle only studied him for a moment or two, then apparently decided it was best to remain silent. It wasn't as if Rùnach hadn't already heard everything Sìle had to say on the subject already. His grandfather stood up, then turned himself around to attempt to scorch his own backside against the roaring fire.

"You know what she is, don't you?"

"Who?"

"Your Aisling."

Rùnach couldn't decide why the question was beginning to bother him, though he suspected it had much to do with feeling like he was missing something he should have seen. What he needed was half a day in a safe place with nothing pressing to do so he might consider things he simply hadn't had the peace and quiet to consider before. He looked at his grandfather. "She's a girl?"

Sìle slapped him briskly on the back of the head as if he'd been a lad of ten. "Disrespectful whelp. Too much time with that young rogue from Cothromaiche has ruined your courtly manners."

Rùnach attempted a smile. "Forgive me, Grandfather. I meant no disrespect."

Sìle shifted, then scowled. "Nay, I'm the one who should be begging your pardon." He put his hand on Rùnach's shoulder briefly. "She unsettles me," he said, looking unsettled indeed. He looked at Rùnach seriously. "Do you know what she is, in truth?"

"I'm honestly afraid to speculate," Rùnach said.

"Do you know whence she hails?"

Rùnach looked at his grandfather but decided that perhaps he should take refuge in silence as well.

Sìle pursed his lips. "Very well, do you know *anything* about her?"

"I know she spins air."

"Aye, as I saw. Very unusual, if you ask me."

"And water. And fire, if you want to be thorough about it."

"Interesting talents."

"Do *you* know what she is?"

Sìle looked at him for a moment or two, then shook his head. "I've lived centuries upon centuries, grandson, and have seen and heard many things." He started to speak again, then shook his head. "I can say no more."

Rùnach suppressed the urge to thank his grandfather for being so helpful, which he supposed saved him another cuff to the back of the head. "They will have treated her well, won't they?"

"Your grandmother?" Sìle asked in surprise. "Well, of course. The servants as well, I'm sure. Why?"

"She has had a difficult life. That and we've had a long journey here."

"Where have you been?"

"Gobhann, Lismòr, Chagailt, Tor Neroche," Rùnach said, finding even giving the list was wearying. "We were most recently in Diarmailt at the library."

"Your pony says you left in great haste."

Rùnach suppressed the urge to roll his eyes. That horse would change himself into a man and demand to sit at the head of any table they frequented if he could.

"Aye, so we were."

Sìle only waited, watching Rùnach closely.

Rùnach dragged his hand through his hair. "We were discovered as being something less than ordinary scholars, Simeon was informed, then on our way out of the library, I learned Gàrlach was nearby. Not caring for another encounter with him—"

"Another?" Sìle asked sharply.

Rùnach sighed. "He caught Aisling out in the wilds and invited her to tea. Was I to leave her there for him to slay her?"

"Of course not," Sìle said quietly. "What then?"

"Out in the open, he tried to take my non-existent power, then Aisling rescued me by taking the spells he was spewing out at us and spinning them around him, accompanied by a little fire." Rùnach couldn't help a smirk. "I imagine he was still smoldering in Eòlas, though I can't say for sure as I didn't have the opportunity to see him."

Sìle pursed his lips. "I can't say I don't enjoy the thought of his humiliation, though I'm sorry you encountered him."

"It was a dodgy business," Rùnach admitted, and that was sadly understating it. He would have died—or worse—if it hadn't been for Aisling and her ability to spin things others couldn't.

It was uncanny, wasn't it, the things the woman could do with elements that weren't usually associated with the production of yarn?

"In Eòlas, we avoided him by hastening back inside the library," Rùnach continued, deciding it was best to avoid discussing exactly why he'd decided on that as an escape route. "We opened one of the windows, then jumped onto the back of our waiting dragon and flew off into the distance, leaving behind persons we didn't want to encounter and places we were finished visiting."

"No doubt." Sìle frowned thoughtfully. "Why Diarmailt?"

"Aisling thinks she's under a curse for leaving her country. I wanted to prove to her otherwise. I thought a trip to the library at Eòlas would help."

"And you didn't think that my library might have what you're looking for?"

Rùnach smiled. "Grandfather, it had nothing to do with the quality or breadth of your offerings downstairs. It was simply that until a se'nnight ago, Aisling thought that elves, dwarves, dragons, and mages were creatures from myth. Lads from Neroche apparently passed the test, but not the rest of us. I hadn't even contemplated bringing her here."

"Where she could attempt to unravel my border," Sìle said with a shiver. "That girl . . ." He shook his head. "What sort of mischief is she about?"

Rùnach chose his words carefully. "She needs a soldier to dethrone a usurper."

Sìle nodded, then froze. He looked at Rùnach as if he simply couldn't believe where his thoughts might possibly be taking him. "She needs a soldier?"

"So she says."

"Don't tell me you intend to be that lad."

"Actually, aye," Rùnach said evenly. "I am considering it."

Sìle's mouth worked for a moment or two in silence, then he sighed the sigh of a man who had long since given up trying to have any effect on the actions of those around him. "I suppose that's nobler than languishing in some unnamed garrison in some hellish locale such as Gairn."

"I'm not worried about being noble."

"I know," Sìle said. "I know that as well as I know anything, son. What you will have instead if you continue down this path is something not even you can control, which I should rejoice over but I haven't the heart to."

Rùnach smiled. "I'm not sure I envy you your sight."

His grandfather looked at him suddenly as if Sìle could see through him to a future Rùnach thought he might not want to know anything about.

"It comes with the blood," Sìle said, pulling himself back from whatever he had seen, "which you'll know eventually." He studied Rùnach. "You wear a Diarmailtian spell of clarity. I assume that's Nicholas's doing."

"A gift whilst we were at Lismòr."

Sìle smiled, a little sadly. "I'm not sure I appreciated him as I should have when he was my daughter's husband. He has given great gifts to my grandchildren when I could not." He took a deep breath, then stepped away from the fire. "I'm assuming you might want to get to the library before your Aisling does."

Rùnach started to protest that she was not his but realized immediately the futility of that. She wasn't his, true, but that wasn't because of any lack of interest on his part. At the very least, she was in his care whilst they were at his grandfather's hall.

What she would be anywhere else, he supposed, was yet to be seen.

His grandfather was watching him expectantly. He supposed it wouldn't do to blurt out that he had a book in his pack he needed to look at first. Sìle would no doubt offer to stay and look at it with him, and then he would be answering all manner of questions about its origin that he wasn't going to want to answer. He was fairly sure shouting might ensue—and that wouldn't be what was coming from him.

Rùnach left his pack on the floor, tossed his cloak over a chair, then turned and looked at his grandfather.

"Coming with me?"

"*I* already have all the answers," Sìle said with a shrug. "What need have I to haunt my library?"

Rùnach smiled. "Simply for the pleasure of it?"

"I made certain that that officious Leabhrach was properly cowed earlier in the week, which leaves me at my leisure to stroll with your grandmother in her favorite garden or, alternately, put my feet up in my private chambers and consider how I should further torture any grandsons who might wander inside my gates." He lifted an eyebrow. "Never leave these sorts of thing to chance, Rùnach."

"I'll keep that in mind," Rùnach said dryly.

"I will walk you downstairs, though, to make certain you arrive in the right place."

"A bit of caretaking for which I thank you kindly," Rùnach said, ignoring the impulse to see just how long it would take to get his grandfather to make sail, as it were, to enjoy that desired stroll so he himself could get back to his chamber and crack open a particular book. "Shall we?"

Sìle preceded him out of his chamber without delay. Rùnach glanced behind him once more, shivered a bit at the sensation of having done just that for the last time at ten-and-eight, then turned away, pulling the door shut behind him. He walked with his grandfather without haste down passageways and along porticos until they reached the steps that led down into the library. He stopped and looked at his grandfather.

"Thank you for being kind to her this morning," he said.

"What? Oh, that," Sìle said. He shook his head dismissively. "It was worth any little spot of trouble to see Ehrne in his nightcap, the reckless fool."

"I wasn't talking about the border, though I appreciate that as well. I was talking about afterward."

"Well, even *I* have manners now and again," Sìle said archly.

He paused, then looked at Rùnach seriously. "She will need protection from a great many things. I think serving as a soldier for her may be the least of the things you see to, if this is the road you choose to follow."

"You're beginning to sound a little like Soilléir with your mysterious references to things you won't name."

"Bite your tongue," Sìle said shortly. "That I should ever become anything like that young rogue from Cothromaiche . . ."

Who was several centuries older than Sìle, something Rùnach supposed his grandfather would have absolutely no interest in discussing. He supposed Soilléir could have been centuries older still and he would have seemed as youthful as if he had just attained his majority. Perhaps there was something in the water at Cothromaiche.

Sìle nodded toward the stairs. "I left something downstairs for you, along with sustenance for your labors. A page awaits your lady when she arises from her rest. I assume you can find the kitchens for lunch if you require it. We'll have supper at the usual hour."

"Thank you, Grandfather."

"You're quite welcome, Rùnach."

Rùnach bowed to his grandfather as he left, then considered. He could lean negligently against the wall until Sìle was out of sight, then trot back to his bedchamber, true, but there was food downstairs and that book that apparently his grandfather had set aside especially for him. He supposed he could safely concede that if his mother had been the one to feed the fires of his unwholesome curiosity, his grandfather had been the one behind her chopping the wood. The difference lay only in their method of enticing him. His mother had always sent him on a hunt of sorts, laying out clues, dropping little hints here and there about a tangle she was convinced only he could unravel.

Sìle, on the other hand, had been far less subtle. Rùnach

couldn't begin to count the number of times his grandfather had simply come to stand next to wherever Rùnach had been reading only to hand him a scrap of paper outlining some question that needed answering. That had without fail been accompanied by Sìle wondering if there might be a lad in the palace equal to solving the problem.

The quandaries had been simple ones at first with most of the answer provided in the query. As time had marched relentlessly on, the queries had become more and more vague and the solutions exponentially more difficult to come by. In the end, Sìle had limited himself to a word or two and an eyebrow raised in challenge, leaving Rùnach to search out or invent the most mighty piece of magic possible to unravel the tangle.

His grandfather, he had to admit, was a sterling soul.

And if Sìle of Tòrr Dòrainn had provided him with a little something in the library, who was he not to seek that out? His own mystery, he suspected, would keep for another hour or two.

The king's library was a marvelous place containing a staggering number of books in a setting made for reading and researching in comfort. Rùnach walked in and sighed a little at the sight that greeted him. A fire burned continually in the hearth, inviting the weary scholar to seek his ease in one of the chairs there and take his time with whatever tome had been selected. There were tables and chairs aplenty as well, which there needed to be. Past the reading area the stacks of books not visible from where he stood stretched back under the palace in lengthy rows. But those were just the things collected for general use. The most interesting things were to be found behind the velvet ropes and imposing desk of the master librarian, Leabhrach, who stood at his post to Rùnach's right.

Rùnach went to greet the man he'd spent half a lifetime trying to woo.

"Master Leabhrach," Rùnach said pleasantly.

"Your Highness," Leabhrach said, sounding almost cheerful, if such a thing were possible. "Your grandfather was here earlier and told me I could expect you. What can I find for you?"

Rùnach leaned his hip against the desk Leabhrach used more as a barricade than anything else. "I'm not exactly sure," he said carefully. "I've read most of what we have over there in the stacks for general consumption, and you have been kind enough to bring me scores of things from behind your rope there."

Leabhrach looked torn between accepting the thanks and defending his domain. "His Majesty is very particular about his books."

"As well he should be." And Rùnach would save asking for what his grandfather had left for him until he'd had a few other things first for his trouble. He lowered his voice. "The truth is, my errand is private and extreme discretion is an absolute must."

Leabhrach's ears perked up. "I understand discretion."

"You are famous for it," Rùnach said honestly. Most would have termed it *pigheadedness completely unnecessary for any given circumstance* but Rùnach knew on which side his toast was buttered, as the saying went. "I don't think I would be remiss in considering you the only man who can help me with my present business."

Flattery was apparently winning the day. Leabhrach unhooked the rope.

"How can I assist you?"

Rùnach considered the opening, trying not to smile at the memories of all the times he had unhooked that rope for himself—when he'd bothered to instead of simply vaulting over it—then walked through and paused. "I am looking for legends," he said, supposing that was as good a place to begin as any. "Legends about places hidden, histories of countries that might not be so well known."

Leabhrach beamed. "This way, Your Highness."

Rùnach was happy to follow.

He spent half an hour in the stacks behind the gilt rope, stacks he knew as thoroughly as he knew the scars on the back of his hands. He never would have told Leabhrach that, though. No sense in not leaving the man his pride. If Leabhrach had had any inkling how many times his kingdom had been invaded, he might have been feistier than he was already. Besides, there was something to be said for having the aid of the man who knew and had read all but the most private of journals kept by the king and his relations.

Rùnach collected a handful of obscure history books and one having to do with myths. He was fairly sure he wouldn't read about any relatives in the last one, which he supposed he should have found comforting.

"Your grandfather left something for you, Prince Rùnach," Leabhrach said after he'd fastened the rope back up behind Rùnach. "I'll fetch it for you."

Rùnach didn't suppose he dared hope for anything that wouldn't break his back to cart across the room, but Leabhrach returned and handed him a slim, unadorned volume without any markings or title on the cover.

"He removed this from his own particular case that only he has the key to," Leabhrach said. "Very precious, indeed."

"I'll be careful with it."

"I wouldn't presume to suggest such a thing myself, but I do agree that that might be wise."

Rùnach nodded, then walked over to the fire. He set his books down next to a bit of breakfast on a low table, then made himself at home in one of the comfortable chairs there. He considered, then decided he would start with the least interesting book and work his way through the stack, leaving his grandfather's offering for last.

By the time he'd worked his way through half a dozen things, he realized that the thing that surprised him the most about Bruadair was how little was known about the place. It wasn't an insignificant territory. From what he could see, it had been a thousand years since any Bruadairian king had sat on the Council of Kings until King Frèam had done so half a century earlier. His voice there had been silent until a little over a score of years ago when his only contribution to the proceedings had been the addition of a single *aye* when asked if he wanted to have Morag of An-uallach take over his seat for him.

Rùnach paused and considered the unlikelihood of that. Perhaps Morag had had a sword in Frèam's back at the time to wring such a statement from him. After that one reference, the entire country had simply faded into obscurity.

As if it had disappeared into a dream.

He frowned thoughtfully as he reached for the unmarked book his grandsire had set aside for him. He didn't dare speculate on its age nor its origin. The cover was, as he'd noted before, unadorned. The pages were gilt with gold, however, and the book was bound not only with very fine thread, but a hint of spells he wasn't familiar with.

He smiled. A mystery in the offing, apparently.

He studied the spells for a moment or two, then decided that perhaps their deciphering would be aided by a peek inside the book itself. He took a deep breath, then opened the front cover. There was a title there, to be sure, written in beautiful golden scrollwork and again laced with spells.

He read the title, then closed his eyes briefly. He and his grandfather would have words, and sooner rather than later.

He read the entire tome, of course, because that's what he did when presented with a literary gift of unimaginable value. He supposed he was surprised by what he read, though perhaps less surprised than he would have been if he hadn't spent twenty years in the company of Soilléir of Cothromaiche, learning all sorts of appalling things.

He had the feeling, however, that there was someone in the

palace who might be rather more surprised than not at the things she might read.

He closed the book, held it between his hands, and looked off into the fire.

Now all he had to do was show it to her.

Five

❧

Aisling stood at the door of her chamber and put her hand on the wood, feeling as if she were still in a waking dream. The only thing that had changed was the fact that thanks to that thread she had held, she could now understand a bit of the elven tongue. That very fact was a bit disconcerting, but she decided there was no point in thinking about it. If nothing else, her newfound ability made King Sìle's glamour less unsettling than it had been when she'd first found herself inside the border, which was definitely a boon.

Still, she couldn't help but wish for a bench in some garden spot where she could simply sit and listen to the speech of the flora and fauna, even if that wouldn't have aided her in finding the answer she needed.

She had asked her maid how long she'd slept in that comfortable chair near the fire, but the girl had merely smiled and told her not long at all. Aisling had declined the tea and cakes the maid had tried to tempt her with and kept to her course. What she needed to do was find Rùnach and see if he would show her the library. Thinking about where she was and what remained still to do was like an unexpected spray of cold seawater against her face. She'd experienced that a time or two on her journey aboard ship from Istaur to Melksham Island, on those rare occasions when she'd left the captain's cabin to venture forth for a bit of air. She took a deep breath, opened the door, then walked out into the passageway.

A young lad stood leaning against a pillar, but he straightened immediately when he saw her. She jumped a little, then remembered that the queen had promised to send someone along to fetch her. Aisling looked past the lad into the garden that opened up on the other side of the portico, but Rùnach was not there. Perhaps he was in the kitchens, helping himself to lunch. She looked at the lad standing there and attempted to address him in his own tongue.

"Do you know where Prince Rùnach is?" she asked.

He looked momentarily startled, then he smiled. "Of course. I was to wait with you until he came to fetch you, but I can take you to him, if you like."

"Thank you."

She had no idea how to make small talk either in her own language or in the common tongue, so she was perfectly happy to forgo the effort of speaking in Fadaire and settle instead for simply accompanying the lad in silence. It was distracting enough to have the palace itself whispering at her.

The lad led her along passageways and hallways, then finally down a set of wide steps. He stopped in front of imposing doors, then opened one of them for her and made her a small bow.

"Safely delivered," he said kindly. "I will wait without for your pleasure."

"Oh," she said, taken aback. "I think I'll be fine now."

He bowed again. "As you wish, though the king himself appointed me to be your page whilst you remain within our borders."

She blinked, not sure she'd heard him properly. "A page?"

"To see to your messages and bring useful things to you," he said. "Perhaps now I should fetch you and His Highness something strengthening, shall I?"

"Ah," she began.

"My name is Giollan, my lady. I'll return posthaste."

Aisling supposed there was no way to stop him since he was already trotting off. She turned and looked hesitantly inside the library.

To her right stood a man behind a very important-looking desk, obviously guarding his tomes. He looked only slightly less intimidating than any of the other librarians she had met so far on her journey. She supposed it behooved her not to make an enemy of him right off, so she smiled, inclined her head with what she hoped was an appropriate amount of respect, then turned to see if Rùnach might be there, ready to save her.

He was sitting in a large, comfortable-looking chair in front of a fire.

A fire that whispered her name.

Rùnach looked over his shoulder, smiled, then rose immediately. He crossed the room to her.

"Forgive me," he said. "I had intended to come and fetch you, but I fear I became distracted."

She looked up at him. "Reading about myths, Your Highness?"

"That seems appropriate in a place like this, doesn't it?" He offered her his arm and nodded toward the fire. "Come and sit. The fire seems to know you already, so I won't bother with introductions there."

"Did you hear it?"

"To my profound surprise, yes, I did."

"Have you not always been able to hear?"

"Oh, well, there's a boring tale to be sure," he said with a small smile. "I lost my sight—and I suppose any ability I might have had to hear as well—during a particularly unpleasant skirmish we won't discuss here."

"Oh, Rùnach," she said quietly.

"Oh, Aisling," he said in return. "You do realize that was three questions, don't you?"

"How did your sight return—and that's part of the third question. And you owe me six answers, in case you've forgotten."

He took her hand and led her over to the fire. "Nicholas slapped a spell of clarity over me at Lismòr, and I'm the first to admit that that Diarmailtian magic is odd. I'm a little surprised it worked given my utter lack of the same, but there are many things that surprise me these days. And now I can see and hear all sorts of things I couldn't before, including a fire that apparently knows you without your having been introduced to it. But let's change the subject to something more interesting." He saw her seated, then resumed his seat. He rubbed his hands together purposefully. "Now to my questions."

"Two days left," she said, "no and no."

He smiled. "Volunteering the answers doesn't count."

"Doesn't it?"

"It doesn't. Did you sleep a little?"

"I think I fell asleep in a chair by the fire, but I'm honestly not sure. I feel as if I'm trapped in a dream from which I can't wake." She paused. "The wood had many tales to tell."

"You poor gel. Did you eat?"

"Nay, but Giollan promised to bring us something. That's two questions I've given you absolutely honest answers to." She had to admit she couldn't help but feel a slight bit of relief knowing that she was almost out of danger. "What's left?"

"Will you read something?"

"Of course," she said, then she caught sight of the look on his face. Her words hung in the air between them for several moments before they simply fell slowly and softly to the earth and lay there on the fine carpet at her feet.

Rùnach studied her for so long, she thought she might soon regret having spoken at all. Finally he reached over to his left and picked up a small book from off the little table there. The cover was unmarked and unmarred, but she could see even without touching it that it was very old indeed. He held the book in his hands for a moment or two, then handed it over without comment.

Aisling took it, feeling somehow as if she had just taken her destiny in her hands. That was ridiculous, of course. It was nothing more than a book. An old book, but a book nonetheless. She reined in her rampaging imagination, then looked at the book in her hands. She glanced at Rùnach, but he was simply watching her, silent and grave. She took a deep breath, then opened the cover:

A True History of Bruadair

The book fell from her trembling fingers. She looked at Rùnach and saw the knowledge there in his eyes. A cascade of thoughts crashed down upon her, so many that she didn't know where to begin sorting them out. All she knew was that there was only one thing left for her to do.

She leapt to her feet and bolted.

She thought she might have upended the tray Giollan was carrying as she fled through the library doors, but she honestly wasn't sure. Somehow, beyond any terrible thing the most fiendish of bards could have imagined to horrify the most jaded of listeners, Rùnach of Ceangail had discovered her secret.

And now she would die.

She didn't blame Rùnach for it. He was fond of a good mystery. Bruadair certainly would have taken the prize for the most tantalizing mystery in the whole of the Nine Kingdoms. How could he resist the solving of it?

She ran through passageways, through gardens, through gates that seemed to open just at the proper time to aid her the most. She ran until she simply couldn't breathe any longer.

Then she stopped.

She realized she was standing in the midst of a little glade surrounded by stately pines. It took her a moment or two before she caught enough breath to lift her face to a pale, warm shaft of sunlight that fell down upon her, filtered as it was through Sìle's glamour.

The trees whispered of strength; the dark earth beneath her feet told tales of a deep elven magic that held nothing evil. She closed her eyes, tempted almost beyond measure to take up some of that magic and spin it into something she could wrap around herself and be safe.

The fact that something such as that would have occurred to her was perhaps the oddest thing she had encountered in the whole of her journey to that point.

She continued to relish the warmth of the sunlight until she realized that her breaths weren't coming so frantically anymore. Perhaps they would simply slow, then finally come to a stop. She hated to clutter up Tòrr Dòrainn with her lifeless self, but she wasn't exactly sure how she was going to get across its border to perish in a lesser place. She supposed that with enough effort she could determine which direction west was and keep walking that way until she walked into Ainneamh, but that seemed like it might take a bit. She wasn't sure how much longer she had before the curse fell fully upon her.

Though nothing seemed to be falling at present besides sunlight.

She stood there until merely standing began to make her restless. Perhaps there were properties to the country of Tòrr Dòrainn she didn't understand, some sort of elvish thing that affected curses in a way their original spewer might not have been able to account for. She turned around to look at the trees, half hoping but not truly expecting them to have any sort of answer for her—

But there was a man standing beneath those trees who might have one or two.

He was leaning against a tree with his arms folded over his chest. Sadly, he wasn't gasping for air as he likely should have been after obviously having run after her. Whatever he'd been doing over the past several years, he hadn't been merely sitting in a chair reading.

He was better at remaining silent than she was, as if he had honed for years the skill of simply breathing without speaking. She gave in first because she supposed they would have stood there all day otherwise, staring at each other in silence.

"How did you know?" she asked, trying not to choke on the words.

He pushed away from his tree and walked out into the glade, stopping but a pace away from her. He looked at her and smiled, a ghost of a smile that she might have missed had she not been looking at him.

"I believe you've lost a few of your hairpins."

She put her hand up to her hair and found that was indeed the case. "The maid put it up for me."

"I should have mentioned earlier how lovely you look, but I was distracted." He held up his hand to reveal half a dozen golden hairpins. "If you turn around, I'll see what I can do."

"Do you have any skill as a lady's maid?"

"Absolutely none, but I have braided more than my share of horses' manes."

"That's something I suppose."

"It is," he agreed.

She turned around, because it gave her something useful to do. Listening to Rùnach curse under his breath as he fussed with her

hair gave her something to do besides listen to her own somewhat
unsteady heartbeat.

"Well," he said finally, "it's back up but rather a disaster. We'll
have to find your maid to fix it unless you care to go for another
run, then we can claim it isn't my fault."

She turned and pursed her lips at him. "It *is* your fault."

He smiled. "How is it my fault?"

"You . . . well, you read things you shouldn't have."

"You hedged."

"You snooped," she countered.

"It's what I do, and just so you know, you are absolutely stunning here in this glade with the sunshine falling down on you." He
smiled. "I wish I could decide what color your eyes are."

She could hardly believe her ears. He had revealed her most
closely guarded secret as if it had been no more serious than what
his grandfather's cook might be preparing for supper, and now he
had the cheek to stand there and compliment her? She put her
hands on her hips and glared at him again, because that seemed
like a reasonable thing to do.

"Is that all you have to say?" she demanded.

"Nay." He reached for her hand. "Let's go find your maid."

The man was going to make her daft long before any Bruadairian curse finished her off. "*That's* it?"

He stopped. "Should there be more?"

She would have thrown up her hands in frustration, but he was
holding one, which was comforting enough that she didn't particularly want to disturb the pleasure it brought her.

"Of course there should be more," she said, settling for exasperation in her tone. "You have revealed things that needed to stay
hidden, secrets of state that should have been preserved, secrets
that might possibly spell the end of my *life*!"

"You seem to still be breathing—"

"Rùnach!"

His smile faded. "Aisling, do you honestly believe that I would have risked your life in such a manner?"

"I don't know," she said miserably. "I only know people who put very little value on the lives of others."

"That was before," he said simply. "Now, you know me. You know half a dozen others—including a pair of kings and queens who happen to be in my family—who value life very highly, including yours. And you can trust that none of us would ever do anything to harm you."

She thought she might like to find somewhere to sit down sooner rather than later. Outside of Mistress Muinear—and perhaps the peddler who needed her to fulfill a quest—Aisling didn't suppose there was another soul alive who cared whether she lived or died. She took a deep breath and looked at him.

"I don't understand why you took the trouble," she said very quietly.

"Because Mistress Aisling of Bruadair, I didn't want you to walk anymore in the shadow of rumor and falsehood when I had the means of dispelling them both."

She looked at him standing there with the sun falling down on his dark hair and casting the scarred side of his face in shadows and knew quite suddenly and without a doubt that if there was one person in the world she could trust with terrible secrets, it was Rùnach of Ceangail. Because he had faced death himself, going places he likely hadn't wanted to but had just the same because he valued the lives of his siblings and his mother.

And now he had done the same thing for her.

"You are very kind," she managed.

"And as I have said before, you are very easy to be kind to." He smiled and nodded back the way they had come. "Let's walk. You'll feel happier if you're wandering through trees who will no doubt favor you with a tuneful bit of singing only you'll be able to hear."

She supposed he might be right. She nodded, then allowed him to lead her out of the glade. It only took walking a bit down the path that seemingly opened up just for them for her to realize what still bothered her. She sighed. "It seems terribly anticlimactic, you know."

He smiled. "What does?"

"You, finding out all my secrets."

"It was just one very big secret, Aisling."

She took a deep breath. "Apparently not."

"Oh, I wouldn't say that. You Bruadairians are a secretive lot. There are indeed many tales—where there are tales to be found—of the lengths you will go to in order to maintain the veil drawn over your country." He lifted an eyebrow briefly. "I know details, if you're curious."

She managed to dredge up a scowl. "Someday, Rùnach of Tòrr Dòrainn, I will know a secret you do not, and I will make you work very hard for the details, believe you me."

He laughed a little and nodded back toward the palace. "Let's go, woman, before you enjoy that thought overmuch. And before I forget my manners in the enjoyment of your giving me my mother's birthplace instead of my father's chosen locale, let me ask how you feel."

She considered the condition of her poor form. "Remarkably good, actually."

"I'm exhausted from chasing you, so why don't we go sit in front of the fire in the library and read for a bit? We might be able to look in the same books for a change, or I can watch you read what I handed you earlier. It was very enlightening."

She nodded absently, then looked over as much of herself as she could. No telltale signs of impending death or untoward swelling or discoloration signaling her innards preparing to suddenly adorn the outside of her flesh. She frowned, then looked up at Rùnach.

"I believe I've been lied to."

He chewed on his words for a moment or two. "In essentials, I would say aye. I believe there may be some truth to rumors of terrible things happening to those who cross your borders, but I imagine that is only because those souls are likely hunted down and dispatched by means of a very pedestrian sword."

"Do you think so?"

"I do. Mansourah of Neroche didn't dispute the fact that the borders are tightly controlled, though I'm not sure I understand the reasons for it."

"Mansourah of Neroche?" she asked in astonishment. "How would he know?"

"He travels a great deal, something I believe he first engaged in to escape the annoyance that was his late brother Adhémar. He knows your ousted king Frèam. He also, if you can believe it, speaks your tongue."

"I knew there was a reason I liked him."

Rùnach pursed his lips. "It is his only redeeming feature, believe me. And *I* could learn your tongue if you would teach it to me."

"Would you?" she asked, surprised. "Why?"

"Because then I would understand what you mutter under your breath when you think no one is listening."

"Then I won't have any secrets at all," she said.

"Save the ones you keep by virtue of the fact that you're a woman," he said dryly. "Those of us belonging to the other persuasion are continually baffled by your kind."

She suspected Rùnach wasn't baffled by anything of the sort, but she didn't say as much. She walked with him through the trees of his grandfather's forest, relieved that the trees were courteous enough not to trip her when a handful of them didn't have very kind thoughts about Rùnach himself. Apparently several of them had served as training partners in his youth and still felt the slight keenly.

"Did you guess?" she asked finally, when she thought her curiosity might get the better of her if she didn't speak.

"What do you think?"

"I think you are going to poke your nose into a mystery one of these days that truly will be deadly, and then you'll regret it."

He smiled. "No doubt. But as for your mystery, the first clues I had were words you murmured not only at Gobhann but at Lismòr as you were descending into understandable senselessness."

"And you couldn't help but memorize those words."

He shrugged. "Habit."

"How did you know what the words meant?"

"That was more difficult. I had no idea what language they were and found nothing in any lexicon I searched, so I was at a bit of a loss."

She looked at him in surprise. "Is *that* what you were doing in those libraries?"

He smiled, and she was pleased to see it was done with a fair bit of sheepishness.

"I had to keep myself awake somehow."

She realized she was gaping at him. She shut her mouth with a snap. "I can't believe you were . . . well, what would you call it?"

"Unraveling a mystery surrounding a very lovely woman who was plagued by things I knew couldn't possibly be true."

She walked with him for a bit longer before she could ask what she supposed had bothered her from the moment she'd seen her truth in his eyes. She took a deep breath. "And if speaking of, ah—"

"Bruadair," he supplied.

She had to take another, deeper breath. "Bruadair," she said, half afraid she would be struck down right there on the soft path leading to the king's hall. She breathed still, which was encouraging. "If speaking of Bruadair had meant death in truth, what would you have done?"

"Kept my bloody mouth shut."

She looked at him then. "To spare me?"

"Aye, Aisling, to spare you."

She couldn't respond, so she concentrated on simply watching where she was going and enjoying the brisk chill that lingered beneath the shadows of the trees. The forest was lovely, the ground was soft beneath her feet, and Rùnach's hand was warm around hers. And under it all was the hint of a song that flowed as if it had been a river. She listened for a bit, then looked at Rùnach.

"I'm sorry you had to leave this."

"There are many beautiful places in the world," he said with a faint smile. "And if I'd done nothing but linger here, I believe I would have turned to fat or become as insufferable as my cousins, ever looking in their polished mirrors."

"Well, you would have had reason, I suppose."

He beamed at her. "Ah, another dip into that most interesting of conversational topics, namely your opinion of the fairness of my poor face. Tell me more."

She rolled her eyes. "I refuse to add to your conceit. Tell me how you unraveled your latest mystery instead."

"Are you sure—"

"That you are well aware of the fairness of your face and the fine figure you cut? Aye, I'm quite sure of that. Now, tell me what I want to know."

He smiled. "Well, if you must know—and this will no doubt reveal more about my methods than I'm comfortable with—I spent a fruitless search or two in various lexicons. It was when we reached Tor Neroche—"

"Where the king is your brother-in-law and the queen your sister," she said pointedly.

"Well, aye, they are," he admitted, apparently without any shame. "I decided perhaps it might be useful to determine where you could possibly have come from. So, knowing that the unwashed and ill-kempt Mansourah of Neroche had traveled a great deal, I repeated to him the words I'd heard you murmur, hoping beyond hope that he might know of their origin."

"And he did," she finished for him. "Very clever, that one."

"But unpleasantly fragrant and possessing no table manners. You wouldn't want anything to do with him."

She realized then what his words actually meant. She looked at him in surprise. "Are you saying that you've known since we left Tor Neroche?"

He nodded.

"And you didn't tell me?" she said, aghast.

"And have you bolt when I wasn't looking? Of course not."

She started to protest the accusation, then realized he had a point given that she'd done exactly that not a half an hour earlier. "Very well, so you're exceptionally good at keeping secrets. What did you learn about my country this morning when you no doubt read that book you handed me?"

"That Bruadair is littered with so many lakes, rivers, and streams that it is thoroughly impossible to go a league in any direction without getting wet." He looked at her. "What do you know about your country?"

"I only know the Guild."

"But that wasn't where you were born, was it?"

She shook her head. "I don't remember very much about where I was born. In fact, I'm not sure what I remember isn't something I instead read in a book."

He walked with her in silence for another moment or two, then stopped. He turned her to him, then pulled her into his arms.

She supposed that if all her tears hadn't already been spent, she might have wept. As it was, all she could do was simply stand there and continue to breathe, in and out.

"I'm so sorry," he said quietly. "I wish things had been different for you."

She shrugged, because there was nothing she could do to call back any of the years she had lost. "'Tis over and done, though I don't particularly care to think on it."

"Then let's speak of other things. I believe there's a bench over there that might suit us for a moment or two. Let's sit whilst you're about the work of telling me how it was you left Bruadair."

She supposed there was little point in keeping that a secret any longer. Not now that Rùnach knew the most important secret of all. She sat down with him, rather more grateful for a solid seat than perhaps she should have been. She sighed, then looked at Rùnach.

"I may have told you some of this already," she said.

"Context," Rùnach said wryly. "I was imagining you in some tiny little village, not Beul."

She blinked. "How did you know that?"

He rubbed his hands over his face briefly, then looked at her with a weary smile. "That was a guess. It is the capital of Bruadair. That's all."

"That's something," she said. She had to take a deep breath and clasp her hands tightly in her lap to keep them from shaking, perhaps, though she wasn't sure why. "I was out on my day of liberty from the Guild and had been looking in a shop window when I saw a very finely dressed couple coming out of a very fine restaurant. I was in the midst of gaping at them when I realized they were my parents."

"They won't eat so well when they're slaving away in a mine."

She smiled. "Perhaps not. Anyway, I think I would have spoken to them if it hadn't been for a man suddenly distracting me by asking for directions to somewhere I can't remember. The only reason I remember him is that later in the evening, he rushed me through streets I was unfamiliar with."

"Wait," Rùnach said, holding up his hand. "What happened between those points?"

"I had run to the pub I often frequented to meet friends, terri-

fied that my parents had seen me and would be sending guards
after me." She had to stop for a moment or two because the memory was too fresh. "I knew the only reason they would have been
in Beul was to indenture me again, so I had two choices: I could
either go back to the Guild and give up another seven years of my
life or I would have to run."

"And you ran?"

"I ran," she agreed. "Two of my friends—if they can be called
that, I suppose—had been talking about overthrowing the gov-
ernment."

"Interesting friends," he noted.

"Very," she said. "One of them pulled me out the back when
guards came in the front door, shoved a trader's license into my
hands, and told me to go. I ran and had not only a city guard but
the gentleman from outside the shop get me to the border. I then
ran bodily into the weaving mistress, Muinear, who put money
into my hands and pushed me into the queue to leave the country."
She paused. "The Guildmistress slew her for that."

"How do you know?"

"I saw the bloodstained sword."

He let out his breath slowly. "I'm sorry, Aisling."

"I am too," she said quietly. "Mistress Muinear was kind to
me." She took a deep breath. "After I escaped across the border,
the peddler who sold me Ochadius's book cut my hair and gave me
clothes and money, then I ran into the night and caught the carriage that dropped me in Istaur. You know the rest from there."

He leaned forward with his elbows on his knees and stared off
over the land that surrounded the palace walls, walls that seemed
to be more suggestions of a border than a barrier to anything
determined, for quite some time in silence. Then he looked at her.

"Why you, do you think?"

"I have no idea," she said helplessly. "The peddler told me to
find a mercenary to save Bruadair, told me to do so in three weeks

or I would die, then told me to have the lad meet him at Taigh Hall
in three fortnights or I would die. And he told me that I wasn't to
speak of my errand or I would die."

"He wasn't very original, was he?"

"I daresay he didn't need to be with me."

Rùnach smiled at her, then straightened. "Ah, but look at how
jaded you are now. I don't think you would be taken in by his tales
were you to meet him tomorrow."

She attempted a smile and was fairly surprised when she managed it. "I believe the scales have indeed fallen from my eyes."

"It might have been the pegasus."

"I think it was Iteach as a dragon," she countered. "Elves,
mages, dragons . . . I hate to think of what I might encounter next."

"Something to eat, then an hour or two of comfort in a very
lovely library." He rose, then held out his hand for hers. "Shall we?"

She put her hand in his, rose, then started toward the palace
with him. She looked up at him as they walked. "Thank you."

He looked at her in surprise. "For what?"

"For opening my eyes."

He shook his head. "You give me credit I don't deserve. All I
did is give you rides on a shapechanging horse. You've done the
rest."

She knew that wasn't true. It was substantially less true when
she dared give thought to her future. She might have been slightly
more jaded than she had been several se'nnights earlier, but she
was no more courageous. The thought of going anywhere near
Bruadair filled her with dread. She couldn't breathe past it; she
couldn't swallow past it; she couldn't rid herself of it as it curled in
her stomach. She looked up at Rùnach.

"I don't know what to do now."

"What do you want to do?"

She struggled to swallow normally. "I want to run."

"I think you already did that."

"You know what I mean," she said. "I want to run very far away and never think about Bruadair ever again." She knew her voice was shaking, but she couldn't seem to control it. "How did you ever force yourself to go to that well?"

He looked at her gravely. "I went to protect those I loved."

"Weren't you afraid?"

"I was too arrogant and stupid to be afraid."

She wrapped the arm not attached to the hand he was holding around herself. "I am very afraid. And there is nothing left in Bruadair that I love."

"Then run."

She felt her mouth fall open. "Do you think so?"

He squeezed her hand. "Aisling, I think this might be a decision you could put off for another day or two."

"I only have two days left."

"See? The timing is ideal. Let's go take our ease in the library, and you can read that book you dropped. My grandfather left it for me with the intention that I would show it to you, I'm sure."

"Your *grandfather* knows?"

Rùnach laughed uneasily. "I don't think either of us should be surprised by what he knows. You can, however, count on his absolute discretion. I am perfectly sure he will remain silent on your origins unless you say otherwise. He wouldn't even divulge them to me."

"Did you ask?"

He smiled a small, serious smile. "Nay, Aisling, I did not."

If she had been fond of him before, then at that moment . . . well, she supposed she could safely say she was extremely fond of him then. She continued on with him in silence, trying not to shake her head. She was walking with a man who knew her darkest secret, and she hadn't been slain for it.

That thought kept reverberating in her mind like a great tolling bell until they reached the edge of the forest. Another step would take her out of the trees and onto the finely laid paths that led to the palace proper, and for some reason, that brought her up short. Rùnach stopped alongside her and looked at her with a faint frown.

"What is it?"

She could hardly believe she was doubting her doubts, but it was hard to do anything else. "They lied to me."

"Aye," he agreed, "it certainly seems so."

"I just don't understand why."

"That is definitely something I think you could put off thinking about until later. Perhaps after supper, after you've had a decent meal. You never know what might happen then."

That thought was almost enough to convince her that she should sneak off to the kitchens to beg scraps, then hide somewhere discreet where no one could find her. She wasn't sure she was equal to having anything else happen. After all, she'd already been favored with rides on a shapechanging horse, encounters with creatures from myth, meetings with kings and queens of legendary realms, and a journey with a man who had kept her secrets until he couldn't reasonably keep his knowledge of them from her any longer. She wasn't sure what the evening would bring after her recent adventures.

She sincerely hoped she was equal to facing it.

Six

❧

Rùnach walked along pathways he had walked innumerable times in his youth, now and again with extremely eligible and desirable maidens from other kingdoms, and considered the changes that had happened in his life.

He was without magic, though if he were to be honest with himself, he had to admit that he had suspected that would be the price he would have to pay at the well if he failed. He was without any elven beauty he may or may not have once possessed, but he supposed that was no great loss to any but those who had to look at him. He was without any fame or fortune he particularly cared to claim, which would likely render him very unattractive to any women he might or might not have known in a former lifetime.

But he was walking next to a lass from Bruadair who was looking around her as if she still couldn't quite believe where she was or that she was still breathing. She was also seemingly examining her surroundings for creatures she'd been led to believe only existed between the pages of a book.

Somehow that went a long way in making up for things he might otherwise have been mourning the lack of.

He paused several feet away from his bedchamber door and turned to Aisling. "I'll only be a minute. You can come inside if you like, though the view isn't particularly inspiring."

She considered, then nodded toward the garden to her right. "Might I wander there?"

"Of course," he said with a smile. "I'll fetch you straightway after I've finished, shall I?"

"No hurry," she said faintly.

And her voice was faint because she had already abandoned him and wandered into one of the innumerable gardens dotting the palace grounds. Rùnach supposed the worst she would find there was a horse who had escaped his confines in the stables and gone in search of tastier fare, so he left her to her ramble and went inside his chamber.

All was as he had left it, which didn't surprise him. He supposed the servants had sighed enough times in his youth over muddy boots deposited just inside the door and too many weapons stuffed into corners and under the bed that they were accustomed, even after all this time, to simply leaving things to lie where they'd been dropped. His pack was still in its place where he'd stuffed it under the chair.

He pulled the book out and ignored the shiver that went through him at the sight of it. He'd thought about it often over the years, as it happened, but he'd been able to do about it exactly what he'd been able to do about most events in his past, which was absolutely nothing. It had been madness perhaps to depend on the witchwoman of Fàs for anything but a hearty case of food poisoning after eating at her table, but he'd had no other choice. It wasn't as if he could have left the damned thing with either of his grandfathers. Sgath would have misplaced it in some tackle box or other, and Sìle would have immediately opened it and thereafter had an attack over what he'd read.

Rùnach could safely say he hadn't been dabbling in anything untoward, but he had been creating and refining spells intended to counter every single one of his father's. By the very nature of that task, he'd had to use a few things that others might have found . . . unsavoury. Well, Sìle would have found them unsavoury. His mother had found them nothing more than necessary.

He wondered if the library would catch on fire if he dared open the book downstairs.

He decided there was nothing to be done but make the attempt, so he took the book in hand and went to look for that still-breathing Bruadairian lass who was likely having a conversation with the flora and fauna of his grandfather's garden.

He just hadn't expected her to be singing.

It wasn't loud singing, though he could hear it once he'd wandered the garden long enough to catch sight of her, standing beneath a flowering linden tree, holding a blossom in her hand. He came to a skidding halt and gaped at her.

He had no idea where they'd found that gown for her, or if someone had merely conjured it up to suit her coloring, but it had been very well done on some industrious seamstress's part. It was blue, as if the shadows of dawn were lying just so on snow, giving it just a hint of color. He would have liked to have been able to say that he'd never given heed to a woman's gown before, or her hair, or her face, but he would have been lying, because he'd been a connoisseur of all three. The gown was perfect for her; it made her hair—which he had done a terrible job of putting back up actually— seem like the finest of pale, spun gold, and it didn't do anything to her face, her face needed nothing done to it save a goodly bit of admiring lavished upon it.

Very well, so he had ceased to think of her as plain directly after she'd stopped puking at Gobhann, and he'd been struggling to come up with some sort of worthy adjective ever since. He supposed he might spend the rest of his life trying to come up with something useful and never manage it.

It was difficult to describe a dream.

He had to sit down on the first bench he found, because he couldn't stand any longer. He wondered if the day would come when she ceased to surprise him with the things she did.

Her song was nothing he'd ever heard before, but for some reason it seemed familiar in a way he couldn't divine at first. It was enough for the moment to simply sit there and watch as she and the tree—and several of the flowers, it had to be said—engaged in an ethereal bit of music making. It was truthfully the most beautiful thing he had ever heard, and that was saying something because the musicians who graced his grandfather's hall were unequalled in any elvish hall he'd ever visited.

And then he realized why what she was doing sounded so familiar.

She was singing in Fadaire.

He grasped for the rapidly disappearing shreds of anything resembling coherent thought, but it was useless. All he could do was sit on a very cold stone bench and listen to a woman who had hardly set foot past her place of incarceration sing a song in his mother's native tongue that would have brought any elf in the vicinity to tears if he had heard it. He knew, because it was nigh onto bringing him to that place and that in spite of his sorry, jaded self.

He saw something out of the corner of his eye and found that there were several elves standing nearby, hidden discreetly behind this garden ornament and that, most with their eyes closed and expressions of wonder on their faces. He was fairly sure he'd seen a male cousin or two amongst the lot—in fact, he knew that was the case because one of them started forward. Rùnach frowned him back into his place and decided that perhaps he should make his own presence known before Aisling was made uncomfortable by her audience.

He rose, then walked unsteadily toward her, stopping a few feet away. He cleared his throat, which he expected would make her jump. He hadn't expected the smile she turned on him when she saw him. She looked as if she were, for the first time he'd ever seen, completely at peace.

"The garden is magnificent," she said happily.

In Fadaire.

"It is," he managed. "Very tuneful trees, apparently."

She laughed a little. "Did you hear us?"

"Willingly," he said honestly. "It was unmatched in all the performances I've ever attended."

She sighed deeply, but in satisfaction. "Their dreams are so lovely. Your grandparents are blessed to live here. 'Tis no wonder they don't noise their existence about. The land would be overrun in no time otherwise."

"Either that or my grandfather is simply not a good host," Rùnach managed. "I never can decide which it is."

She smiled and patted the tree before she turned away and walked toward him. "Did you find your book?"

"Do you realize you're speaking my tongue?"

"So are you, so it seemed fair."

He opened his mouth to point out to her that her recently acquired ability was a little, ah, *unusual*, but he supposed that when it came to Aisling of Bruadair, unusual was the order of the day. Unusual and, it could be said, almost magical.

He was obviously missing something important.

"When are you going to teach me Deuraich?" he managed.

She blinked a little, then shook her head. "You know too much about my land."

"Yet we both still breathe." He offered her his arm. "Fair is fair, if you're insisting on that. You've left me gaping time and time again, so I must have a bit of my own back when I can. So, when shall we begin our lessons?"

She considered. "Learning it is perilous, you know."

"What isn't in Bruadair?"

"That's true," she agreed. "You'll have to tell me what you want to learn, I suppose. I can teach you the dialect we were allowed to speak in the Guild or I can teach you the forbidden but admittedly more beautiful High Deuraich that I shouldn't have known. That is reserved only for nobility and those of a loftier and more worthy social standing."

"What absolute rot."

She smiled at him as if he had pleased her in some way. He supposed that he would have done jongleur's tricks all down the portico's pathway to have another of those looks, poor fool that he was.

"Mistress Muinear taught me the more refined tongue so I could read her books."

"Did you sharpen your skills reading edicts from the king?"

She laughed. "Aye, I did, as it happens. I could easily command you to be tidier with your rubbish or instruct you on the proper way to bow as I passed so you didn't trouble me with your impudent gaze."

The whole country was daft. He wasn't sure how to express that politely, so he decided that perhaps he would do well to simply keep his thoughts to himself. "Perhaps we can find a pile of edicts or myths for you to use for my lessons," he said.

"I suppose we could do that." She nodded at the book in his hands. "What do you have there? Not more revealing secrets about secret places, I hope."

He started to speak, then decided perhaps it wasn't a good idea when there might be listening ears he couldn't see lurking around some corner or other. "I'll tell you in the library."

"Do you think that other book will still be there?"

"I have the feeling it might, because I hid it under the chair."

Which was exactly where he found it not a quarter hour later. He saw Aisling seated comfortably in the chair next to him, made sure there was food and drink within reach for her, then took his own book in hand and hoped he wouldn't bring the library down around his ears when he opened it.

"Are you unwell?"

He looked at Aisling sitting next to him, watching him. He shook his head.

"I'm fine."

"You look pale."

"I need food."

She looked skeptical. "Are you going to tell me what that book is that's making you look pale?"

He supposed there was no reason to deny its effect on him. "If I survive the opening of it, aye, possibly."

"Is it worse than mine?"

"I'll let you know," he said grimly, "and that was three questions I answered. I believe I've answered all the questions we bargained for, so we're back to even."

"I'll keep that in mind."

He nodded, then looked at the book in his hands. He remembered vividly the tooling of the cover and the binding of the pages. He had laced the thing liberally with spells, of course, and he was faintly surprised to find there was still the echo of them on the cover.

But not the pages.

There was no time like the present, he supposed, to have something unpleasant over with, so he opened the book, fully expecting to see his own hand staring back at him.

But it wasn't.

In fact, not only was the hand not his, the words there made no sense because they weren't words; they were scratches. Scratches that made a sound, actually, that he quickly realized had set his grandfather's glamour to protesting quite loudly what it was being assaulted by. Rùnach shut the book, the sound ceased, and calm was restored. He glanced at Aisling to see her sitting there with her hands over her ears.

She pulled her hands away carefully, then took an unsteady breath. "What was that?" she managed.

"I'm honestly not at all sure," he said.

"Are you going to tell me what that book is?"

He took a deep breath. "You know, that delicate little bell we're hearing is the supper gong. Why don't we deposit our treasures in our chambers, then spend a lovely evening thinking about things that have nothing to do with quests, books, or countries that are shrouded in mystery." He looked at the book in her lap that she hadn't had time to open yet. "Want to take that with you?"

She hesitated, then shook her head. "I'll come back tomorrow and look at it, if you think they won't mind."

He imagined they wouldn't, though he suspected he wouldn't find the same sort of forbearance when it came to his own reading. Obviously he was going to have to get out of the palace's reach before he dared look again at what was in his book.

There was something foul afoot in the world, and he didn't care for it at all.

A handful of hours later, he was convinced there were things afoot in his grandfather's kingdom, as well. Several of those foul things were in the middle of the hall, slobbering on an ethereal Bruadairian lass—they likely would have termed it dancing, but he knew better—and if they didn't stop, blood would be spilt. His grandmother had abandoned him to his fate half an hour earlier, and his grandfather was sitting a chair or two away, smirking at him. It was shaping up to be a perfectly horrendous evening.

And all he could think about was why in the world his book would have been hidden in the library at Eòlas, who had put it there, and why his spells were missing from between those inexpertly tooled leather covers.

Someone dropped down in the chair next to him, interrupting his gloomy thoughts. He looked to find his uncle Sosar sitting there, looking unpleasantly cheerful.

"How are you?" Sosar asked.

"Trying to make my way in the world without magic," Rùnach asked, "which leaves me singularly unable to glue a handful of my cousins to their seats."

Sosar laughed a little. "Poor you."

Rùnach looked at him seriously. "I'm sorry, Sosar, about what happened to you at the well. For what that's worth."

"It's worth a great deal, actually," Sosar said frankly. "At least you'll speak of it. No one else will."

Rùnach wasn't sure quite what to say. He and Sosar had talked at Mhorghain's wedding and Ruith's as well, of course, but they hadn't discussed anything of substance. Rùnach had quite frankly been too overwhelmed at the return to the boyhood home he hadn't dared hope he would ever see again, and Sosar had no doubt been too raw still from the recent loss of his power. Rùnach hadn't asked the details, though Miach had mentioned very briefly that Sosar had been with them at the closing of the well and been attacked by Lothar. That had been more than enough to know at the time.

Now, though, sitting in comfort at his grandfather's table and looking at the uncle he'd not only always admired but been quite good friends with, he couldn't help but mourn a bit for the loss. His own loss of power had come because he had deliberately risked it for the chance to stop his father's madness; Sosar's had been lost simply because he'd been in the wrong place at the wrong time. Rùnach toyed idly with the glass of wine he hadn't touched.

"It isn't fair," he remarked.

Sosar smiled. "You're too old to believe that life is fair, Rùnach."

"I know," Rùnach said with a sigh, "but one does hope for it now and again, don't you think?"

"And how dull things would be if that were the case, don't you think?"

"Oh, I don't know," Rùnach said dryly. "I could do with a bit of boredom."

"Didn't you have enough of that haunting Soilléir for all those years?" Sosar asked innocently.

Rùnach laughed a little in spite of himself. "Now you sound like Ruith. I'm not sure what Soilléir ever did to him to earn his endless irritation, but it must have been terrible." He looked at his uncle sitting there next to him and couldn't help but pity the man in a way he never allowed himself to pity himself.

Sosar of Tòrr Dòrainn could have perhaps gotten lost a bit in the press of the seven children Sìle had sired, but somehow he hadn't. He had the full complement of power from both his parents—or he once had, rather—and possessed more beauty than was good for him, all wrapped up in a wry wit that annoyed his father and baffled potential brides' fathers. It was no wonder he was still unwed.

There were times, Rùnach had to admit, that elves took themselves far too seriously.

"You know what she is, don't you?"

Rùnach pulled himself back to the present and focused on Sosar. "Aisling?"

Sosar only nodded.

Rùnach blew out his breath. "You know, I'm never quite sure what anyone is driving at with that question. Is she a woman? Why, yes, I believe she is. Does she have magic? Why, nay, I believe she doesn't."

Sosar smiled, obviously amused. "Are you sure?"

Rùnach rubbed his hand over his face before he could stop himself. "Tonight I'm not sure of anything save that I am going to do damage to a cousin or two if they don't leave that girl alone long enough for me to dance with her. Do *you* think she has magic?"

"I think they all do, in one form or another."

"Who?"

"Those Bruadairians."

Rùnach looked at him narrowly. "How did you know where she was from?"

"How could you *not* know?"

"Because I'm an idiot?"

"Well," Sosar said, smiling deeply, "I wouldn't go that far. Blinded by the fairness of her face, aye, perhaps, which I can understand. She is very lovely in a very unusual way—and here she comes to perhaps give you the opportunity to rescue her from the slobbering clutches of your dastardly cousins."

Rùnach looked up to see that was indeed the case. He stood up as Aisling was escorted around to the back of the table by some cousin he feared to identify lest he feel the need to take him outside the hall and explain to him just exactly where his interest in the woman standing there should end. Sosar had stood as well, vacating what had been Aisling's supper chair.

"I think she likes me," he said, elbowing Rùnach firmly in the ribs. "She's watching me."

"She's dazed by your bad manners," Rùnach said with a snort.

"Introduce us and we'll see which of us she likes better."

Rùnach rolled his eyes briefly, then turned a pleasant look on Aisling. "Uncle, if I might present Mistress Aisling, who is my, ah . . . well, my—"

"Questing companion," Aisling supplied.

Sosar laughed. Rùnach wasn't sure he found anything particularly amusing about that, but there it was. It was perhaps ridiculous to even be contemplating any sort of alliance with the woman in front of him, but he was beginning to wonder if he could bear even the thought of anything else.

"Rùnach always has had the best of fortune in finding questing companions whose loveliness leaves the entire room gasping for breath."

Aisling was looking at Sosar gravely. "I imagine he has."

"I, on the other hand, am always looking for a lovely woman to take pity on me and lower herself to at least sit with me at table. I don't suppose we could shove Rùnach down to one of the lower tables and you take his seat whilst I have yours, could we?"

"Of course, Prince Sosar."

Sosar looked at Rùnach. "You've been talking about me," he said with a knowing nod.

"Not a word," Rùnach said.

Sosar smiled slightly, then looked back at Aisling. "Then my father told you who I was."

She shook her head. "I just knew."

"What else do you know?"

Rùnach would have warned his uncle he was wading out into deep waters, but his elbow in Sosar's ribs went unheeded.

"I know you're one of Sìle's sons," she said slowly. "The youngest."

"As it happens," Sosar agreed.

"And you've lost your power."

Sosar went very still. "How do you know that?"

Her expression was very grave. "Because I know who has it." She reached out and put her hand on Sosar's arm. "I don't think you would want your magic back now."

"Ah," Sosar managed, "I imagine not."

She studied him a bit longer. "You know, he didn't take your birthright."

Sosar sat down abruptly on the edge of the table. Rùnach wasn't exactly sure Sosar hadn't sat down in a bit of Aisling's unfinished dinner, but since he'd joined his uncle in that sitting activity, he supposed he couldn't complain about the condition of his uncle's backside when his likely looked the same.

"What are you talking about?" he asked faintly, realizing only after the fact that Sosar had said the same thing.

Aisling winced. "I shouldn't have said anything."

"Nay," Sosar said faintly, "go on. I'm curious."

"A trait you share with your nephew," she noted.

"Aye, and look at what trouble it lands him in. I know I should avoid all displays of it, but I'll take my own advice tomorrow. What were you saying?"

Rùnach found himself the recipient of a questioning look from Aisling, which he answered with a helpless shrug. Sosar had asked, after all, and he was not a weak-stomached fop. Aisling took a deep breath.

"Lothar of Wychweald," she said very carefully. "He didn't take your birthright."

"I believe I need to sit," Sosar said thickly.

"You are sitting," Rùnach pointed out. "In Aisling's supper."

"Did you tell her?"

"About her supper? Nay, not yet."

Sosar shot him a weak glare. "About me."

"What do you think?"

"I think I need to sit closer to the floor, but that may happen all on its own." He looked at Aisling with a mixture of astonishment and horror. "What do you mean?"

Aisling struggled to put it into words. "It is," she began slowly, "as though he came along and cut down a mighty forest that had been growing for several centuries." She paused. "You have been alive for several centuries, haven't you?"

"To my continued surprise, aye."

"Well," she said, "I don't imagine you were born with a full complement of skills, were you?"

"I was too young at the time to remember."

She smiled. "I like you."

"Thank heavens."

Rùnach would have laughed, but he was too busy watching Aisling and wondering where indeed she had come from. Obviously he knew *where* she had come from, but as to the things she could do . . . He shook his head.

There was a mystery there.

And because he was who he was, he could hardly allow that sort of intriguing bit of unknowing to pass by without his notice. Her ability to see was something he could explain away readily enough, having known Soilléir of Cothromaiche for so many years. Perhaps there was something in the water in the north that infected both Bruadairians and Cothromaichians. But that was where understandable ended and things too odd for coincidence began.

For example, it was odd, wasn't it, that ability she had of spinning things most spinners wouldn't dream of putting on a bobbin? Not to mention what she was capable of fashioning the wheel itself from; that was something he'd never heard of in the whole of his life spent haunting libraries reading the obscure and usual. And what of that business in the garden earlier? She had touched that tree, held one of its blossoms, and suddenly she was speaking his tongue as if she had grown up doing just that.

None of that was magic, at least not in the traditional sense of the same.

He focused on the conversation going on in front of him and forced himself to catch up the thread of it. He didn't particularly care to let a mystery slip by him, but he would revisit it very soon.

"Just as a mighty forest doesn't grow overnight," Aisling was saying, "I would think your power grew as time passed." She paused. "Is that right? I don't know, you see, never having had much to do with elves."

Sosar looked at his nephew. "I feel like I'm talking to Soilléir."

"I understand," Rùnach said, with feeling, "believe me."

Sosar looked at her. "I think that might be right. That bit about growing."

"Then," she began, "if I could offer an opinion, I think the roots are still there. Rather scorched, I'm afraid, but still there. If you want the truth."

Sosar put his hand over his eyes. "I'm not sure I can bear any more truth."

"You might have to find a particular sort of soil to grow in for a bit, if you know what I mean." She paused. "Not that this wouldn't be a lovely place to garden." She looked at him. "I'm not sure it can give you what you need."

"What I need, I believe, is a very strong drink." He pushed himself up off the table, took Aisling's hand, and bent low over it. "I thank you, lady, for that." He straightened and looked at her seriously. "You have given me hope."

Aisling only nodded, looking slightly green. Rùnach would have pulled her down to sit next to him and asked her to explain what she had seen, but he hardly had the chance to open his mouth before another one of his cousins—one of his aunt Ciatach's extremely handsome lads who seemed to move quite easily between his mother's home in Tòrr Dòrainn and his father's in Ainneamh— had appeared at Aisling's side and lured her away to the middle of the hall for yet another dance. Rùnach watched her go, sighed, then dropped down into his chair. He looked up at his uncle who was far greener in the face than Aisling had been.

"How are you?"

"Almost speechless," Sosar said faintly. He shook his head slowly. "I also have a lovely chicken supper on the seat of my trousers."

"So you do."

Sosar eyed him. "I was going to spell them clean, but I don't suppose that's possible."

"Well, don't look at me."

Sosar bowed his head and laughed, though it sounded a miserable laugh indeed. He shot Rùnach a look. "We are quite a pair."

"So we are, but I avoided my plate."

"Which was clean anyway, so you needn't have worried."

"You could ask Còir or one of the other lads for aid," Rùnach pointed out.

"They would make the cloth disappear with the chicken remains, and then where would I be?"

Rùnach clucked his tongue. "Wishing you had instilled the proper fear and loathing into them several decades ago."

"I've been too busy being my charming and sunny self. Where is my mother? She wouldn't leave me humiliated."

Rùnach watched his uncle stumble away and had to admit there was something about what Aisling had said that left him feeling just the faintest bit of envy.

And no small bit of curiosity, it had to be said.

If Sosar's birthright were still there in his veins, then perhaps . . .

He cut off the thought before it had the chance to grow. It didn't matter what his own birthright might or might not have been; what mattered was the power of the mage who had stripped that birthright away. And the simple but undeniable truth was that Lothar of Wychweald, for all his bluster and arrogance, had never been and never would be anything but a neophyte when compared to Gair of Ceangail.

Would that the roles were reversed and his own power had been taken by someone with Lothar's lack of skill.

He immediately turned away from the thought, because it smacked too much of self-pity and because he wouldn't have traded the possibility of his having his own power back for Sosar's hope of the same.

Never mind that, in spite of the fact that he sat there in absolute mythological luxury, surrounded by souls whose beauty it was almost difficult for him to look at and he'd grown to manhood looking at them, all he had to his name was his name, his father's reputation that clung to him despite any attempts to dispel it, a pair of mysteries that perplexed him, and his own poor magicless self and ruined face.

It was almost enough to have him trotting after Sosar to see what his uncle might have languishing in bottles that needed to be emptied.

Instead, the moment the current song ended and another threatened to begin, he popped up out of his chair, walked with all due haste around the end of the table, and marched out purpose-fully onto the floor where he relieved yet another damned cousin of the exertion of partnering Aisling of Bruadair in yet another dance.

"You dance as well?" she asked in surprise, then she laughed a little. "I'm sorry. I forget who you are."

"I think, my lady, that *that* was a compliment." And he would have accepted those sorts of compliments far into the evening if it meant he could see her for a change looking as if the sword of death wasn't hanging over her head.

So he danced with her. He was slightly surprised that he remembered any of the steps but somehow less than surprised that she seemed to have learned a great many that evening thanks to her numerous tutors. When he thought he might fall asleep on his feet if he didn't close his eyes, he begged her to put him out of his misery and allow him to walk her back to her bedchamber. The older members of his family had already retired, and he wasn't about to humor the younger ones with any more time spent in Ais-ling's presence, so he led her out of the hall without saying any fond farewells.

She was silent on the way to her chamber, but she didn't look unhappy. Perhaps she was mulling over her choices for dancing partners on the morrow.

He stopped in front of her doorway and looked at her gravely. "How are you?"

"Tonight was a great diversion," she said slowly, "but even though I've eliminated a handful of things that should have sent me to an early grave, I still face one."

"The need for a mercenary?" he said.

She nodded. "You know, 'tis one thing to consider something from the safety and distance of time and place. It's another thing entirely to be coming up hard against it and know there is no more time for considering." She looked up at him. "But you know that, don't you?"

He had to lean against the wall, not because his knees were weak, but because she said the damndest things. "I think I might."

"There might still be something attached to the finding of my mercenary," she said reluctantly. "I can't be sure about that."

He supposed that now most of her secrets were out in the open there was no point in not telling her what he'd been planning, yet something stopped him. He reached out and tucked a stray strand of hair behind her ear. "You'll find what you need."

"I'm supposed to be at Taigh Hall tomorrow."

"Mercenary in tow?"

She nodded. "Unless I've counted amiss." She drew her hand over her eyes. "At the moment, I'm not sure of anything. Perhaps all I must do is secure a lad by tomorrow. The peddler didn't tell me I had to be at Taigh Hall myself." She started to speak, then shook her head. "I don't know what must happen exactly."

"I have a suggestion," he said. "Why don't you go to bed, have a beautiful-dream-filled rest thanks to the bedding that will no doubt tell you tales all night, and we'll discuss this tomorrow? All will be well."

"How?"

He took her hand, kissed the back of it, then smiled at her. "We'll discuss it tomorrow. My grandfather has a garrison, you know, and those lads are always ready for an adventure." Never mind that he had no intention of sending any of them off on any kind of journey.

She frowned at him, but that was ruined by an enormous yawn she hid behind her hand. She looked at him blearily.

"Tomorrow, then."

"Of course."

She shot him a warning look, then went inside. He gave vent to his own yawn, then stumbled to his own chamber where he managed to do nothing more than get his boots off before he cast himself down onto his bed and felt himself falling under sleep's spell.

But with his last conscious thought, he realized he was more lighthearted than he had been in years.

Perhaps there was something about the contemplation of a quest that was good for the soul of a man who had been too many years without one. Or perhaps it was the thought of coming back home—potentially—to a lass with pale hair and colorless eyes who might look on him with approval if he managed to see to that quest for her. He wasn't sure which it was. He just knew, with the accompanying feeling of destiny being satisfied, that he was on the right path.

He could only hope setting foot to that path wouldn't get him killed.

Seven

❧

Aisling woke to a sudden weight upon her chest. She opened her eyes and looked into the bluish-brown eyes of an extremely noisy chestnut cat who had apparently decided that her throat was the perfect place to put his nose and purr. She would have dislodged him without hesitation, but two things occurred to her in rapid succession.

First, that purring feline was Iteach. If she hadn't already suspected as much, his *goooood morrrrrrning* whispering across her mind would have identified him beyond any doubt.

Second, she was waking on a comfortable cot, which told her that either she had sleepwalked back to her bed or someone had seen her keeping watch over Rùnach's door and taken pity on her by lifting her off the ground. That was useful for her back, she supposed, but it hadn't done as much toward keeping her awake as repeated encounters with cold, dew-laden grass might have.

She squinted up at the sky above her and judged that whilst it might have been past dawn, it wasn't that far past dawn. With any luck, Rùnach hadn't managed to go anywhere yet.

Perhaps another might not have fretted over his whereabouts, but another likely wouldn't have realized approximately five heart-beats after she had closed her bedchamber door just exactly what Rùnach of Tòrr Dòrainn intended to do.

He intended to go off and save Bruadair.

The moment the thought had crossed her mind the night before, she'd known with dread certainty that it was true. He would take his sword in hand, trot off into the darkness with a grace and courage that no lad from Neroche could ever have hoped to match, and then he would get himself killed.

She had toyed with the idea of either clunking him on the head to stop him or, as seemed to have worked well enough in the past, stealing his horse to prevent him from taking wing into the deepening gloom. The second option seemed more likely at present given that she had his horse now sitting on her belly, kneading her flesh to apparently see if he could elicit more flinches. She sat up, scratched Iteach absently behind the ears, then noted the luxuriousness of the couch and the delightful softness of the blanket she was covered with.

Dastardly elves about their foul business during the night, no doubt. In fact, she wouldn't have been surprised to learn the chief instigator of her profound night's sleep had been the very man she had been spying on. Or, rather, attempting to spy on. Which hadn't gone all that well, she had to admit.

She put Iteach down on the ground, stood, then folded her blanket and left it on the couch. Then she looked down at Rùnach's horse.

"Do you know where he is?"

Iteach stared unblinkingly at her for a moment or two, then licked his paw and commenced washing his face.

She scowled at him and looked about herself for other potential sources of aid. She jumped a little when she realized her page was standing twenty feet away, trying to be unobtrusive. "Do you know where Prince Rùnach is, Giollan?" she asked.

"I believe, my lady, that he was last spotted walking near the lists."

Which was uncomfortably close to the gates. She suppressed the urge to indulge in one or two of Rùnach's favorite curses. "I need to speak with him immediately. Let's hurry and find him."

Giollan didn't seem inclined to question her, which she found somewhat terrifying. She had never been given charge of someone else. Even befriending other weavers in the Guild was severely frowned upon. There were times she wondered how she managed to move about in decent society with any success at all given the way she had passed almost the whole of her life. If it hadn't been for Mistress Muinear, she wouldn't have had any useful manners at all.

She hurried with Giollan through the palace itself, then had to stop at the gates to catch her breath, something she imagined Rùnach hadn't needed to do. She put her hand on the metal—ignoring the tales it had to tell of its trip through the king's forge—and waited until she thought she could carry on. She looked at Giollan, who was watching her with wide eyes.

"I'll be fine from here," she managed.

He didn't look convinced. "But your safety, my lady—"

"The king's glamour is impervious to assault, or so I understand," she said, sincerely hoping that was the case. "I will deliver my message to Prince Rùnach, then return posthaste."

Giollan didn't move back toward the palace. "I'll await you here."

She supposed she could argue with him all day and never move him, so she simply nodded, then strode away purposefully. It occurred to her that she should have brought a cloak of some kind, but perhaps her enthusiastic striding would keep her warm. It was definitely useful in getting her to her quarry that much more quickly.

She stopped herself just before she stumbled out into a little clearing that looked remarkably familiar. It was, she realized, the same place where she'd come to a stop the day before after she had run from the library. That she hadn't recognized her path already said much, perhaps, about her level of anxiety.

Rùnach stood in the middle of that glade, dressed for travel. She nodded to herself over the sight. She'd been right to suspect him of nefarious intentions—

Or perhaps not.

She brought her stampeding thoughts to an abrupt halt. She supposed she didn't know terribly much about the man, but she did know he would never have gone on any sort of journey without his gear, and at the moment he was definitely not wearing his pack. She wondered what he was doing until he turned a little to use the sunlight falling down on him to better read the book in his hands.

She considered him for a few minutes, then nodded to herself over the decision she'd made the night before. He was not at all what she'd been thinking of when she'd set out to find an assassin. She had contemplated at great length on her way to Gobhann the type of man she would need to find for the peddler to take back to Bruadair. She had envisioned a rather craggy, battle-hardened, disposable sort of lad who cared little for his life and was willing to risk it all for a hefty bag of gold. She'd assumed that rough sort of lad would be willing to march off into the fray, hopeless as the battle might have been, leaving her free to scamper off to some-where less dangerous.

She had never in her wildest dreams thought that the grandson of an elven king would be the one willing to do something she certainly wasn't willing to do herself.

Not only did she not want to return to Bruadair and unseat

Sglaimir, she also knew she *couldn't* do it. She was just a weaver who hated the art and wished for nothing more than to do something different, far away from where she'd spent almost the whole of her life as a slave to a loom. She had no interest in political intrigues and no skill with any sort of weapon save a modest ability to bend a bow and send an arrow in the vicinity of where she wanted it to go. Add to that her absolute terror over the thought of crossing back over the border into her land where she would immediately be captured and returned to the Guild, and she supposed she could consider herself singularly unqualified to take on any sort of noble quest.

I was too arrogant and stupid to be afraid.

Rùnach had told her that when she'd asked about his going to that horrible well of evil to try to save his family. The trouble was, she wasn't arrogant, and she didn't think she was particularly stupid. She was, however, definitely terrified. Though what she would face if she returned to Bruadair could be perhaps now classified as speculation, she had enough experience with the Guild to know what those who lived within Bruadair's borders were capable of.

She didn't want to die.

But she also didn't want to see Rùnach die.

She wasn't quite sure how to go about telling him either politely, so perhaps she would have to simply be impolite. She took a step forward but he didn't turn. He seemed to be particularly engrossed in the text he was holding. Perhaps it was the same book he'd been looking at the day before, the book that had set his grandfather's library to complaining so loudly.

She eased forward to have a look before he realized she was there and shut it up again. He was taller than she was by several inches, which made looking over his shoulder difficult but not impossible. She hadn't merely learned to weave at the Guild. Eavesdropping and knowing how to steal peeks at forbidden correspondence had been invaluable skills. She could bring to mind many times when both had proved her salvation.

Well, save that once when she'd been a score and one and gone to listen at the Guildmistress's door thanks to a suggestion from one of the less untrustworthy inhabitants of the place. She had listened to her parents sell her yet again without so much as a twinge of regret. She would have preferred to have been able to say that she hadn't eavesdropped since, but things were what they were, and she had a keen sense of self-preservation.

She moved around Rùnach's shoulder to get a better look at the pages in his hands. The writing there was in no language she had ever read. In fact, it looked like nothing more than scratches on the page, nonsensical and quite random.

Only when she looked at it, it felt as if she could indeed see a pattern. It was slippery somehow in a way that left her feeling as if she'd put her foot to the bank of a river and begun to slide toward its icy depths.

She looked up at Rùnach, but she couldn't see him. All she could hear was the rushing in her ears, and all she could see were the shadowy outstretched arms that waited there to welcome her into a cold, watery grave. She tried to clutch at something to keep herself from falling, but everything she reached for slipped away from her.

Aisling.

Aye, that was her name, but she couldn't hold on to it either.

She slid helplessly into oblivion.

Waking was, she had to admit, worse than falling. She couldn't move her head or her limbs, and she couldn't open her eyes. All she could do was struggle to breathe in and out, and hope she didn't soon retch on whoever was holding her.

"Aisling?"

She couldn't answer. All she could do was breathe.

"Can you open your eyes?"

She supposed if he could ask, she could try to oblige. She opened her eyes, then shut them up again right away to spare herself the humiliation of losing anything that might or might not have potentially been left inside her from supper the night before. It took her several minutes, she was fairly sure, before she had a sense of herself again.

She realized after a bit that she was sitting on Rùnach's lap with his arms around her.

"I feel terrible," she whispered.

"What in the world are you doing out here?" he asked.

She started to say *stopping you from going off to save my country*, but she realized immediately that if she admitted that whilst he had perhaps been merely out for a walk, she would make a colossal fool of herself. "Ah," she said, "well, what are you doing out here?"

"Trying to get out from underneath my grandfather's glamour so it wouldn't shout at me when I attempted to open this book. And that wasn't an answer to my question."

"Best you'll get at the moment," she said. She put her hand over her eyes for a moment or two, then pushed herself out of his arms and stood. That lasted only a heartbeat before she found herself sitting quite hard on the bench next to him. She realized she had sat upon his book, which unsettled her almost as much as looking inside its covers. She stood up and waited for him to remove it before she collapsed back down next to him. "What *is* that thing?"

He dragged his hand through his hair. "I'm not sure I can answer that at the moment." He hesitated, then shook his head. "I'm not sure what it is. Why don't you tell me instead what you saw?"

She leaned forward and put her face in her hands. "I'm not sure I saw anything," she managed. "Writing that didn't look like writing, perhaps."

"But you cried out," he pressed. "What did you see that inspired that?"

"A river," she said, though the memory of it wasn't a pleasant one. "I slipped down its bank and into freezing water. I was sure I would drown. That is, as you might imagine, the sort of thing that tends to unsettle a body." She shivered. "I feel as if I've been swimming in that icy stream in truth."

"Well, if it explains anything, you've been unconscious for an hour, and I couldn't call you back from wherever you were. If you hadn't still been breathing, I would have been sending for someone with spells to see to you. You absolutely won't be looking inside this bloody thing again."

"I think I should," she said gingerly. "I might see something useful."

"And I might be regretting the fact that I had to bury you under one of those trees you are so chummy with in Queen Brèagha's garden." He shook his head. "This has nothing to do with your present business. How it figures into mine is something I don't want to speculate on. Filching it was a whim; one I do truly regret. Now can you walk, or shall I carry you?"

She started to stand up, then realized immediately there was no point. "Neither. Not yet, at least."

He put his arm around her shoulders. "Then lean on me, if you like, for a bit until you're recovered."

She did like, so she leaned on him. She closed her eyes and wished that made things better. "You can't not tell me," she said, wondering if she might find a distraction in conversation. "About that book, that is."

He was silent for a moment or two, then sighed. "Very well, I'll tell you, though I hesitate to do so. The truth is, the book is mine."

"What do you mean, 'it's mine'?" she asked faintly. "*That* book?"

"Aye."

"But that's impossible. It's so dark."

"Thank you," he said ruefully. "I think."

She waited for him to say more, but all he did was rub the back of his neck. She could feel the tension in him, so she lifted her head and waved him away.

"Go pace," she said.

"Why do you think I need to?"

"Because this subject makes you uncomfortable and you think better when you're pacing." She looked in his general direction because she still couldn't quite focus on him. "I've watched you do it before."

He reached for her hand, squeezed it, then rose. "I might make you dizzy."

"I won't watch you." She put her hand over her eyes. "Go ahead and trot about to your heart's content. And I believe you owe me three answers, so speak whilst you're trotting."

"I owe you nothing," he said with a snort, "which you have obviously forgotten in your enthusiasm over my recent lengthy and readily given responses. We can perhaps trade a few answers if you care to."

She peeked at him from between her fingers. "I don't have any more answers, yet you apparently have quite a few secrets left."

He attempted a scowl, but he was either too unsettled to do it properly or he was simply too kind to frown at her. She took her hand away from her eyes and rested her chin on her fists instead. She smiled encouragingly.

"Go ahead. Spew away."

"I want it noted that I am much more inclined to answer questions than you have been," he grumbled.

"I'm not sure, Your Highness, that I would be boasting of anything in that regard, but I'll let that go. Why was your book in Diarmailt, and did you leave it there?"

He started to speak, then apparently changed his mind about something. "I have never been to Diarmailt until I went with you.

As to the other question, I have no idea why it would find itself there."

She watched him pace for several minutes before she thought he might be willing to address what troubled her most. "Did you write what was on those pages? I know 'tis none of my affair, but . . ." She took a careful breath. "It was evil, Rùnach. I can't believe you made those marks."

He smiled grimly. "I appreciate the confidence in my goodness, and nay, I didn't write what was there. It would seem that at some point in the past, my pages had been removed and others inserted."

"I wonder why?"

"I honestly don't know."

"Perhaps someone wanted what you had written down before."

He came to a stop, rubbed his hands over his face briefly, then sighed before he looked at her. "I suppose they might have. It was my private book of spells."

It was odd to think that at some point in the past, Rùnach had spent time writing down spells. She was so accustomed to him in his current incarnation, she could hardly imagine him with magic. She looked at him standing there with sunlight filtering down through his grandfather's glamour and wondered what he had been like before.

It occurred to her as well that while she had still seen echoes of Sosar's magic in his soul, in Rùnach's there was nothing left.

She rubbed her eyes because the sunlight was bright, not because they were stinging. "Were they good spells?" she asked, forcing herself to move past what she had—or, rather, hadn't—just seen.

"For the most part."

She looked at him in surprise. "Indeed? And for the other part?"

He walked away again. It took a bit before he stopped and looked at her. "Let's say this: my grandfather wouldn't have been pleased with them. Most were of my own making, using whatever magic seemed to suit the spell best. There were a handful, though, that were fashioned from . . ." He took a deep breath. "From less pleasant sources."

"I don't know anything about less pleasant sources."

"Be grateful."

"I think I am," she said honestly. "What happened to these spells, do you think?"

He walked for a minute or two more, then came and collapsed on the bench next to her with a sigh. "I can speculate, I suppose. They could have been taken by any number of souls, though perhaps common sense would suggest that whoever inserted the new pages was the one to take the old pages out. I'm not sure why anyone would have bothered. I'm even less sure why anyone would have hidden the book in the library at Eòlas. And lastly, I have no idea what those marks mean, but they make me ill to look at them myself, though not nearly as ill as they made you."

She would have gotten up to pace a bit herself, but she wasn't sure that wouldn't end with her pitching forward onto her face. She had trouble enough with her looks without adding injury to herself. She frowned a bit more, then looked at Rùnach.

"When did you leave the book behind?"

"A score of years ago."

"Oh," she said, and she needed no further elaboration to know why. Obviously he'd left it somewhere before he'd gone to the well with his family. "Here?"

He smiled grimly. "And have my grandfather stumble upon it? Nay, I left it in the care of the witchwoman of Fàs."

"Who is that?"

"The mother of my father's natural sons."

She made a valiant effort not to gape at him. "Is she a good person?"

"Well," he said slowly, "I'm not sure that's the word I would use to describe her. I trusted her, as odd as that sounds. She had little reason to allow the counters to all my father's spells to find their way into the world."

"Is that what the book was?"

He looked heavenward, then at her. "Aye, if you can believe my arrogance. My father honed his spells for a thousand years, and I thought I could counter them whilst still in my youth. I will admit that the spell that covers the pages was well done, but for the rest?" He shrugged. "I'm not the best one to judge. I'm not even sure I could write them down properly again. I've tried not to think about them over the years."

"And if someone found them and could use them?"

He considered, then shook his head. "I wouldn't want to speculate. The only mercy is that the spells can't be unlocked without the proper key, no one knows that particular spell but me, and I haven't the power to use it. Convenient, isn't it?"

"I think magic is a very dangerous thing."

"And that, my lady, is something we definitely can agree on." He rubbed his hands over his face, then smiled at her wearily. "I fear I didn't sleep very well last night."

Neither had she—or, rather, she had slept too well, but she wasn't ready to tell him why. She couldn't imagine that he hadn't seen her sprawled out on the little cot across from his bedchamber door, but perhaps he was too much of a gentleman to speak of it. She would have to talk to him about it soon, but she thought she might safely leave it for another hour or two.

"What you need then, my lad, is a nap somewhere beautiful." She pushed herself to her feet, swayed, then offered him her arm just as he had done so many times for her. "These lovely trees here have suggested that you might enjoy your grandmother's garden. I assume you know where that is?"

"I imagine I do."

"Then let's be on our way."

• • •

Aquarter hour later, she was walking with him into his grandmother's garden, a garden that seemed somehow much more private than anything she'd seen before. She supposed that was just as well because she suspected Rùnach wasn't going to last another five minutes before he fell asleep on his feet.

She sat down on a very lovely bench of smooth wood, then handed him the blanket she found sitting suddenly next to her. "You sleep. I'll keep watch, though I'm not sure with what. I think Iteach lost our bows."

"But fortunately not my sword, but that is currently propped up in a corner of my bedchamber." He stood and pulled a knife from his boot and handed it to her. "You won't need this, but studying the runes might keep you entertained for a bit." He spread out the blanket, then looked at her. "Care to join me?"

"I have too much to think on."

"But you would otherwise?"

She frowned at him. "Is this the sort of question you generally ask when in your grandmother's garden?"

He stretched out. "In truth, Aisling, I can't bring to mind a single woman I would have cared to nap with beneath my grandparent's trees save you." He folded his hands over his belly and looked up at her. "But since you're denying me that pleasure, you could at least send me off to sleep with a tale."

"What sort of tale?"

"Something told in Deuraich."

She wondered if she would get to the point where she stopped flinching at the things he knew. "What sort of something?"

"Do you have any myths?" he asked politely. "You know, involving pointy-eared creatures?"

"Aye, ugly little brutes who hide in closets and come out at night to vex naughty children."

He laughed a little. "No doubt."

"I'm not sure I should even tell you any of those stories. You'll just memorize the words."

"Most likely." He looked up at her, clear-eyed. "Because that's just what I do. That, and it might come in handy for me to know a bit of your tongue."

She had the feeling she knew exactly why he wanted to know what he wanted to know. Worse still, she knew that if she didn't humor him, he would just go behind her back and learn her language anyway.

She couldn't bring herself to tell him about sharp-eyed, sharp-nosed deirbs who tormented guilty sleepers, so she told him a tale about Maraiache of Clomhais who had set off on a journey to obtain a certain sort of spice he preferred for his stew and wound up finding much more than he'd bargained for. She had hardly gotten the poor mariner out to sea before Rùnach was asleep.

She watched him for quite a while, marveling at who—and what—he was, then she simply sat and listened to the garden murmuring as it did of endless spring and the conversations that had been held within its confines. The last light before twilight suffused the air, casting a soft glow over everything before her. She looked at that air, heavy with a golden glow, and wondered if it would permit her a liberty.

She took her pointer finger and spun the air to her right, a small circle only because she wasn't entirely sure what she intended to do. She created a bobbin spun by that flywheel and put things onto it: snatches of dreams dreamed by flowers that sang with soft, sleepy voices, and other things offered by the trees near her and the earth beneath her feet that weren't quite dreams but weren't exactly conscious thoughts either. And throughout the invisible thread she was creating, she added the bits of Fadaire she knew. She couldn't decide if those last things were magic or merely words, but they were exquisite and she couldn't resist them.

She stopped her flywheel and wondered what to do then. She took the bobbin she found she could actually handle now, unwound what seemed to be thread that was handled with equal ease, then looked down at it in her hands.

It was the stuff of dreams.

She looked at it until an idea came to her. She wound it from her hand to her elbow and back until the entire spun length was a circle, twisted it to keep it from unraveling, then leaned over and put it on Rùnach's head like a crown. It disappeared.

He sighed deeply.

Aisling jumped a little as she realized she and Rùnach were not alone. The queen of Tòrr Dòrainn stood to her left, watching her with a faint smile. Aisling pushed herself to her feet, but Brèagha shook her head, waving her back down to her spot on the bench. Rùnach's grandmother joined her there.

"How are you, darling?" the queen whispered.

"Unsettled."

Brèagha smiled. "Why is that?"

"Do you believe in curses, Your Majesty?"

"If you mean the sort of curse that is supposedly attached to speaking of one's homeland, then nay, I do not."

"What an interesting idea," Aisling managed. "A curse attached to a country."

"Isn't it, though?" Brèagha smiled. "Do you believe in such a thing?"

Aisling had to consider her answer for a moment before she could speak. Then she looked at the queen. "I don't believe I do, Your Majesty. Not any longer."

"I hoped not." She seemed to consider her words carefully. "You know, darling, there is a difference between a country supposedly protected by curses and a country that is simply shrouded in secrecy. Let me tell you of such a place. I don't imagine you've heard of An Céin, have you?"

Aisling shook her head. "I'm sorry, but nay."

"There is a reason for that," Brèagha said. "It is my homeland, but few know of it because my great-grandfather willed it so." She smiled. "Secret, not cursed, as it happens."

Aisling managed a smile. "I appreciate the difference."

"I think you do. We are a small country, unlike other countries that might or might not want to remain secret. We don't have treasures interesting enough for anyone to want to steal, and our magic is of a kind that isn't readily available to those who might want it. I daresay perhaps my great-grandfather didn't think we were important enough in the grander scheme of things to pay much heed to. It does lead one to have a certain perspective about one's place in the world." She looked out into her garden for a few minutes, in silence, then sighed. "I suppose that gave me an overconfidence when it came to discounting the potential for harm from other sources."

Aisling looked at Rùnach's grandmother and suspected she knew what Queen Brèagha was referring to. "Prince Gair?"

The queen nodded. "I feared what he could do to my daughter, but what mother doesn't want her daughter's mate to be beyond reproach?" She paused and seemed to choose her words carefully. "There is much damage a mage without scruples can do, I'll admit. And those who become too enamored of their own power tend to always want more of it, no matter who they hurt in the process. Gair was no different, I fear." She shrugged. "As for myself, I did not fear him. He was powerful, true, but my magic was—and is—nothing he wanted. We move very slowly in my country, keeping ourselves occupied with simpler things. Not even the elves here or to the west care overmuch about us."

"Save King Sìle, of course."

Brèagha smiled. "Well, Sìle is different. He was also young and arrogant when we first met, as well as terribly handsome. He didn't walk into a room that women didn't swoon. Rùnach is very much like him, I must say."

Aisling glanced at Rùnach. He was terribly handsome, true, in spite of his scars.

"I think the only reason Sìle looked at me twice was because I didn't swoon."

Aisling smiled at the queen. "Your Majesty, I would suspect that wasn't the only reason. King Mochriadhemiach told us a tale or two about your husband."

"I can only imagine," Brèagha said with a bit of a laugh. "Sìle has tormented Miach endlessly, so it wouldn't surprise me to know the tales were not all that flattering."

"Oh, they were," Aisling assured her. "Full of glory and brave deeds and the accomplishing of the latter that he might impress his future bride." She looked at Rùnach. "I can imagine, though, how Rùnach might fell an entire room."

Brèagha looked at Rùnach snoozing peacefully there at their feet. "I love all my grandchildren, of course, but I will admit to having a particular fondness for that one there. There is something to his character that is particularly pleasing." She studied him for a moment or two more. "He's dreaming. I think he has you to thank for that."

Aisling shifted uneasily. "I hope I didn't hurt him."

"I don't think that's in your nature."

"I don't know how to use this gift," Aisling said slowly. She met the queen's eyes. "If it is a gift."

Brèagha laughed a little. "Aisling, my darling girl, your art is far beyond anything of mine. I have no advice to offer you on how to use what has been given you."

Aisling shifted uncomfortably. "You can't mean that."

Brèagha took her hand and patted it. "I know you can't see it yet, but your destiny . . . nay, it would be imprudent to speak of it now. But I will say this much: I think in the end you will know far more about dreams than I do."

"But elves are creatures from dreams," Aisling said.

"Rubbish," Brèagha said with a merry smile. "Fanciful tales begun, I can assure you, by the elves of Ainneamh to keep lesser mortals from crossing their borders and pinching their daughters."

"I hesitate to mention this, Your Majesty, but those aren't the only elves there are tales about."

"Well, Sìle can't control everything, in spite of what he thinks. Neither can the rulers of Bruadair," Brèagha added very quietly, "though I imagine your current usurper might want to try."

Aisling supposed the only reason she didn't flinch was because she'd had so many shocks already that day. She took a deep breath and met the queen's lovely blue eyes. "How did you know where I was from?"

"I saw," Brèagha said simply. "You've already begun to, haven't you?"

"I fear so."

The queen smiled. "Aisling, there is so much loveliness ahead of you."

"But?"

The queen smiled. "You perhaps wouldn't value it then if you hadn't suffered in the past. As for anything more specific, I'll say that I don't know the state of Bruadairian politics these days save that Frèam and his lady are in exile. How are things inside your borders?"

"A man named Sglaimir rules," Aisling said, finding the words tumbling out of her mouth and hardly able to believe she was allowing them such free rein. "There are lads who want our country back from him. I wasn't privy to their conversations save the last one I heard where they discussed how they might accomplish that."

"What is their plan?" Brèagha asked.

"After ruling out an army or a powerful mage, they settled for the scheme of acquiring a mercenary who might, I assume, slip in the palace and do what needed to be done. They planned to be about the search themselves, of course, but things went awry and I was the only one available."

"Is that what you were told?" Brèagha asked with a faint smile.

Aisling blinked. "Well, aye. It's the truth. I was just in the wrong place at the wrong time."

"Which led you by means of a very circuitous route here, to this garden, to spin dreams to give my grandson something he hasn't had in a score of years? That's an interesting journey, don't you think?"

"Your Majesty, after the past few weeks I've had, I'm not sure I should think anymore."

Brèagha laughed. "I don't believe in coincidence, love. But before I say too much, I'll leave you to your thinking and Rùnach to his dreaming, and be pleased with both." She rose gracefully and smiled. "Dinner is in an hour, if you're interested."

Aisling nodded, thanked her, then watched her walk away. She took a deep breath and looked at Rùnach.

He was watching her.

"Are you awake?" she asked, jumping a little in surprise.

"I'm not sure."

"Why not?"

"I dreamed."

"Were they good dreams?"

He sat up and patted his head, as if he couldn't quite trust that his head was still attached. "Exceptionally lovely." He frowned. "I wonder why."

"I have no idea," she lied, because she couldn't bring herself to speak of what she'd done. "Your grandmother said supper was in an hour."

He heaved himself to his feet, picked up the blanket and

returned it to its place, then sat down next to her. "That will give you just enough time to finish the tale I fell asleep during, won't it?"

"Are you awake enough to hear it?"

He looked thoroughly bemused. "I'm honestly not sure, but I'll give it my best attention." He started to speak, then he frowned. He reached out and plucked something off her finger. "Have you been spinning?"

"It's possible," she managed.

He held up a strand of something that shimmered in the diffused light of the afternoon garden. "I think this is a dream."

"Is it?"

He looked at her, as if he might have been working something out in his head that he wasn't quite ready to discuss.

"Your grandmother said supper was in an hour," she reminded him.

"You said that already," he said slowly.

She bounced up, then rubbed her hands together. "We should go before we're late."

"I have a question for you—"

"Oh, isn't that the dinner bell?"

He harrumphed at her, then wound up the strand of whatever it was and tucked it into his pocket. "I'm not finished with you."

"I might need a lie-down before supper. I'm feeling faint."

"What you're feeling is the heavy weight of my disapproving glance at your hedging, but we'll discuss it after supper, when you're not feeling so faint." He took her hand. "Let's see what the lord of the hall has on the fire."

She walked with him, but her thoughts were less on food than they were on the things she had learned that day, more particularly what his grandmother had told her. She didn't think Sglaimir was a mage, but what did she know? And if he were capable of enslaving Bruadair, what else might he do if not stopped, though why he would have simply sat on his stolen throne for a score of years without looking further afield, she couldn't have said. Perhaps with too much power came madness.

At least she had survived the afternoon and kept Rùnach from fleeing his grandfather's hall to go off and do heroic deeds that would surely spell his end.

What the morrow would bring, she didn't dare begin to speculate.

Eight

Rùnach left his grandfather's hall and walked out into the lists as the sun was coming up. It was something he'd done for so many years during his youth that doing so as a man—with the ability to hold a sword, thankfully—was almost a bit startling. He could only hope to find a swordsman out there who might be able to put aside any hesitance he might have felt at treating an heir to the throne—however far the distance might have been—as just another lad. Rùnach supposed that might be the only thing that saved his sanity that morning.

He'd already gone to check on Aisling only to hear a report from her maid that she was sleeping peacefully. At least she hadn't been sitting, sound asleep, against a pillar in the garden outside his room again. He had found a cot for her that first night they'd been in Seanagarra, moved her to it, and covered her with a blanket before he'd returned to his own rest. He didn't suppose she would simply up and run off into the distance to be about her quest, but then again, he supposed he honestly wouldn't have been surprised by anything she did. He had woken from a nap he hadn't been able to put off the day before fully expecting to find she had bolted. He surely wouldn't have been in any condition to have trotted off after her.

Because he had, and he could hardly believe he hadn't imagined the whole thing, dreamed.

He had managed to escort Aisling back to her chamber for her maid to repair her hair, run to his chamber to change for supper himself, then get back to her chamber in time to be rendered speechless by the sight of her.

Beautiful? Nay, not beautiful.

He had found himself unequal to latching onto any adjective that described her. The elves of Ainneamh were famous for noising about the tale that they looked as if they had just stepped from a dream. Rùnach could safely say that he had seen a creature who fit that description, and it wasn't any of the lads or lassies to the west.

He had escorted her to supper, unable to muster up even the most banal of conversations. It had given him ample time to simply look at her and admire, but it had also left an opening—again— for a steady and quite annoying stream of cousins to present themselves at her elbow and request her company for a dance.

Of course that dancing had required instruction in new steps, which had required more time with the aforementioned cousins he sincerely hoped he would soon see in the lists where he might help them understand that good manners set limits on the number of times one might monopolize a woman who had been escorted to supper by someone else.

He had managed a dance or two with her himself, then finally escorted her to her room when she looked as if she had had almost as much as she could bear. They hadn't spoken any more of Bruadair, his missing spells, or the fact that he knew that this was her last day to find a mercenary willing to travel north and save her country from its villainous ruler.

He had been happy to let those topics lie, and he hadn't dared even speculate on what she was thinking about them. If she'd been a dab hand at courtly intrigues or one to tap him smartly on the shoulder with a rolled up list of men she had rejected simply for the sport of it, he might have known how to take her. As it was, all he could do was stare at her and wonder what in the world was going on in her head.

He couldn't help but believe she had been affected adversely by her time in that damned Guild, forced into servitude by her parents. If she had visions of her sire and dam slaving away in a mine, he had far worse.

He shook his head. Bruadair. She had been tasked with finding someone to save the whole bloody country. He could scarce believe it.

He walked out into his grandfather's lists and through someone. The sensation was so breath stealing, he almost fainted. He gasped, then whirled around to find himself looking, well, at himself.

Or, rather, his youngest brother, who was, he supposed anyone would admit, much more handsome than he himself was at the moment.

"Ruith," he said, wishing he had the breath to laugh a little as he so desperately wanted to, "what are you doing here?"

Ruith hadn't changed in a score of years. He had been driven and hopelessly serious as a young lad. He was terrifyingly so as a man full grown.

"I wanted to talk to you."

"But I just saw you—"

"Two months ago."

"I suppose that's true," Rùnach allowed. He looked around himself, then smiled politely. "I don't see any means of travel, nor do I see your wife. Forget them both, did you?"

Ruith dragged his hands through his hair, looking as scattered as the wind he'd just blown in as. "Nay, actually, I didn't. I was in haste, and Sarah agreed to stay behind and prepare to entertain guests who stand to arrive in a fortnight or so."

"And who are you entertaining these days?" Rùnach asked politely.

"King Frèam and Queen Leaghra of Bruadair."

Rùnach choked. Or at least he thought he had choked. He wasn't entirely sure. All he knew was that he suddenly found himself hunched over with his hands on his knees, sucking in very unsuccessful breaths.

"They're bringing us a wedding present," Ruith said. "Some tapestry, no doubt adorned with half-dressed figures and swords and flowers. I can scarce wait to see it. Why do you ask?"

Rùnach straightened in time to find Aisling standing five paces away, looking at him as if she thought he might soon perish from lack of air. He lost his breath yet again and wondered if it might be better if he simply went back to bed.

Aisling moved closer to him. Well, closer and a bit in front of him, if he were to describe her location exactly.

He paused. Very well, so she put herself directly in front of him, between him and his brother. He was winded; there was no point in attempting to save his pride. Between his shapechanging brother and his, ah, his overprotective *questing companion*, he was simply not at his best.

"You look like Rùnach," she announced.

"We're brothers."

"Which one are you?"

"Ruithneadh," Ruith said. "The youngest of all save Mhorghain. Has Rùnach talked of me?"

Rùnach rolled his eyes and heaved himself upright. "Aye, to give her a detailed recounting of all your faults. Aisling, this is Ruith. Ruith, this is Aisling."

"I see," Ruith said.

Rùnach had the feeling he did, far too clearly. He ignored his brother and shuffled a step forward until he was standing next to Aisling.

"You're up early," he said to her.

"Your cousin Còir told me last night that he was a marvelous swordsman. He promised to show me this morning what he could do."

"I imagine he did," Ruith said mildly.

Rùnach shot his brother a dark look, then smiled at Aisling. "Keep in mind he's not very bright."

"He seemed fairly bright last evening."

"It was an aberration, believe me."

Aisling started to speak, then caught sight of the very eligible, highly intelligent, and hopelessly skilled Còir of Tòrr Dòrainn striding out into the lists as if he owned them.

Rùnach suppressed the urge to grind his teeth.

"I'd better go," she said.

"I'll be here, polishing up my meager sword skill with my brother," Rùnach said, but he supposed she hadn't heard him. She had wandered away to go bask in the glow of an elven princeling whose perfection was only matched by his ego. Rùnach watched her go, then turned to his brother. "I hate him."

"I believe you always have."

"He makes me feel old."

"Rùnach, he's three centuries older than you are," Ruith said with a snort. "And he's a shameless flirt. Even I remember him as such."

"Which she won't understand, which means he'll hurt her and I'll have to kill him. I think that will result in my being banished."

Ruith smiled. "Who is she?"

"Someone I met in Gobhann."

"What was she doing in Gobhann?"

"Looking for an assassin."

Ruith looked at him in surprise. "A what?"

"Someone to sneak inside her village and rid it of the lad who has taken it upon himself to make everyone miserable," Rùnach said evenly. "Only it's not just a village."

"Isn't it?"

"Nay, it isn't."

Ruith waited, then rolled his eyes. "Do you want me to guess?"

"Can I stop you?"

"Where would be the sport in that?" He studied Aisling for a moment or two. "She has magic—"

"Why does everyone insist on saying that?" Rùnach asked, feeling slightly irritated. "Hell, Ruith, until a fortnight ago, she thought elves, dwarves, dragons, and their ilk were creatures from myth. Why would she have magic?"

Ruith looked at him. "Why wouldn't she?"

"Because she can't cast a spell or shapechange or do anything a normal mage can do. And even if she did have magic, which she doesn't, she wouldn't believe it."

It was odd, though, wasn't it, how everyone seemed determined to credit her with what she couldn't possibly have? He knew he'd considered it before and taken into consideration the fact that she could admittedly spin unusual things—

He shook his head. It was impossible. Perhaps the ability to spin was something all Bruadairian lassies had. Ruith's wife Sarah could spin and she could See. Admittedly, he'd never seen her spin air or water or fire, but he hadn't spent all that much time with her nor had he asked her if she could.

"There is something different about her," Ruith mused. "Something . . ." He thought for a moment, then shook his head. "She's haunting. Like something from a dream."

Dreams. Rùnach suppressed the urge to swear. If he had to hear anything more about dreams . . .

"Not an elf, definitely, but not exactly mortal either, is she?"

Rùnach froze. "What do you mean?"

Ruith considered for several long moments in silence, then finally shrugged. "I don't know what I mean. She's just different. She reminds me a bit of Soilléir, though I couldn't say why." He looked back at Rùnach. "Who is she, in truth?"

Rùnach hardly knew where to begin, but he supposed the wrong place would be with telling secrets that weren't his. He was the first to admit he hadn't seen his brother in two decades, but he could remember very well how even as a child Ruith had had an uncanny sense of discernment. Perhaps he would have to reveal less than he feared.

"She's a weaver," he said finally, "who was sent on a quest to find an assassin to rid her village of a usurper."

"So you said before." Ruith turned to look at Aisling. "Is she auditioning helpers over there, do you suppose?"

Rùnach turned to follow his brother's gaze only to wish he hadn't. Damn that Còir if he hadn't ordered up a dozen longbows of various rare and valuable woods with which to tempt a Bruadairian lass who Rùnach had to admit was somewhat terrifying with a bow in her hand.

"You can't kill him," Ruith said mildly.

"A man can dream. And aye, I believe she's testing the mercenary waters."

Ruith studied Aisling a bit longer. "There is something about her that seems familiar—" He froze, then shook his head as if something had occurred to him that he simply couldn't believe. He attempted speech for a moment or two, then he simply looked at Rùnach in shock. "Is she from *Bruadair*?"

"I can't say."

"You don't have to. Bloody hell, Rùnach, why in the world would she be off on a quest to rescue *that* place?"

"Is it so terrible?" Rùnach asked. "That place?"

"I've never been and neither has Sarah, so I'm not the one to ask, though I've heard rumors." He paused, then shook his head. "Their king and queen are quite lovely people, but . . ." He shook his head. "I'm not sure *terrible* is the right word for it. Odd things happen there. And nay, I can tell you no more than that. You would have to ask Soilléir, perhaps, for more details. I just know that no one crosses the border."

"But Aisling did."

"Then she had help. If she's not royalty, then she was aided either by a trader or someone else with enough gold to bribe the guards to let her pass." He frowned. "Haven't you asked her for the details?"

Rùnach shook his head. "'Tis only since yesterday that she knows I know where she's from. She was told that if she divulged any of the details of her quest, she would die."

"What absolute rot."

"I agree. I think whoever has taken over her country has done his work well. At least Aisling seems to believe—or, rather, she used to believe—that she is absolutely powerless in the face of whatever curses are attached to the land. I don't suppose you would have any details about the current political situation, would you?"

"I doubt any more than you do," Ruith said. "I could ask Frèam and Leaghra for you, if you like, but that might reveal more than you care for to souls you might want to keep in the dark until you've given them a vacant throne to return to. I assume you're going to be in the thick of things."

"Who, me?" Rùnach asked. "Me, with hands that barely work and not a drop of magic to my name?"

"Battles have been won with less."

"By whom?" Rùnach grumbled.

"Perhaps by you," Ruith said seriously, "and perhaps in a way that songs will be sung about it for centuries to come. If your lady will allow you to hoist your sword in her country's defense, which still seems to be in some doubt."

Rùnach didn't bother telling his brother what his plans were because he had the feeling that Ruith could see them written rather plainly on his face. He rubbed his hands over that face and wondered how long he would have to watch Aisling kept captive in the clutches of the embodiment of elven perfection before he could march over to liberate her—

"You know we all wanted to be you."

Rùnach wondered if he would ever again manage to pass any time at all without being winded from directions he hadn't been looking. He looked at his brother.

"I honestly can't imagine why."

"Because you were fearless," Ruith said. "And possessing sword skill and spell skill we all despaired of ever having for ourselves. If you want to know the truth, I think Father disliked you the most."

Rùnach smiled in spite of himself. "Now, that is something to be proud of, I suppose."

"It would gall him to know you were alive."

"Are you going to tell him?"

"I honestly had never intended to return to his little hovel in the woods, but the pleasure of giving him those tidings might change my mind on that. And speaking of Father, I brought you something."

Rùnach felt time slow to a crawl. He supposed he should have realized that Ruith wouldn't have made a journey to find him without having had a good reason to do so, but he honestly couldn't imagine what his brother had for him. He frowned.

"I already have Father's ring. What else can I possibly need?"

Ruith shrugged out of a small pack, opened it, then pulled out a book. He held it out without comment.

Rùnach knew without opening it what it contained. He drew back as if his brother were trying to hand him a Natharian viper. He'd seen more of those slither out from beneath Droch of

Saothair's door in Buidseachd than was polite, so he knew of what he spoke.

"I don't want them," he said without hesitation.

"I don't want to give them to you," Ruith said. "Which I imagine you know."

Rùnach had to admit that was true. Miach had been willing to give those spells to Rùnach, to replace the memories Rùnach had lost, but Ruith had not only never offered, he had been adamantly opposed to the idea. Why he had changed his mind was something Rùnach thought he might not particularly want to know. He looked at the book in his brother's hand with distaste.

"Tell me the old bastard didn't write them down himself. Again."

"Nay, I wrote them all down," Ruith said calmly. "And because you and Keir taught us to memorize things instantly, I know they're a perfect copy of what Father had written down himself in that damned book of his."

"Ruith, I do not want these."

"I know, brother, but what you want and what you need are often two separate things."

Rùnach pursed his lips. "Why does that sound as if you're quoting someone?"

"I believe I'm quoting you."

"I don't remember saying such a . . ." He searched for the right word, but all that came to mind were curses he didn't have the energy to utter. "What a stupid thing to have ever said. Stupid and rather unoriginal." He blew out his breath in frustration. "I'm not off to fight Father, so what good will his spells do me? In fact, all that having them will do is make me worth the effort being spent trying to find me."

Ruith looked at him in surprise. "Is someone looking for you?"

Rùnach nodded at a bench set against a low wall to his right. "I'll leave my gear there, then let's walk. I'm not equal to facing this conversation whilst standing still."

Ruith nodded and followed him across the lists. Rùnach made a point of not commenting on the fact that his brother had put the book back into the pack he had been wearing but subsequently shrugged out of. He understood why Ruith had done so. There was no point in someone accidentally stumbling upon those pages full of evil.

An elegant, impossibly powerful bit of evil, it had to be said, damn their father to hell and back a thousand times.

"A turn about the lists," Ruith suggested. "I wonder if it will take us near your lady and her bowmaster?"

"Let's go see," Rùnach said, starting off on a circle near the wall with his brother. "And to answer your question, whilst it is merely Gàrlach I had the misfortune of encountering several days ago, it is Acair who seeks me. Actually, for all I know, the whole damned litter of bastard brothers is out there looking for me."

"Well, they are rather homeless at the moment, so I suppose that's possible."

Rùnach smiled briefly. "Are you still enjoying bringing Ceangail down around their ears?"

"It wasn't me, it was Franciscus of Cothromaiche who was responsible, but aye, I do relive the moment now and again with pleasure."

Rùnach considered. "Miach claimed that Acair was slain by Lothar several months ago."

Ruith shook his head. "We discussed that very briefly when I saw him at Tor Neroche yesterday, being as I was on the hunt for you. Acair was definitely at Ceangail when last I was there. I can't say I was paying too much attention to him, though I did note that he was very quiet and looked as if he'd been through something he didn't particularly care to discuss."

"I don't want to imagine what."

"Perhaps it was his escape from Riamh." He considered for a bit, then frowned. "What does he want from you, do you think?"

"The same thing all of them always want," Rùnach said grimly. "Father's spells."

"You know, brother, I have never understood why they don't have them already. I went to Ceangail precisely because I assumed the spells would be in the library."

"I imagine they were at one time," Rùnach said. "Obviously Father had put them somewhere else before we went to the well. I know without a doubt that he didn't trust any of the lads with them." He shook his head. "Those spells are the very last thing I should know whilst I have no way to protect myself."

Ruith stopped, then turned to face him. "Rùnach, I'll be perfectly honest and tell you I wouldn't have traveled first to Lismòr, then Tor Neroche to find you if I hadn't felt an overpowering sense of urgency that you have these in your hands."

"In case you've forgotten, brother, you absolutely refused to give these to me two months ago when you and Miach were discussing the idea."

"Things change."

"I'm not interested in this change."

Ruith rolled his eyes. "You've spent too much time with Soilléir. Stop being such a purist."

"I note that you weren't so fastidious about not using his spells of essence changing recently."

Ruith snorted. "Neither was Miach, though he'll just look at you blankly if you press him on it. He used several things at the well that he won't discuss."

Rùnach rubbed his hands over his face. It was so damned tempting to take the book and just have a look at the spells, perhaps to see if he remembered anything of them or if seeing his father's work again after a score of years might show him things he hadn't seen before—

He shook his head sharply, then looked at his brother. "No," he said firmly.

Ruith's expression was grim. "I think you may wish you had at some point."

"I can't imagine why."

"Better that you're prepared if you discover that reason than not, wouldn't you say?"

Rùnach set his jaw. "I don't want them."

Ruith looked at him for several very long minutes in silence, then sighed. "As you will, then. I'll destroy the book."

"Very wise. I assume you're staying for supper?"

"After I've stayed for breakfast and luncheon, aye, most likely."

Rùnach sighed. Aye, it was indeed just after sunrise. "It's been a very long pair of fortnights."

"I can imagine it has been, but whilst we're out here, shall we work a bit? It might take your mind off that rather robust line that seems to be forming to court your future wife."

Rùnach choked. He managed to regain his breath without his brother having to slap it back into him, then he gaped at him.

"My *what*?"

"Well," Ruith said with a shrug, "that's a bit of quest to go on for merely a comrade-in-arms, don't you think?"

"What I think is I would be daft to think to wed the first female I meet after twenty years at Buidseachd."

Ruith turned and walked back to where they'd left their gear. "It worked for me," he tossed over his shoulder as he started across the field, "but perhaps you're just not as clever as I am."

Rùnach found he had absolutely no answer for that. But he did have a swordsman of decent mettle with which to distract himself for a bit, so perhaps that was all he could ask for.

S even.
       That was the number of his cousins who had annoyed him that morning in the lists. Seven was still the number of cousins

who had annoyed him as he'd left the lists. Seven was the number of cousins he would likely do damage to if they did as they threatened, which was to find Aisling and escort her to supper.

Perhaps the look he had shot the lot had done what it was intended to do, for he'd managed to get Aisling free of the lists without anyone else having come with them.

Family. What had he been thinking to make a visit?

He glanced at Aisling to see how she fared. She was walking alongside him, looking grave. He reached for her hand and found it cold to the touch. He frowned but continued on along the path until they had reached his grandmother's garden. He made certain they were alone, then led her over to his favorite bench. He invited her to sit, then sat down next to her.

"How are you?" he asked.

"It's a bit like being trapped in a dream," she admitted.

Well, at least it wasn't a heroic tale with a lad from Neroche in the lead role.

And then he realized that she'd said it in Fadaire. He realized that at some point he was going to have to stop simply gaping at her every time she did something startling. The truth was, she continually startled him, which left him, he supposed, looking rather less suave and composed than he might have liked.

She tilted her head briefly as if she listened, then smiled at him. "He is dreaming."

"He—who?"

"This tree. He's very proud of his blossoms, you know. And quite aware of his place in the queen's favorite garden." She looked at him solemnly. "He's taught me quite a bit of your tongue."

"So I hear," Rùnach managed. "How exactly is he doing that?"

"Well, I held one of his blossoms earlier, so now his words are flowing into my mind. I suppose that's one way to describe it, though it's not completely accurate." She paused. "He has more to say than the one in the garden near your bedchamber, but I think that might be because he's much older." She smiled at Rùnach. "Have you never heard them?"

"In my youth I could hear the trees singing here, but I've never had them tell me their tales."

"Never?"

He lifted an eyebrow briefly. "Not anything I would want to repeat to you, if you want me to be entirely truthful. And if you want more truth, I *have* heard from the trees surrounding my paternal grandfather's lake. Repeatedly. Perhaps not in the dulcet tones you've heard here."

She smiled. "What terrible thing did you do there?"

"Fixed targets to several of them when I was a lad and used those targets for their intended purposes."

"I suspect they were happy to be of use to you."

"And I suspect they weren't," he said with a snort, "which you might believe as well if you'd been counting the number of roots that have tripped me up where roots hadn't been but a moment before."

She laughed a little, and the tree rustled along with her in his dreams.

Rùnach thought he might need to remain seated on his current perch longer than he might have suspected previously. How was it that a cloistered weaver from an obscure city in a country that reputedly didn't exist could now be speaking to him with the bulk of her words being in Fadaire?

"Do you mind?" she asked.

He pulled himself away from his ruminations. "Mind what?"

"If I speak your tongue?"

"Only in that you haven't yet taught me a like number of words in yours."

Her smile faded. "I'm not sure I want to teach you any."

"Then how will I fight your battles for you?"

She put her hands over her face. He realized then that she was trembling, and he didn't think it was from laughter. He wondered if perhaps he should have spent a bit more time with the fairer sex over the past several years. He was, he could admit without any undue pride, adept at picking up the purposely discarded handkerchief, understanding delicate flirtations engaged in over fans and nosegays, and unsurpassed at sidestepping blatant and unwanted advances from women who should have known better. But unraveling the thoughts of a woman who never quite reacted the way he expected?

He was swimming in very deep waters indeed.

"I realize," he said finally when he thought she might never speak again, "that perhaps you were hoping for someone else, someone with magic perhaps or more sword skill—"

She looked at him so quickly, she startled him. "That isn't it at all."

"Then what is it?"

"I'm not sure I can admit to such craven thoughts."

"I imagine I've had many of the like," he said, "so go ahead and admit your darkest secrets."

She looked at him then, her pale, almost colorless eyes full of what he supposed might have been a mixture of grief and shame, though over what he couldn't imagine.

"I was hoping to send the lad off, then run the other way."

He could understand that, perhaps more fully than she might suspect. After all, he'd spent twenty years hiding in the shadows.

"Given that I hadn't intended to take you with me," he said carefully, "I'm not sure that matters."

"But that was before I ever considered that the lad might be you," she continued, as if she hadn't heard him.

He started to tell her that she didn't need to worry about that, but he was interrupted by her page Giollan suddenly appearing a discreet distance away.

"Aye, lad?"

"Your Highness, the king extends his invitation for you and the lady Aisling to attend him in his private solar for luncheon. He bid me inform you that unfortunately none of the princes your cousins will be able to be there."

"What a pity," Rùnach said, wondering if the day might be brightening in spite of itself. "When does he want us?"

"At noon, Your Highness."

"We'll be there," Rùnach said. "Thank you, lad." He looked at Aisling. "Your bedchamber is just around the corner. What do you say to a wee rest before the rigors of an afternoon in my grandfather's solar are upon us?"

She nodded and rose with him, but she said nothing, which worried him. He supposed she wouldn't run off into the woods on a whim, at least not without his grandfather's glamour having told him so first.

He wasn't altogether sure he wanted to listen to what his grandfather himself would have to say when Rùnach announced his plans for the immediate future.

He walked Aisling to her door, then studied her face to see if he could see any indication there that she was about to do something rash. All he saw there was a deep misery that he suspected no words of his would assuage. He would have drawn her into his arms, but he suspected that might not go very well. So he simply watched her until she apparently remembered she was supposed to be going inside. She looked up at him for a very long moment, then turned and walked into her bedchamber, shutting the door softly behind her.

He turned and walked swiftly down the portico. He would have a wash, change his clothes, then take up a post in the garden outside her bedchamber door so he would be there to stop her before she did something foolish. It occurred to him that that was exactly what she'd done, but all he could do was say he understood.

Completely.

Nine

Aisling opened the door and looked carefully out into the passageway. Finding no one there she knew, she stepped out of her bedchamber and pulled the door shut behind her.

She had been in her chamber for all of five minutes, and that had been enough for her. If she didn't find a place where she could walk in peace and escape her thoughts, she was going to have some sort of an attack. Despite their beauty and gracious manners, she was finished for the moment with elves. Dancing with them, talking to them, looking at bows with them: she was finished. Well, unless that elf was Rùnach, perhaps, but he was part wizard, so perhaps that streak of something wild was what rescued him from being just too perfect.

Nay, the truth was, she needed peace for thinking—and her thoughts were not pleasant ones.

She walked for perhaps a quarter hour before she could even

face what was troubling her the most. She'd known it all along, of course, but having to face the truth was more difficult than she'd suspected. It wasn't that she didn't want Rùnach to go to Bruadair, though that was certainly the case. It wasn't even that she had discovered that the curses she had lived under the threat of for the whole of her life weren't true.

It was that she was a coward.

She had suspected it before, of course. After all, how many times had she slipped off into the shadows when another inmate in the Guild had run afoul of the Guildmistress's ire lest she find herself in the woman's sights as well? That had been in her youth, of course, but she couldn't say she had improved since then. She had simply learned to keep her head down and not attract any attention.

Nay, she had to be honest. She had ignored things she should have spoken up about. She had ignored the souls around her who could have likely benefitted from her aid, even in the smallest measure. She had been a coward of the worst sort.

Things hadn't changed recently. She had had her quest thrust upon her, true, but she had been, in the back of her mind, in the place where she kept her most difficult-to-look-at thoughts, fully prepared to find a rough lad and send him off to Taigh Hall without another thought whilst she ran off in a different direction entirely. She had made plans, in a different place in her mind where she visited slightly more often, to hoard the peddler's gold he'd intended for her until she could find a safe place, a little village where she could do whatever work was available and earn enough money to feed and clothe herself.

But return to Bruadair?

Not if her life depended on it.

She wasn't sure anything had changed, if she were to be completely honest with herself. The very last thing she wanted to do was go anywhere near the place.

Courage is not the absence of fear.

She was fairly sure she'd read that somewhere, buried in amongst Weger's strictures, perhaps. The problem was, she wasn't afraid.

She was paralyzed with terror.

To call Beul a hellhole was to sadly understate its flaws. It was the embodiment of misery, street after street full of hopeless souls wandering aimlessly through lives so bleak, she would fall on the nearest sword before she would become one of them again. Just thinking about her own life where the days had been filled with endless toil and there had never been any thought of anything else—

She turned a corner, then pulled back immediately. Rùnach was standing there with his brother. She leaned forward and looked again, but they had their backs to her. Though she couldn't see their faces, she knew well enough what they looked like. They looked to be of the same age and resembled each other closely enough that no one would have any trouble knowing they were brothers, scarred as Rùnach was.

That was where the similarities ended. Ruith had been a perfect gentleman earlier in the lists, and she couldn't imagine there would be a soul in the world who wouldn't have been happy to pass any number of hours in his pleasant company. Yet even with that, she preferred Rùnach. He had an elegance about him that his brother did not, something she supposed that had been honed very well in the palace behind her: a fondness for a well-turned phrase, pleasure in fine music and tasty edibles, and a wry sense of humor it hadn't taken her any time at all to learn to appreciate.

Well, all those fine qualities augmented by the fact that he was obviously going to do what she should have been willing to do without waiting for her even to have the courage to leave her room.

She closed her eyes, took a deep breath, and pulled back behind the corner. Perhaps she wouldn't go with him all the way to Bruadair, but she would at least tell him what she'd been told and where he would need to go first. Craven, aye, but who could blame her?

Besides, no one had to know that she was so sick with fear over the thought of returning home that her legs were like jelly beneath her and she thought she might lose the lovely breakfast she'd ingested a pair of hours earlier. She could send Rùnach off into the darkness, then disappear where no one would ever find her again.

After all, it was what she did best. She had spent a score of years as a virtual prisoner in a Guild where the work never ended, and she had absolutely no desire to endure it for even a single day more. If cowardice saved her from that fate, then so be it.

Though she had the feeling Weger wouldn't have approved of that thinking, and he would have told her as much quite loudly whilst at the same time telling her to stop looking at the ground.

If only all her troubles could have been solved by the application of a stricture written by a man who lived a life of simplicity far away from troubles such as hers.

She heard voices approaching, so she quickly looked for the nearest place to hide. She found nothing, so she simply flattened herself against the wall and hoped she would be overlooked.

The brothers had come to the end of the passageway, but they turned right instead of left, something for which she was extremely grateful. She watched them walk off, discussing something she couldn't see.

"You're mad to have it."

"And I should have instead left it in that damned library of Simeon's? I shudder to think who would have filched it at some point—or, more to the point, returned for it."

"I'll allow the thought is sobering. Very well, who do you think this belongs to?"

"I don't recognize the hand, which I suppose doesn't mean anything. I would hazard a guess it's one of the lads, though—"

Aisling heard nothing after that, though she was half tempted to follow them to find out who the lads were. She had the feeling she knew the book they were discussing, that horrible book that

Rùnach had been looking at the day before. She wondered who had taken his spells out and replaced them with marks that had created something evil right there in front of her.

Well, she didn't know that, but what she did know was that Rùnach was dabbling in things she had absolutely no ability to face. She couldn't even face the thought of going back toward her past. It would have been worse than going to prison, she supposed, not having gone to prison before. At least with a dungeon, it was only one's imagination that conjured up scenes of torment and misery. With the Guild, she knew exactly what she would face.

And if she crossed Bruadair's thin, glowing border, she would be caught, taken back to the Guild, and then her parents and the Guildmistress would put their heads together to invent a way to keep her there for the rest of her life. She would never again see Rùnach, never again see the stars from the back of a pegasus, never again hear the delicate rustle of flowers in an elven king's garden or listen to the deep, endless dreams of trees that bloomed with gladness because they loved the queenly mistress who tended them so faithfully.

She continued to walk aimlessly, trying to keep some sort of respectable distance between her and her thoughts, until she realized she was standing in front of King Sìle's library without really knowing how she'd gotten there. She supposed it was distraction enough. Heaven knew she needed something to do besides wallow in her own terrible thoughts.

She put her hand on the door and opened it slowly. She looked inside but found it empty. Well, the spots in front of the fire were empty, as were the tables where more serious scholarship could take place. The librarian—she couldn't remember his name at the moment—was most definitely in his place, though she suspected he never left that place. Perhaps elvish librarians took naps whilst their patrons were engrossed in whatever texts they were reading so they could always be ready and waiting to direct newcomers to what they were looking for.

She didn't have the courage to simply stride back into the stacks as if she knew where she was going, so she sidled up to his table and looked at him.

"Um," she began.

"My lady," he said inclining his head.

She didn't want to tell him she was no lady and ruin his graciousness, so she simply nodded. That was all she could manage though, because she wasn't quite sure what she wanted. All she knew was what she didn't want, and that was to read anything about a country she had no desire to save or see saved.

"Is there something I can find for you?"

She shifted uncomfortably. "I'm not sure."

"Then if you'll permit me the liberty of selecting something for you, I believe I have just the thing."

It wasn't long before he returned with a rather large book that looked less like a book and more like a collection of pages contained inside sturdy covers and kept there by string and insistence alone. She accepted the burden and looked at him in surprise.

"What is this?"

Leabhrach smiled. "A collection of paintings done by Her Majesty the Queen. I could provide you with a history as well, but if your time is limited and you want to know how the country feels to those who live there, I recommend this."

"What country?" Aisling asked.

He looked at her in surprise. "Why, Bruadair, of course."

Aisling supposed it wouldn't serve her to fall over in a faint at the mere hearing of the word. The librarian didn't seem to find the saying of the word to be dangerous, which she supposed was one more bit of proof that curses were the stuff of legends.

And then she realized what he'd said. To know how the country felt to those who lived there? It took her a moment or two before she thought she might manage speech.

"Have you looked at these?" she asked.

"Occasionally," he said, "when my memory of them fades." He hesitated, then looked at her seriously. "It is a place of deep magic, my lady. Magic that lingers on in dreams long after mortal sight has faded."

Aisling could hardly believe they were talking about the place where she'd spent so much of her life, but Leabhrach seemed to think they were.

"There is a table over there you could use, if it suits you."

Aisling nodded, clutching the collection to her. She managed to get herself over to the table indicated and set Queen Brèagha's sketches down before she dropped them. She sat down, then looked at what was in front of her.

The coverings were fairly nondescript, dark brown leather that folded in half and shielded the contents from dirt and questing fingers both. It was tied shut with a simple silk ribbon in the same color brown as the leather. Aisling pulled one end of the ribbon to undo the bow, then she undid the half knot before she thought better of it. She opened the cover and turned the whole thing so the pieces were facing her in the position they were meant to go. How bad could it be to see her country there on the table in front of her? She knew what it looked like.

Or perhaps not.

The first was a simple landscape with a road running through it, a road that disappeared between two sheer sides of mountains. It wasn't particularly welcoming, that scene, and Aisling thought that there was a place on the mountain to the left where it looked as if a doorway had been carved into the rock, but what did she know? Perhaps the queen had looked at it and found that doorway to be an interesting bit of scenery. Aisling didn't care for it personally—there was something about it that left her with the faint impulse to look over her shoulder and see who might be lurking there—but she was no artist, so her taste was not to be trusted. She lifted the page and set it aside carefully, then looked at the second picture there.

And she caught her breath.

It was Beul, though as she'd never seen it before. She looked closer and realized that they weren't sketches with colored pencils but some sort of colors that had to have been blended with magic. It was, she was quite sure, impossible to capture those images on paper without both amazing skill and a useful amount of something extra. She ran her fingers over the paper and was almost surprised to find that the scene felt as real as it looked. If she could have looked closely enough, she was fairly sure she would have seen the handful of wonderfully dressed people strolling down that street, breathing and talking and laughing.

Was that how her city had looked before Sglaimir?

She could hardly believe the colors, not only on the inhabitants and the flowers, but shimmering there in the air as well.

Astonishing.

She set it aside and continued to look deeper into the small stack of paintings, feeling herself being pulled into her country in a way she had never imagined possible.

It was breathtakingly beautiful.

By the time she had turned the last sheaf, she couldn't decide if she was overcome or devastated. She sat back in her chair, stunned. To think she had lived her entire life in a place that beautiful, yet she had never seen anything but dingy grey.

How was that possible?

She stared off into the fire, trying to reconcile what she'd seen with what she knew. When she moved finally, she realized that she had obviously been still for too long because she was stiff. She looked at the queen's final picture, a haunting view of a forested bluff on the edge of the sea. She looked at the path that led down to the sea, something she hadn't noticed the first time she'd looked at it. She wondered how many people had walked along that path to reach the shore and couldn't help but wish that she had been one of them.

Perhaps the path had lain fallow since Sglaimir had taken over the throne.

She sighed, then turned the pages back one by one until she was left looking at the pathway past the mountain with the sheer face. She closed the cover, because the sight of that unsettled her, then retied the ribbon the way she'd found it. She rose, stood for a moment or two until her foot that had fallen asleep woke up, then carried her burden back to Leabhrach. He was waiting at his post, apparently as usual.

"Did you enjoy them?"

"Very much," Aisling said honestly. "The queen is a marvelous artist."

"She is," he agreed. "I would wish for the chance to actually see for myself the views she has painted, though I'm not sure they would be any more beautiful than what Queen Brèagha has done here."

Especially not now was on the tip of her tongue, but she let the words go without speaking them. She nodded, thanked Leabhrach for his aid, then left the library. She wandered through the passageways slowly, looking around her and feeling as if she were seeing things for the first time. The elves she passed were more arrestingly beautiful than she remembered them being. The flagstones beneath her feet spoke of the quarry from which they'd been mined, the wood of the doors told of the forest from which it had been hewn, the walls whispered of those who had adorned their surfaces with scenes to please those who would walk past them. She smelled flowers she hadn't smelled before, heard songs of Fadaire sung in gardens she hadn't paid heed to until that moment, felt the faintest hint of Sìle's spells of protection and peace as if they were exceedingly fine mist on a morning after a good rain.

And all because she had seen her country as it once had been.

It occurred to her at that moment that no one she had known in Bruadair would ever see anything like what she had seen, not their own country, not Seanagarra. Not only that, they would never experience anything like it in the future. There were girls much younger than she who had been given to the Guild at an even younger age than she had been. There were women who were older than she was, women without families, women without anyone to rescue them who were so poor that there was no choice but to stay in the Guild and live out the rest of their lives without any hope of anything more beautiful.

Yet there she stood, her hand on a marble pillar that supported the roof over a pathway that was open on one side to a garden full of such beauty, she could scarce look at it. She, who was not even a particularly good weaver, had seen things with her own eyes that her companions in the Guild couldn't possibly imagine. She, who was no one, had seen creatures from myth. She had ridden on the back of a dragon and watched magic trail from his wings. She had stood in Seanagarra's gardens and listened to trees singing in Fadaire. She had been witness to things she wouldn't have thought even to dream of three months ago.

And now, just that morning, she had seen pictures drawn and colored by an elven queen's hand, paintings that showed her country to have a breathtaking beauty all its own.

She looked into the garden full of morning light, heard the laughter of trees in the rustling of their leaves, saw the flowers lifting their faces to the sun in delight, and wondered if perhaps her own country might once have had an equal amount of magic and loveliness.

No other Bruadairian might have wondered that, but she did.

The question was, what was she going to do with that knowledge?

She caught sight of someone and turned her head to see Rùn-ach standing some ten paces away from her, looking at her as if he'd never seen her before.

"Are you unwell?"

She took a deep breath, then turned and walked over to him. And into his arms, it had to be said. She wasn't sure what his family would think, but he seemed to think nothing of it for his arms went immediately around her. He held her in silence for so long, she began to wonder if they might be finding themselves turned into statues by an elven king who had somehow caught wind of what his grandson thought to do and supposed that keeping him immobile was the best solution.

"I've been looking for you," he said finally.

"I was in the library," she croaked. She cleared her throat, because apparently it was full of things she wasn't quite ready to say. "Master Leabhrach gave me something to do."

"Hopefully it didn't involve shelving his books."

She would have smiled, but she wasn't sure her face was equal to it. "Nay," she said. "It didn't."

"Are you going to tell me what it was you were doing there?"

"Just looking at art."

"Do you like art?"

"I don't have enough experience to judge," she said, her words somewhat muffled against his shoulder. "I've only seen what was on the walls at Tor Neroche. Well, and here. And now down in the library."

"Did you like what you saw?"

"It was breathtaking," she said. She took a deep breath, then pulled away. "They were paintings your grandmother had done."

He blinked. "She paints?"

"Apparently so."

"Tell me it wasn't of me and my brothers in short pants."

She smiled. "Nay, it wasn't. I'll show you later, if you like. Master Leabhrach was very kind to me."

"Then I imagine you'll be doing my requests for me from now on," he said. He reached for her hand, then frowned. "Your fingers are like ice."

"I forgot to sit near the fire," she lied. In fact, she thought the whole of her felt like ice, but perhaps that was something she didn't need to say. "I think I am nervous about such a small gathering. I'm not sure I'll know what fork to use when at luncheon."

"'Tis a pity my cousins aren't coming," he said, "for they would simply eat with their hands and take the attention off the rest of us."

She looked at him in surprise, then almost laughed. "You don't care for them?"

He nodded down the path. "I just feel compelled to warn you about their atrocious table manners and other glaring flaws lest you think you might want to spend more time with them than is polite."

"But they are quite handsome."

"Skin deep, as they say, and no further."

"They dance very well, though," she pointed out. "Not that I have much experience in that area—"

"But I do, so let me warn you that more than one maiden has limped back to her bedchamber sporting sore toes thanks to their stomping about. I think even Mansourah of Neroche might surpass them in many areas."

"Shocking."

"Isn't it, though?"

She wasn't sure if she should laugh or scold him for being so hard on his kin, but she was also not exactly sure if he was being serious or simply mocking them for sport. She glanced at him.

"Are they truly so awful, or are you having me on?"

He smiled, a hint of a smile that was there and gone before she could mark it properly.

"I think, Aisling, that I'm trying to discourage you from look-ing too closely at them lest you compare them to me and see only my flaws."

"Do you have flaws?"

He stopped in mid-step, then continued on. "Now I believe you are making sport of me."

"I'm not sure I know how."

"And I think if I think on that any longer before this endless luncheon we're about to attend, I will spirit you off into some secret garden where I can have you all to myself and beg you to distract me with tales of pointy-eared gnomes before I do something to frighten you off."

"I'm not sure what that would be."

"I know," he said, shooting her a quick smile. "I know that as well as I know anything, which is part of your charm. And here we are at my grandfather's most exclusive of chambers, just in time."

"For luncheon?"

"Nay, to save me from making an ass of myself." He embraced her briefly, then looked at her, his smile fading. "He can be rather loud when faced with things that he hasn't planned himself."

"Such as quests?"

Rùnach nodded. "Such as quests."

She would have told him right there in a passageway flanked by walls covered by intricately carved wood that spoke eloquently of the glories and triumphs of the house of Seanagarra that perhaps Sìle didn't need to shout, because if she could, she would force Rùnach to stay behind and take up her quest herself. But she had the feeling Rùnach wouldn't stay behind, no matter what she said to discourage him. She took a deep breath, then looked up at him.

"Why are you doing this?"

"Doing what?" he asked. "Standing here?"

She suppressed the urge to frown at him because things had now become all too serious. "Nay, taking on this quest."

He opened his mouth, but before he could say anything, the door had opened and Sìle stood there, a grave yet welcoming smile on his face.

"Come in, children," he said, standing back to allow them to pass. "Come in and take your ease."

Aisling wasn't sure she was going to have any ease at all any time soon, but she supposed no poor fool did who was contemplating the doing of impossible deeds. She would have found a way to escape if—

Nay. She wouldn't have. It was difficult to even allow that thought to linger for any time at all in her mind, but she realized with a startling flash of clarity that she could run no longer.

She knew too much about too many things.

She very much feared that she had seen too much to turn her back on things that needed to be done.

She had been a coward before, but that was before. She could be a coward no longer. And if that meant she would have to walk back into the very place that she had barely escaped from with her life and face those who would most certainly want her dead, that was what she would do. Worse, she suspected that facing down the Guildmistress might be the least of the things she would have to do if she had any intention of setting things aright that were wrong.

She, who had no beauty of her own, thinking she could give beauty back to a country of dreams. A no-name weaver with no sword skill, no magic, and a deplorable lack of courage thinking to overthrow a mage who had stripped Bruadair of all its magic.

It was entirely possible she was mad.

And if she had to tie Rùnach of Tòrr Dòrainn to a chair and flee in the middle of the night so that she was the only one partaking in her madness, that was what she would do.

Ten

❈

Rùnach sat at the table in his grandfather's private solar and wondered how a luncheon that had been so pleasant at the start could run afoul of such trouble after dessert.

The first clue, he supposed, should have been the guest list. His grandmother had been there along with Sosar, Ruith, and Aisling, but no others. The second should have been the way Sìle had waved off all but clear soup for lunch and a small plate of fruit for dessert. Nothing heavy to get in the way of a bit of friendly shouting.

The third had been the way his grandfather had continued to smile at Aisling and occasionally reach out to pat her hand, reassuring her several times that he loved a robust discussion during the afternoon and would it offend her if he engaged in the same that particular afternoon?

It had started off as just a mild rumble delivered after yet another apology to Aisling about his tone. Rùnach had been the

recipient of his grandfather's opinions more than once over the
course of his life, so he had been fully prepared for what he knew
was to come. What he hadn't been prepared for—which in hindsight should have been the first thing he'd thought of—was the
look on Aisling's face when Sìle truly began to roar.

"Grandfather," he said loudly, interrupting the king during the
very brief respite provided by Sìle taking a breath, "you're fright-
ening your guest."

Sìle blinked, then looked at Aisling. "Oh, forgive me, missy.
Just voicing my opinion, of course."

"I don't believe I've yet said anything that merits an opinion,"
Rùnach said mildly.

"You didn't have to," Sìle said shortly. "Your grandmother told
me what you're about."

Rùnach shot his grandmother a look, but she only smiled at
him serenely. His mother had had the ability to push just the right
amount in precisely the right direction. Obviously that ability
hadn't come from her father. He looked back at his grandfather
and dredged up all the patience he could.

"Grandfather, whilst I am grateful for your opinion on the matter, the simple fact is Aisling has been charged with a quest to
locate and secure a soldier to see to a little trouble in her village.
Today is the deadline she was given for accomplishing her task—"

"I know all about what needs to be done," Sìle said shortly,
"and I'm telling you this is madness."

"I don't see—"

"You cannot go into a country, Rùnach, all on your own and
overthrow a king!"

Rùnach suppressed the urge to say something he was certain
he would regret. He'd known what his grandfather would say, and
he'd already prepared an entire list of reasons why he could indeed
slip inside Bruadair, toss Sglaimir out on his arse, then get back
out without anyone noticing—

"He won't be going alone."

He heard the words, but it took him a moment to realize it was Aisling who had said them. He looked at her in surprise, but before he could say anything, she launched the next bolt.

"In fact, he won't be going at all."

"What are you talking about?" Rùnach said. He realized his grandfather had said the same thing in rather the same tone of surprise.

"There is no need," she said, hardly any sound to her voice. "It is my quest, after all, and I think I should be the one to see to it."

Sìle blinked. "Without my grandson?"

"Aye, Your Majesty."

To his credit, Sìle looked rather appalled. Rùnach started to speak but found whatever he'd planned to say stopped in mid-flight by the hand his grandfather put out practically against his face.

"But Aisling, my dearest girl, he has taken your quest as his own. You cannot deny him this chance to exercise his chivalry in this manner."

Rùnach exchanged a look with his grandmother because his mother wasn't there. He saw in Brèagha's eyes that she understood exactly what he was thinking, both about her daughter and her husband. She smiled gravely, then sent Rùnach back a look that disavowed all responsibility for her husband's mercurial behavior. Rùnach turned back and would have spoken, but again, his grandfather's hand was annoyingly near his face.

Aisling blinked. "But you're so upset, Your Majesty."

Sìle frowned, looking thoroughly perplexed. "I'm not upset at you, Aisling, though perhaps I didn't make that as clear as I should have. I'm upset with Rùnach."

"Because he offered to join my quest?"

"Nay, my gel, because he thinks to go by himself. Very foolish."

"Thank you," Rùnach said dryly.

Sìle shot him a look that in spite of himself had him biting his tongue. He rubbed his hand over his face before he could stop himself and suppressed the urge to laugh. He was a man full grown, yet when he was sitting at his grandfather's elbow, there were times he felt like a lad of ten-and-eight. He could bring to mind several episodes of looking at his grandfather's hand as he had just recently done.

"Of course, you will stay here and pass your days in safety whilst he sees to what must be done," Sìle said, in a tone that he no doubt thought would brook no argument. "I don't care for the idea of women going off on quests."

And that perhaps was the most egregious understatement ever spoken in the entire history of the Nine Kingdoms. Rùnach glanced at his grandmother who only lifted her eyebrows briefly and turned back to her wine.

"But, Your Majesty, I can't allow him to go," Aisling protested.

"Oh, he'll go," Sìle said without hesitation. "We're just negotiating the details, which will include the number and identities of his retinue." He reached out and patted her hand again. "You'll stay here, Aisling, and reside under my protection until he's finished with this unpleasantness."

Rùnach watched Aisling's face, partly because he had a hard time not watching her whenever she was within view and partly because there were things going on in her head that left him wondering just what she had seen in the library that morning—and what decision she had made because of it. He'd known, of course, that she wasn't particularly keen on his taking up the sword, as it were, but unless he'd heard her awrong, she had just recently said that she hadn't intended to go either.

He wondered what had happened to change her mind.

"Let's have luncheon cleared, and then we'll discuss details."

Rùnach tried to stay out of the way as Sìle's servants cleared the dishes and disappeared almost before Rùnach could rescue his glass of wine. He wasn't much for wine, as it happened, but even

Sgath would admit that Sìle's cellars were without compare and their contents never seemed to leave one without full possession of his wits. He set his glass back down, then realized that he had somehow missed an exchange between Aisling and his grandfather. Gone was the roaring lion. In his place was an old man who was looking at Aisling with the same gentleness he would have used for one of his own daughters or granddaughters.

"I think, my girl, that we can be nothing but honest from this point on if we're to see to discharging your task, something you will not be seeing to yourself."

Rùnach watched Aisling close her eyes briefly, then look at an elf who knew a thing or two about protecting the sanctity of his homeland.

"Do you know where I was born, Your Majesty?"

Sìle's expression was very grave. "I do, Aisling. Shall I say it aloud?"

"If you wish, Your Majesty."

Sìle covered her hands folded on the table with his own briefly, gave vent to a brief and relatively quiet exclamation of dismay, then looked about him for someone useful. "Ruith, lad, run and fetch something warm from the kitchen, if you would. And perhaps something strong for your brother. He'll be requiring it later."

"I'm fine, Grandfather," Rùnach said dryly.

Sìle shot him a look that made him wonder if he'd spoken too soon, then turned back to Aisling. He considered for a moment or two, then leaned forward with his elbows on the table.

"First, it might ease you to know Rùnach has divulged none of your secrets."

"Oh, I never thought he would, Your Majesty," Aisling said quickly.

Rùnach supposed that might have been one of the most satisfying though least-deserved compliments he'd ever received.

"Well, in that at least, he has no room for improvement," Sìle conceded. "As for other things, I will tell you that whilst there are always mysteries of one kind or another swirling around Bruadair, those rumors having to do with death and curses are absolutely untrue."

Aisling was looking at him as if she simply didn't dare hope he was speaking the truth. "Rùnach said he thought as much," she managed, "and I have personally disproved several. But how do you know for certain, Your Majesty?"

"Because I have known several Bruadairian kings over the course of my life, and one does talk after supper." He paused, then shook his head. "It is a strange country, though that is perhaps describing it poorly. *Exclusive* is perhaps a better term for it. Beautiful in a way I almost don't know how to describe."

Rùnach blinked. "Have you been there, Grandfather?" he asked, thoroughly surprised. "You never said anything."

"And what would I have said?" Sìle asked. "I know how to hold my tongue." He looked at his wife. "When was it, Brèagha? Eight? Nine?"

"Twelve," Brèagha said mildly. "Twelve centuries ago, darling, when Frèam's great-grandfather sat on the throne."

"Aye, that's it," Sìle said. He looked at Aisling. "The current king, or at least the man who should be the current king, is Frèam, and it was his great-grandfather who was king last time I crossed the border." He smiled at the queen. "It was beautiful, wasn't it, my dear?"

"It was past that somehow," Brèagha said with a wistful smile. "I'm not sure quite how to describe it in those days. Of course the landscape was beautiful, as it is here, but there was something more than just magic in the air and the soil. It was as if when you first put your foot onto the land, you crossed over into a dream. I've never seen colors so vibrant or smelled trees and flowers so perfectly scented, yet it lingered with a delicateness that persists in my mind even until now."

Rùnach looked at Aisling. She looked rather ill, truth be told. She looked at him in misery, then turned to his grandfather.

"It isn't like that now," was all she said.

"Obviously something foul is at work," Sìle said. "What is the name of that foul thing?"

"Sglaimir," she said hollowly. "I don't know him, of course, because I'm just a weaver, but I've heard terrible tales of him."

"What has been done to remove him from power?"

Aisling looked at Sìle. "I don't think anything. No one dares. I had mates down at the pub who wanted to start a rebellion, but they spent most of their time arguing about how best to go about it." She paused. "I think they were forced to act by circumstances beyond their control. That last night they managed, in a round-about way, to get me across the border. A peddler gave me gold and sent me off to Gobhann to look for a mercenary."

"An interesting idea," Sìle said with a frown. "I wonder why they wanted a man and not a mage?"

"I think they thought a single man without magic would have a better chance of sneaking in and overthrowing Sglaimir than an army would, or even a handful of mages."

"And how was this mercenary lad to know what to do?"

"I am to have him meet an unidentified party at Taigh Hall at a predetermined time." She paused. "That day was, as Rùnach said, today."

"I'm sure they'll wait for you," Sìle said dismissively. "Does this Sglaimir have magic?"

"I don't know, Your Majesty."

"Well, I've never heard of him, so we'll assume he's a self-important wizardling who has simply managed to convince gullible inhabitants of his mighty power. I shouldn't think it would take more than a score of elves to unseat him."

"I think you're forgetting something, husband."

Rùnach could hardly wait to hear what his grandmother planned to say.

"I never forget anything," Sìle huffed.

"Our magic doesn't work there."

Rùnach would have enjoyed his grandfather's choking if the tidings hadn't caught him quite firmly in the midsection as well. Perhaps it was a blessing that he had no magic. At least he wouldn't be counting on something that wasn't going to work.

Sìle harrumphed. "I don't know that we can say that with authority. With enough force it might."

"But it has been tried, hasn't it?" Brèagha asked.

"Has it?" Rùnach asked. "When?"

She shrugged. "Your grandfather has made more than one journey to Bruadair; two to be exact. The second was many centuries ago during the reign of Sealladh, who was Frèam's grandfather. A good man, but not a wise one. He allowed himself to be beguiled by a mage whose name escapes me at the moment."

Rùnach glanced at his grandfather and suspected by the look on the king's face that the name didn't escape him at all. He turned back to his grandmother.

"And?"

She lifted her eyebrows briefly. "Sealladh sent out a call for aid, and your grandfather responded. Only it happened that our magic was not useful within Bruadair's borders." She paused. "Not simply not useful, but the spells your grandfather attempted to use went awry somehow. I think that if we had had the time to learn their ways, we might have been successful, but haste was the order of the day." She paused again. "It did not go well. In the end, Sealladh restored the sanctity of his throne, but the price was his life."

"I moved too gingerly the last time," Sìle said darkly.

Brèagha shook her head. "My dear, you of all people know that force does not work, not with the precious souls around you and not with magic that isn't yours."

Sìle dragged his hand through his hair. "Damnation," he said wearily. "Very well, Rùnach. You win."

"It wasn't a battle, Your Grace," Rùnach said quietly. "Not this time. Not ever."

Sìle grunted. "That's debatable on several points, but I'll accept the sentiment." He looked at Aisling. "Very well, my dear, we'll send for maps from the library and plot his strategy with him—"

Sìle stopped speaking abruptly at the entrance unaccompanied by a knock of someone into the room, and protested the rudeness. Rùnach would have complained as well, but he was too surprised by the sight of his eldest uncle Làidir walking into the room to do so. Làidir made his father and mother a bow, then paused.

"Oh, who's this?"

"Rùnach's comrade-in-arms," Sosar announced helpfully, "Aisling. She's from Bruadair."

"I'm just a weaver," Aisling said quickly.

Làidir walked around the table, took her hand, then made her a bow as well. "I am Làidir, Sìle's eldest. A pleasure, Mistress Aisling."

Rùnach would have complimented his uncle on his pretty manners, but he found himself too busy not liking the look on the crown prince's face. Làidir continued his way around the end of the table, putting his hand briefly on his father's shoulder. He stopped in front of Rùnach.

"Nephew."

"Uncle."

Làidir pulled a folded note from within his cloak. "I'm not sure how to announce this without perhaps attaching more importance to it than it deserves, but I was given this just outside the border as I was riding homeward early this morning from Slighe."

Rùnach took it, knowing without reading it who had written it.

He was tempted to see if he couldn't guess what it said as well, but he had no interest in self-torture. He unfolded the sheaf of parchment and read the untidy scrawl there. It was, he had to admit, a hand he had seen recently. In Tor Neroche, as it happened.

I have the notes, such as they are, that you left on the plains of Ailean. You have my book. We might trade, or I can find you and kill you and keep both, which means your life is measured in days.

Fair warning, Rùnach
Acair

Rùnach folded the note up and stuck it in a pocket. "Did you see the author himself or one of his representatives?"

"The author himself," Làidir said, pursing his lips in distaste.

Rùnach looked his uncle over but saw no marks. "I assume he didn't challenge you."

Làidir lifted an eyebrow. "He's a fool but not stupid. You understand the difference very well, I know."

Rùnach thanked his uncle, then rose and started to pace. He listened absently to Làidir describing to his father whom he'd encountered and what the message had been. He listened to his grandfather express his displeasure in less-than-dulcet tones. He listened to Ruith, Làidir, and Sosar discuss what utter asses Gair's natural sons were, but that they were powerful enough not to be taken lightly. He listened with half an ear as Ruith described the truly bizarre markings to be found in the book that had once been Rùnach's but the innards of which had now been identified as Acair's, though no one seemed overly interested in having a look at it.

He finally leaned against the wall near a window and looked out into the garden that was drenched in afternoon sunlight. How fortunate his grandfather was to have had that view to admire every day for the whole of his very lengthy life.

Rùnach sighed. He hadn't thought about the length of his own life recently, though at the moment two things came to mind that bothered him.

First, he wondered how long Aisling would live and if she would be willing to live with him for the duration of that life.

Second, he realized at that moment that he didn't particularly want to die, especially at the hands of a runt who whilst powerful had absolutely no redeeming qualities. He could bring to mind scores of incidents where Acair had been cruel not even for the pleasure of it. He'd been cruel simply because he could be.

Obviously he was going to have to determine what those markings were and why Acair wanted the book so badly.

A pity he could think of only one place where the master of the house—or mistress, as the case was—might have the knowledge to help him with that. Fortunately for them all, it was on the way to the country under discussion. If one looked at a map in the right way. With a great deal of imagination and folded in the middle.

He looked away from his contemplation of the garden and realized that Aisling was watching him with those fathomless eyes of hers. And he realized at that moment something that had absolutely nothing to do with his quest or her but seemed to have a great deal to do with all those days he wasn't quite ready to surrender yet.

He loved her.

He pushed away from the wall, pulled her up out of her seat, then took her face in his hands.

"What are you doing?" she managed.

"I think I'm going to kiss you."

"Why?"

Someone laughed. He was fairly sure it was his brother, so he shot Ruith a dark look.

"I believe it's best if you court the girl for a bit before you begin kissing her," Sosar put in. "Just a suggestion."

"I don't need any help," Rùnach growled.

"Well, she seems to think you do."

Rùnach looked at Aisling. "Are you confused?"

"Very."

He sighed, then put his arms around her and pulled her close. "Very well. I'll clarify later." He looked down at her. "You may want to go sit by my grandmother."

"Why is that?"

"Because I'm about to say something my grandfather isn't going to like."

She considered, then pushed out of his arms and resumed her seat. She looked up at him. "I'll be fine here."

He looked at her for a moment or two and considered. There was something different about her. Something steely he hadn't seen there before.

It made him a little nervous, truth be told.

He shot her a warning look she completely ignored, then he cleared his throat and looked at the men of his family assembled there. That gave him pause, he had to admit. He was fairly sure he had made important announcements at several like gatherings during his youth, announcements having to do with plans to unman, unnerve, or unhorse—in a manner of speaking—his illustrious sire. To their credit, not a man had ever mocked his plans. His grandfather had roared, of course, because that was what Sìle tended to do when things weren't his idea to begin with, but that had been somewhat comforting.

He had the feeling the roar that would no doubt ensue at his current announcement was going to deafen everyone in the room.

"I appreciate the aid," he said, sweeping them all with a look he hoped bespoke just how much he had appreciated it, "and because of that, I've settled on a plan."

Sìle motioned for him to move away from Aisling. "She'll be safer that way."

Rùnach would have done so, but Aisling reached up and covered his hand that was resting on the back of her chair with her very cold fingers.

"Stay," she said.

Rùnach wished he were better at handling trouble coming from two different directions than he was. It was obviously a skill he was going to have to hone—and quickly—if he planned on spending any time with Aisling of Bruadair. He cleared his throat.

"I'm going to go to Taigh Hall," he said, happy to at least have some idea where he needed to wind up, "but I must resolve this issue with Acair as well. I think I can do both by traveling in a fairly straight direction."

"And I worry about your map-reading skills," Sosar said with exaggerated slowness. "There isn't anything of substance between here and Taigh Hall, if memory serves."

"Save Léige," Làidir said dryly.

"I said *fairly* straight," Rùnach said. "I need to know what Acair's book means."

"It's rubbish," Sìle said dismissively.

Ruith cleared his throat politely. "I wouldn't say that, Grandfather," he said carefully. "I had a look at it earlier today, and I believe it to be actually fairly perilous." He looked up. "Where are you planning on going to find out details, brother?"

Rùnach took a deep breath. "I'm going to see the witchwoman of Fàs."

The room erupted. Actually, only one end of the table erupted, but the sound was so loud, it seemed as if the roof might soon come off the chamber.

"Absolutely not!" Sìle thundered.

"She's on the way north," Rùnach said reasonably.

"And you will go into that harridan's house with no magic?" Sìle roared. "Have you lost *all* sense?"

"I think I've finally found some."

Sìle seemed to realize that he needed to breathe. He took a deep breath, then released a gusty sigh. "She's a village witch. Hardly worthy of your time."

"She's very powerful."

"Her power is of a common sort," Sìle said shortly.

Rùnach suppressed the urge to sigh. "Grandfather, she knows everyone and everything. There is not a more meticulous diarist in all the Nine Kingdoms. If anyone knows what these marks mean, it will be her."

"She looks as if rats have been nesting in her hair!"

"Her grooming leaves aught to be desired," Rùnach allowed, "but I believe she prefers to look as if she's just rolled out of bed. It puts her visitors into a state of underestimating her."

"And you never underestimate her," Aisling said.

He shot her a brief smile. "Never."

"She's evil," Sìle insisted.

"She's missing a functioning moral compass," Rùnach said, "which doesn't necessarily make her evil."

"It does make her reprehensible."

"But understandable."

"And unpleasant."

"She likes me."

Sìle looked momentarily stymied, then he shook his head sharply. "You won't go alone."

"I can't ask anyone—"

"You aren't asking," Sìle said firmly. "I'm insisting. Làidir, you'll find my crown is in the cabinet behind—"

"Grandfather, nay," Rùnach said, stunned. "I couldn't allow it."

"Allow it?" Sìle repeated, looking as if the gale were readying for another good blow. "Who do you think you are, *whelp*, to tell me what to do?"

"I believe, Your Majesty," Aisling said quietly, "he's someone who loves you."

Rùnach didn't dare smile, because his grandfather would have made the effort to get up out of his chair so he could deliver a brisk blow to the back of a grandson's head, of that Rùnach was certain. He wasn't even pleased to see that his grandfather was momentarily winded. That might have been because Aisling's next words had stolen his own breath.

"Besides, I'm going to go along to keep him safe."

Sìle closed his eyes briefly before he leaned forward and looked at Aisling seriously. "You, my girl?"

"Me, Your Majesty."

Sìle chewed on his words for a moment or two. "I don't hold with the idea of women going on quests, which I believe I said before. It's unseemly. And dangerous."

"But necessary."

Rùnach watched his grandfather look at his wife in consternation.

"Are you listening to this?" he asked in disbelief. "She isn't even spawn of mine, and yet she exhibits this unsettling independence."

"I find it quite admirable, husband."

Sìle pursed his lips at her, then turned a frown on Aisling. "I don't want to be impolite, my gel, but how will you keep Rùnach safe?" He snorted suddenly. "As if that is the question here! How will either of you be safe on this road that I can guarantee will lead you places neither of you will want to go?"

"I can spin things," Aisling said. "Air and water and fire. It tends to unnerve those we meet who have less than honorable intentions."

"Aye, Aisling, you can," Sìle conceded, "but you've had the element of surprise on your side until now. What do you do if you and Rùnach come upon a clutch of mages? All seven of his bastard brothers at once? That is enough to give any mage pause."

"Even you, Your Majesty?"

"Well, not me, of course, but I am not afraid of little magelings."

"Neither am I."

Which was, Rùnach had to admit with a terrible feeling in the pit of his stomach, perhaps more truth than was good for her. He pushed away from the wall and walked over to squat down by her chair. He looked up at her.

"I want you to stay here."

She looked at him for a moment or two, then reached out and touched his scarred cheek. "I am too old to be stupid and arrogant," she said very quietly, "but this is my quest, and I must see it through to the end, wherever that end might lie."

And then she leaned over and kissed him.

On the end of the nose, but he supposed it was a start. At least she wasn't looking at the tips of his ears any longer.

"I'll think about it," he said, and by that he meant *not a chance in hell*.

She only looked at him steadily. Rùnach was vaguely unnerved by her look, but he was nothing if not confident when he'd made a decision for someone else. He rose and glanced at his grandfather.

"I appreciate your concern, but I'm going alone."

Sìle rubbed his hands over his face. "Brèagha?"

"Aye, my love?"

"When did I lose control over my progeny?"

"Several centuries ago, I believe, dear."

"It seems more recent than that."

"I don't think so, darling."

Rùnach stood back from the table as his grandfather rose and called for maps to be brought. He was happy to watch his grandmother rescue Aisling and draw her over to sit by the fire, no doubt to keep her out of the fray until absolutely necessary.

Rùnach didn't need to watch to know what would happen. His family would gather around the map laid out on the table, then discussion would begin about strategy. He supposed the conversation might be more involved than usual given the destination and his own particular weaknesses.

He jumped a little when he realized Aisling was watching him. He smiled at her and had a very faint smile in return. He considered, then went to join the lads, but that was almost more of a diversionary tactic than anything useful.

That woman was plotting something; he would have staked his horse on it.

He had the feeling he wasn't going to like her plan at all when he discovered what it was.

Eleven

❊

Aisling wandered along the passageway, trying to clear her head. She had spent the afternoon in Sìle's private study listening to more discussion about Bruadair than she thought she would ever hear in the entirety of her life.

Map after map had been produced, and she'd had an education in just what her country looked like. She'd had no idea that it was so full of mountains and lakes and rivers. She supposed she should have realized as much, but the memories she had of her childhood were few and honestly not terribly pleasant, most of them having to do with her mother and yet another task to see accomplished.

It was odd how few memories she had of her father. He had been there, she was sure, but she honestly couldn't remember him having spoken overmuch. Then again, her mother had never taken a breath, so perhaps he had never been able to find an appropriate space in which to insert a comment or two.

After maps in the king's chamber had been studied to everyone's satisfaction, the conversation had turned to kingdoms and rulers, and how the latter had affected the former and what was perhaps to be found once the dust had settled.

By the time the sun had set and a vibrant twilight had covered the garden outside King Sìle's window, the talk had turned to mages, and she had turned to the door. The queen had decamped an hour earlier so Aisling didn't feel too terribly guilty about abandoning the men to their talk of things she didn't want to listen to. The queen had promised to return after she'd seen to preparations for supper. Rùnach had made her promise to return as well, which she supposed she should do—to keep him from escaping, if nothing else.

She considered going back to her chamber and fetching the book King Nicholas had given her, but she wasn't sure that she wouldn't find more unsettling things inside, so perhaps that wasn't a safe idea either.

Not that safety was going to be factoring into her future any time soon.

She walked more swiftly in an effort to escape several truths that were nipping at her heels, but it was futile. She couldn't outrun them, couldn't elude them, couldn't avoid facing them.

The first truth was, no matter what the lads down at the pub in Beul had said, she had the feeling it would take an army to overthrow Sglaimir, and that army would be well-served to have quite a bit of magic at its disposal. Sneaking back across the border—if such a thing could even be done successfully—and marching up to Sglaimir sitting on his throne to tap him on the shoulder and ask him politely to go sit somewhere else wasn't going to work. She doubted that, even with the superior qualities of the elven bows she'd shot that morning, she was going to be allowed to simply walk into his audience hall and put an arrow through his heart. And somehow, the thought of Rùnach slipping into the palace to

attempt to stab Sglaimir whilst he was about his morning ablutions was one she simply couldn't contemplate.

But to do nothing was, now, unthinkable.

How could she possibly leave her country in the state it was
when she knew what it could be? And how could she leave the man
who had volunteered to save that country to see to the deed alone
when she might be of use to him?

She rubbed her hands over her face and considered briefly
going to bed early, but she knew that wouldn't serve her for she
would dream. After the things she had seen in Rùnach's book, she
was genuinely afraid of what might find its way into those dreams.

She stopped suddenly and frowned. Just what had he meant
when he said he thought he was going to kiss her?

"My lady, are you unwell?"

She blinked and realized that Giollan was standing in front of
her, looking at her carefully as if he feared that startling her might
send her into some sort of fit. Given the fact that she couldn't seem
to string two thoughts together in any semblance of coherence, she
thought he might have something there. But how was she to ask a
lad about the ridiculous statements a grown man had made?

He couldn't have meant that he *wanted* to kiss her. He was a
prince, and she was, well, she was a weaver from a country that
might be the cause of his death. If he had any sense, which she
knew he did, he would satisfy his chivalry that wasn't all that
rusty and then hastily hurry off to some salon or other where he
would find a lengthy line of very eligible maids from noble houses
waiting for their turn to have his attentions.

Damn them all anyway.

"Who, my lady?"

She looked at Giollan in surprise. "Ah, no one, lad. Just thinking aloud." And hopefully not so loudly that he'd heard all her
thoughts. She attempted a smile. "I'm fine. How is the conference
going?"

"They're still closeted in King Sìle's solar. I was sent to watch over you and see to your needs."

"Very kind," she said. "I think I'll make for the library for a bit. I can find my way back, I think."

He nodded but didn't move. She nodded back, then walked away in the direction she thought she should have been going. It only took one glance over her shoulder to find that her page was following along behind her at a discreet distance. She wasn't sure if she should have been offended that he didn't trust her to get anywhere without aid or moved that someone had obviously sent him after her to . . . well, if it had been Rùnach to do so, it had been to make sure she didn't do something untoward.

It was unusual, she had to admit, to have someone looking after her. Unusual and somehow quite lovely.

She found the library after only a mistaken turn or two, then presented herself at Leabhrach's desk. He smiled pleasantly.

"Mistress Aisling, what can I provide you with?"

She hesitated, then supposed there was no reason not to be frank. "I was wondering if I might see the queen's paintings again."

"Of course," he said, not looking the least bit unsettled by the topic. "I have them right here."

She took the large leather case, then hesitated. "I'm not sure this is appropriate," she said slowly, "but I would like Prince Rùnach to see these. If that might be possible."

He waved her on. "Take them with you, of course. The queen gave specific instruction that you be allowed free rein with them."

"Did she?" Aisling asked in surprise. "She is very kind."

"She is that, my lady. And if you're interested, she is the one who came down last night and suggested that there might be things you might want to see."

Aisling was somehow unsurprised. She thanked him, then left the library, Queen Brèagha's paintings under her arm. She made her way slowly back to King Sìle's study, only having to look at

Giollan twice for the slightest tipping of his head to indicate the proper passageway to turn down. An elf stood guard at the door, but he opened it for her without hesitation. Aisling smiled at him, then stepped just inside the doorway and paused to judge how things were proceeding.

Sìle, his son Sosar, and Ruith were sitting at the table, still deep in talk. Rùnach was sitting there as well, but his eyes were closed as if he simply couldn't bear any more. Perhaps he'd heard all the talk he could stand, perhaps he was simply soaking up the time with people who loved him. She could understand why they did, for there was something about him that was so compelling, she wondered how anyone could not want to be next to him.

"He has always been that way."

Aisling was somehow unsurprised to find Rùnach's grandmother standing next to her. She looked at her but couldn't smile. "Has he?"

Brèagha looked at Aisling and smiled. "There is something unusual about him, isn't there?"

"Aye, Your Majesty, there is."

"He has always had an elegance far above his brothers and cousins, though he would likely deny it." Brèagha studied him for a bit longer. "I think he would make a good king."

Aisling had to agree, though she couldn't quite bring herself to give voice to the thought. He was far enough above her as it was.

"He wouldn't be interested in such a thing, of course," Brèagha said. "When he announced to Sìle that he intended to go off and be a lowly garrison knight for some nameless, yet-to-be-identified lord, my husband was not pleased."

"I can imagine."

Brèagha smiled and put her hand on Aisling's arm. "Come over to the fire with me, darling, and let's be comfortable. Have I ever told you the tale of Caileag of Tòsan?"

"I don't believe you have, Your Majesty."

"Then I shall, if you have the patience for it. Ah, there is Rùn-ach setting out chairs for us. Shall we?"

Aisling thought she should perhaps agree. She walked over to the hearth with the queen of Tòrr Dòrainn, accepted a chair pro-vided by that queen's most elegant grandson, then sat down grate-fully next to that grandson.

"What do you have there?" Rùnach asked politely.

Aisling handed him the collection of paintings. "Bruadair, painted by your grandmother."

Rùnach looked at his grandmother. "May I?"

"Of course," Brèagha said with a smile. "They're poor rendi-tions, but I thought Aisling might enjoy them. They're not nearly as useful as a strategy session, so be forewarned. But it will keep you occupied whilst I entertain your lady for a bit."

"Telling tales, Grandmother?"

"Caileag of Tòsan and her handsome prince."

"I'm not sure I've ever heard that one."

"I believe you might find it very interesting."

He started to nod, then he froze. Aisling supposed that might have been because he was looking at the first of his grandmother's paintings. He looked at Brèagha in astonishment.

"You did this."

Brèagha shrugged slightly. "I fell in love. It seemed a shame not to make some sort of tribute."

Aisling watched Rùnach glance her way, smile faintly, then turn back to what was in his hands. She looked at the queen expectantly.

Brèagha smiled. "Caileag is associated with Tòsan, but the truth is, she was instead from a very small, very unimportant town near to it that no one remembers. What they do remember is her deeds, which I won't relate now, and the man she married."

"Elf," Rùnach said absently, turning another sheaf of parchment.

"Of course," Brèagha said, nodding. "Elf." She looked at Aisling. "She wed an elven prince, you see."

Aisling could hardly bring herself to say the words lingering just inside her mouth. "But," she managed, "elves live forever."

"Not forever," Brèagha said, "but long enough, I suppose."

"And what did he do when she died?"

Brèagha frowned thoughtfully. "You know, I'm not sure."

"But surely it must have grieved him."

"I think, darling, that the time he had with her was so marvelous that he was forever afterward lost in the dream of her. There never seems to be any passage of time in dreams, does there?"

"Nay, Your Majesty," Aisling managed. "There doesn't."

"He loved her very much," Brèagha said, "and she him." She smiled faintly. "Some candles burn very brightly for a brief time."

"I don't think I want to burn briefly," Aisling whispered.

"Darling, I don't think that is your fate," Brèagha said. "But I'll tell you the tale just the same."

Aisling listened to the queen talk about the impossible romance between a simple village girl and an elven prince from Ainneamh and couldn't help but wish that such a tale could be hers. Caileag had been courageous beyond measure and ferocious in her love for Brathadair of Ainneamh who had fought a terrible battle to rescue her from things Brèagha said were too dark to name so late in the day.

It would never happen for Aisling, of course, but she couldn't help but wish it would, just the same.

She watched Rùnach continuing to study each painting before he turned the page. He reached out and covered her hand as it rested on the arm of her chair, as if he had done the same thing dozens of times before. She supposed he had, though she wondered if he knew what he was doing. She looked at his grandmother, who was watching her with a small smile.

"My hands are cold," Aisling explained. "He's very generous to warm them."

"Aye, I'm sure that's all he's doing," Brèagha said with a deep smile. "Very chivalrous."

Aisling wasn't sure if the queen were jesting or not, so she smiled as best she could and abandoned the idea of pulling her hand away from Rùnach's. The truth was, she liked the feel of his hand around hers, and not just because his hands were always warm.

Poor fool that she was.

She watched him as he came to the last piece, and then simply sat there for several moments in silence as he looked at the painting of the coastline that had moved her so. He took a deep breath finally and looked at her.

There were tears in his eyes.

She felt her eyes begin to burn immediately. Sympathy, perhaps, or relief over finding someone who was touched by something that had touched her.

"The sea," he said softly.

"Apparently so," she managed.

"Perhaps we should make a visit there, after we've restored Frèam to his throne."

"It is beautiful."

"And so are you."

She smiled. "Ethereal."

He smiled, leaned over, and kissed her on the cheek. "Beautiful *and* ethereal. A very potent combination."

"And so it begins," Brèagha said dryly, "though I have the feeling this began slightly before this moment." She rose, leaned over, and kissed Aisling's cheek. "You should sleep whilst you can, darling. And you, Rùnach my love, should seek out your own bed as well. They'll have a plan ready for you, I'm sure, that you can ignore as you will."

Aisling watched the queen move about the room, kissing and

patting husband and descendants, before she left, taking a little bit of light with her.

She looked at Rùnach. "I like her," she said honestly.

"She likes you," he said. He leaned back in his chair. "She's a remarkable woman. There are many qualities that she possesses without effort that I wish I had. Developing them will, I fear, take a lifetime."

Aisling nodded and wondered if it was too late in her life to start a list of qualities she might like to acquire for herself. The one thing she thought she might have already acquired thanks to Brèagha of Tòrr Dòrainn was an awe for the country of her birth, a country she had never seen until she had looked at it through the eyes of an elegant elvish queen who had fallen in love with a land not her own.

Aisling wondered if she might manage to fall in love with it just as easily.

Rùnach rearranged the pages, then leaned forward to set them on the table at his elbow. He blinked, then held up a small leather folio folded in half.

"I wonder what this is—oh, wait. There's a note." He unfolded it, then handed it to her. "Sorry. It's for you."

Aisling opened the note and looked at the words written there in the most beautiful hand she'd ever seen.

Copies of what pleased you, Aisling darling. So you don't forget what you love.

Aisling took the book Rùnach handed her, untied the ribbon, then blinked. She looked at Rùnach in surprise.

"She's made copies of her paintings for me."

"Magic can be handy," he said.

"Apparently so."

He nodded toward the doorway. "I think we should take my grandmother's advice and seek our rest. If I'm to leave tomorrow, I might need at least a pair of hours of sleep."

She gaped at him. "Tomorrow?"

"I'm already late for the appointment at Taigh Hall."

She found words eluded her. All she could do was follow him from his grandfather's solar, silently wondering how she was going to slow down events to a pace where she could face them individually and successfully. As it was, she felt as if she were standing in the middle of a raging river, fighting for her balance and knowing she was but one more heartbeat from being pulled under.

She didn't care for that comparison, actually.

She considered what she could say but found nothing, not even when she was standing in front of her bedchamber door and Rùnach was tucking her hair behind her ear.

"Sleep well," he said quietly.

"Why are you doing this?" she blurted out.

He frowned, looking slightly confused. "Leaving you here?"

"Nay, going on this quest!"

He opened his mouth, then shut it. It took him a moment or two before he apparently found what he wanted to say. "Because it needs to be done."

"That isn't a good reason," she said, though she supposed many quests had been started with lesser reasons.

"Because *you* need it to be done."

"Those aren't the reasons. Why are you doing this?"

He looked at her in surprise. "Those seem like perfectly acceptable reasons to me."

"For someone else, but not you." She wrapped her arms around herself. "Why are you doing this when it would be so much easier to do something else?"

"Apart from the fact that my most powerful bastard brother has, for all intents and purposes, put a bounty on my head and I need to find a way to hobble him?"

She swallowed, but her mouth was very dry so it didn't go very well. "I'd forgotten about him." She nodded. "Then you're off to save the world from him."

"Nay, Aisling, I'm off to save Bruadair for you. Saving the world is secondary. And though it might reveal more about my miserable self than I would like, I'm doing it partly for purely self-ish reasons."

She blinked. "Do you want to be king?"

He looked at her blankly for a moment, then laughed a little. "Of course not. Can you imagine?"

"Actually, I can."

He reached for her hands, unwrapping her arms as he did so, then kissed each hand in turn. "And that is why the only thing I will mourn on my journey is the lack of your company."

She clutched his hands, hard. "Don't waste any strength on that."

He looked at her evenly. "Don't think you're coming along."

"Of course I'm coming along," she said shortly. "Do you think I would actually let you wander off into the night without me?"

"Haven't we discussed this before?"

"Aye, and I said I was a craven coward. I'm not a coward any longer."

He looked at her for so long, she half wondered if he'd forgotten what she'd said. Then he smiled, a small, grave smile, and pulled her into his arms. She went, because she realized that of all the places she could be, that was where she felt safest. He rested his cheek against her hair and sighed.

"Nay."

"Aye."

"Very well."

She pulled back and looked at him in surprise. "That easily?"

"Did you think I would go off without you?"

"Ah—"

He shook his head. "I don't like it, of course, but unfortunately this quest is just as much yours as it is mine. As for anything else, you might be interested in knowing I went down on bended knee before my grandfather and begged him for spells that come with their own power, that I might keep you safe."

She closed her eyes briefly. "You didn't."

"Oh, I did. Earlier, when you escaped the madness in his solar. He limited himself to a spell of protection wrapped in his own terrible glamour, but I think it will serve us well enough." He put his arm around her shoulders. "Let's go sit under the trees one last night. You can sing with them if I bore you."

She imagined that wouldn't happen any time soon, but she didn't say as much. She was too taken aback by the things he'd just said.

He had begged a spell to keep her safe.

"I'll give you the absolute truth."

She winced. "Can I bear any more truth?"

"I think, love, that you can bear more things than you think you can." He took one of her hands in both his own, looked at their hands together for a few moments, then looked at her. "I think, apart from anything else, that if you don't see this thing done, it will eat at you until there is nothing left of you but regret."

She attempted a light laugh. "You credit me with too much sentiment for a place I do not love."

"Do you not?"

She started to tell him she most certainly didn't, then found that she couldn't quite get the words out.

"I saw your face, Aisling," he said very quietly. "When you watched me look at those paintings of my grandmother's."

She could only watch him, mute.

"There is something in Bruadair, love, that has been lost or stolen or simply drained away. I don't know what it is, and I'm not sure we'll manage to find it before whoever has taken it has killed us, but I think we have to try to restore it. I think, if I might be so bold, that *you* have to try."

She found that her mouth was utterly parched. "I am no one."

"Aren't you?" he mused. "Funny, then, that you were the one who had so much help getting across the border. Even stranger that you were the one charged with this quest."

"Coincidence," she said.

"I don't believe in coincidence."

"Neither does your grandmother."

"I learned it from her," he said with a grave smile. "I don't believe you were chosen to fulfill this quest because there was no one else available. I don't believe that you were in the wrong place at the wrong time. I believe that if we were to look deeper into your past, we would see that there were those who knew exactly what was in your heart and kept you safe until the moment when the time was right for you to find the tools you needed to save your country."

"But I'm no one—"

He shook his head sharply. "Aisling, you are not a soul who could live and die and no one would notice. *I* would notice. My family would notice. And I have the feeling that there would be people in Bruadair who would notice." He laughed a little, a sound that was equal parts exasperation and wonder. "In a country of weavers, love, you can *spin*. In a country of those who haven't the means or the courage to do something, you can weave dreams." He slid her a look. "I can attest to that personally, I believe."

She pursed her lips. "Did your grandmother tell you?"

"That you wove a crown of dreams and draped it over my poor head? Nay, I figured it out all on my own, clever lad that I am." He shook his head and smiled wryly. "I haven't dreamed in a score of years, yet I woke from slumber in my grandmother's garden and couldn't decide for several minutes if I were awake or still dreaming. Perhaps you don't have magic in the usual sense, but I have to

admit there is something about what you spin that comes perilously close to it."

"I imagine many can spin," she said quietly. "Perhaps in places
other than the Guild where they are free to do so."

"Perhaps or perhaps not. I think that might be something we
want to find out. All I know is that there has been something missing in the world for the past twenty years. Part of that might be
Frèam having been exiled, part of it might have to do with your
Sglaimir grinding the populace into the dust. I suspect that it has
more to do with Bruadair as a whole than who might be the rightful sitter on that throne."

She looked at the topmost painting on her lap, the copy of the
original that Brèagha had created for her, shimmering as it was
with elven magic. "It does seem as if it might have perhaps been
lost in a dream."

"Or perhaps lost without dreams, which I think is what the
world is missing." He looked at her seriously. "There is mischief
afoot in the world, Aisling, and I have the sinking feeling Acair of
Ceangail has all ten of his questing fingers in the middle of it. I
can't imagine that it has anything to do with Bruadair, but perhaps it does."

"Do you think so?"

He sighed. "I have no proof nor any real reason to think so, but
I can't shake the feeling that there are things he is doing that
are . . ." He shook his head. "I'm not sure what to call it. He wants
my father's spell of Diminishing, that much I know."

"What's that?"

"Remember how Gàrlach tried to take my power—my nonexis-
tent power?"

"That's what black mages do," she said, then met his gaze. "Isn't
that right?"

"Unfortunately," he agreed. "I don't know what spell Gàrlach
was using. Some rot of his own making, I daresay. My father, on

the other hand, had a spell for it—Diminishing—that could strip a
mage of every last drop of his power." He rubbed his hand over his
face before he covered hers with it again. "Lothar calls his *Taking*,
I believe. Droch of Saothair calls his *Gifting*, but to my continual
surprise he does have at least a decent sense of irony. There are
other things out there in the world for the same purpose, but nothing to equal Diminishing."

"But why create such a thing?" she asked, shivering.

"Power," he said succinctly. "No mage ever has enough."

She looked at him carefully. "Not even you?"

"Well," he said with a faint smile, "I suppose not even me, though
I was content to go about stretching my power by honorable means.
Diminishing was a shortcut, but as with all things you don't earn,
along with the power came things that might not have been so
desirable. In the case of mageish power, my father acquired the
occasional character flaw or tendency to madness from the mage
so diminished. There are times I think that by the time he got to
the well, he was mad."

"Terrible," she murmured.

He smiled briefly. "It was, but it's in the past now."

"Is it?"

He looked at her sharply, then laughed a little. "You see too
much."

"You're worried about things you haven't shared."

He lifted an eyebrow briefly. "Unfortunately, I suppose I am.
And whilst I don't want to worry you overmuch, I'll say that it
bothers me to have Acair out in the world stirring up trouble. He
has a lust for power that I don't think he will ever slake. If he had
the spell of Diminishing to hand . . ." He seemingly considered his
words for quite some time before he looked at her. "I'll only say
that I find several things odd about what is afoot in the world.
Simeon of Diarmailt telling his chief librarian that he was about
to have more power and Sglaimir of Bruadair—or wherever he's

from—sitting on the throne of a country stripped of its magic." He shrugged. "I'm curious."

"You know what curiosity killed, don't you?"

He smiled, a quick smile that was utterly charming. "My mother said that to me more times than I can count."

"A very wise woman, your mother."

He brought her hand to his mouth, kissed it, then rose, pulling her up with him. "You should sleep."

"You'll be here in the morning."

He sighed. "Aye, against my better judgment, I will."

"And we'll go together."

He looked at her seriously. "Aye, Aisling, we will. Because I think Bruadair needs you far more than it needs me. How, I don't know yet, but I have the feeling that is a mystery we'll solve in time."

She couldn't imagine it, but she wasn't going to argue with him. She had committed herself to a quest that might well result in her death, yet she felt no thrill of fear, no dread that left her wanting to find something to hide behind.

"You know," he said as he stopped with her in front of her door, "if Bruadair falls, then perhaps the last bastion of dreams will cease to exist as well."

"I don't want that."

"Neither do I," he agreed. He reached up to touch her cheek, then smiled at her. "Goodnight, love. Sweet dreams."

"You as well."

"Well, that might be why I'm allowing you to come along on this doomed errand," he said dryly.

She pursed her lips and pulled away from him. "If I knew how to give you nightmares, I might just for that."

He leaned against the wall and looked at her. "Aisling, I'm not sure you have that in you." He nodded toward her chamber. "Go on and go inside so I can watch you do it. I don't want you poaching my horse."

She opened her door, looked inside, then looked back at him. "He's asleep on the foot of my bed."

"Tell me he's masquerading as a puss."

"I think he likes that shape."

"Heaven help us," he muttered, then he smiled. "I'll see you in the morning."

She nodded, went inside, then closed the door softly behind her. She supposed she perhaps should have been tempted to leave him behind, but the truth was, she didn't want to. It was madness, but there it was. Besides, his horse didn't look inclined to do anything but roll over on his back where she might more readily scratch his tum.

She went to bed, the tale of Caileag of Tòsan running through the back of her mind like a river in her dreams.

Twelve

❧

Rùnach stood just inside Tòrr Dòrainn's border and suppressed the urge to pace. He had enough practice in that that it shouldn't have been difficult, but there was something about his current straits that seemed to inspire it.

He held on to Iteach's withers with one hand and Aisling's hand with the other. Iteach was absolutely immobile, which Rùnach appreciated. Aisling was equally still, and her hands were freezing. He smiled briefly at her.

"Not to worry."

"Me, worry?" she said uneasily. "Surely you jest."

Rùnach patted Iteach, then turned and pulled Aisling into his arms. He realized he was beginning to do that with regularity, but who could blame him? She was, as his cousins had pointed out to him several times the night before, an angel in human form, surely worthy of the most ardent and sustained pursuit by the most jaded of elven princes. They had tripped over each other to also assure her of that.

Rùnach just thought she was lovely.

He rested his cheek against her hair and watched his cousin Còir, second son of the crown prince, stand as silent as a sapling with his hand outstretched and as light as a strand of sunlight against the glamour that even Rùnach could see. Unorthodox, perhaps, but a very easy way to tell when Sìle and his company had breached that security and begun their purposely frantic but utterly pointless journey east toward Beinn òrain.

It was a plan Rùnach hadn't dared disagree with, especially given that his grandfather had been the one to suggest it. The idea was that Sìle and a small company would pretend to be Rùnach and an escort making for a logical place, namely the schools of wizardry. Whilst that company was heading east, Rùnach would slip over the border and fly under cover of night and spell toward Ceangail, which was perhaps the very last place Acair would expect him to go.

Còir stirred, then looked at Rùnach. He nodded.

Rùnach patted Aisling on the back. "We're off," he breathed against her ear. "Up you go, but don't leave without me."

She shook her head, then accepted his leg up. She settled herself on Iteach's back in the very lovely saddle provided, then drew her cloak more closely around herself. Rùnach watched Còir walk over, look up at Aisling, then make her a low bow. Rùnach would have given in to the urge to reach out and slap his cousin smartly on the back of the head whilst he was almost folded in half, but there was something about the sight that brought him up short.

Aisling continued to believe she was a simple weaver of no importance in the world, yet the grandson of a king was making her an obeisance better fit for the queen of some important realm. Rùnach wished he'd had some means of painting the scene so Aisling might have enjoyed it at another time.

Còir turned to him and stepped forward. "Guard her well," he said in a low voice.

"I will."

Còir reached out and touched the back of Rùnach's right hand. "Last night Grandfather gave you a spell of glamour that when laid under Mochriadhemiach's will make you impenetrably invisible to anyone, including any of Prince Gair's get. I will give you something far different. It will reside here amongst the runes until you need it."

Rùnach looked at Còir in surprise. "That's very generous."

Còir didn't look at all happy, but perhaps his ale that morning had been unusually bitter. "Aye, it is," he said briskly. "Keep in mind you can use this only once."

"Interesting—"

Còir reached out and touched the back of Rùnach's left hand. Rùnach caught only a flash of gold and silver before something sank into his flesh. It burned like hellfire, rivaling even Weger's worst efforts.

"What *was* that?" he gasped.

"Don't ask," Còir said grimly.

"Còir, you can't simply embed something into the back of my hand without telling me what it is."

"It's one of my own runes," Còir said almost angrily. "I gouged it out of my own flesh and gave it to you."

Rùnach felt his mouth fall open. "Why?"

Còir jerked his head sharply toward Aisling. "Because of her, and I'll tell you now that you don't deserve her and if I find out you've mistreated her, I will come dig out not only that rune from your hand but your heart from your chest. Are we clear?"

"Perfectly," Rùnach said, feeling as if he were suddenly facing an angry elven father who thought Rùnach might have had less than honorable designs upon his daughter.

Còir glared at him again, then moved to stand next to Aisling. He pulled a handkerchief from the bosom of his tunic and held it up toward her.

"For you, lady."

Aisling looked at him blankly. "What is it?"

"A gift. There is a spell woven into the cloth."

"What does it do?"

"It tattles on Rùnach if he doesn't treat you well."

She smiled. "In truth?"

Còir pursed his lips. "Aye. I might also have enspelled the threads with the delicate scent of twilight from my grandmother's garden, though I'll never admit as much. If you find yourself in trouble, pull that cloth out, write a message with your finger upon it, and the spell will send the words to me instantly. I will then come either to rescue you or to kill this young rogue without delay; your choice."

Rùnach had other suggestions about what Aisling might do with Còir's offering, but he supposed it would be wise not to give voice to those. He shook his cousin's hand, promised him Aisling would be perfectly safe—never mind that he had little to no idea exactly how he would manage that—and swung up upon Iteach's back behind Aisling.

Còir looked at him seriously. "Be careful."

Rùnach nodded, then turned his attentions to the parting his cousin had made in the king's glamour. Iteach stepped daintily across the border, sprouted wings, then leapt up into the air with all the magnificence of a horse who was absolutely aware of his own spectacular self.

Rùnach settled himself in for a rather long ride and supposed he would have ample time to think about all the things his family had done for him and more particularly the protections they had offered him.

He just wished he hadn't needed them.

• • •

It was mid-morning the next day when he found himself walking through woods near his father's keep of Ceangail, woods he had frequented as a child and young man. He could safely say that he disliked them every bit as much at present as he had a score of years ago. Aisling walked next to him, her expression guarded. Iteach trailed at their heels in the shape of a hound that Rùnach certainly wouldn't have petted had he not known who lurked behind those very impressive fangs.

They were all wearing not only Miach's spell of un-noticing, but Sìle's glamour underneath it as well. Rùnach found the combination oddly comforting, though he would be the first to admit the rune Còir had gifted him itched well past ignoring. It wouldn't have surprised him to learn that was on purpose.

He walked to the edge of a clearing, then paused and looked at Aisling to see her reaction.

She looked past him into that break in the trees, blinked, then looked up at him in disbelief.

"You can't be serious."

"I am."

She pointed into the glade. "*That* is where the witchwoman of Fàs lives?"

"Amazingly enough."

"Rùnach, it looks edible."

He had to admit that was the case. The house wasn't overly large, but it was constructed and then painted in a way that left it resembling a rather tall, plump sugared bun such as he might have had for tea as a boy. The thatching of the roof didn't mitigate the desire the house had ever inspired in him to simply go up to one of the walls and lick it to see if it tasted as good as it looked. He looked at Aisling and smiled. "She lures people inside with the exceptionally tasty shutters."

Aisling pursed her lips. "She does not."

"Very well, she doesn't, but I think the whole effect is to soothe and put at ease."

"Someone will someday write a tale about her and her house," Aisling said, "but it won't be me. I'm too terrified standing here just looking at it."

"Well, I won't tell you that she isn't dangerous, but she doesn't see very well and she has more interesting things to do than put us in cages and prod us with sticks."

"Such as?"

"Such as looking for pencils and quills in her hair. She is, as I've said before, a very committed diarist. She possesses the necessary tools of the trade, you know."

"I'll take your word for it. How do we proceed now?"

"We trot right up to the front door and knock."

She looked at him in alarm. "You can't be serious."

"The only other alternative is to trot up to the back door and knock, which I don't think will go very well."

She seemed to be having trouble swallowing. "Why would that be?"

"Because there is a spell there that slays anyone immediately upon their touching the wood." He shivered delicately. "Very nasty."

Her mouth was moving but no sound was coming out. "You," she finally managed, "are mad. Utterly mad. What's come over you?"

He smiled, wishing he dared kiss her as he so desperately wanted to. "There's nothing I like better than questing with an exceptionally fetching weaver from Bru—"

"Shhh!"

He smiled. "I had a lovely nap on the back of our charming lad there, I'm not required to return to Ceangail to sleep in a bed that belongs in the rubbish heap, and I have you to look at. How can I be anything but happy?"

She pursed her lips at him. "You worry me."

"Perhaps I should, but the truth is, I'm fairly certain this will be the least terrifying thing we face," he said, unable to be less than honest. "I'll keep my grandfather's spell handy."

"Will it work here, do you think?"

"Aye." He supposed it wasn't the time to explain exactly why he knew Sìle's glamour would work on his father's soil or enumerate how many times he had used the same spell himself in his youth for various and sundry purposes. "We'll be safe enough."

"I trust you."

He smiled at her, but she wasn't paying him any heed. She was looking with alarm at the house in front of them that looked indeed as if it had sprung from some sort of book of tales for children. Only inside that house was not a kindly old granny with sweets and stories for any and all who knocked on her door. Rùnach had managed to never run afoul of her ire, but he knew others who hadn't been so fortunate—including her own sons.

Nay, the witchwoman of Fàs was not to be underestimated, no matter how many innocent-looking birds might have been nesting in her hair.

He took a deep breath, then had a final look around before he stepped out into the glade and walked with Aisling up to the front door. He and Aisling were still wearing not only his grandfather's glamour, but Miach of Neroche's spell of un-noticing. They would be safe enough out in the open. He knocked and prepared himself for a bit of a wait.

The door creaked open eventually. With again absolutely no concession to haste, the door was opened wide to reveal a hunched-over, warty-nosed crone. The old woman stuck that nose out into the sunshine, sniffed, then frowned. She then tilted her head and looked down at Iteach who was sitting at Aisling's feet.

"Oh, a nice doggy for lunch," she said, sounding pleased. "Come in, little one, and we'll put you right on the fire."

Iteach whinnied indignantly at her.

The witchwoman of Fàs patted herself, presumably looking for spectacles that were neither on her nose nor residing in her hair, then frowned.

"You, little one, are obviously not what you seem." She frowned and looked up. "Who else is there?"

Rùnach hoped he wasn't making a colossal mistake as he drew both spells aside and tucked them into his pocket, unmagically speaking. The witchwoman of Fàs looked at him for a moment or two without a spark of recognition, looked at Aisling in the same manner, then back at him.

"Hmmm," was all she said.

"Indeed," Rùnach agreed.

She looked at the side of his face, then reached for one of his hands and studied the scars there. She frowned, then released him.

"You'd best come in, the both of you."

Aisling gulped audibly, but the witchwoman of Fàs didn't seem to notice. Rùnach stepped across the threshold and drew Aisling through the doorway behind him. He hadn't but closed the door behind him before his father's erstwhile paramour turned and tossed a spell over them both.

The runes on his hand blazed forth with a light that almost blinded him. When he could see again, the witchwoman of Fàs's spell lay in a tidy pile at his feet.

The witchwoman of Fàs harrumphed in displeasure.

Rùnach shrugged and attempted a polite smile. "So sorry."

"Sìle's glamour has a very long reach, I see."

"I think those were just the runes," Rùnach offered, "though the spell he gifted me is useful enough."

"As is that little something you hold from the youngest prince of Neroche."

"King now," Rùnach said.

"So he is." She patted herself, then muttered a curse or two.

"Lost my spectacles." She looked at Aisling. "Don't suppose you'd go hunting for them, dearie, would you?"

Rùnach would have stopped Aisling from moving, but she seemed thankfully and quite conveniently frozen to the spot.

"Where?" Aisling managed.

"Over there in my comfortable chair."

"And what else will I find there?"

The witchwoman of Fàs smiled, looking almost pleased. "The odd coin, perhaps my favorite pencil. Who knows? You might find out, though, if you have the courage to go and look."

"And if I agree," Aisling said slowly, "will you promise not to do anything untoward to Prince Rùnach?"

The witchwoman of Fàs peered at her. "Hmmm," she said again. "So that's how it is. And what, my young miss, will you do if I damage him?"

Aisling lifted her chin. "Something dire, I assure you."

"But, my girl, your magic will not work in my house."

"I don't have any magic."

The witchwoman of Fàs studied her for another long moment, then looked at Rùnach. "What does she have except your heart?"

"Vast amounts of courage," Rùnach said, vowing he would at his earliest opportunity sit down and see if he couldn't determine exactly why others seemed so damned determined to credit Aisling with what she most definitely couldn't possibly have. She had no more magic running through her veins that he did. She would have known it otherwise, surely.

"Even the rudest village brat can possess courage," the witchwoman of Fàs said with a snort. She looked at Aisling. "Enlighten me further about your possible plans for revenge. Would they involve spells?"

"I don't have any spells," Aisling conceded, "though I could spin yours into something I could hide along with your spectacles so thoroughly that you never found either again."

The witchwoman of Fàs looked positively delighted. "I might have to have you spin something after all, just to see how you do it. And nay, I won't damage your lad."

"He isn't my lad."

The witchwoman of Fàs looked up at Rùnach with a jaundiced eye. "Well, I'll allow that he is no longer a boy. And I'll concede that he turned out well, in spite of the path he chose. Quite a mighty mage in his youth, though perhaps he hasn't said as much. I'm not opposed to the odd display of modesty. My boys could certainly benefit from the like."

"I believe, my lady, that you have that aright," Aisling said without hesitation, "though one of them did offer me tea several days ago."

"I assume you didn't drink it."

"That seemed prudent."

The witchwoman of Fàs laughed merrily. "I like you. Off you go, my girl. I'll be much more at ease when I can see you both, then we'll have a lovely tea and make a proper visit of this."

Rùnach watched Aisling go off to look for the witchwoman of Fàs's glasses, then looked at their hostess. She was watching him from watery blue eyes that he was quite certain needed no ground glass to sharpen their vision.

"Yes, Mother Fàs?" he asked politely.

"Nasty business at Ruamharaiche's well."

"So it was."

She shook her head. "I tried to tell your mother that the location was the wrong one for what she wanted to accomplish, but she saw no other alternative." She shrugged. "We do what we must, I suppose, with the means we have at the moment."

Rùnach had always thought after what he'd seen over the course of his life that he was past surprise. Obviously not. "You spoke to my *mother*?"

"*Conversed* with your mother, ye wee fool, and more than once, at that. Does that come as a surprise?"

"A very great one," he said honestly.

She straightened the collar of her dress. "I have manners, just like the next lass. I'm just sorry things went so poorly for her. As for your father, however, he deserved what he got, the arrogant bastard. I heard tell Ruithneadh dealt him a rather confining blow recently."

"I might know details about that."

"I imagine you might. That'll do for a start. I'll also have the guest list for Princess Mhorghain's wedding."

"That too," Rùnach agreed.

"Anything else of interest?"

"Name it and 'tis yours."

"Done, then." The witchwoman of Fàs took her glasses from Aisling, polished them on a bit of her skirt, then put them on. She looked at Rùnach. "You haven't changed."

"Thank you," he said dryly.

She looked at Aisling, then went very still. "Ah, what do we have here? I think I may have missed a thing or two before."

"She's a weaver," Rùnach said.

"A nobody," Aisling added. "No one of importance."

"Hmmm," the witchwoman of Fàs said. "Very interesting. As I said, I perhaps missed things before, but perhaps those things should stay missed. Not terribly pretty, are you, dear?"

Rùnach made a noise in protest, had a wrinkled wink as a reward, then found his input was apparently not necessary.

"I'm not," Aisling agreed.

"The word doesn't apply to you," the witchwoman of Fàs said bluntly. "Nor beautiful. What does Rùnach call you?"

"Ethereal."

"And so you are, little one. Not all Bruadairians are, but there are some right handsome girls there and even more extremely handsome men. Preening fowl they are, but there you have it."

Rùnach found Aisling looking at him as if she weren't sure if she should laugh or weep.

"I imagine you knocked that one there flat when he realized how he felt about you," the witchwoman of Fàs said wisely.

Aisling gaped at her. "Oh, I don't think he—"

"Am I spoiling something?" The witchwoman of Fàs looked at Rùnach and blinked owlishly. "Don't you like her, Rùnach?"

"Very much."

The witchwoman of Fàs grunted, then looked at Aisling. "And you?"

"Are you a matchmaker, my lady?"

The witchwoman of Fàs laughed. "I'm no lady, girl, and no matchmaker. Miserable people are more interesting, you see, and I'm interested in interesting. What do you think of my erstwhile lover's least favorite son?"

Rùnach wasn't sure what Aisling thought, but *he* thought she looked as if she might like to run back out the front door and take her chances in the forest.

"Oh," Aisling said miserably, "that isn't a very nice thing to say to him."

The witchwoman of Fàs looked at Aisling shrewdly. "And so you see who I am. But have no fears for young Rùnach's feelings." She took Aisling by the elbow. "Let's go see what sort of poison is in the pot, then I'll tell you all about your would-be lover there and how thoroughly his father loathed him."

Rùnach clasped his hands behind his back and walked behind them, suppressing his smile. He had to admit that he was actually rather fond of his father's first, er, well, he supposed she wasn't his father's first anything. Whatever she might have been, he couldn't help but appreciate her unstinting honesty and her robust collection of facts. He considered that until he was called upon to carry a surprisingly elegant tea service that produced a tea that was nothing but tea and cakes that were definitely not laced with anything magical. He was vastly relieved to realize he could see that thanks to the spell of clarity his uncle had gifted him.

He was going to have to be about writing the odd thank-you sooner rather than later.

"I suppose his scars bother you."

Rùnach pulled himself away from the contemplation of the bottom of his cup to realize the ladies were discussing him.

"I don't see them anymore," Aisling said.

"Of course you do," the witchwoman of Fàs said with a hearty snort. "How can you miss those damned things? But count yourself fortunate he has them else you wouldn't be able to look at him twice. Too handsome by half, that one."

Aisling seemed to be having trouble picking her jaw up off the floor. "But, Mistress Fàs—"

"Fionne," the witchwoman of Fàs corrected her. "You may use my name."

"Thank you," Aisling said faintly.

"You," the witchwoman of Fàs said to Rùnach, "may not."

"Of course, Mother Fàs."

The witchwoman of Fàs smiled pleasantly. "Haven't heard that in years."

"But don't your sons call you that?" Aisling asked.

"My sons," she groused. "They call me nothing. They live within shouting distance, but do they ever come to visit? Do they send missives? Of course not, the worthless little sods. Useless, every last one of them."

Rùnach had a far different opinion of those bastard sons, but he decided there was no use in saying as much.

"Of course, my sisters didn't fare any better with their children, but that's a cold comfort indeed."

Rùnach blinked. "You have sisters?"

"Well, of course I have sisters, dolt," the witchwoman of Fàs said impatiently. "Fiunne and Leannagan, though we never talk about Leannagan." She shook her head in disgust. "Always had an unwholesome fascination with doing good, that one did. You try

to show family the error of their ways, but there's only so much a
body can do when another is determined to ruin her life." She
looked at Aisling and nodded in Rùnach's direction. "Didn't have
any success with that one either."

"Did his father try?" Aisling asked hesitantly.

"*I* tried, but failed miserably. Gair could scarce bear the sight of
him. And why not? Rùnach was extremely handsome, terribly
bright, and hopelessly skilled with a sword, something his sire never
managed even after all his years of living. Used to tell others he
never cared for steel, but what a liar he was. And to find his second
son with all those annoyingly appealing characteristics wrapped up
in a healthy dose of delicious elven glamour?" She shook her head.
"I'm surprised Gair didn't murder him in his sleep long before now."

"Not much chance of that any longer," Rùnach said dryly.
"Thankfully."

"Aye, and fortunately so—you with no magic to use against
him," the witchwoman of Fàs agreed. She pushed away her tea
and looked at them expectantly. "Very well, time is short, so let's
begin the negotiations."

Aisling jumped a little, but Rùnach reached out and tapped the
toe of her boot with his.

"That was *my* foot, you wee oaf," the witchwoman of Fàs
groused.

Aisling looked faintly appalled. "You aren't very nice to him."

"Imagine how awful I am to those I don't care for," the witchwoman of Fàs said with a sly smile. "Now, what is it you need from
me, children?"

"My lady needs a safe place to rest," Rùnach said. "I need an
opinion on a book I found in the library at Eòlas."

"Found it," she repeated with a snort. "I daresay you stole it,
did you?"

"Without remorse." Then again, the book was his, so perhaps
the method of its liberation could remain safely uncategorized.

"There's hope for you yet, lad." The witchwoman of Fàs nodded. "Very well, what else?"

"That's all."

"And in return?"

"Those details you might want about happenings out in the world."

"That seems rather thin, as far as offerings go," she said doubtfully. "On the whole."

"What else would suit?" he asked.

"I have wood that needs chopped."

"Seems a bit perilous to be outside," Rùnach pointed out.

"Wear that spell from young Miach and that blasted glamour of your grandfather's. I'll use something of my own to muffle the sounds."

Rùnach supposed that if the muffling was limited to the sound of an axe falling on wood instead of his head, he couldn't argue.

The witchwoman of Fàs looked at Aisling. "You, Mistress Aisling, will stay inside and keep your hound from chewing on the legs of my furniture."

Aisling looked at her with the expression of one who had had enough surprises for the day. "How did you know my name?"

"Rùnach mentioned it, I'm sure."

"He didn't."

The witchwoman of Fàs shrugged. "It's written plainly enough on your soul, gel. You might want to learn to hide that eventually, but I doubt you'll learn that from me." She rose. "Come along, Rùnach my lad. Off to your labors."

Rùnach hesitated. "Perhaps Aisling would rather come sit in the sunshine."

"Don't be daft," the witchwoman of Fàs said. "It isn't as if I'm going to pop her into my oven and roast her for supper, now, is it?"

"I should hope not."

She pursed her lips. "She's too ethereal and skinny for that.

Now, one of those sturdy lassies from Gairn might tempt me. Ever been to Gairn, Rùnach?"

"Never, Mother Fàs."

"Don't go. They're rough and tumble there in the north. Might offend your delicate elven sensibilities. Now, come along and bring your best efforts with you. Your lady will be safe enough with me inside."

Rùnach shuddered to think what might happen to Aisling during the afternoon with Fionne of Fàs manning the tea table, but perhaps since they'd already eaten, she might be safe for an hour or two. He rose, then stood with his hand on his chair and wondered what sort of parting words he should leave with Aisling before he went to pay the purchase price of what he wanted to know.

"Good hell, Rùnach," the witchwoman of Fàs said impatiently, "I said I wouldn't harm her."

"You said you wouldn't roast her," he said pointedly. "That leaves several options still quite open."

The witchwoman of Fàs winked at Aisling. "Don't think he didn't hone some of that decent thinking here at my hearth. Did he tell you that he built on to my greenhouse and created a spell for my plants that waters them just enough at precisely the right moments? He had one of my best spells as payment and more than a few details about Gair's weaknesses as well."

"What spell was that?" Aisling asked.

The witchwoman of Fàs frowned thoughtfully. "Can't say as I remember. You, Rùnach?"

"I believe it was a spell that when laid upon a mage caused his nose and ears to grow in direct proportion to the evil intent behind whatever unsavoury spell he might lay on another."

Mother Fàs slapped her thigh and cackled. "That was the one." She shot Aisling a look. "Not particularly useful for protection, but good for a chuckle. You should have seen Gair's face the first time Rùnach cast it on him. Rùnach blamed it on one of my boys. Can't remember which one."

"Amitàn," Rùnach said dryly. "I imagine he still hasn't forgiven me for it."

"Likely not." She looked at Aisling. "Sadly, my gel, that was the one and only nasty thing Rùnach did in the whole of his youth—and that despite my efforts to show him the error of his ways. I imagine he still feels guilty over it." She nodded toward her back door. "We may as well go with him, girl. He'll fret else and not do justice to my wood pile. You would think one of my sons would be interested in seeing my fire fed, wouldn't you?"

"Don't you have a spell for that sort of thing?" Aisling asked.

"It never yields as fine a blaze as does some decent labor from a lad who knows how to wield an axe. Come along, Rùnach, and show your lady here something useful. Did I tell you, Aisling, how handsome he was as a youth?"

"Not fully, Mistress Fionne."

"Mistress Fionne," the witchwoman of Fàs echoed with a snorting laugh. "Pretty manners from—what did you say you were?"

"A weaver."

"Why do I have the feeling you don't care for the art?"

"It might be the sneer attached to the word."

The witchwoman of Fàs laughed heartily and shot Rùnach a look. "A worthy mate for you, this one. Well, come along, Rùnach. Show her you can do something besides sit upon your prissy elven ar—"

"Mother Fàs," Rùnach warned.

The witchwoman of Fàs rolled her eyes. "See, Aisling? *Prissy* is the perfect word for those elves. Don't know how I put up with Gair for all those centuries, but I was younger then, and I stole him from someone else. Hard to put away a trophy you've stolen from someone else is my thinking."

What Rùnach thought was that he might have to sit down soon

and digest what he was hearing. He had never thought to ask about his father's past, and now he understood why. He could only hope that Fionne of Fàs would leave off with her revelations whilst he had an axe in his hands. He wasn't concerned about her, but he was quite concerned about his toes.

He followed the ladies out a side door that fortunately wasn't the portal that sat under Mother Fàs's eminently useful spell of death and saw them seated before he retreated to the chopping block. He stole a look at them sitting in chairs half in and half out of the sunlight and smiled to himself. The witchwoman of Fàs was obviously enjoying shocking Aisling, and Aisling was perhaps unwittingly giving her pleasure by gaping at her as if she simply couldn't believe anyone could be that plainspoken. It was an unlikely pairing, but one he couldn't help but enjoy for a moment.

"Rùnach! Chop, you lazy—"

He smiled and set to his work.

Thirteen

✤

Aisling sat in the sunshine, in what had to be one of the most unlikely spots for comfort in all the Nine Kingdoms, and wondered how much stranger her life could become.

The witchwoman of Fàs, Fionne by name, was snoozing in a chair that looked to have been fashioned with that sort of activity in mind. One of her wild white locks had come free of her bun—and Aisling used that term lightly—and fallen over one eye and somehow over her nose. It seemed to bother their hostess even in her dreams, because every time it would tickle her lips, she would snort, curse, and blow it out of her way only to have it return to its former position when she succumbed again to slumber.

Aisling would have suspected Rùnach of laying an untoward spell on her, but even if he'd had magic, he didn't look as if he had it in him. He was simply leaning upon his axe, looking somehow quite harmless and terribly perilous at the same time. He dragged his sleeve across his forehead and smiled.

"She terrifies her sons."

"I can see why."

"I think she terrified my father."

"And you irritated him."

"Apparently so. I had no idea to what extent." He smiled. "That was likely for the best. I think I might have been quite impossible to live with otherwise. Badge of honor and all that."

She rose, tip-toed past their hostess, and sat down on a stump near where Rùnach was standing. He was finished with the enormous pile of wood he'd been given, so she supposed she was in no danger of flying splinters.

"Does it bother you?" she asked. "In truth?"

"To know my father loathed me?"

"Did she use the word *loathe*?"

"I believe she did." He shrugged and propped a foot up on his chopping block. "Gair of Ceangail is not the sort I think you want having a good opinion of your character. If he had approved of me, I think I might be worried." He looked at her. "What do you think?"

"About you or about her?"

"Me, of course."

She smiled at him. "I think Mistress Fionne hasn't damaged your ego."

"I saved her plants; she can't be too hard on me." He drove the corner of the axe blade into the stump, then sat down in front of it and looked at her. "And?"

"You chop a very fine pile of wood."

"Prissily?"

She smiled. "Of course not."

"My cousins are very delicate, just so you know."

"Which ones?"

"The ones who slobbered all over you at Seanagarra."

"Còir wasn't prissy," she said. "He gave me a handkerchief, you know."

"And I've given you all kinds of perilous adventures," Rùnach said. "Far better than a handkerchief, I'd say, if you know what I mean."

"And what he means," said a voice that sounded as if it had just woken from a satisfying nap, "is that he doesn't want you thinking his cousins are worth looking at a second time, whilst he himself most certainly is. Arrogant thing, isn't he?"

Aisling looked at the witchwoman of Fàs. "His cousins aren't interested in me. Whyever would they be?"

"*He* is interested in you, which is what he wants you to think about instead of those prancing lads from Tòrr Dòrainn." The witchwoman of Fàs rolled her eyes. "My girl, you need a few lessons in the art of flirtation."

"From you?" Aisling asked, realizing only after she'd already said it how horrified she'd sounded.

The witchwoman of Fàs pursed her lips. "Well, of course not from me. I've no patience for that sort of thing, and I certainly have no experience with the elves of Tòrr Dòrainn. An exclusive lot, those, though even I'll admit one of the best is there beside you." She paused. "Well, before he ruined his looks trying to rid himself of his sire. I suppose he's still handsome enough from the proper side."

Aisling wasn't sure if she should laugh or gasp. The woman could say the most appalling things without so much as a flinch.

"I don't see his scars," she managed finally.

"So you said before. I didn't believe you before, but I'm slightly disappointed to find you're in earnest now. I wouldn't manage the like, but perhaps I have a more discriminating eye than you do." She dragged her sleeve over her eyes, smacked her lips a time or two, then nodded at Rùnach. "Bring your wee tome, laddie, and let's have a look. It seems as if you've done a proper day's labor."

"I haven't stacked it yet," Rùnach pointed out.

"Not to worry," she said dismissively. "I'll have one of my sons do that, whether he wants to or not. I think Acair will be here later this afternoon." She looked at Rùnach blandly. "Did I forget to mention that?"

Rùnach cursed fluently, which only left the witchwoman of Fàs smirking. Aisling found herself too busy trying to breathe to make any noise. Rùnach cursed a bit more as he walked over to his pack, dug about in it, and pulled out the book that Aisling hadn't dared look in after that first time. He sat down on a stool at the witchwoman's feet, then handed it to her.

"Your book of spells," she said mildly.

"Which I left here, if memory serves."

The witchwoman of Fàs looked, remarkably enough, slightly sheepish. "I believe it was, as the young hooligans say these days, nicked whilst I was napping."

Rùnach looked at her sternly. "You knew it was gone?"

Aisling watched them lock gazes and engage in what even she could tell from where she sat was a fairly serious battle of wills. She had to admit she was slightly surprised when the witchwoman of Fàs broke first.

"Well, of course I knew it was gone," she muttered, sitting back. "Saw someone leaving with it out the back door before I could wake my feet up enough to give chase. I couldn't say for sure who it was. Didn't have my spectacles on, you know."

"Did you know where it had been taken?"

Mistress Fionne shrugged. "It's possible someone might have tossed a chipper *I'm off to Diarmailt, Mother!* over his shoulder as he skipped merrily away, but I'm a bit foggy on the whole episode." She looked at Rùnach with wide eyes. "Don't tell me *that's* where you found it."

Rùnach pursed his lips. "What I am going to tell you is that I'm disappointed in you that you didn't keep it behind a boring collection of herbals."

"You wound me, Rùnach my boy, truly you do. I thought you were dead—very well, I knew you weren't, but I wasn't about to spill your secret for you. And if you must know, I knew exactly which little demon was in here, rifling through my books. I *assumed* you had actually managed the spell to keep the innards locked as you'd claimed—very well, I knew you had because I tried my damndest to unlock it myself and failed. I thought it might keep the little wretch occupied for a few decades." She shrugged. "Overly altruistic of me, as you can see, which goes to show where that sort of thing generally leads."

"Acair?"

"Well, of course Acair," she grumbled. "Who else would bother with anything of yours?" She paused, then rolled her eyes. "Very well, there is a very *long* list of mages who would have sold their souls to bother with your book of spells, but I knew Acair would suffer the most from not being able to have them, the heartless worm. It's kept him busy for the past twenty years, hasn't it?"

"I wouldn't know," Rùnach said grimly. "What I do know is that my spells are no longer in this book."

"A pity, though perhaps they'll turn up. What is inside instead?"

"Open the cover and see."

The witchwoman of Fàs looked at the book in her hands, then a stillness fell over the glade. Aisling would have found it peaceful in perhaps another location, but not where she was at present. She watched Mistress Fionne open the cover of Rùnach's book, then she began to frown.

Aisling looked at Rùnach to see what he was thinking, but his expression gave nothing away. He glanced at her briefly, lifted an eyebrow just as briefly, then went back to watching their hostess.

The old woman flipped through the pages without haste, frowning every now and again and finally resorting to a steady stream of muttering under her breath.

She reached the end of the book, then turned back to the first page. She looked at Rùnach.

"Hmmm."

"Acair knows I have this. He also said he had the notes I lost over the plains of Ailean, though I'm not sure of what use they would be to him."

"What sorts of tidbits were in your notes?"

"The sources for my father's spells," Rùnach said with a sigh. "Or what I could find in the library at Buidseachd."

The witchwoman of Fàs shuddered delicately. "That place is crawling with terrible things."

"I would have to agree," Rùnach said, "and most of them are slithering out from underneath Droch's chamber door."

"Bah, Droch of Saothair," the witchwoman of Fàs said dismissively. "A neophyte."

"And what would you do if *he* came knocking at your door?" Rùnach asked politely.

"Invite him in to tea and poison him."

"He's merciless."

She shot Rùnach a look. "And you think I'm not?"

"I think, Mother Fàs, that you're far more charming than you would like anyone to believe, and I'm desperately curious to know your opinion of that book."

The witchwoman of Fàs puffed up a little with pleasure. "Don't you be spreading that about, young Rùnach, or I will be simply overrun with guests clamoring for my company. As for the book, I'm not sure I care for it. I daresay it will spoil my dreams, but it wouldn't be the first thing to do so."

"Are they spells, do you think?"

Aisling watched Mistress Fionne's face, though she supposed the woman had too many years of practice in not giving anything away to reveal aught but what she cared to.

"Symbols, rather," she said slowly.

"Representing spells?"

Mistress Fionne considered the book in her hands for several moments without speaking, then looked at Rùnach. "That, my lad, is something not even I can tell." She shot him a look. "You have a bit of a mystery on your hands here."

"So it seems."

She handed him the book, then sat back. "It galls me not to have a better answer for you than that, but there it is." She considered, then shook her head. "Symbols, as you well know, can represent many things. Spells, the effect a spell might have on a body, the proper time of year for the use of a particular spell." She looked at him casually. "Landmarks on a map, even."

He blinked. "A map?"

"Stranger things have been drawn, haven't they? Your sire was famous for his scribblings that meant nothing except to him."

"Was he?" Rùnach asked. "I don't remember that."

"That's because he never let you see anything that wasn't perfect. Works in progress were those scribblings, which may be what you have there." She looked at him blandly. "You know he came here that first night."

"My father? After the well?"

"Aye." She looked off into the distance. "I called him a dozen kinds of fool, but I could see why he'd done what he'd done."

"And why was that?"

She looked at Rùnach. "You didn't goad him into it, if that worries you, nor did your dam. The blame lies entirely at his feet—or, rather, at the feet of his walloping ego. He had been, if you can fathom this, desperate to show the lot of you that he was a mage without peer."

Aisling watched Rùnach consider, then shake his head.

"That is the part I suppose I'll never understand. Why us? Why not take a collection of mages of consequence there?"

The witchwoman of Fàs looked at Rùnach seriously. "I believe he thought he had."

Rùnach closed his eyes briefly, then rubbed his hands over his face. "Hell," he said finally.

"I understand that's where he is now, courtesy of that little fiend Ruithneadh." She smiled. "Always had a soft spot for that one I did, though I can't say he holds me in any esteem."

"He's terrified of you," Rùnach said seriously.

"Well, then perhaps all is as it should be," she said, sounding pleased. She shot Rùnach a look. "You don't look particularly terrified."

"I rebuilt your greenhouse for you. That grants me some sort of immunity, doesn't it?"

"You know, lad, that excuse is only good for the first five hundred years. You may have bought yourself another century with that decent chopping, but after that you'll need to refill the well, as it were."

Aisling listened to the woman—and she really had no idea how old she was—talk about Rùnach in terms of centuries and realized something she hadn't been able to face to that point.

He was an elf who would live hundreds of years whilst she would be dead in less than sixty if she lived to be an old, bent crone, hunched in front of her spinning wheel and complaining about her joints.

"I wouldn't be so sure of that."

Aisling realized the witchwoman of Fàs was speaking to her. "I beg your pardon?"

"Don't measure your life in years, girl, measure it in memories." She paused, then smiled smugly. "That was poetic, wasn't it? I believe I shall become a philosopher when my magic runs dry."

"Will it?" Rùnach asked in surprise.

"Of course not, dimwit, but one must make contingency plans."
She looked at him sharply. "The reason I was telling you about
your sire is that I convinced him to make a copy of his spells and
leave it here with me."

"Why in the hell would I care about that?" Rùnach asked.

"I suppose that depends on whether or not you have them all
still memorized, or did all that time at Buidseachd drive their
superior structure and elegance from your wee brain?"

Rùnach pursed his lips. "I struck my head—"

"Face, rather," the witchwoman of Fàs said mildly.

"Very well, I struck my face against the side of the well, which
seems to have blotted out several pertinent memories," Rùnach
said grimly.

"I would say it was Gair taking your power that did the like, but
we could argue the point and never restore what was lost." She nodded toward the house. "Go fetch the book and memorize the spells."

"Thank you, but nay."

"Don't be so fastidious," the witchwoman of Fàs said sharply.
"How will you ever fight Acair without them?"

"Does _he_ know them?" Rùnach asked, looking slightly winded.

"Of course not," the witchwoman of Fàs snorted. "How colos-
sally stupid do you think I am? I wouldn't trust my youngest son
with the key to my front door, much less anything of import. But
if he's found your notes, he might accidentally put something
together. He's certainly had the time over the years to attempt a bit
of purposeful thought." She pointed to the house. "Go."

He looked at her evenly. "I don't want them."

Aisling found herself being pinned to the spot by the witchwoman of Fàs's surprisingly piercing gaze.

"The book's down the side of my comfortable chair near where
you found my spectacles. Go get it and put it in your satchel with
the other two."

"No," Rùnach said.

Aisling looked first at Rùnach, who was adamant, then at the witchwoman of Fàs, who was insistent. She took a deep breath.

"Why would you want to keep those spells here?" she managed.

"Because I am a keeper of important records," the witchwoman of Fàs said sharply, "which Rùnach of all people should understand."

"But if they fell into the wrong hands—" Rùnach protested.

"I believe you forget, my boy, just whom you're dealing with," she said frankly. "Do you think my sons have their power only from your father?"

"Nay, Mother Fàs, I don't," Rùnach said quietly.

"If I die or if the book is stolen, there is a spell attached to both copies that will blot them out of existence."

"Both?" Rùnach echoed faintly.

"Both," the witchwoman of Fàs said firmly. "The other one will be perfectly safe here."

Aisling glanced at Rùnach and had the feeling she knew exactly what he was thinking. The witchwoman of Fàs hadn't done a smashing job of keeping his book under wraps, as it were, so what was to say she would do any better with a copy of his father's spells?

"Aisling, go fetch the book. You'll know it when you see it."

Aisling looked at Rùnach but didn't speak. He merely looked at her as if he had seen something he knew he had to do but couldn't bring himself to say how badly he wanted to avoid it.

"I don't think he wants me to do this," she ventured.

"What he wants and what he needs may be two entirely different things," the witchwoman of Fàs said briskly. She looked at Rùnach. "My son he might be, but even I won't sacrifice the world for his ambitions. If you ever hope to face Acair and come away the victor, you had best have weapons of your own."

"I will not use Gair's spells," Rùnach said flatly.

"Didn't say you had to, did I?" she asked tartly. "But you'd best have something on hand to counter them with, and you won't have that unless you know what the originals were."

"I have no magic."

"Well, I can't solve everything for you, can I?"

Rùnach chewed on that for a bit, looking as if he didn't care at all for the taste, then looked at Aisling. "You stay here. I'll go."

She had no intention of arguing with him over that. She watched him go into the house, then looked at the witchwoman of Fàs. "I'm not sure we can keep them safe. You realize that neither of us has any magic."

"I'd suggest you find a way," Mistress Fionne said.

"I'm not sure I understand why you would force them on him," Aisling said slowly. "You have to know that your son will hunt him down for them."

The witchwoman of Fàs shrugged. "It is as I said. He'll need to have the originals to counter Acair. And if he can't keep Acair at bay, then I've sadly misjudged his cleverness. As for the book, you'll find a way to destroy it after it's outlived its usefulness. If you want my suggestion, you'll keep it in that little satchel you have along with the two books—nay, it's three, isn't it?—already there."

"How did you know that?"

The witchwoman of Fàs looked at her, clear-eyed and unrepentant. "I would tell you that I know many things, but actually I just snooped when you went to use the loo and Rùnach was inspecting his work in my greenhouse. Doesn't look as if you've cracked open that tome from Nicholas, though."

"Do you know him?" Aisling asked faintly.

"I know everyone," she said smugly. "And I'll tell you this much: that Nicholas of Diarmailt was quite the looker in his youth. 'Twas no wonder Lismòrian of Tòrr Dòrainn couldn't resist him." She patted her hair into place. "Don't know that I wouldn't have set my cap for him myself if I hadn't already had my sights on that handsome rogue from down the way."

Aisling couldn't imagine King Nicholas being pursued by the woman in front of her. She considered, then shook her head. It made her head hurt just thinking about thinking about it.

"Why haven't you read his book?"

"King Nicholas's?" Aisling asked. She shrugged. "I didn't want to know what was in it."

"You have paintings of Bruadair. Is that Brèagha's mark I see in the corner of them?"

Aisling shot her a look. "You're thorough."

"It's what makes me a good recorder of history," Mistress Fionne said. "And I have to admit, though the words fair burn my mouth, that your country wasn't too hard on the eye in its heyday."

Aisling looked at the old witch sitting in front of her and wondered if she dared ask such an unreliable source the question that popped into her head, then supposed there was little harm in it.

"Why do you think the magic is gone?"

"Why do *you* think the magic is gone?"

Aisling looked at her thoughtfully. "I suppose someone took it."

"I was afraid there for a minute that you weren't too quick on the uptake," the witchwoman of Fàs said bluntly. "I still have my worries, but fewer of them. Of *course* someone took the magic, you silly girl. The magic from an entire country doesn't simply up and walk off on its own."

"But why?" She could hardly believe she was asking the woman for her opinion, but there it was.

The witchwoman of Fàs blew that stray lock of her hair out of her eye. "You are an innocent, aren't you?" She leaned forward and looked at Aisling. "Because of *power*, my girl. That's what all mages want and there is never enough of it to suit them."

"But Rùnach isn't like that."

"That's because he hasn't got any of his magic left, but don't think for a moment he wasn't as happy as any of the rest of them to have any power he could lay his grasping hands on." She paused, then scowled. "Very well, I'll allow that perhaps *grasping* was unfair. And I'll also admit that he did always use his power for good, an annoying habit that no amount of my attempting to talk sense into him could erase." She pursed her lips. "He's a terrible do-gooder, that one. But don't think any of them wouldn't be happy with a bit more *oomph* behind the old spells."

Aisling smiled in spite of herself. "And you, Mistress Fionne?"

"My oomph vanished into the ether long ago, my wee lass, but I'm still powerful enough. And as for your books, I don't think Nicholas would have given you anything harmful. A lamentable trait to be sure, but there you have it."

It was hard not to like the woman on a certain level. "I appreciate your honesty."

"When your looks are gone—which in your case I daresay will never happen—it's all you have left."

Aisling smiled in spite of herself. "I'll remember that."

"And remember something else." The witchwoman of Fàs leaned closer. "I've been having bad dreams. See if you can attend to that when you have the chance of it, will you?"

Aisling was spared from having to disappoint her hostess with her certainty that she would never have the means of doing the like by Rùnach coming back out of the house. She rose, took the book from him, and put it in her bag without looking at it.

She could hear it, though, whispering things she was certain would give her nightmares if she listened.

"Hark, I think I hear someone coming," the witchwoman of Fàs said, putting her hand to her ear.

"Mother!" a voice bellowed in irritation from the other side of the house. "Mother, damn you, let me in!"

Aisling felt her heart stop. She looked at Rùnach. "Who is that?"

Rùnach cursed and shot the witchwoman of Fàs a glare. "Acair, I daresay."

The witchwoman of Fàs only smiled. "Best be on your way, hadn't you?"

"I thought you said he didn't have a key."

"That's why he is shouting instead of just barging in. Doesn't dare come through the back now, does he?" She heaved herself out of her chair, patted Rùnach on the cheek, then pinched Aisling's arm as if she tested for substance there. "You wouldn't have been worth the effort to spit, girl. Come back when you're fatter."

"I think I don't dare," Aisling said uneasily.

The witchwoman of Fàs laughed, winked at Rùnach, then walked back toward her house. "Stop your bellowing, you stupid git," she shouted, her voice and curses fading as she apparently wended her way to her front door.

Rùnach donned his cloak and his pack, then looked at Aisling. "Can you run?"

"How far?"

"Out of earshot, then we'll fly."

"I imagine I can," she said breathlessly. "Where are we going?"

"Somewhere safe."

"Does that exist?"

He took her by the hand and pulled her along with him. "In the realm of myths, love, all sorts of things exist."

Aye, mages and magic and those of the first persuasion who had no scruples about using the latter for evil ends. She was sure that in the realm of all things mythical, all manner of things existed, things she had likely never read about even in Mistress Muinear's most treasured of books.

She just wasn't sure she wanted to meet them.

Fourteen

❧

Rùnach stood at the gates of Léige, soaked to the skin and weary beyond belief. He wasn't sure if he should be grateful for the cover of darkness or worried that because of the darkness, he couldn't tell if he was being followed or not. He hadn't seen Acair along the way, not even a hint of him, but he didn't suppose that should be reassuring. It wasn't as if Acair didn't have his own spell of un-noticing, however inelegantly it might have been woven. It also wasn't as if the witchwoman of Fàs could possibly be trusted to keep their visit a secret, though he supposed he could rely on her oft-stated desire to cause her son as much grief as possible. Perhaps they had managed to get away without being noticed.

At least the only thing he was noticing at present was the looks of perfect boredom adorning the faces of the guards. They didn't even flinch as the fierce black dragon waddling along behind Rùnach and Aisling changed himself back into a lovely chestnut stallion with a blaze down his nose. They also weren't looking at Iteach as if he had been spat up from the depths of hell to torment them, though Rùnach supposed those lads from Léige had seen too much during their days to be surprised by anything.

The lad in charge stared at Iteach for a moment, frowned thoughtfully, then looked at Rùnach. He motioned with his sword for him to remove his hood, which Rùnach did.

The man's mouth fell open, but just briefly. "Your Highness," he said, dropping his slightly less-than-starched pose like a dirty cloth. "We had not expected such a distinguished guest, one of King Sìle's grandsons, obviously, so late in the evening. I would guess Prince Rùnach, but perhaps I guess amiss."

Rùnach wondered if the time would come when he wasn't surprised at being recognized in far-away places. He supposed he was less surprised at that than he was at not being sent away immediately simply because he was an elf, but perhaps his grandfather had caused more of a thawing of relations between Tòrr Dòrainn and Léige than Rùnach been aware of.

He smiled at the guard. "Nay, you have it aright. I compliment you for your keen eye."

"Thank you, Your Highness." He nodded to one of his fellows, and the portcullis was immediately raised. "Please, come inside the gates and take your ease by our fire. I'll have word sent to the king immediately."

"Oh, no need for that," Rùnach said quickly. "We would simply be grateful for a dry place to pass the night, if someone can be found to grant us that request. I wouldn't want to trouble the king so far into the night."

The guard hesitated only briefly. "Your courtesy does you credit, Prince Rùnach. I'll have word sent about that as well."

Which, Rùnach supposed, was all that could be done. He didn't imagine dragging King Uachdaran out of bed was going to smooth their path for them, but it wasn't his place to order about men who weren't his. He kept Iteach's reins in one hand and held Aisling's hand with the other as he walked under the barbican. At least they were out of the rain.

The portcullis was lowered discreetly behind them, and he and Aisling were offered pewter mugs of something steaming. He didn't ask, he merely drank and was grateful for watered-down mulled wine instead of that strong ale he'd sampled at Mansourah of Neroche's table.

He looked at Aisling to see how she fared. She looked much as he suspected he looked: bedraggled and exhausted. Léige wasn't as far from Ceangail as the inhabitants of Durial might have preferred, but still it was a fair distance. Rùnach was surprised Iteach had traveled that distance so quickly, but that pony had magic at his disposal for which Rùnach was extremely grateful. It had to have been close to midnight, which he regretted, but perhaps at the very least they might manage to sleep in a stall. Far better that than arousing the ire of a sleeping dwarf king.

He hadn't but finished the last sip of ale before a page came running out toward the gate. The captain of the night guardsmen spoke briefly with him, then came to stand in front of Rùnach.

"My apologies for keeping you waiting here, Your Highness. If you don't mind following young Seamus there, he'll lead you to the hall where others will be waiting to see to your comfort and the comfort of your lady."

Rùnach wanted to protest, but he supposed it was too late. "Thank you," he said simply. "You've been very kind."

The guardsman acknowledged the comment with the slightest of nods, then hesitated. "About your horse, Your Highness. There are obviously, er, *unusual* qualities about him. What sort of housing does he require?"

"I think at this point he would be content with a dry stall and a bucket of warm grain. If he wants something else, I imagine he'll find it."

"As you say, of course." He looked at Iteach. "I cannot leave my post to see to him, but I imagine the stablemaster—ah, there he is, striding this way with every intention of taking over your steed's care."

Rùnach shot Iteach a warning look, had an indignant tossing of the head in answer, then handed over the reins to the stablemaster who was already making noises of appreciation and admiration as he reached up to stroke Iteach's neck reverently. Iteach allowed himself to be led off to what would no doubt be kingly accommodations.

Rùnach thanked the guard for his aid, then smiled politely at the page who stood ready to lead them into the hall. He glanced at Aisling as they started across the courtyard.

"How are you?" he asked in Fadaire.

She blinked, then smiled. "Surviving in spite of my intense discomfort at not being grand enough for this place."

"That's quite a mouthful for a lass who just learned my tongue. Do you want to borrow a thread from one of these lads here so you can greet the king in his own language?"

"Dare I, do you think?"

"At this point, love, I think you can dare whatever you like."

He meant it. He was beginning to think that not only *might* she do whatever she liked, but she quite possibly had the . . . well, to be honest, he wasn't quite sure what to call what she had. Others seemed to think it was magic. He wasn't sure he was ready to call it that, but there was no denying that she had ability far beyond the norm.

Besides, what did he know? He knew of elven magic because he possessed it as his blood right, had encountered all sorts of other types of magic over the course of his life because he had sought them out, and he had admittedly seen some very strange things in places he hadn't particularly wanted to go. Unfortunately, he had never been to Bruadair, nor did he know anyone who had been born and grown to adulthood there, so he certainly wasn't in a position to know anything about what sorts of otherworldly powers they possessed.

Well, save Aisling.

"I think I'll leave the guards be," she said. "I'm not sure I can take in anything else tonight."

"Then I'll flatter the king until you've had a chat with your pillow," he said, suppressing a yawn. "I speak the king's tongue, which will please him, and apparently my grandfather during a recent visit made great strides in giving the relations between our countries a firm turn toward warm. I think we'll at least be granted beds, not just a spot on the floor."

She looked up at him. "How do you know their tongue?"

"Well, whilst my grandfather was in the past never a welcome guest—I'm not sure in all the years he's been alive he's ever made it past the front gates—my mother most certainly was. I've been here at least thrice I can bring to mind."

"And you thought learning their tongue before your visits might flatter the king enough to earn you a spell or two?"

He smiled. "It seemed wise."

She started to say something else, then she looked at the massive doors in front of them and fell silent. Rùnach found himself, as he had been on the previous trio of times he'd been inside those gates, rendered absolutely speechless by the sight of the dwarf king's hall. Seanagarra was light and delicate song and a beauty that was not quite of the world. Léige could not have been more opposite.

The entrance to the palace looked as if it had been carved from the stone of the mountain itself, though he seriously doubted any mortal hands could have managed the feat. He wasn't entirely sure that the hall hadn't simply pushed itself out from the rock to offer itself as refuge for the first king of Durial who had demanded it. Where rock failed, heavy wood continued along with a floor so polished, it seemed as if they walked on water.

A solemn dwarf awaited them there just inside the front doors, introducing himself as Riaraiche, the king's steward. Rùnach was surprised to find he recognized the man, but perhaps it hadn't been so long since he'd been a guest at Léige.

"You are most welcome, Prince Rùnach," Riaraiche said. "And your companion . . . er . . ."

"Aisling," she supplied. "Just Aisling."

Riaraiche, to his credit, didn't bat an eye. He did, however, hesitate. "I would say you hail from the north, but perhaps I am speaking out of turn about things you would rather keep unsaid."

Rùnach felt Aisling's fingers twitch in his hand, but she didn't bolt.

"I think that would be best," she managed.

"Of course," Riaraiche said promptly. "Now, if you'll follow me, I'll take you to the king. Your gear will be brought in, of course, and settled in your chambers for you." He looked at Aisling's satchel. "Shall I—"

"Nay," Aisling said quickly. "I mean, thank you, but nay."

Riaraiche nodded. "As you will, of course."

Rùnach exchanged a glance with Aisling after the steward had turned away to lead them through the palace. He winked, had a weak smile in return, then supposed they would both survive the evening. At the very least, they would have a safe place to sleep.

It occurred to him after a bit that Riaraiche wasn't taking them to the king's main audience chamber, but his private solar. He was very surprised by that. Perhaps the man was in his nightclothes. It wasn't possible that he and Aisling would have merited any other sort of welcome.

Riaraiche knocked, was bidden to enter, then opened the door and led the way.

"Prince Rùnach of Tòrr Dòrainn and Mistress Aisling, Your Majesty."

"And at this unearthly hour," the king grumbled. "Very well, might as well have a chat before I have them put to the sword."

Rùnach wasn't sure what startled him more: the sound of the
king's voice or the sensation of walking over his own grave. The
last time he'd been in the king's private solar, he had been hunting
down Miach and Ruith who had been about the poaching of a
spell. Rùnach had always supposed the king left that spell of hiding easily accessible to incorrigible mage's get so they would leave
his more perilous spells alone, but who knew for certain? Uachdaran of Léige was an unknown quantity to all but a select few.

Riaraiche stood aside. "Please enter, honored quests." He bowed
to them both, then departed, pulling the door shut behind him.

Rùnach took a deep breath, then put on his best company manners. He made the king a low bow and felt Aisling attempt the same.

"Your Majesty," he said, straightening. "Your kindness for
weary travelers knows no bounds."

"Travelers as well as soggy elven get, you mean," Uachdaran
said with a snort. He glanced at Rùnach—well, glared at him,
actually—then turned a fierce frown on Aisling.

Or, rather, he did for the space of approximately two heart-
beats before his mouth fell open and he pushed himself to his feet.
He stared at her in silence for several moments.

"Well," he said, finally. He stepped forward and offered Aisling
his arm. "Come sit by the fire, gel."

Rùnach caught the quick, panicked glance Aisling sent him,
smiled encouragingly at her, then watched as the king escorted
her with grave formality to a chair across from his near the fire.

"Thank you, Your Majesty," Aisling said faintly.

"You're very welcome, lass." Uachdaran shot him a look. "Rùnach, you go find your own chair—*after* you pour us wine. What
were you thinking to have this wee thing out in the wet so late?"

"An inescapable exigency, Your Majesty," Rùnach said.

The king grunted. "I can just imagine. Well, you'll dry off,
warm up, then we'll see this girl settled in a comfortable chamber.
If that suits, Mistress Aisling—or may I call you Aisling?"

"Of course, Your Majesty."

"This incorrigible rogue has obviously been dragging you all over the Nine Kingdoms without a thought for your proper care."

"Oh, it isn't his fault," Aisling said. "You see, we're on a quest."

"I would be surprised by anything else," the king said. "Ah, thank you, Rùnach. Most welcome. Have some wine, Aisling. It's warm and not from my own cellars, both of which should be considered boons. Now, if you can, tell me of your journey here. I assume you didn't walk."

Rùnach fetched himself a cup of wine, grateful still that he could do so with hands that worked as they should, then sat down in a chair next to Aisling. He supposed at another time he would have paid full attention to the conversation going on next to him, but at the moment, all he could do was fight to stay awake.

Supper arrived soon after their wine was finished, and Aisling fell asleep soon after that. Rùnach didn't suppose she would fall out of her chair, but he thought there was no harm in moving his chair closer to her and providing her with a shoulder against which to rest her head.

She slept through the entire affair.

"Well, you know what she is."

Rùnach looked at the king. "I can't tell you how many times I've been asked that question."

"And your answers have been?"

"In no particular order, a girl, a lass from a northern country, and a very lovely gel with no magic but an uncanny ability to pull things out of thin air."

"Lost your magic, did you?"

"Aye."

Uachdaran shook his head. "That grieves me, Rùnach, and I don't mind telling you so. I wasn't fond of your father, but you and your brothers inherited none of his evil. Your brother Keir was a fine man." He looked at Rùnach from under bushy eyebrows. "And unlike your wee brother Ruithneadh, you never once snuck into my solar and poached any of my spells."

"Nay, Your Majesty," Rùnach said solemnly, "I just took the ones you left like chocolates on my pillow."

"Are you complaining?"

Rùnach smiled. "King Uachdaran, one of my deepest regrets is that I no longer have the power to use any of them, for they were mighty spells indeed."

"And those weren't even the best ones. Imagine what lengths your brother and that dratted king of Neroche would have gone to otherwise."

"The world trembles at the thought."

The king pursed his lips. "It does, indeed." He studied Aisling for a moment or two, then looked at Rùnach. "A quest?"

Rùnach supposed since the quest was now his, there was no reason not to be frank. "She was tasked with finding a lad to overthrow her country's current, ah, usurper."

The king considered a bit longer. "Interesting. Are you going to share with me which country needs a bit of pruning at the top?"

"Do I need to?"

Uachdaran smiled. "I imagine you don't. I've had occasion to have speech with Frèam of Bruadair more than once over the past score of years. But I sense there is more to it than just your lass's quest. On the run from something untoward, are you?"

"Is it obvious?"

"Rather, my boy. I generally don't have visitors during the middle of the night who aren't flying under cover of darkness, so to speak. What are you running from? Or should I ask who?"

"My bastard brothers."

"I imagine that galls you," Uachdaran said with a snort. "Any one of them in particular, or the whole writhing pile of them?"

"Acair primarily," Rùnach said with a shrug. "He wants me dead."

"Lad, I would imagine Acair always wanted you dead."

Rùnach studied the king for a moment or two and couldn't help but smile a little. "You know, Your Majesty, I wouldn't have believed a score of years ago that you knew anything about my family."

"Much less give any of your family sanctuary here, is that it?" Uachdaran asked. "'Tis a bit of a shock to me as well, as you might imagine, but I suppose you can blame Miach of Neroche for starting the whole sorry state of affairs. Or that might have been the very charming Queen Mehar. The details escape me now, but I can tell you that I seem to find myself overrun with regularity by some or other of your relations. I allowed your grandfather into my hall—a *first*, if you'll have the truth—only because Miach had begged it of me."

"Did he behave?"

"Sìle?" Uachdaran scratched his cheek thoughtfully. "To my continued surprise, he did. I'm tempted to let him in again if the occasion arises." He considered, then nodded toward Aisling. "Is this quest she's on hers, or are you joining her in it?"

"What I would have preferred was to replace her on it," Rùnach said, "but she insisted on coming along."

"And you couldn't say her nay."

"I might have had an ulterior motive," Rùnach said.

Uachdaran smiled. "I should certainly hope so. How is that working?"

"Not as well as I would like. She seems reluctant to entertain any of my advances."

"Do you think?" the king asked with a bit of a smirk.

"I try not to," Rùnach said honestly, "especially where she is concerned. Then again, it isn't as if we've had much chance to do anything but run."

"That would tend to put a damper on amorous adventures, I'll allow." Uachdaran looked at him over the top of his cup. "You do know what she is in truth, don't you? And if you say *a girl*, I will stick you for it."

Rùnach couldn't see Aisling, but he did notice that at some point during the recent conversation he'd scarce managed to stay awake for, she had put her hand over his. She was assuredly asleep, so perhaps she had done it in her dreams. He looked at her hand over his for a moment or two, then looked at the dwarf king.

"Do you?"

"I know many things," Uachdaran said mildly.

Rùnach sighed. "I know she's Bruadairian. I know she has abilities that I don't understand, but I don't know why she has them or how she came by him. I thought only Bruadairian royalty had any sort of"—he couldn't bring himself to say magic, so he looked for another word—"unusual gifts."

Uachdaran leaned back in his chair and cradled his mug in his hands. "You don't know anything about the place and you're keeping company with that lass there?"

"In my defense, her details have been a bit hard to come by," Rùnach said. "It isn't as if she was willing to divulge anything."

"Bad luck to do so."

"She was told it was death."

Uachdaran snorted. "Here's something to learn now, which is something I'm surprised you didn't learn at Soilléir's knee: people exaggerate."

"Do Bruadairians exaggerate more than most?"

"I wouldn't go that far. Let's just say they have reason enough to want to protect what's theirs."

Rùnach considered, then cast caution to the wind. There was obviously no point in hedging.

"So," he said slowly, "do most everyday Bruadairians have magic?" He attempted to ask the question as casually as possible lest it appear more important than he wanted it to.

Uachdaran lifted an eyebrow. "Not that I've seen."

Rùnach looked at him then. "None of them?"

The king shrugged. "Again, not that I've seen, though perhaps

I'm not the best one to ask. I know what Frèam and his wife possess, but other than their sight, their abilities seem to end at their
border. As for what magic they can call upon inside Bruadair, it
is very powerful, but wielded in a way that I wouldn't have the
patience for. As for anyone else, I suppose it's possible that there
are ordinary Bruadairian lads and lassies who possess a rudimentary sort of magic." He nodded knowingly. "You know, the ability
to blurt out the odd charm of ward or create a love potion."

"Useful."

"For you, aye, it might be, especially considering the lack of
progress you've made so far with that gel there."

"She's a difficult case."

"Either that, or you've been too long out of decent society. Obviously Soilléir wasn't of any use to you in this area. Then again, it
isn't as if he's had any success with the fairer sex."

"He's intimidating."

"He a bit of a bungler when it comes to impressing a woman, or
so I would say. He'll need vast amounts of help if he's ever to wed.
Don't look at me for that sort of thing where you're concerned."

Rùnach wasn't sure Uachdaran of Léige was the one he wanted
advising him in matters of the heart, but he thought it prudent not
to say as much. He rubbed his hands together, wondering why
they ached so much. The rain, perhaps. He looked at his hands, his
hands that had once shaped magic beneath them without his having to think about it overmuch. He frowned, then looked at the
king.

"Soilléir has magic."

"So he does," Uachdaran said with a nod. "Mighty magic,
indeed."

"Do they all in Cothromaiche, do you suppose?"

"Didn't you think to ask him?"

Rùnach shook his head. "I never did."

"Too busy memorizing his spells, I'll warrant," the king said with a snort. "And don't look at me for that answer either. I would imagine 'tis like anywhere else. There is the odd strain of magic in the general populace, but I would imagine it finds itself there courtesy of some encounter with nobility back in the branches of the family tree. Magic always comes from a bloodline somewhere, wouldn't you agree?"

"Is it the same thing in Bruadair, I wonder?"

"Ah, now we come to it," Uachdaran said.

Rùnach waited, but the king didn't seem inclined to elaborate. "I'm not sure what to think."

"Aren't you?"

Rùnach shook his head. "My sister-in-law doesn't have magic, does she?"

"Apart from the fact that she Sees?"

"Which I would suspect she inherited from Artair of Cothromaiche. She inherited nothing from her mother, yet Sorcha was Bruadairian royalty."

"And?"

"Aisling is not royalty," he said. "She's a weaver."

"Are you sure of that?"

"I think she would know if her parents were related to the king," Rùnach said pointedly. "I think they had aspirations of being nobility, at least, but I think we can say with a fair amount of certainty that if they had been of royal blood, they wouldn't have sold her to the weaver's guild."

"Perhaps she was a changeling left on their doorstep."

Rùnach laughed a little, then he realized the king was perfectly serious. He looked at him in disbelief. "A changeling?"

"Stranger things have happened, I daresay," the king said with a shrug. "Did they sell any of her siblings to the weaver's prison?"

"Nay, but . . ." Rùnach paused, but couldn't bring himself to go down that path. "Perhaps she annoyed them."

"Perhaps she annoyed them because she wasn't theirs."

He shook his head, because he couldn't imagine that. Her parents had sold her because they were selfish and stupid, not because of anything more . . . well, anything more. Surely.

But they hadn't sold her siblings.

"It is interesting, isn't it," Uachdaran mused, "that you should meet a gel from Bruadair. Coincidental, even."

"I'm not sure I believe in coincidence."

"Then perhaps you should see if there's someone pulling your strings, shouldn't you?"

Rùnach blinked. "What?"

"Just what I said." He set his cup aside. "Think about that when you can't sleep, my boy, and see if you can't come up with an idea or two."

Rùnach shook his head. "Your Majesty, I believe your thoughts are simply too deep for my poor head tonight."

"You asked."

"I think I wish I hadn't."

Uachdaran slapped his hands on his knees and laughed as he rose. "Ah, what I live for: to confuse and confound any elf cheeky enough to enter my gates. Best be off to bed, lad, before your wee brain gives up entirely."

"Thank you, Your Majesty," Rùnach said dryly. "I'll take that advice to heart."

"I seriously doubt you will, but I've done what I can. Let's get your lady to a proper bed before she wakes with a kink in her neck. We'll talk more in the morning."

"I appreciate the refuge, King Uachdaran."

"Oh, don't think I won't have something out of you in return for it," Uachdaran promised. "Just haven't decided what yet."

"I'll pay it gladly."

"I imagine you will," the king said mildly. "Goodnight, lad. I'll send someone along to show you to your chambers."

"Thank you, Your Majesty. You've been exceedingly kind."

"Don't noise that about," the king said on his way out the door.

Rùnach sat in front of the king's fire until he heard a discreet tap on the door and knew his escort had come. He put his hand over Aisling's.

"Aisling? Time for bed."

She sat up so suddenly, she put her hand to her head, apparently to stop things from spinning around her. She looked at him, then rubbed her eyes.

"Tell me I didn't drool."

He smiled. "Not once."

She looked around herself. "Where is the king?"

"He went to bed, which is where you need to be off to." He set his wine aside, then rose and held down his hand for her. "I'm sure even the bedclothes will take pity on you tonight and allow you to sleep."

"One could hope."

He left the king's solar with her, then followed the servant down the passageway to where they were to be offered chambers. The dwarf made them both a low bow.

"This is for my lady's pleasure," he said. "Your Highness, your chamber is a bit farther down the way. I will await you there, if you like."

Rùnach nodded, and the man bowed again before he withdrew discreetly down the way. Aisling looked up at him.

"This seems like a safe place," she ventured.

"It is a fortress," Rùnach agreed. "I don't think all seven of my half brothers would dare assault it. You may sleep in perfect peace."

She smiled wearily, then followed a serving girl into the chamber provided. Rùnach reached in and pulled the door shut, trusting that she would be well taken care of. He had no reason to suspect anything else.

He walked thoughtfully to his own bedchamber, thanked their

guide, then went inside and wasted no time in putting himself to bed.

Sleep was long in coming, though he supposed he had reasons enough for that. Most of his discomfort came from his very location. He had to admit he didn't much care for having to run from refuge to refuge in an effort to keep himself alive. He just wasn't exactly sure what he was going to do to change that. He supposed his grandfather's glamour he'd asked for and the runes on his hands he hadn't might provide him with defense and Miach's spell might provide him with anonymity, but how far would that go in seeing Sglaimir off Frèam's throne or convincing Acair that he would be better off amusing himself with the pursuit of other mages?

Then perhaps you should see if there's someone pulling your strings, shouldn't you?

Of all the thoughts he'd had that day, that one was, he could safely say, the most unsettling.

And the most ridiculous. There was no one leading him down a path he hadn't chosen himself, much less forcing him down that path. He had an entire world full of possibilities in front of him, all waiting for him to choose the one that pleased him the most. After, of course, he saw to Aisling's business for her, then took care of his own.

Besides, who would possibly be interested in either of them? She was a simple weaver and he a man with no power. Surely they weren't of interest to anyone but themselves.

Surely.

Fifteen

❧

Aisling followed Rùnach and the king down a passageway that descended at a slow but steady decline. Actually, the truth was she was stumbling along behind them, but it was the best she could do at the moment. It had nothing to do with her sleep, which had been deep and restful, or the supper the night before, which had been wonderful. It didn't even have anything to do with the company, which was delightful.

It was that the rock was talking to her.

She hadn't heard it whilst she'd been sleeping. She would have remembered that, she was sure. In fact, her chamber had been comfortingly silent. Even the fire had simply burned in a cheery but voiceless way, leaving her to her own thoughts.

It hadn't been until noon, when she'd managed to get herself to the king's great hall and the king had asked them if they wanted a tour of his palace, that she had realized that it was as if the entire place were holding its collective breath for something. She had walked behind the king and Rùnach only because she continued to be distracted by the intricate carvings on the walls, which led her to endlessly fall behind.

And then she'd put her hand on one of the walls.

Even the king had looked back at her then, the torchlight and shadows playing equally over his expression of surprise. His surprise had soon turned to something else that she hadn't been able to identify. She thought it might have been approval, but she honestly couldn't tell. She was too busy being deafened by all the things the rock was telling her.

She took her hand away, but the cacophony continued. It wasn't a single voice; it was a plethora of voices that sounded as if the whole mountain were sliding down on top of her with an endless rumble. The only way any of it made any sense was if she trailed her fingers along the cold stone, for then at least she could understand what was being said. Or at least that had been the case in the beginning. Now, she found she could understand the stories being whispered to her without touching anything at all.

She supposed it might not have been so shocking if her only other experience with the sudden learning of a tongue hadn't come in Tòrr Dòrainn. The language of the elves there and the corresponding expression of the spells permeating the realm had been flowers and streams and endless sunlight falling down unless it had been interrupted by a gentle rain to freshen and renew.

The king of Léige's tongue had all the delicacy of an enormous stone being dropped on her head.

The language was a perfect reflection of the palace, she supposed: hard, unyielding, full of complicated twists and unexpected turns. The king and Rùnach were speaking in the common tongue—or so she thought; she wasn't sure she was capable of distinguishing anything from the low rumbling speech of the rock all around her. She couldn't tell what was speech, what was magic, and what was simply the stone that had borne the footsteps of tens of thousands of souls over the millennia of the palace's existence.

She realized, perhaps belatedly, that she didn't much care for being underground, but she couldn't bring herself to admit as much. Not when the king was doing them the courtesy of giving them a personal tour of his keep.

She tugged at the neck of her gown. It hadn't occurred to her that it would be so warm beneath the palace—if that's where they were. Actually, she hadn't expected many things, beginning and ending with being treated like royalty. In Seanagarra, she had been shown every courtesy she could have imagined, but she had assumed that had been because she had come with Rùnach and they had been humoring him.

At Léige, for some reason things were different. Rùnach was a guest, not a family member, and she was nothing. They could have easily put her in a closet and invited her to work for her food.

Instead, she had woken in a bed so soft, she felt as if she'd been sleeping on a cloud. She didn't remember having put on a nightgown of material so soft, she half feared to touch it, though she could tell well enough where it had come from and who had woven and subsequently sewn it.

She'd had a bath, breakfast in front of a roaring fire whilst she lounged about in a luxurious dressing gown, then she'd been dressed in a velvet gown of ice blue trimmed with lace and things that sparkled. Putting her hands on the gems made her slightly dizzy, but she supposed that might have been because they had come from the ground beneath her feet.

It apparently had that effect on others as well, which she had clearly seen in Rùnach that morning. After a very late brunch, she had been led to what she had assumed was the king's great hall where she had found Rùnach and the king sitting in front of one of the hearths, chatting about politics. Uachdaran had kept his seat as she approached, which she had expected him to. Rùnach, however, had jumped to his feet and looked at her in astonishment. She had looked quickly down to make certain she was adequately dressed, but had seen nothing untoward happening with her gown.

"What is it?" she had asked him.

He had made her a bow that made the very formal bow Còir of Tòrr Dòrainn had made her look like nothing more than a bit of a stumble. She had frowned at him, then asked the king what Rùnach had had for breakfast and if it had been accompanied by too much ale. The king had laughed, then offered her a tour of his palace, which she had accepted.

All of which had led her to where she was at present, coming to a halt after the floor had ceased to have a slope.

"Take her hand, Rùnach. I want to see her face when she sees what lies ahead. Close your eyes, Mistress Aisling, if you can bear to. I won't plunge you into anything perilous."

Aisling didn't suppose she was a particularly trusting soul, but she did trust Rùnach. That and she had the feeling the rock would tell her in its deep whisper if she was about to meet some unwholesome fate.

She closed her eyes as Rùnach took her hand, then continued to walk with him until he stopped.

"You may open your eyes now," the king said.

Aisling did, to complete blackness. She wondered if it were just her eyes failing her or if there was indeed no light. Then she heard the king whisper a word of command.

At that word, the song the rock was singing changed to a dirge, though it wasn't unpleasant or terrifying. It was simply the lowest voice in a mighty chorus.

Other voices were added, almost imperceptibly at first. As they became clear to her, as she was able to hear their harmony layered upon the dirge, she realized that the passageway she was standing in was growing lighter—and that the light was coming from within the walls.

Gold, silver, other colors she had names for and some she didn't: they lit themselves until the entire passageway was alight and the air was full of their song. Aisling looked at the king and found his sharp eyes full of something that wasn't quite passion and definitely not madness, but something that had good quantities of both things. He looked up at her intensely.

"What do you think?"

"I don't have words."

He smiled. "Wait." He nodded toward the end of the passageway. "Wait."

Rùnach took her hand and pulled her forward to walk between him and the king. She could do little besides look around her and marvel at what was contained in the rock, beautiful things that revealed themselves because their king had commanded them to. She suspected they would have leapt from the walls into his hands if he had asked them to.

Without warning, the passageway opened up into a cavern that was dark for only a heartbeat before it erupted into light.

She gasped.

The king only looked up at her and smiled. "The stuff of dreams, eh, gel?"

She could only nod. She started forward, then hesitated. "May I?"

"Of course."

The floor was the same polished stone that she had seen in the king's throne room as she passed it on her way to find Rùnach that morning. She walked out across it, into light and into a wall of song. She wasn't sure she was capable of deciphering it—if such a thing could be done anyway—so she simply walked through it, unsure where she was in relation to the floor and the ceiling. There were huge pillars of things she couldn't name hanging down from the ceiling, but for all she knew they had been carved specifically to cast light into the cavern. She walked through the middle of the cavern first, then along the wall, trailing her fingers over the stone. She wasn't at all surprised to realize that what she was seeing, all that light, all that music, came from things buried deeply in the rock.

She made the circle a second time, only this time the chorus had faded to a whisper and what she heard over it were the tales the silver and gold and gems had to tell her, tales of their creation, tales of gifting parts of themselves to miners who created heavy jewelry and crowns to adorn the kings and queens of Durial who had passed on before.

She walked along the edge of the cavern a final time, only this time the lights began to go out in the walls as she passed. She listened shamelessly to the dreams of the veins of ore and gems as they returned to slumber. They were dreams of a deep magic that grew slowly and waited patiently until it was called upon.

She paused. She could have sworn she also heard the sound of something running, a faint stream perhaps, but she saw nothing there.

She frowned and continued on, the lights extinguishing themselves behind her, until she reached where the king and Rùnach were chatting.

"Don't know what it is," the king was saying, "but I know I don't care for it."

Aisling came to a stop next to Rùnach who was frowning a little himself.

"Water running?"

"Not water," the king said. "Something running beneath my mountains. I can feel it under the roots."

"I heard it," Aisling agreed, then froze when both men turned to look at her. "I'm sorry. Perhaps I spoke out of turn."

The king shook his head. "Of course you didn't. What did you hear?"

"I thought it was a stream," Aisling said, "but I couldn't see anything. Is there an underground stream nearby?"

"There isn't," Uachdaran said slowly, "but I will admit there are many things that even I haven't had a chance to explore in spite of all my time on the throne. Perhaps I've just missed something." He seemed to shake aside a thought that bothered him. "Now, lass, what did you think of the bowels of my mine here?"

"Spectacular," she said. "They were happy to have you come visit."

"Well, one could hope," he said with a smile. "Now, which would you two prefer: a tour of the smithy or something to eat?"

"You know what I'll say," Rùnach said cheerfully, "so perhaps Aisling should make the decision."

"I would like to see the smithy," she admitted.

"Interested in the musing of ore as it becomes the finest swords available?"

She smiled. "I can only imagine the boasting that goes on and the plans that are made for future glory and honor."

The king laughed a little. "Aye, lass, there is that in abundance. You can tell your wee elven princeling what's said, as I imagine he's never heard his sword say anything at all, eh, Rùnach?"

"Oh, I wouldn't go that far," Rùnach protested. "I would imagine I've had swords that had plenty to say about my paltry skill."

The king looked him over. "I see you have a blade there, but it doesn't look as if it has any magical properties."

"A gift from Sgath," Rùnach said. "He was humoring me, I believe."

"Well, if you're interested, we'll see if Mistress Aisling hears anything in my forge that can't face a lifetime of not being at your side. Don't get your hopes up, though."

"I wouldn't dare," Rùnach said seriously.

The king started back up the passageway. "I don't suppose, Mistress Aisling, that he has told you anything about his adventures with the sword, has he?"

"Nay, Your Majesty, he hasn't. I've seen him wield a sword, though, at Gobhann."

"And just what did the master there have to say about him?"

"Many things," Aisling said, though she supposed she didn't need to repeat the slurs and insults. "In the end, Weger told him that he had nothing to teach him."

"A wise man, that Scrymgeour Weger," the king said, nodding. "Knows a thing or two about steel and its wielders. Your young lad walking behind us, trying not to salivate over the possibility of having one of my swords, went through a very long and distinguished list of swordmasters."

"Did you know him so well as a lad, then, Your Majesty?"

The king shook his head. "Relations between our houses weren't what one might call warm, though I did allow his mother to bring a selection of her spawn here a time or two. The reason I know about his swordmasters is because I supplied Princess Sarait with a pair of them, but only after she promised me I wouldn't have to sit next to her father on the Council of Kings if I complied."

Aisling smiled. "And that went well, I take it?"

"It went as well as you might expect with my having to be in the same room with that feisty old elf, but that was before I found myself unwillingly breaking bread with him and being forced to admit that with a mug of ale in his hand he wasn't as intolerable as he is whilst sitting in a chair pontificating about the glories of his realm."

Aisling looked at Rùnach who was walking behind them with his hands clasped behind his back, his head bowed. He looked at her briefly, smiled, then resumed his contemplation of the floor in front of him.

The king seemed content to walk and be silent, so she joined him in that. It was growing easier to listen to the rock, perhaps because it had finished with the telling of its most important tales or perhaps the mountain had decided she needed to rest her ears.

Or, she realized a short time later, perhaps it had taken pity on her because it knew what she would face in the forge. She realized that was the case when she walked into the smithy and a chorus of steel greeted her.

The king looked at her, chuckled, then touched her elbow before he went to talk to his smith.

She stood next to Rùnach near the door and looked up at him. He was watching her with a grave smile.

"How are you?"

"Distracted."

"I understand that the rock has things to say if you have ears to hear it."

"It sings as well."

He blinked, then laughed a little. "I didn't know that. Is it a good song?"

"It's majestic."

"I think I envy you," he said quietly. "All I heard was the drip of water. I didn't see any, though, did you?"

She shook her head. She hadn't heard a drip; she had heard a small stream, in a place where she'd seen no trace of water.

Very odd, that.

She wondered what it meant and why the king seemed so bothered by it.

Supper was a very difficult affair. She sat on the king's right hand, in the place of honor, with Rùnach on her right and didn't mind the feeling of security that provided. The players were equally superb, weaving melodies that seemed to mingle with the tales whispered by the stone of the walls. The conversation was pleasant and the king's household very kind. But she couldn't hear any of it.

Or perhaps it was that she could hear all of it.

"Aisling, would you care to dance?"

She focused on Rùnach with difficulty. "What?"

He rose and held out his hand for her. She put her hand in his because that's what she was accustomed to doing, only this time she hadn't expected what would happen.

The moment she touched him, the tumult stopped.

She sighed deeply and walked with him out into the middle of the hall. She had learned one pattern from one of his cousins—she couldn't remember which one at the moment—and fortunately the musicians seemed to know a tune that fit the steps. She looked up at Rùnach.

"I'm distracted."

"I noticed."

She winced. "Have I been rude?"

"Nay, just distracted." He tilted his head as he looked at her. "Too much going on?"

"Much too much," she said honestly. "It's as if the walls are competing to tell me their tales in the loudest voices possible. I have no idea why they're concerned that I hear what they have to say, but they seem to be." She looked up at him. "Do you hear it too? Here in the king's hall, at least?"

"Not anymore," he said with a smile, "but I did once or twice in my youth."

"Do you think the king hears it? The tales the walls tell, I mean."

"I imagine he does, though I also imagine he doesn't pay attention unless those tales concern him."

She smiled. "He's very kind."

"He can be," Rùnach agreed. "He can also be impossibly ruthless. It's what makes a good king, I suppose."

"Does he enjoy it, do you think? Being in charge of his realm?"

"I think he loves it," Rùnach said dryly. "In spite of their differences, he and my grandfather share a few important characteristics, most notably the opinion that they know best in every situation. I suppose after all the years of sitting on the throne, they have earned the right to think so."

"Would you want to be in that place?" she asked. "King of some realm?"

He laughed. "You know I wouldn't. I'm perfectly happy to slip into obscurity."

"Are you?" she mused. "How is that possible?"

"We'll finish your task, then I'll quite happily show just how 'tis done." He smiled. "A little house, a garden, a place for Iteach to graze. Sheep to trim the weeds under the fruit trees."

"No sea?"

"Is it impossible to have that as well, do you think?"

"I don't know," she said. "Is it?"

"Why don't we find out?"

"I think of the two of us, you'll find out first," she said seriously. "I have many years to work before I could afford anything like it."

He smiled. "Nay, Aisling, I mean, why don't the two of us find out together?"

She stumbled to a halt, right there in the midst of the king's great hall. "What are you talking about?" she managed.

"What I'm talking about," he said seriously, "is me, seeing to a house for you."

She considered that idea for the space of approximately two heartbeats before she shook her head. "I couldn't," she said quietly, because the idea that he should look at her and see anything but a runaway weaver with ruined hands and no beauty in her face was . . .

Well, it was the stuff of dreams, and not even in her most fanciful dreams did she see herself walking off into the sunset with the grandson of an elven king.

She looked up at him. "I'm not sure how to repay you for everything you've done for me so far as it is." She said the words, but she didn't mean them. She just couldn't bring herself to talk about the reason why her face felt as if it had caught fire and how absolutely preposterous it was that he should even talk about building her a house . . .

Unless he merely meant he would build her a house and leave her to it.

She fought the urge to turn and walk out of the hall. It was true that he had spent a goodly amount of time at Seanagarra glaring at his cousins when they would seek to accompany her here or there, or seek out her hand for a dance, but perhaps he simply didn't like them—

"You could," he said slowly, "allow me to build a little house for you."

She did her best to nod casually. "Lovely," she managed. "Terribly generous."

"Isn't it, though? Let's discuss it further. A little house on the edge of the sea. With no doors."

She started to ask him why no doors, but she had the most astonishing sensation of having envisioned just such a thing. She was distracted enough by that to find that whilst she had been trying to remember when she'd thought of a doorless house, she had begun dancing with Rùnach again. She looked up at him.

"Did I dream that?"

"I think you might have."

She took his hand again and picked up the pattern of the dance, though it was certainly not easily done on her part. It took her another set before she thought she could ask the question that bothered her. She was very grateful for the pause in the music as the players decided on which tune to choose next. She looked up at Rùnach. "Why would you want to build me a house like that?"

"Why do you think?"

"I have no idea," she said, because she didn't dare say anything else. "Because you pity me?"

"Nay, Aisling of Bruadair, I do not pity you," he said very seriously. He looked at her for a moment or two, then he smiled. "You know, I'm beginning to think I should have asked Mother Fàs for a book on proper courting methods. I'll admit I'm at a bit of a loss."

"Well, I understand there is a contingent of very lovely women coming with traders tomorrow. If we're still here, you might want to look them over."

Though she had to admit the thought of Rùnach pursuing other women was not one she entertained with pleasure. Hard on the heels of that came the thought that she was absolutely the most foolish woman in the Nine Kingdoms to think a man of Rùnach's lineage would ever look at her with anything more serious in mind than helping her with her quest—

"You know, you think too much."

She looked up at him. "Do I?"

"I believe you do. Perhaps we should ask the king if we might go sit in his solar. I think it might be fairly quiet there."

"Aye, please," she said, finding that she was suddenly very out of sorts. Perhaps dwarvish food didn't agree with her.

Or perhaps she was vexed by the thought of beautiful traders' daughters looking at Rùnach and finding him lacking because of his scars. Aye, that was it. She might have to do damage to them if they were unkind to him.

She was still contemplating what she might reasonably do or say to unruly females half an hour later as she sat with Rùnach in front of the fire in the dwarf king's solar. In front of her sat a spinning wheel, provided apparently by the king for reasons she didn't dare ask, and to her left, away from the flames, sat a basket full of wool dyed in a riot of colors. She sat with her hands in her lap, not sure she dared touch anything. She looked over the wheel at Rùnach who was sitting on a very comfortable sofa with his hands behind his head, watching her with a faint smile.

"I might bring the mountain down atop us," she warned.

"I'm not sure you give Uachdaran's spells of protection the credit they deserve," he said mildly.

"I moved your grandfather's border."

"Aye, well, he moves it himself with regularity."

"Does he?" she asked in surprise.

"Now and again, when things feel a little too peaceful for his taste. Besides, then you were spinning air which seems to lend itself to more esoteric substances. This is just a pedestrian wheel with ordinary wool. How much damage can you possibly do—nay"—he laughed a little—"don't answer that. Start slowly and we'll see what happens."

She couldn't argue with that. She found yarn, tied a leader as Mistress Ceana had taught her, then selected a deep red that was almost a burgundy color.

"I don't normally like red," she said, thinking that perhaps if she talked as she spun, she might not do anything untoward.

"Then why did you choose it?"

She looked at him. "I might make you a cap. It would go very well with your eyes."

He lifted an eyebrow. "Ah, you've noticed the color of my eyes."

"I've looked in them often enough."

"I'm flattered."

"Rùnach, it's difficult not to look at you," she said, focusing on the fiber twisting beneath her fingers. "Which I'm sure you know already."

"I've forgotten."

"I'm sure you haven't."

"Remind me."

She shot him a look. "I'm busy."

He only smiled and folded his hands across his belly as he stretched his long legs out toward the fire. "How do they woo in Bruadair?"

"I have no idea. I suppose they must, but I've never seen it happen."

"None of your mates down at the pub tried to win your favor with a bit of flattery?"

She looked at him in astonishment. "Those lads? Me? You must be mad. They never would have paid me any heed. Not that I would have been interested," she added under her breath.

"Not interested," he echoed. "Why not?"

"Because they were mannerless louts full of ego and bluster."

"Ah, so you want a lad with manners and no ego. Anything else? He should perhaps be easy on the eye, I suppose."

"Tolerably so, I should think."

"How tolerable is tolerable?"

She stopped treadling. "Honestly, I hadn't thought about it seriously."

"Truly, Aisling? Not once?"

She put her hand on her flywheel, the wood solid and sturdy beneath her fingers. She looked at that very lovely wood for a bit, then looked at him.

"I suppose," she said slowly, "that I never thought to escape the Guild, so what was the use in thinking about something I could never have?"

He closed his eyes briefly. The look he gave her then almost brought tears to her eyes. "I'm sorry," he said very quietly. "You deserved better."

She spun the wheel and went back to her work. "It's over, and I'll give them no more of my time than they've had already." She shrugged. "As a young girl, of course, I imagined things that could never be."

"Heroes from legend coming to rescue you?"

"They were usually lads from Neroche," she said solemnly.

He pursed his lips. "Unsurprising."

"Well, it is the sort of thing they do."

"Badly, with bad manners and too much ego," he said darkly. "I think you should look in a different direction. Here, we'll make a list of places that don't qualify."

She watched him fetch paper and pen, then resume his seat.

She turned back to her spinning, grateful for a generous host who had provided her not only with a wheel but a comfortable place to use it.

She listened to Rùnach name then discard a lengthy list of places she absolutely shouldn't go to look for a suitor. He then began a list of qualities she might be interested in. She commented on them when she heard them, though the truth was, she was too distracted by the wheel and her own thoughts. In time, though, even her thoughts ceased to distract her and she was able to look at other things.

She found herself watching Rùnach's hands as he continued with a list she could no longer hear. She realized she could see the runes on the back of his hands, runes she was tempted to sketch out that she might study them and see if she could understand what they meant. The impression they gave was one of power and protection, gifts from his grandfather who loved him so dearly.

She could have sworn she saw something else there, a thread of something that was neither silver nor gold, but multihued. It reminded her sharply of a cluster of raw gems she had seen in the cavern below.

She considered that for a bit, then shrugged it aside. It was obviously something that was part of the Fadaire his grandfather had used. She would have to ask him how that all worked, but perhaps on the morrow, when she wasn't so tired.

At least the hum of the rocks and veins of ore had subsided. In fact, she could hardly hear it at all. Instead, there was simply a solid and very lovely sense of security. All that was left to hear was the whir of her wheel, the crackle and pop of the wood in the hearth, and Rùnach's mutterings over the undesirable characters foisted off upon the world, characters who always seemed to have their roots in Neroche somehow.

"I dreamed of a house with no doors," she said finally.

"I know."

She looked at him to find he was watching her gravely. "Did you?"

"That's why I want to build it for you," he said quietly. "Because it is something from your dreams, Aisling."

She considered, then met his eyes. "I'm not sure Prince Mansourah would build a house with no doors."

"I daresay he wouldn't, but then again, he has no imagination and never tends to his teeth. You don't want him."

"Nay, I don't think I do."

But she knew what she did want. He was sitting across from her, holding a list of things she might want in a mate in his hand, and offering to build her something so beautiful, it resided only in her dreams.

Queen Brèagha's words came back to her, that in her future lay something so beautiful and sweet that perhaps the path she would walk to get there would be especially difficult.

She wondered if she would be equal to paying that price.

Or if the prize would still be there when she was finished.

Sixteen

❧

Rùnach sat on the floor in the middle of Uachdaran of Léige's lists, such as they were, and looked at the book he held in his lap.

The book of his father's spells.

Looking inside was the last thing he wanted to do. Well, that wasn't entirely true. The last thing he wanted to do was watch Aisling rush off to her wedding with someone he didn't much care for—his cousin Còir, for instance—but memorizing his father's spells came a very close second.

He looked at the ceiling above him, sparing a moment to marvel at its height when he knew the entire chamber was below ground, then sighed deeply. He didn't want the spells, but he could see the wisdom of having them. What he couldn't believe was that another copy of the book existed. Nay, another *two* copies, though he supposed the witchwoman of Fàs was canny enough to know what would happen to her if one of her sons had Gair's spell of Diminishing to hand. She would find herself drained of all her power without hesitation, and then perhaps repaid for all the manual labor she'd put her sons to in order to attempt to curry her favor. The thought of those attempts was almost enough to leave Rùnach with the urge to smile.

Almost, but not quite.

He opened the book, looked at the first page, then sighed and set to work.

It was easier than he'd feared it might be and more distasteful than he'd imagined it would be. Worse still, by the time he was finished, he had reacquired a very grudging respect for his father's skill as a mage. Admittedly, the man had had a thousand years to perfect his craft, but that wasn't it. The spells were elegant, to the point, and ruthlessly effective. Rùnach could vouch personally for the last bit. He couldn't imagine why in the world he would ever need to know them given that he had no magic with which to use them, but perhaps they would be useful as a bartering tool.

He didn't want to think about what sort of bargain might require them.

He set the first book aside, then reached for the other one he'd brought with him, Acair's pages of indecipherable gibberish sewn into the cover of his book of spells. He could assume, hopefully not wrongly, that Acair hadn't managed to unlock those spells he had obviously removed. If he had, Rùnach suspected he would have known by the trail of destruction Acair would have left in his wake.

As far as the scratches went, though, he had to admit they baffled him. He would have chalked that up to his bastard brother's stupidity, but Acair was far from stupid.

Rùnach turned the pages carefully, but they made no more sense to him at present than the previous times he'd looked at them. There wasn't a single spell written on the pages, nor anything that looked like even half a spell. He wondered absently if perhaps the pages themselves were enspelled, only revealing their contents if commanded to in precisely the right way, but surely if that had been the case, Fionne of Fàs would have said as much. She was dangerous and treacherous, but she kept her word. He had paid the price of her opinion and felt sure she had told him the truth—

She had said the symbols might represent points on a map.

He started from the beginning again and tried to force the symbols into some semblance of a pattern. He read from front to back and back to front, all whilst holding the book from various angles. It made no more sense than it had from the start, which was no sense at all.

He shut the book with a curse, then picked up both books and rose. He tested his memory and found to his disgust that there were bits of his father's things he couldn't remember properly. What he'd wanted to do was toss the book into Uachdaran's hottest furnace, but it looked as if he would be holding on to it a bit longer.

He left the lists and wandered aimlessly through the passage-ways, wondering where Aisling might be keeping herself at present. He turned a corner only to hear the unmistakable sound of traders hunting for chambers and food. He couldn't imagine that any of those fathers would want to send their daughters off with a damaged, magicless elf, but stranger things had happened.

He wondered, with a sharpness that brought him up short, what Aisling's father would say if he were to present himself at the family hearth and ask the man for his daughter's hand. Or, perhaps more fittingly, if he presented himself to the man in the most uncomfortable part of the mine available for the laboring of parents who deserved far worse. He supposed he would have preferred the latter, for Aisling's sake, and he also supposed he should congratulate himself on his good manners even though he had the feeling that Aisling wouldn't care what her father said.

All of which assumed that he could convince her that what he wanted was the sort of arrangement requiring a father's permission and that she would be interested in such an arrangement to start with.

He could hardly believe that he was so turned about by a slip of a girl who sang with trees and listened to the dreams of a dwarf king's veins of ore, but there it was. His mother would have considered it nothing more than he deserved, no doubt.

He found his own bedchamber by sheer dumb luck, quickly shoved his books into his pack, then ventured to poke his nose out his door. Finding the passageway empty, he made straight for Uachdaran's solar. It was the one place where Aisling had any peace, so he supposed it was the place he would find her.

He knocked, was invited to enter, then walked inside and shut the door behind him. Aisling and Uachdaran were sitting in front of the fire, chatting animatedly in the dwarvish tongue. Rùnach was somehow not at all surprised at Aisling's newfound skill. The king's delight in her mastering his language was obvious. He looked up and beckoned.

"Come and sit, Rùnach my boy."

Rùnach did. He listened for a bit, though he found it increasingly difficult to stay awake. He had to admit it had been a very long morning so far, begun too early after a terrible night's sleep full of dreams of rivers running under things. Again. If he had to either dream about that sort of thing or hear about it from almost everyone he met—all of whom seemed determined to bludgeon him with details about their own foul dreams—he would . . . well, he would walk away from them whilst they were still speaking, that's what he would do.

The fire was very warm, which he appreciated. He appreciated it for an indeterminate amount of time before he fell asleep to the soothing conversation of a weaver and a king speaking of things that sparkled.

• • •

He woke, which is the only way he knew he had slept. It took him a moment or two to find his way out of his dream of rivers of diamonds and colored gems so he could focus on Aisling and Uachdaran. The king was still sitting in his chair, nursing a mug of something useful. Rùnach realized that Aisling, however, had vacated her chair and was currently leaning over his own poor self, looking at his hands. He frowned at her, then at the king.

"What did you say?"

They both ignored him.

"I'm not the one to ask, gel," Uachdaran said, shaking his head. "Ask the elf. Those are his grandpappy's runes, after all."

Rùnach looked at Aisling. "What are you talking about?"

She sank down into the chair next to him, a chair he didn't remember having seen there before he fell asleep. Perhaps they had moved it there whilst he was otherwise occupied. She took his hand.

"I was wondering about these," she said, pointing to his scars. "Or, rather, the runes, actually."

Rùnach decided if that sort of wondering left her with a desire to hold his hand, he would explain runes to her all day long.

"What do you want to know?"

She frowned thoughtfully. "I wonder if you could draw them out for me." She met his eyes. "So I could see exactly how they lay there on your hands."

"Happily," he said. "You know, men often write down things for the women they woo. Poetry. Lays to their beauty." He looked at her solemnly. "That sort of thing."

Uachdaran blew his breath out and rolled his eyes. Aisling simply looked at Rùnach as if she feared he had lost his wits and it was her sole responsibility to help him find them again.

Uachdaran shoved paper and a sharp pencil at him. "Take that before you frighten the girl off."

Rùnach considered that rather good advice. He drew the runes on his left hand and on his right, adding with a good deal of reluctance what Còir had buried in his flesh. Not because of the rune itself, which might come in handy, but because he didn't want Aisling thinking about that enspelled handkerchief any more than necessary. Especially since it would do for her what he could not.

"Why are they laid one atop the other?" she asked after several minutes of studying what he'd drawn.

"It has to do with their importance, partly," he said, "and partly with how the magic is best used." He pointed to the first rune he'd sketched. "That is a rune of protection," he said, "but only of any efficacy at night or in shadow or under the shadow of a dark spell. It could mean just one of those things or all three depending on where it finds itself."

"On your hand, you mean?" she asked.

"Partly, but also what it is linked to. That particular rune, Teasraig, lies next to and is intertwined with courage, Sonairte, which could mean that the protection only reaches its full power when the elf so marked finds himself lacking courage whilst facing an assault by a dark spell. Or it could mean that possessing courage in abundance causes Teasraig to drive back a spell of darkness that courage alone cannot best."

"Or it could mean that Sìle was just slapping them on your hands randomly to leave you scratching your head for the rest of your very long life," Uachdaran said dryly.

Rùnach smiled briefly. "There is that."

Uachdaran looked at Aisling. "You can speculate all day, gel, and never understand what Sìle was thinking, though I imagine in the end you can assume he marked that lad there because he loved him. I suppose of any of Sìle's grandchildren, Rùnach might have the best guess at what his grandfather intended."

Aisling looked at his hand for a bit longer, then up at his face. "There is something over your brow."

"I imagine it's a rune of protection and something to utterly rebuff Weger's branding iron."

She smiled. "I imagine so." She looked back down at his hands. "What is that one there? It seems to cover the rest."

Rùnach looked at his hands. "What do you mean?"

She traced something on the back of his right hand, a rune that flashed to life, sparkling silver and gold in the firelight. He looked at it in surprise because he hadn't known it was there. It seemed to be under the other runes, though he couldn't have said what its purpose was. He never would have noticed it if it hadn't been for Aisling having touched it.

"It seems to be something that extends . . ." He studied it for quite a while before he shook his head. "It would take centuries to learn all the runes of Tòrr Dòrainn, then even longer to know what they mean in conjunction with something else. I have never seen that particular rune, though it resembles another that is used for, well, hiding things. But not hiding, for that is too strong a term." He looked at Aisling and shrugged. "Let's say it inspires a lack of interest."

She nodded, returned his hand to his knee, then rose and began to pace. Rùnach watched her, then looked at the king who was watching him with an expression Rùnach didn't dare attempt to identify.

Aisling came to a stop suddenly and looked at the king.

"Where does your power come from, Your Majesty?" she asked. "What are the sources?"

Rùnach found the words to tell her she shouldn't ask on the tip of his tongue, but he bit them back at the look on Uachdaran's face. The king wasn't angry. In fact, his expression indicated the opposite. He looked as if a prized student had asked a question he'd been waiting forever for her to ask.

"A very interesting question, indeed. Shall I tell you or would you prefer to guess?"

Aisling wrapped her arms around herself. "I would guess it comes from underground."

Uachdaran nodded. "My magic reaches deep, like veins of ore, down into places in the earth too deep for man or dwarf to reach. It is, as you might imagine, an endless source of magic and might."

"So, it is possible," she said slowly, "to have power lying underneath, say—"

"Rock?" Uachdaran finished for her. "Not just possible, lass, but imperative. It isn't as if anyone else could take my magic, not after all these years of my having been connected to the land. I suppose they might try, but my spells for hiding that magic from view are impenetrable. It is for that reason that you could look at my hall for years upon years and never see what lies beneath it."

"I can."

He smiled, a small twisting of his mouth that wasn't at all unkind, but rather unsurprised. "Aisling, lass, I don't doubt that for a moment." He tilted his head toward Rùnach. "See something there that interests you?"

"I'm not sure," she whispered. "What I think I see is so faint, so far down, so remote . . ." She took a deep breath. "I think I might be imagining it."

"Imagination is the daylight counterpart to dreams, my gel, and the start of all sorts of things that seem impossible at first."

"Is that so," Aisling said, and it wasn't a question.

"It is so." He set his mug down on the floor. "I hear you once believed elves were mythical creatures."

Rùnach wondered just what in the hell they were talking about. He would have asked, but he was too busy wondering why Uachdaran was now carrying over to the fire a small table such as might be used to hold drinks or a light supper.

"Ah," Aisling began, "aye, I did."

"Pointy ears and all that, eh?"

"That too."

The king of the dwarves banged a rather large pewter cup down in front of Rùnach, then poured a liberal amount of something amber. Rùnach looked at the king.

"What's that for?"

"You elves have rather delicate constitutions," he said without a shred of levity. "Best to get you drunk before one does anything painful to you."

"Painful," Rùnach echoed. He looked at the king, who didn't have anything sharp in his hands, then at Aisling, who was only watching him as if he were something she intended to experiment on. "What," he managed, "are you talking about?"

"Ask your lady," the king said with a shrug.

Rùnach wasn't sure he dared. She looked as if she were fair to falling over in a faint as it was. He would have gotten up to put his arms around her, or lead her to a chair, but he wasn't at all sure he wouldn't fall over as well. There was something afoot that he couldn't name, and it frightened the hell out of him.

Aisling looked at him for an eternal moment, as if she were gathering her courage for something truly dire. Then she took a deep breath.

And then she started a flywheel of air.

"Well, isn't that interesting," Uachdaran said softly.

Rùnach thought it was less interesting than it was unsettling, but he didn't suppose anyone cared at that point what he thought. Aisling was looking around, apparently for something to put on her flywheel and connect it to the bobbin he could see hanging there motionless in the air. The king was just watching her work with what Rùnach considered to be an unseemly amount of interest.

Aisling pulled a single strand of flame into it.

And then she looked at him again.

He had the feeling, ridiculous as it was, that he was somehow going to factor into what she was doing at present. There were many things he thought he wouldn't have minded where she was concerned. A long walk along the shore, a morning outside where they shot pointy things into targets pinned to subsequently irritated trees, a quiet evening spent in front of the fire.

But he didn't like the look of that fire that was spinning not only her flywheel but the bobbin as well.

"What," he managed in what sounded to his ears like a very garbled tone, "are you doing?"

She met his gaze. He thought he could safely say that he had never seen her look more unsettled, but at the same time, he was fairly sure she had never looked more determined.

It was profoundly alarming.

"I think," she said slowly, "that there is something beneath your scars."

"Aye, my flesh!" he exclaimed.

Uachdaran sighed gustily. "Don't unman yourself in front of the woman you're wishing to woo."

"Woo?" Aisling echoed.

Uachdaran looked at them both, then laughed. "If the two of you manage to do anything but stare at each other in confusion and consternation for the rest of your days, I'll be thoroughly surprised. Here, let me set things along on the right path before you do damage to him. Aisling, he wants to woo you, presumably for the usual reasons. Rùnach, if she weren't busy preparing to spin things out of thin air, she would possibly tell you that you are looking too far above yourself. Now, Aisling, tell him what you see."

She looked at the king. "Do you see it too?"

He only smiled.

"See what?" Rùnach demanded. "What *are* you two talking about?"

Aisling took a pair of deep, steadying breaths, then looked at him.

"I think your power lies under your scars," she said.

He was absolutely sure he was hearing things. "You can't be serious."

"And here,"—she reached out and touched the corner of his mouth—"and here and here," she continued, touching the corner of his eye and the place where the scar terminated near his ear.

He wondered if somehow his hearing had begun to fail him, because she couldn't possibly be saying what the words sounded like.

"Impossible," he said, but there was no sound to the word, because he couldn't bring himself to even entertain the thought.

She touched his hand. "Rùnach, I don't think your sight was taken from you, or your magic, or your voice. I think it's buried under your scars."

He shook his head, because he had to convince her she was wrong before she got her hopes up. "Miach and Ruith worked on my hands for hours. So did my grandfather. They would have seen something."

"Would they?" Uachdaran put in. "Funny that a gel from Bruadair can see what they could not, isn't it?"

"Sarah would have seen it," Rùnach protested.

Then he watched his words fade away into something that fell into the fire with a soft hiss.

Sarah hadn't been there for any of it.

He couldn't remember why not, now, though he supposed she had gone on with Sgath and Eulasaid to Lake Cladach, leaving Ruithneadh behind. Soilléir had been there for the wedding, of course, but he had been his usual self, pleasant but not offering too many words.

He looked at Aisling—nay, he could hardly look at her. The thought of having, well, he couldn't dare hope.

He shook his head. "Impossible."

She put her hand over his. He watched as she traced a rune there, the rune that was revealed very briefly as a discreet, elegant thing of silver and gold that lay under all the other runes. It covered his scars completely, as it happened.

She touched the edge of that rune, then drew a long strand of Fadaire out of it and wound it around her finger.

"I'll be damned," Uachdaran whispered.

Rùnach was afraid he would be more than damned, he would be shattered if she were able to pull anything out of him but agony over what he had lost, what his father had taken from him. Because hadn't his father taken everything? In truth, the whole sordid episode was blurry in his mind despite how many years he'd had to think about it. His mother had rushed forward, his brothers had fallen, he had . . .

He couldn't remember clearly what he had done. He was fairly sure his mother had blurted out a spell that had shielded him from the brunt of his father's spell of Diminishing, for all the good it had done him. Or perhaps she had laid that spell over Keir. He simply didn't know.

But what he did know was that the cap of the well had gouged his cheek as it had fallen shut on his hands.

"Your Majesty?"

"Aye, gel?"

"What do I do with his power once 'tis spun?"

Rùnach realized they were discussing him, his life, his long-dismissed, gravely mourned . . .

Nay, to say his loss of magic had been gravely mourned didn't come close to describing it. He had grieved for it every moment of every day for so long, he'd stopped counting the days as they passed. He had initially wished for death, but been too cowardly to take his own life. In the end, he had told himself he was resigned to the loss of his birthright, content to simply go about as an ordinary man, happy with his lot in life.

He had been a terrible liar, actually.

"Well, I don't know, gel," Uachdaran said, stroking his chin thoughtfully, as if they discussed what they might have for supper later that night. "Can you weave?"

Aisling made a sound that was something akin to a sob. Rùnach turned his head to look at her and saw that she was very pale. He felt very pale, so perhaps they were evenly matched there.

"Aye, Your Majesty, I can weave."

"I suppose you could weave his power and we could throw it over him like a cloak, but that doesn't get it back in his blood where it belongs, does it?"

Rùnach felt the room begin to spin.

Spinning. It was what she did best, after all. Hadn't he watched her spin all kinds of things: air, fire, spells . . .

"I don't suppose you have a spell that might suit," Aisling asked carefully. "Do you?"

The king held up his hands. "Aisling, I have spells for all sorts of things, but opening the soul of an elf and putting his power back inside him is beyond whatever art I might call my own."

Well, at least her notice was off him for a moment or two. Rùnach drew in breaths, trying to ignore how ragged they sounded. He felt as if he had just run endless numbers of stairs at Gobhann in the predawn air that tore at one's lungs and left a body wanting nothing more than to go back to bed.

"How does your kingship come to you," Aisling pressed, "if that isn't too personal a question. I've read that in Neroche it is a mantel that falls upon the man so chosen."

Uachdaran shook his head. "Here, it just sinks in . . ." He looked at her. "Well, I suppose we could try that sort of spell, if you like."

"I have no magic, so you'll have to do it."

"Of course, my girl."

Rùnach watched with a fair bit of alarm as Aisling bent over his left hand again. "I need something to pry up one of the edges of this rune here," she muttered. "It's covering too much of the scar."

"The boy has a knife down the side of his boot."

Aisling considered. "Well, his grandfather did give it to him. I think it might have magical properties."

"I imagine it does."

Rùnach tried to pull the knife free—quite possibly to stab himself with it, for the thought did cross his mind quite strongly—but his hands were shaking too badly to do so. He couldn't even bring himself to reach for what Uachdaran had so graciously poured for him there on the table. All he could do was watch Aisling and wonder if he would howl or weep.

Or if she would fail.

Or succeed.

He honestly wasn't sure which would have been worse.

Uachdaran pulled the knife from his boot and wielded it where Aisling told him to, quickly and without any mercy. Rùnach would have cursed him, but he had no breath for it. He could only gape at the multihued strand that Aisling pulled from under the scar on his right hand.

"The end of this is what I saw," she said, frowning thoughtfully. "It made me wonder."

"I can see why. Lovely thing, isn't it, for it being fashioned not of anything my land produced. Why don't you spin it up and let's see what it is."

It was agony, that's what it was. Rùnach felt as if she were pulling his soul out of him through the back of his hands, first one, then the other, then the scar on his face. It could have taken a handful of minutes or a handful of hours. All he knew was that when she stopped, he was so empty of himself, he could scarce breathe.

"Best hurry, hadn't you, lass? He doesn't look at all well."

Rùnach managed to get his eyes open to watch Aisling string a loom of air and fire. She quickly wove what she'd pulled from him into a long, wide scarf of sorts.

"Put it around his shoulders, Aisling, then we'll use the spell together. You hold on to his magic, and I'll put my hands over yours."

Oh, please don't was what Rùnach would have said if he could have. He knew what happened when a mage joined his power to another mage that way. His own sister had tried to heal a cut on his hand by having little Miach of Neroche put his hands over hers and speak the words of a spell with her. Well, Miach had only spoken the last word, but Mhorghain had fainted just the same. Rùnach had felt a white-hot something streak through him. It had almost killed him, truth be told.

"Don't . . . hurt . . . her," Rùnach managed. "Not . . . worth . . . it . . ."

He looked up, because he could hear the spell beginning to fall on him. He could feel Aisling's fingers digging into his shoulders and Uachdaran's voice sounding a great deal like the entire mountain collapsing.

And then it fell.

Rùnach found himself suddenly on the floor, watching a heavy bottle of wine come with agonizing slowness toward his face.

"Oh, sorry, lad," Uachdaran said from a great distance. "I only had hands to catch one of you, and I fear you weren't my first choice. Can you blame me?"

Indeed, he could not.

Rùnach closed his eyes and knew no more.

Seventeen

❦

Aisling sat by Rùnach's bed and wondered if she'd killed him. He was pale as death, still as death, perhaps even dead. She reached out quickly and put her fingers to his neck, then sighed in relief. His heart was beating, for all the good it apparently was doing him. She would have looked around her for aid, but there was none to give it to her. She was there alone with the remains of her actions.

It hadn't been very long ago—a pair of hours at best—that she'd woken from a terrible dream about attempting to run away from rocks rushing down a mountainside toward her, to find herself instead of being crushed by the slide, lying comfortably on the sofa in front of the king's fire.

Rùnach, however, had been lying on the floor, an angry red mark over one eye that she hoped hadn't come from her fist. The bottle from which the king had poured him a cup of wine had been lying next to him, so perhaps that had been the perpetrator of the assault. She had knelt down by his side, ignoring the way the chamber spun at such a minimal movement, and felt for his pulse. Her relief over the fact that he lived still had been almost over-whelming. She might have indulged in another swoon, but she'd been interrupted by the arrival of the king.

He had marched inside with a small army of helpers who had heaved Rùnach up and onto their shoulders to then carry him to his chamber and put him to bed. Aisling had followed, trying not to wring her hands. If she had killed him, how would she be able to go on?

If King Uachdaran had found anything unusual about the sit-uation, he had given no indication of it. He had merely advised her to keep watch, promised to send along sustenance, then sauntered off to see to his other guests with a whistle and a light heart.

She hadn't shared his optimism.

That had been a pair of hours ago and Rùnach had still not stirred. She hadn't dared even sit on his bed at first, preferring to limit herself to the bedpost where she could clutch the wood that remained blessedly silent instead of chiding her for killing an elven prince, and wonder if he would ever wake. By the time she had dared perch on the edge of his bed, she had wondered less about whether or not he would wake again than she had whether or not he would wake to himself.

The issue of his magic was something she still couldn't bring herself to face.

That was, she supposed, an issue she would only be required to face if he awoke. She looked at him, lying there still as death, and wondered what his grandfather would say when he listened to her discharging the unenviable duty of telling him she had slain his grandson.

She closed her eyes because that blocked out the sight in front of her, but it left her seeing the loom of air she had strung with fire and woven his power into, so she decided there was no comfort in that. Instead, she looked at the man lying there on the bed and forced herself to mark if there was anything changed about him.

Well, whatever she'd done to him, she had changed his aspect more than she'd anticipated. The scar that had webbed his cheek wasn't entirely gone, but it was so faint, she supposed that unless a body looked closely, he wouldn't notice it. She reached out and brushed his hair from his brow. She could see King Sìle's rune there, of course, because it was difficult to overlook, but she could also see a hint of Weger's mark as well. His grandfather wouldn't be pleased to see that, she was sure.

She put her hand on his chest, over his heart, and tried to concentrate on feeling the beating there, strong and steady. Unfortunately, all she could do was look at his face and wonder how it was possible one man could be so beautiful.

It wasn't as if she didn't now have a rather large number of other exceptionally handsome men to compare him to. One could say what one cared to about their egos, but only a fool would say that those lads from Neroche were not exceptionally easy on the eye. And if that hadn't been enough, she had spent a trio of days in Seanagarra, trying to concentrate on testing different bows whilst simultaneously being presented with an endless array of elven males to admire. But neither they nor even Rùnach's brother Ruith, as great as the familial resemblance was, could compare to the man lying senseless before her.

She almost wished he were still wearing the entirety of the scar on his face.

A soft knock on the door almost left her clinging to the marvelously carved stone of the ceiling. She got to her feet, smoothed down her gown, then hastened to open the door. A very serious-looking man stood there with a satchel over his shoulder.

"I am His Majesty's physick," he announced, "Ollamh."

"Oh," she managed. "How lovely. Unfortunately, Prince Rùnach is still sleeping—"

"Nay, my lady, I was sent to see to you."

She blinked in surprise. "Me?"

He nodded. "The king said the prince would recover on his own but that you might need a draught of something strengthening."

Aisling had the feeling the king would enjoy telling Rùnach that, assuming Rùnach woke with the ability to hear it. She considered Ollamh's offer of a medicine, then shook her head.

"I am well," she managed. "You could, if you were willing, have a look at the prince." She hesitated, then decided if there were anyone who might be able to offer an opinion on Rùnach's health, it was the dwarf standing in front of her. "I worry about him."

Ollamh frowned at her as if he thought she might indeed still be the one who needed tending, but he nodded just the same. "If you like. The king said he'd had a bit of a shock."

Well, that was one way to describe it. She supposed it was best to keep her thoughts to herself and allow the king's physick to make his own assessment of the damage she'd caused. She stood back and welcomed the man into the chamber. He didn't seem shocked to see Rùnach lying on the bed with his boots still on, but perhaps he had seen worse.

Ollamh felt Rùnach's pulse, checked for fever, then pried open his eyes and looked in them. Or, rather, pried open one eye and looked in it. The other was rather too swollen to do anything with.

"A bottle fell on him," Aisling said quickly. "An accident."

"I wouldn't have thought otherwise," Ollamh said absently. He considered for a bit, then looked at her. "A shock, was it?"

"Of a magical sort," Aisling said carefully. There was perhaps no point in giving him too many details. "A very great shock, I believe."

Ollamh stroked his chin. "There's little to be done for that, I'm afraid. Time will either heal that or it won't." He looked at her. "I think, however, that you, my lady, might be best served at present by a bit of fresh air. You look as if you've had a bit of a shock as well."

She wasn't sure that quite described it. The truth was, she felt as if *her* soul had been the one to be cracked open instead of Rùnach's. It wasn't a physical weariness. She simply didn't feel as if she were quite who she had been before. She was rather surprised to find, quite suddenly, that she thought she could hear something running.

A thread of the king's dreams running under her feet.

She looked at Ollamh. "Where is the king, if you don't mind my asking?"

The dwarf looked rather apologetic. "I believe he has retired to his chamber, my lady." He hesitated, then leaned closer. "These particular traders try the limits of his patience, I fear. I have on more than one occasion in the past given him the odd though very small sleeping draught, though he didn't seem to require it today."

Aisling nodded. "If you think the prince will be well enough for a few minutes, I think I will take your advice and seek out some fresh air."

Ollamh smiled and nodded back over his shoulder. "I have brought an entire group of assistants with me. We will take perfect care of His Highness the Prince of Tòrr Dòrainn. The air in the king's garden is particularly healthful, if you're interested."

She supposed Rùnach would be safe enough in the care of a small battalion of healers. She nodded, had a final look at Rùnach, then made her way from the chamber.

She hadn't gone twenty paces before she had bowled a dwarf over before she realized he was in her way. She thought he might have reached out to steady her, or perhaps that had been her to keep him on his feet. All she knew was they both were suddenly leaning heavily against one of the passageway walls.

"My lady," the dwarf said, his hand to his heart. "Forgive me."

"My fault," she said quickly. "I didn't see you." She started to move past him only to realize that he was moving with her. She stopped and looked at him. "Can I help you?"

"I am Eachdraidh," he said nervously. "Bard to the king and keeper of perilous books."

Heaven help her, she didn't need any more of either of those. She looked at the book he was holding in front of him as if it were so hot it was fair to scorching his hands. "Is that a perilous book there?"

"Extremely."

Of course. She wondered why she would have thought anything else. She looked at him hopefully. "Taking it to the king, are you?"

"Nay, my lady, I was asked to bring it to you. By the king himself, if you must know." Eachdraidh swallowed with difficulty. "Very dangerous if you ask me, but no one generally asks me my opinion on these matters."

Aisling took the book only because he shoved it into her hands and scurried away before she could shove it back at him. She supposed she had two choices: she could either put it with the other extremely perilous tomes she was carrying—tomes she realized at the moment she had left in the king's solar—or she could keep the book and do what the king had obviously intended, which was to read it.

She hesitated, then cast caution to the wind and opened the plain cover of the book in her hand to read the title page:

The Lore of Bruadair.

She supposed it said something about the state of her life over the past pair of months that she didn't even flinch. She shut the book, tucked it under her arm, and decided that she might as well try to find the king's garden. Master Ollamh would see to Rùnach well enough for a bit, she supposed, no doubt much better than she could have.

She was halfway down a passageway she'd never seen before when it occurred to her that she had no idea where she was going. She stopped the first likely looking soul she came across and asked for directions. It was entirely possible that she didn't take a decent breath until she found herself being allowed through heavy wooden doors. She stepped outside, then looked at what was in front of her.

She wasn't sure even *garden* could describe what she was seeing. It was more of a maze of trees adorned with the first tentative blooms of trees used to the vagaries of a mountain spring. She stepped down onto a path of finely laid stone and walked through the trees there until the perfect spot for a bit of reading appeared in front of her. A stone bench sat there, surrounded by torches that weren't lit as yet. Perhaps someone would come later to light them, perhaps even whilst the sky was still light so that there would be no chance of a guest having to strain her eyes whilst about the heavy labor of reading things about the country of her birth she might not particularly want to read.

She shivered briefly, wishing she had thought to fetch a cloak out of her chamber, then opened the book and hoped she would survive the reading of it.

It was less taxing than she'd feared it might be. The initial few chapters at least seemed to be more of a history of her country than anything else. She read of rulers and houses that had provided rulers and wars and fierce border disputes with Gairn and An-uallach.

And then things took a turn for the more mythical.

She read about the magic that drenched everything from simple milchmaids to less simple kings and queens, how it ran through the rivers like silver and gold shot through fine cloth, how it turned a spectacularly lovely realm into something that left inhabitants and visitors alike believing that they were dreaming. Not everyone had a mighty magic, of course, but that didn't seem to matter.

The air was full of it, and somehow that left it touching all who breathed that air.

She left her finger in the spot where she was and closed the book around it, then looked off into the distance. It occurred to her that she was holding that book in the same manner Rùnach had been holding the book from his grandfather's library on that fateful day when she'd discovered that he knew far more about her than she'd suspected.

Was he conscious yet or . . .

She found it difficult to swallow all of a sudden, perhaps because whilst she'd been able to ignore it for the past half hour or so, the truth was she wasn't sure she hadn't damaged him permanently. After all, who did she think she was? It wasn't a flawed weave she'd tried to correct or a miswritten pattern she'd tried to amend—not that she'd ever been allowed to do anything but weave plain, dull broadcloth—this was a man's life. It was not only his life, but his magic.

Rùnach had said it hadn't mattered to him, the loss of that magic. She had believed that initially, because she'd had no reason not to. But now that she'd seen Seanagarra for herself, full of magic and beauty and the song of a land that loved those who dwelt within its borders, she had to think differently. It wasn't as if any of his kin had done any mighty magic in her presence, but she had seen it shimmering in their veins, a profoundly lovely something that she suspected was what bards were describing when they talked about elves looking as if they'd stepped from dreams.

She supposed that was what had started her thinking about things perhaps she shouldn't have. Rùnach had claimed his father could drain a mage of all his power, to the very last drop in every single case. Once she had seen the king's cavern so far below his palace, she had started to wonder about things lying hidden far beneath the surface of other things. When she'd seen that strand of magic beneath Rùnach's scars—

She had to take a deep breath. Perhaps she shouldn't have even attempted anything. What if she had taken Rùnach's only chance to have his power back and she had ruined it?

She looked at the mountain to her right to judge how close the sun was to going behind it only to find that the sun had already dipped behind that enormous peak. Then she realized something else.

She wasn't alone.

She stood up, feeling the book slide from her fingers as she did so. Rùnach was standing some twenty paces away, under a tree, watching her. He was breathing, which she supposed was a good sign. He didn't seem to be moving, though, and his expression was unreadable, which worried her. She actually couldn't see him very well, but perhaps her eyes were blurry from too much reading.

The point came when she simply couldn't stand there any longer and look at a man who seemed to have been turned to stone.

"How—" She had to clear her throat. "How are you?"

"Staggered," he said quietly. "And you?"

Where to begin? She was terrified that she had damaged him beyond what even his father had done whilst at the same time appalled by her own presumption in thinking she might do something that no one else could. She swallowed, but that didn't solve anything. It just reminded her that her mouth was as dry as a pile of dusty waste yarn that hadn't been tidied up in months.

"I don't know how I am," she admitted.

He pushed away from his tree. She supposed she might have panicked if it had been anyone but Rùnach, fearing for her life. But he didn't look menacing. He looked . . . staggered.

He walked until he was a pace or two in front of her, then stopped. "I am," he said slowly, "almost completely unable to see out of my right eye."

She blinked, then smiled. "I didn't drop that bottle on you, you know."

"Are you sure?"

She considered. "Honestly, I don't remember."

"I'm a little fuzzy on the whole affair myself," he admitted. "As for anything else, I feel as if Uachdaran has taken his entire collection of mining tailings and dropped them on my head."

"That could be from the bottle somehow having found its way onto your face, which still wasn't my doing even though I can't remember anything about it."

He smiled. It was the same smile he'd been giving her for almost as long as she could remember. Small, grave, full of something she might have called affection if she'd been a more hopeful sort of woman.

"Oh, I don't think it was from the bottle," he said. "I think it came from something else entirely. I wonder what that something else might have been?"

She would have speculated with him, but she just couldn't. She had already spent a pair of hours fretting over what she might or might not have done to him. Spending any more time at it wasn't something she could bear to do. She took her courage in hand and looked him full in the face.

"Do you have your magic back?"

He didn't answer. He simply looked at her with an expression she had great difficulty in identifying. It wasn't horror, surely, nor disgust. It certainly wasn't amusement. She studied him for a moment or two, then decided that the only thing she could say was that the look on his face was one a man might wear after he'd seen something that awed him.

He held out his hand, his open palm facing toward the sky.

A ball of light appeared.

She looked at him in surprise—and no small bit of relief, actually. "Then you do have your magic back?" she asked breathlessly.

He tossed that ball up into the air and above them exploded a canopy of light that turned into petals of various springtime colors, which subsequently fell down toward her as she looked up at them, disappearing with the faintest of scents of the flowers she had smelled in King Sìle's garden before they touched her skin.

She closed her eyes, then she did something she had never done in the course of her whole life.

She burst into loud, noisy, extremely messy tears.

At some point during that truly appalling display of blubbering— she suspected it had been at the very onset—Rùnach had pulled her into his arms. She found herself clinging to him as if he were a life raft and she adrift in perilous seas. He put a handkerchief into one of her hands at one point, which she appreciated, but otherwise, he simply held her. Well, he held her so tightly, she thought she might soon perish from lack of air, but she didn't think she should complain. She thought she might have trembled a bit. She was absolutely sure he had, and she suspected it hadn't been from laughter.

She dabbed at her eyes and wiped her face, finally, then started to lift her head off his soggy shoulder, but he put his hand against the back of her hair.

"Don't."

"Why not?"

"I don't want you to see me weeping."

She pulled her head away from his hand. "Don't be daft." She looked up at him, then dabbed at his cheeks as well. "I take it that means aye."

He looked at her for a moment or two in silence, then he released her only long enough to take her face in his hands. He took a deep breath, turned his face to wipe his eyes against his shoulder briefly, then he turned back to her.

And he kissed her.

Aisling realized just how much she had sobbed onto his shoulder mostly because she could feel his soggy tunic beneath her hands as she clutched him to keep from falling flat upon her, ah, well whatever it was she would have fallen onto from shock.

"Well," she managed, when he lifted his head and looked at her. "Is that a thank-you?"

"Nay," he said with a faint smile. "This is."

He kissed her again. She was no less prepared for it that time than she had been the first. It occurred to her at some point that there was a reason those ladies fair in the tales she'd read as a youth put their arms around their heroes' necks whilst about the activity of being kissed, and it had everything to do with not landing ungracefully upon their . . . well, there was a reason for it.

"If that was a thank-you," she managed finally, "what was the first?"

"Convenient timing."

She laughed because his joy was contagious.

Or at least she laughed until she realized with an unpleasant start that perhaps she shouldn't have been laughing.

He had his power back.

She stepped back away from him, out of his arms, though doing so almost did her in. She dragged her sleeve across her eyes, then looked at what she was now able to allow herself to see: the magic in his veins.

It was beautiful.

"Oh, nay," he said, reaching for her.

She backed up another pair of steps to elude his hands. "I'm fine."

"I wasn't asking you if you were fine," he said. "I don't want you running away."

She wrapped her arms around herself. "Why would you think I intended to run away?"

"Because you have the look a lass gets when she's plotting something," he said, with a knowing nod, "which in your case generally includes running away. You may as well tell me now exactly what you're thinking."

She lifted her chin, because Scrymgeour Weger had taught her to do so. "I've made a decision," she announced, never mind that it was something that came to her at that precise moment. "I can't let you come with me."

He looked unsatisfyingly unsurprised. "Can't you?"

"I can't."

"Why not?"

"Because look at you," she said, feeling suddenly rather irritated. "You need to be back at your grandfather's hall, entertaining beautiful princesses and watching them fight over you."

"Just there?" he asked mildly.

"Of course not," she said shortly. "Every bloody salon from here to Tor Neroche to Tòsan and back will want you to adorn it."

"You forgot Meith."

"Damn Meith!" She blew her hair out of her eyes. "I mean—"

She couldn't speak any longer. That might have been because he had taken two strides and pulled her again into his arms. She lifted her face to protest and found that she most definitely couldn't speak.

He was going to have to cease with that sort of thing or she wasn't going to get anything else done in her life.

"Why don't you," he said after a moment or two, "trust that I am a selfish beast who only makes decisions for my life that are in my best interest?"

"Because I know you aren't," she said miserably. "You're a hopeless do-gooder."

He pulled her close and rested his cheek against her hair. "As, I believe, are you. Isn't it a lovely day?"

She sighed and closed her eyes. "Rùnach—"

"Whilst we are about enjoying the last of this lovely day, tell me a tale," he said. "Perhaps the tale of Roland of Istaur."

"Don't you know it?"

"Aye, I do. I want to see if *you* know it."

She sighed. "Roland of Istaur was a knight who fell in love with Iona of Diarmailt, apparently when Diarmailt was still a powerful kingdom. But because she was the daughter of a king and Roland a mere knight, he had to do something extraordinary to win her hand, so he took on an impossible quest."

"Funny, that," Rùnach said. "The taking on of a quest to win a lady's hand."

"Well, I suppose if a man truly loved the woman in question, then it doesn't seem so silly."

"Nay, it doesn't."

She nodded, then she realized he wasn't speaking anymore. Hard on the heels of that realization came the one that she understood what he was getting at. She pushed out of his arms and looked at him in shock.

"You can't be serious."

"Can't I?"

She turned away. The torches sudden lit themselves, which surprised her. She spun around and looked at him. Very well, so she might have glared. It had been that sort of spring so far.

"You're an elf," she accused.

"Mostly." He smiled. "And a very weary one, as it happens. Would you mind if I sat down?"

"Of course not," she said promptly. "There's a lovely bench there."

He walked over to the bench she'd been perching on earlier, then bent and picked up her book from where she'd dropped it. He opened the cover, smiled, then sat. He set the book aside and looked up at her, his smile fading. "Is my blood an impediment?"

"Of course it is!"

"Why?"

"Because—" Her voice broke. She cleared her throat and drew

on every smidgen of self-control she'd learned during endless days in the Guild. She absolutely would not cry over him now. "Because I am nothing and you are a prince."

He looked down at his hands for several minutes in silence, then held his hands out and looked at her seriously. "Spin it out of me, then."

She frowned. "What?"

"My magic. Spin it out of me."

She blinked. "Why?"

"Because I think it has changed how you look at me."

She sighed, because she couldn't keep herself from it. "How could it not?"

"I don't think it would if you understood exactly what I think it's good for."

"And what is that?"

He pointed at the torches behind them. They leapt to light with a fire so beautiful, she gasped.

"Because that and this"—he snapped his fingers and every single tree in the garden blazed to life with the same light—"and that"—lights exploded in the sky above her—"and even that"—he pointed to a spot in front of him and a fountain simply appeared, singing a song of Fadaire as the water fell softly over its edge—"is all rubbish."

She thought she might want to sit down soon. "Beautiful rubbish, though."

He didn't smile. "There is only one thing my magic, the magic that you had the uncanny, almost *magical* ability to see and then spin out of me as not another single person on the face of the earth could have done, is good for."

"And what is that?" she asked reluctantly.

"To keep you safe."

She smiled uneasily because the thought was so ridiculous, but she felt her smile fade when she realized he was perfectly serious.

"You mean that."

"Of course I mean that." He reached out, took her hand, then pulled her over to sit next to him on the stone bench. "I'm not finished with this conversation," he said, "but I'm not sure I'm equal to doing aught but sitting here for a few minutes and catching my breath."

"I can go—"

"Stay."

Well, if he was going to put it that way, she supposed she wouldn't argue.

She looked at his hands that had taken her hand between them. Before she thought better of it, she reached out and traced the runes there. She drew Teasraig and Sonairte on the back of his right hand, causing them to flash silver and gold briefly in the torchlight. She could also see Còir's rune there, buried in his flesh. She could see the rune he hadn't known the name of, the one that had inspired a goodly bit of uninterest. And beneath them all, covering flesh that was no longer webbed with scars was Comraich.

A rune of gathering.

She frowned thoughtfully at it, then looked at him. "What is Comraich?"

"Comraich?" he echoed in surprise. "It is a rune of gathering, but in the sense of gathering something in and protecting it. Why do you ask?"

"Because that was what was covering your scars. Beneath that other rune you spoke of that inspired disinterest." She traced it a time or two more before she dared tell him what else she saw. She met his gaze. "Your mother put both there."

His eyes grew very red. "Did she, indeed?"

She nodded. "It was she who hid your power."

He rubbed his face against his shoulder, then looked at her. "Aisling, I think you might reduce me to tears. Again, if you're keeping count." He took a deep breath. "How in the world do you know that?"

She continued to trace his runes, because she thought it might bring him some small comfort. "You told me that your mother had managed to deflect your sire's spell so you took only a glancing blow, which was obviously the case. I don't know, not having been at the well, but I believe that what she did was take your power and hide most of it in your hands, then cover it with a rune of Comraich." She met his eyes, but her eyes were too full of tears to see him properly. "She cut it out of her own hand with a spell and gave it to you. Your voice and your sight and your hearing she covered as well, but I fear by then her power was . . . less."

"Less?"

"The spell she used to do so was the last thing she said before she perished."

He caught his breath, then bowed his head. He put his arm around her shoulders and pulled her close. She supposed it was his tale to weep over, but she found instead that she was the one who was falling apart. She put his handkerchief over her face, but it did little to stem the tide, as it were. She wept until she thought she might have wept all of her tears for the foreseeable future, wiped her face, then looked at him. He wasn't weeping.

He looked at peace.

She hiccuped, which seemed particularly out of place, but she couldn't help herself. "She loved you."

"I believe she did," he said quietly. He looked at her and smiled. "I don't know how to thank you. You have given me a gift I can never repay."

"Oh, Rùnach," she said miserably, "I'm not sure I was even thinking that at the time. I did it because I thought I could, which was an arrogant assumption on my part."

"Born of an intense desire to do good," he said seriously. He reached up and tucked a lock of hair behind her ear. "Which is why you and I will go on this quest, save Bruadair, then turn our attentions to more personal things."

"It doesn't bother you that I could have killed you?"

He shrugged. "I didn't hear any spells of death coming out of your mouth."

She looked at him helplessly. "I took a foolish chance with your life because I arrogantly thought I could do something none of your relatives had managed."

"And isn't that interesting?" he said, sliding her a look. "That you managed something none of my relatives could."

"Perhaps they didn't try," she said with a shrug.

"I spent twenty years acting as servant to the son of the crown prince of Cothromaiche, who has all sorts of spells for doing all kinds of things," he said seriously. "He certainly could have done something, I should think, but he didn't. And in this case, I don't think it was because he thought it was better that I suffer. He would have restored my magic to me had he been able to."

She thought she might have rather preferred her life when all she did was weave rough thread. "What are you getting at?"

He smiled, then leaned over, stopping just short of kissing her. "Might I?" he asked politely.

"You're asking?"

"I thought I should."

"Why?"

He blinked, then smiled before he kissed her. He rose, pulling her up with him, then put his arms around her and held her tightly for a moment or two. He pulled back and met her gaze.

"Let's go read your book."

"You didn't answer my question."

"I'm still thinking about what to say, which might take me all day, so why don't we seek out a comfortable spot in front of the king's fire and read your book until I manage it?"

"If you like." She paused. "He has been very kind."

"I'm not sure that describes it," Rùnach said wryly. "I'm not sure even my grandfather has seen the inside of the king's private solar, much less enjoyed the privilege of sitting in it for hours at a time. I think we can safely assume he's doing this because of you, not me."

"Surely not."

He only smiled and took her hand. She didn't find that a particularly satisfactory answer, but she obviously was going to have nothing more from him.

She walked with him back toward the king's hall and tried not to jump as first the fountain disappeared, then the lights above them, then the lights in the trees after they were no longer needed.

"I don't think the king would want to have Fadaire in his garden," Rùnach said.

Aisling imagined not. She continued on with him back into the palace, then through the passageways toward the king's solar. She flinched a little each time someone would bow to them—for it wasn't just to Rùnach. She looked up at him to find him watching her with a small smile.

"Why do they keep doing that, do you suppose?"

"I think they know who you are."

"But I'm just me," she said in surprise. "I'm no one."

"I believe Mehar of Angesand said the exact thing at one point."

"You don't know that."

"Actually, I think I might. And something else you should know is this: there have been several lads who spent much effort and questing to win the heart of a Bruadairian lass. You're quite an exclusive lot."

"I think you're inventing all this on the spot."

"And I think you're beautiful," he said seriously. "I should also mention that Uachdaran has a vein of something special in an easily accessible place. Too fine for picks, too hard for fingers. He was thinking you might want to see if you could spin it out of solid rock."

"I'm not sure I can spin anything else unusual today," she said with a shiver.

"Then let's leave it for tomorrow." He shot her a meaningful look. "There are several things we must needs discuss, Aisling, but perhaps we should leave those for tomorrow as well. But don't think I've forgotten any of them in my delight and profound gratitude over the events of today."

"Events that you can only see out of one eye."

"I'll beg a bit of healing from the king, and you're changing the subject." He leaned over and kissed her cheek. "Thank you."

She nodded, but she could say nothing else. The day had been full of things she hadn't expected, things she wasn't sure she would be able to think about in the future without weeping.

Rùnach had his magic back.

She couldn't help but believe that had changed a great many things.

Eighteen

❧

Rùnach had always suspected it would be magic that would kill him in the end. He just hadn't expected it would be his own.

He stood, hunched over with his hands on his thighs, and wondered if it would be simpler to beg for mercy and lose his pride or let Uachdaran of Léige's very unsettling spells simply do their work and rid him of anything resembling a sentient existence.

"There's ale on the bench over there."

Aye, no doubt laced with spells that would leave him retching far into the evening, which he wasn't sure he wouldn't just do all on his own. He heaved himself upright, nodded his thanks to the king, then staggered over to the wall where he indeed found what had been promised. He downed half a cup of pale, undemanding ale before he realized what he was missing.

Aisling.

"She left an hour ago."

Rùnach looked at the king standing next to him. "Have we been here an hour already?"

"Two," Uachdaran said, his eyes bright with amusement. "Don't you remember?"

"I'm trying not to."

"I told her to go," the king said. "Didn't think she should see you on your knees begging for mercy."

Rùnach couldn't even nod in thanks. Uachdaran inviting him into his private lists had been, he had to admit, a very generous offer. He and Aisling had encountered the king on their way back inside from the garden whereupon the king of the dwarves had invited Rùnach to step into his lists for a bit of late afternoon's exercise. Rùnach had agreed, then experienced a moment's pause when the king had told him he wouldn't need a sword. He'd suppressed a flinch, agreed to Aisling's request that she come along, then hoped he hadn't gotten himself into something he might not emerge from unscathed.

In truth, the entire experience had felt like something out of a dream—and not just the two hours he'd apparently spent in the king's lists. Watching Aisling pull his power from him, power he hadn't realized he still possessed, then spin it into something even he could see was a moment he was sure he would never forget. She had draped that power around his shoulders like a delicate shawl fashioned from something far less tangible than spiderwebs. He had felt it sink into him, though, with the power of a thousand hammers.

Nay, that didn't come close to describing the pain of it, though he supposed that might be a memory he didn't care to entertain until the misery had faded from it.

He'd woken to the sight of some sharp-eyed dwarf peering at him, listened to the man identify himself as Uachdaran's personal physick, then sat up and looked about for Aisling.

And then it had occurred to him what she'd done.

He supposed it was fair to say that he had leapt out of bed with a giddy laugh. Perhaps Ollamh would forget in time that Rùnach had spun him around as if they were both professional players capering about to jovial music. The man likely thought him mad, which perhaps he had been at the time.

He had extinguished the flames in the hearth with a word, then lit the wood again and almost set his bedchamber on fire. It had taken him a moment or two to breathe enough times to calm himself down and use his power in a useful, measured fashion.

And he had Aisling to thank for it.

The truth was, he'd had to bite his tongue to keep himself from proposing to her earlier in the garden. He wasn't sure how that was related to having his magic back. At the moment, he honestly wasn't sure of anything except that he wasn't sure he could look at any more of Uachdaran of Léige's spells without puking.

He looked at the king. "This is very generous."

The king drained his cup and set it down. "It is," he agreed. "I seem to be indulging your family in this regularly. I put Ruithneadh through his paces recently, if memory serves."

"How did he do?"

"Well enough, and so you know, he escorted his lady out after a pair of hours. I did that for you, which I believe I just mentioned."

"I don't remember that," Rùnach said honestly.

"Lad, you were too busy trying not to lose your lunch to remember much of anything. Are you up for more?"

Rùnach took a deep breath. "Why are you doing this?"

"For my own amusement. Are you afraid?"

Rùnach considered. "I am my father's son, as you know."

"Am *I* supposed to be afraid?"

"Confident in my lack of surprise over your spells, rather," Rùnach said dryly. "I did also live in the same keep as Droch for a score of years, as it happens."

"Ah, but did you see anything he fashioned from that bilge he calls magic?"

Rùnach had to concede the point. "I suppose I didn't, but I'm not sure why that would matter."

The king reached up and patted his shoulder. "Hope you've a strong stomach, little one. Let's have another go and see if I can reduce you to tears. Your brother didn't weep, if you're curious. Don't imagine you would want to give him any reason to mock you now, would you?"

Rùnach didn't suppose he would. He took a deep breath, gathered his tolerance for vile things, and followed the king back out into the middle of his chamber.

It was no longer than another hour before he finally threw up.

"Well, at least your lady didn't see that," Uachdaran said with a snort. "What a weakling you've become."

"If you'll forgive my saying so," Rùnach wheezed, "those were exceptionally vile spells."

"Dredged them up just for you, though I have to agree." Uachdaran shivered delicately. "Disgusting, aren't they?"

Rùnach collapsed on the stone bench and looked at his host. "I'm almost afraid to ask where you learned them."

"Oh, you don't really believe your father was the first black mage of note to stride across these nine kingdoms, do you?"

"I'd like to think I'm not that naive," Rùnach managed.

The king sat down next to him and squinted up at the ceiling. "I believe it was my grandfather—nay, my great—or perhaps my great-great-grandfather who found Carach of Mùig slithering around in the passages below, thinking to stir up mischief and perhaps even steal a bit of our magic. Carach was unhappy to be collared, as you might imagine, and challenged my progenitor, Tochail, to a duel of spells. Tochail was, as you also might imagine, very happy to accept."

"And?"

"Well, as skilled as he was—and he was a spectacularly powerful mage, I'll admit—Carach was sorely out of his depth. Perhaps in his own land he might have called upon an advantage, but not here. King Tochail carved out this space with a word, then invited Carach inside to do his best."

"So Tochail could memorize the spells, one would assume."

"Of course."

"But why hand them down?" Rùnach asked. "If they were so vile, that is."

Uachdaran looked at him lazily. "Well, to torment cheeky elves with, of course."

Rùnach managed a smile. He had to admit he was somewhat relieved to learn those spells were not of Uachdaran's make. "So what happened to Carach? I assume he was thoroughly bested."

"He was," Uachdaran agreed, "and sent off into the night. Not sure what happened to him. He likely talked some poor wench into wedding with him and sired a dozen sons on her who were just as vile and stupid as he was." He shrugged. "Not my worry."

Rùnach shared the sentiment. He had enough on his plate without speculating over the landing place of some mage he'd never heard of. He looked at the dwarf king. "Thank you for sending Aisling away."

"Rùnach, my lad, there are some things that shouldn't be seen by the woman you love."

"Agreed."

Uachdaran leaned back against the cold stone of the wall. "She's a strong-willed gel, that one, in spite of her innocence. Full of mighty magic. Perhaps even mightier than yours, whelp."

"Do you think so?" Rùnach asked frankly. "I must admit this is the thing about her that baffles me the most. I'm obviously still unable to even begin to adequately express my gratitude for what she's done for me, but even so, I'm not sure I can call it magic."

Uachdaran looked at him from under his bushy eyebrows.

"Have you considered, Rùnach my lad, that sometimes you think too much?"

Rùnach sighed. "The thought has crossed my mind."

"Allow it freer rein from now on." The king blew out his breath with a gusty sigh. "You're looking at it without any imagination at all, which surprises me given who you are. Not every mage or king or village witch possesses magic in exactly the same way, which you well know."

"But they possess something in their veins that gives them power," Rùnach said slowly. "Wouldn't you agree?"

"For the most part, aye, though you must admit that there are those for whom power is tied to their land. Your grandfather's magic, and mine as well if you'll have the truth of it, transcends boundaries of country and birth—to the everlasting disgust of several other, lesser kings and queens. I will allow that young Mochriadhemiach of Neroche seems to carry most of his power with him, but even he might be prevailed upon to admit that there is something about home that cannot be duplicated anywhere else."

"And Prince Soilléir?"

"He's Cothromaichian," Uachdaran said without hesitation. "He's different."

That was perhaps an understatement. "And Aisling?"

Uachdaran considered for a bit, then shrugged. "I don't know enough about those Bruadairians to say for certain. It just seems to me that it might be very interesting to see what she can do when she is within the confines of her own land."

"I'm not sure she'll actually cross that border again."

"I'm not sure she'll have a choice."

"We *all* have choices."

"And some of us possess the character that allows us to make the choices necessary without thought of self."

Rùnach sighed. "Very true, Your Majesty."

Uachdaran elbowed him. "I'm torturing you, Rùnach. You're

altruistic enough for an elf. But if you want my advice, take that gel of yours and make certain she's never out of your sight. Unless you simply plan on turning her loose in the wide world of kings and queens and fine salons to allow her to fend for herself."

"Of course not."

"Annastashia of Cothromaiche never believed you died at the well, you know."

The change of topic was dizzying, and then it occurred to him that it wasn't much of a change. He looked at the king. "Didn't she?"

"She didn't." He blinked owlishly. "I'm surprised Prince Soilléir didn't send word to her that you were safe."

"He wouldn't have."

Uachdaran smiled faintly. "I suppose not, being who he is." He lifted an eyebrow. "Shall I have word sent to her?"

"Please don't," Rùnach said without hesitation. "I'm not interested."

"You were mightily interested once."

Rùnach sighed deeply. He had been interested in Annastashia of Cothromaiche, very interested, but that had been before, when he'd been full of his own might and magic, and confident that he could walk into any room and be equal to any woman of rank there.

Which he supposed he still was.

He looked at the king. "I'm not interested any longer, Your Majesty," he said with a sigh, "though I thank you for the offer."

"You'd best keep your gel away from them," Uachdaran said seriously. "Those sorts of women, I mean. They'll tear her to shreds."

"I know," Rùnach said quietly.

Uachdaran considered the ceiling a bit longer, then looked at him. "Bruadair is a strange place."

Rùnach shifted a bit on the bench so he could look at the king more closely. "Why is that?"

"It isn't so much the people as what they do."

"The dreamweavers?" Rùnach asked.

The king grunted. "An odd lot, those."

"This is the thing that perplexes me most deeply," Rùnach asked. "How is it they weave dreams?"

"Well, my boy, I think you should probably go find a Bruadairian and put your questions to him yourself. Or you could trot back to Buidseachd and ask Soilléir, not that he'd tell you anything, of course." He put his hands on his knees, then rose. "It does make you wonder what those dreamweavers weave, doesn't it?"

Rùnach pushed himself to his feet with far greater effort than he would have preferred to have been using. "What do you mean?"

Uachdaran shot him a look. "Well, they have to weave with something, wouldn't you say?"

Rùnach frowned. "I seem to remember having had this conversation before with my sister and her husband."

"Did they have any answers?"

"Not a one. Just speculation about how one went about weaving dreams and . . ." He paused and looked at the king. "And who was spinning the dreams they weave."

"An interesting question, isn't it?"

Rùnach would have smiled, but the king's expression stopped him. He shook his head. "I simply can't believe that anyone would spin dreams or weave dreams or anything that—well, what would you call it? Unsubstantial? Ethereal?"

He stopped and wondered when it was the king had put a solid rock wall in front of him. He saw stars, truly he did. He drew his hand over his eyes, then looked off into the king's lists until he thought he could pit what was left of his poor brain against what he'd just encountered.

Ethereal. How many times had he used that word for Aisling? He supposed he had applied it to how she looked . . . or had he?

He'd thought her beautiful for so long, he honestly couldn't re-member.

But handling things of a less-than-tangible nature, now there was something he thought he might be able to describe with a bit more authority. He had watched her spin several things that were a little odd, weren't they? Air, fire, water . . . elven magic out of horribly scarred hands. And what of that dream he'd had in his grandmother's garden? He couldn't remember at the moment if she'd admitted to it, but he had the feeling she had spun the songs of the trees of that garden and given them to him.

She had given him dreams, he who hadn't dreamed in a score of years.

He looked at Uachdaran. "I don't know what to think."

"Maybe you'll find a dreamspinner and ask her what you should think." Uachdaran led him over to the door, then paused. "Be careful with your magic."

"Your Majesty?" Rùnach said in surprise.

Uachdaran considered, then shook his head. "Just be careful. Magic can be unwieldy, as you well know. You did well today."

"But?"

Uachdaran shook his head again. "I've said too much."

"Your Majesty, you've said nothing."

"Which was too much." He shot Rùnach a look from under bushy eyebrows. "Just have a care, with yourself and that girl of yours. Now, would you like supper in my solar or would you pre-fer to take your chances amongst the piles of traders and their daughters who will be cluttering up my table in the hall?"

"Oh, the former, please."

Uachdaran smirked. "I imagined you'd say the like. I don't think I can escape the torture, but I'll allow you to beg off. You keep your hands to yourself, though."

"I think I can manage that, at least."

"One would hope."

• • •

T wo hours later, Rùnach was sitting in a well-appointed solar on a luxurious sofa, and he had almost stopped shaking from his afternoon's adventures. At the moment, he wasn't sure what had taken more out of him: regaining his magic or facing the king of Durial and his exceptionally vile spells.

He had, thankfully, shared a lovely supper with Aisling and caught up with where she'd stopped in the book Uachdaran had given her. Currently, he was sitting with the book on his lap and paying attention instead to the lovely woman who was sitting on a stool in front of the fire, contemplating the ball of deep red wool she held in her hands.

"What is it?" he asked.

"This yarn should be washed," she said thoughtfully, "and that after having been allowed to rest for a bit." She looked at him. "I don't imagine we're going to be here that long, are we?"

"Not if you want to find the lad you're supposed to meet at Taigh Hall," he said. "If you want my opinion, I think we should probably leave in the morning."

She nodded. "Then I'll knit this tonight, though I'm not sure what with. I don't suppose you have any knitting needles in your pack, do you?"

He held open his hand and a pair of knitting needles appeared. She took a deep breath, then rose and reached out to take them from him.

"Handy, aren't you?"

"Trying to be. I think I'm actually just too lazy to go fetch the ones in my pack that Mistress Ceana sent along for you." That and the very act of creating something courtesy of his magic was simply too glorious not to take advantage of. He patted the place next to him on the sofa. "Come sit by the fire, and I'll finish up the book for you."

She hesitated, then sat down—rather far away from him, actually. He shot her a look.

"You could come closer."

"I'm not sure how." She looked at him seriously. "I don't know anything about this . . . this . . ."

"Wooing?"

She winced. "If that's what you're calling it."

He opened his mouth to assure her that's exactly what he was calling it, when something rather unpleasant occurred to him.

What if she wasn't uninterested in just wooing, she was uninterested in *his* wooing? He put her book down and rubbed his hands over his face a time or two.

"Are you unwell?" she asked quickly, putting her hand on his shoulder.

Pity was good, he supposed, but not exactly the emotion he was looking for from her. He looked at her and tried to smile.

"You know," he said with as much of a casual tone as he could muster, "I think I may have pressed on where I shouldn't have."

She blinked. "What do you mean?"

"Well, arrogant clod that I am, I didn't stop to think that perhaps you might not want to be the object of my attentions. I've jested about those lads from Neroche, of course, but they aren't as terrible as I've made them out to be. And my cousin Còir is well worthy of your esteem. It's entirely possible, likely even, that you might not be interested in me."

And then he waited. The words were out, hanging there in the air between them. He supposed she could do with them what she wanted: stomp on them, mock them, take them and rearrange them into a list of his flaws she could add to as she liked.

Instead, she laughed.

He looked at her in surprise. "Is it amusing?"

"Your head pains you, doesn't it?"

"It doesn't," he said, suppressing the urge to scowl at her. "The king restored my eye to its proper form if not its proper beauty, and nay, I do not have pains in my head."

"Then you have fluff in it," she said, rolling her eyes. She looked at him, then shook her head. "You can't be serious."

"I think I might be."

She looked at him as if she were fully convinced he had lost his wits. "I think I must have taken a blow to the head I don't remember. How can you think I wouldn't want you?"

"Ah, so you do want me," he said, putting as much satisfaction as possible into his tone to cover the relief he felt at the thought of a simple weaver not finding him objectionable.

A simple weaver he couldn't help but think was anything but.

She rose suddenly and walked about the king's solar for several minutes, apparently not seeing anything. Rùnach sat perfectly still, partly because he was exhausted beyond reason and partly because he feared that she was coming to some sort of decision about him. He supposed that if any of his former interests of the romantic sort had been witness to the scene, they would have been laughing themselves sick over it. He was many things, he supposed, but unaware of his flaws was not one of them. He had, he could admit now that he was safely far away from his youth, been absolutely insufferable when it came to his awareness of how he affected the opposite sex.

He paused. Very well, he'd been a shameless flirt and had likely merited the concern, as Weger had once told him, of every father in the Nine Kingdoms with daughters of tender ages. He supposed considering the number of hearts he had perhaps wounded that it would have served him right if Aisling had cut his from his chest with a dull blade and stomped on it until what was left of him wept. His former paramours would have enjoyed that, no doubt.

He imagined he would enjoy it far less.

She finally stopped in front of him and looked down at him.

"This is all utterly ridiculous, you know."

He squinted up at her. "Could you ignore the ridiculousness of it and at least entertain the thought?"

"I have entertained it," she admitted with what seemed to him to be an unwholesome amount of reluctance.

"And?" he asked.

She sighed. "I will admit that those lads from Neroche pale by comparison."

He smiled. "I'll build you a house on the seashore."

"I said *pale* not *disappear completely*."

He took her hand and happily pulled her to sit down next to him. She sat on her book, which she had to get up to retrieve, but she sat back down almost as close to him as he would have liked.

"Where is your handkerchief?"

She frowned. "The one you gave me?"

"Nay, Còir's."

"Why?"

"Because I want to write something on it."

She put her hand over her pocket protectively. "I have the feeling it won't be polite."

"And I have the feeling it will be something along the lines of *I want to ask Aisling to wed me but need your advice on when and where to do so*."

She looked at him again as if he'd lost his mind. "You *are* serious."

"Move your feet and I'll go down on bended knee—"

"Oh, please don't," she said quickly. She looked at him, then shook her head. "Rùnach, you are mad. What in the world will your relations think? What will your friends think? What will King Uachdaran think?"

"I'll answer the last first," he said, reaching for her hand. "He told me I would be fortunate if you looked at me twice. I believe my grandfather said much the same thing, as did my grandmother the queen. My brother asked me when the wedding was. And I can assure you, all of them thought you would be mad to consider me."

She sighed. "But you're a prince and I am no one."

"Well, unless we make a quick visit to my father or Acair has somehow acquired spells he shouldn't have, I can't renounce my magic—which you bear some responsibility for, as it happens—but I can renounce my title." He looked at her, then shooed her. "Go on and fetch me paper so I can send my grandfather a missive."

Her mouth had fallen open. "Fetch it yourself."

"But I am a prince and you are a weaver. I don't fetch."

"Neither do I," she said, then she scowled at him. "I think somewhere along this journey you have corrupted me and filled my poor head with thoughts of loftiness. Listen to me now."

"You just told the grandson of the king of Tòrr Dòrainn to fetch his own paper," he said easily. "Lofty behavior there, don't you think?"

She considered her hands, then looked at him. "Ridiculous."

"You know, I will exact some sort of painful recompense for every time you say that."

"You might try."

He smiled and took the book she handed him, then left her to her knitting while he read humorous tales of mages trying to take over Bruadair with their pitiful magic. He was surprised to find notes about parliamentary rules and procedures in the section of the book dealing with magic—

He froze, seeing something there in front of him on the page that startled him so badly, he almost dropped the book. He flipped past the page quickly, then patted his shoulder and looked at Aisling.

"You look weary. Come use me as a place to rest your head."

She covered a yawn with her hand. "It has been an eventful day."

And he suspected the events hadn't ended yet. Aisling put her head on his shoulder and yawned again. A bit of juggling resulted in his managing to capture her hand with his whilst still holding the book, propping it up against his knee.

It only took another long slog through relations with other countries before she was asleep. Once he was certain she was, he flipped back to the page he hadn't wanted her to see, though he supposed he was being overly . . . something. Protective, perhaps. Unable to believe what he'd just read, definitely.

The original charter of Bruadair was drawn up between the three parties, each agreeing to remain confined within their particular disciplines. The ruling class vowed to keep their magic separate from the others and leave them free rein to do as they saw fit with their stewardship. The weavers were to oversee not only the tangible creation of cloth but a select few were to spend their labor attending to their true business of creating the fabric of the world.

The dreamspinners were few and soon faded into memory.

He turned the page only to find the report continued with talk of the noble houses in the land and their gentle disagreements about the colors for their heraldry. He shut the book and shook his head. If that was the worst they'd had to face, they had been fortunate indeed. He set the book aside, then looked into the fire.

Dreamspinners?

He turned that over in his mind for a very long time, but from every angle it still looked like something he wasn't sure he could reduce in such a way that it seemed manageable.

There were dreamspinners in Bruadair?

He looked down at the hands of the Bruadairian lass sitting next to him on the very comfortable sofa he had drawn closer to Uachdaran's fire for Aisling's comfort. One of her hands was held in his own. The other was resting on his arm. He had watched those hands do all sorts of things that left him with more questions than answers.

How was it a simple weaver from a country known for nothing more than buckets of rain and secrecy could reach beneath impervious Fadairian runes of power and protection, beneath scars half created, he was convinced, by not only a bit of his father's dark spells but a well of evil, beneath spells his mother had put there to hide and contain, and pull out a single thread of power that no one he knew had seen before? How was it possible that that same weaver had taken that magic, spun it out of him in spite of what he was sure had been his shrieks of agony, and put it onto a bobbin she had created out of air and fire?

How was it that same weaver had fashioned a shawl of that power, draped it around him, then not been slain immediately when a dwarvish king had put his hands over hers and spoken a spell that Rùnach couldn't help but wish he'd been capable of memorizing?

The door opened behind him, almost sending him off the sofa onto the floor in his surprise. He looked over his shoulder gingerly so as not to wake the woman sleeping next to him. The king stood there, looking grave.

Rùnach sat up before he thought better of it, then had to catch Aisling before she pitched off the sofa. The king strode inside his solar, walked past him, then sat down in the chair facing him.

"There's been an incident."

"What sort?" Rùnach asked, though he had the sinking feeling he wouldn't be surprised by what he heard.

"I just had word that your grandfather and his company were attacked on the plains of Ailean. They're not sure there are any survivors."

Rùnach felt the ground beneath him shift and the room grow dim. He supposed he might have fainted if Aisling hadn't had hold of his arm in a grip that pained him. He hadn't realized she was awake, though perhaps he should have—

He blinked aside the haze, then focused with an effort on the king. "Are they sure?"

Uachdaran looked at him grimly. "The scouts are not mine, and I don't trust any but my own lads. The tidings were from a generally reliable trader. He saw the battle, which was mighty, then saw elves being flown back to Tòrr Dòrainn. He thinks those who came to fetch them were not in the battleguard. But, he could be mistaken. He claims he saw a group of mages—dark ones, he stated—turn and come this way in a frightful hurry. But that would have been yesterday, at least."

"Acair was at Mistress Fionne's house yesterday morning," Aisling said quietly.

Rùnach looked at her and realized she had it aright. He could hardly believe it had been such a short time ago, but it was true. And perhaps now Acair knew he was not traveling toward the schools of wizardry.

The question was, where would Acair believe he might be going?

North, if the witchwoman of Fàs had told him anything.

"You are both weary," the king said, "but if you'll take my advice, you'll leave under cover of darkness."

Aisling stood, swayed slightly, then picked up her knitting. "I'll pack quickly."

"I'll walk you to your chamber—" Rùnach said.

"Nay, I'll find it on my own." She touched his shoulder briefly. "I'm sure your grandfather is well."

He nodded, waited for her to go, then looked at the king. "Is that all?"

"Isn't that enough?" Uachdaran asked grimly.

Rùnach handed him the book on Bruadairian lore. "You might want this back."

"Read it, did you?"

"I couldn't help myself. I learned an interesting fact or two."

"I imagine you did, lad." The king rose. "I'll go see to rations for your journey. I have a blade for you, if you're interested." He shot Rùnach a look. "Something in my forge seemed to think it needed to come on your adventure."

"Very kind," Rùnach managed.

The king grunted. "So it is." He started toward the door, then paused and looked at Rùnach. "Remind your lady about what runs under my land. I don't like that I can't identify it."

Rùnach nodded. It was one more thing to add to the rather robust and unsettlingly long list of things that puzzled him. Spinners, dreamweavers, ethereal weavers who could see and touch things others could not, books of spells gone missing to be replaced by maps he couldn't understand.

Why did he have the feeling all the answers lay in Bruadair?

It was a mystery. And as he'd admitted more than once in the past pair of months, he loved a good mystery.

He only hoped the solving of it didn't kill them all.

Nineteen

❧

Aisling knew she shouldn't have been cold. She was wearing clothing provided by the dwarves of Léige, boots, leggings, a long tunic, and a cloak that was neither too thin nor too heavy. She should have been perfectly comfortable in spite of the fact that twilight had faded and there was no moon. But terror did that to a person, she supposed.

"Not to worry," Rùnach murmured. "I'll keep you safe."

"I'm not worried about me," she said, her teeth chattering. "How will I keep *you* safe?"

"I think you've done that often enough in the past to merit a rest at present," he said with a small smile. "I'll see to it this time."

She could scarce see his expression for the darkness. She could, however, see a hint of his magic running through his veins. "I forgot."

"I never will, believe me."

She nodded, then looked at the hall in the distance. There were torches lit around the perimeter else she might not have seen anything at all. As for how to proceed, she had no idea. She was late arriving to meet, or, rather, sending her mercenary to meet the person responsible for setting in motion the plan to rescue Bruadair. The likelihood of anyone being there to meet her was very slim. Perhaps she had failed utter—

Rùnach's hand was suddenly in front of her, keeping her from moving.

"What?" she managed.

He eased them both back a step, then nodded toward the ground. "Spell."

She wondered how he possibly could have noticed, though now that he pointed it out, she could see it as well. A thin line of shadow that wasn't quite as dark as the rest of the shadows. Rùnach considered, then took a step forward, tripping the spell with the toe of his boot.

"Now we wait."

They didn't wait very long. Aisling jumped a little as a shadow detached itself from the trees and walked toward them. She was fully prepared to find it was one of Rùnach's bastard brothers. The tidings they had had the night before in the dwarf king's solar had been stunning, though she couldn't help but hold out hope that the trader had been mistaken and Rùnach's relatives were unharmed. She was fairly certain Rùnach hadn't believed what he'd heard, though she hadn't had the chance to talk with him about any of it as yet. They had packed their gear, bid farewell to the king in his courtyard, then rushed off into the night without fanfare.

Rùnach had used both his grandfather's glamour and Miach of Neroche's spell of un-noticing to cover their passing, which had

surprised her a little until she'd had the chance to think about it a
bit. Rùnach had had his magic restored to him for less than half a
day. Perhaps he wanted to test it a bit more than just in King
Uachdaran's training lists before he relied on it.

Either that or he had been even wearier than she herself was at
the moment.

Whatever the case was, she couldn't help but think he'd been
wise in his choice. If that shadow coming toward them was one of
his bastard brothers . . .

But it wasn't.

It was the peddler.

There was no mistaking his profile when he turned to look at
the pegasus standing to one side of them. She supposed she shouldn't
have been surprised to see him there. After all, he hadn't said he
wouldn't be the one meeting her mercenary at Taigh Hall. The truth
was, he hadn't said anything past what he'd said to frighten her
into compliance.

The peddler stared at them both for several minutes in silence,
then beckoned for them to follow him. Aisling heard Iteach flap
off up into the sky as something she didn't have the wherewithal to
identify at the moment, then felt Rùnach take her hand. He pulled
her behind him and to his right, so he was between her and the
peddler. She would have told him it was unnecessary, but she supposed it would have been a waste of breath.

They followed the peddler through the woods and around to
the back of Taigh Hall. It was a rather large place, but very rustic.
She stole looks at the shadows in the trees as they walked but saw
nothing untoward. Still, once they reached the back door, she had
to force herself not to turn and bolt. If Rùnach was going to go
inside, then so was she.

Guards stopped them at the back door, saw the peddler, then
allowed them to pass. She looked at Rùnach quickly, but he only
shrugged and flashed her a very brief smile. She frowned, but

what did she know? Perhaps the peddler traveled more than she had suspected and was known in places she wouldn't have suspected.

They walked swiftly along hallways, weaving their way ever inward until the peddler stopped in front of a doorway and knocked. It was opened by what Aisling assumed was a servant, which surprised her. The chamber was opulent, which also surprised her. She saw a couple standing near the hearth, but she didn't know them, so she dismissed them. Perhaps the peddler was acquiring a small army and those two were his first recruits.

He turned around, folded his arms over his chest, and frowned at her. "You're late."

She pushed her hood back and looked at him frankly. "I did the best I could."

He lifted an eyebrow. "My, how cheeky you've grown, little Aisling."

"Being lied to for the whole of your life and finding out the extent of it in uncomfortable ways at inconvenient times will do that to a woman," she said shortly. "Again, I did what I could."

"Who did you bring with you?"

Aisling looked up at Rùnach. He released her hand, then lifted his hood back from his face and looked at the peddler.

The peddler only smiled.

"What an interesting choice." He stepped back and made Rùnach a low bow. "Prince Rùnach, what a pleasure." He lifted an eyebrow briefly. "Rumor has it you perished at Ruamharaiche's well."

"Rumor is ofttimes wrong," Rùnach said mildly, "Prince Ochadius."

Aisling realized her mouth was hanging open. She gaped first at the peddler, then at Rùnach. She shook her head, because she couldn't believe what she'd just heard. She considered, then decided that perhaps the peddler could be addressed first. "Do you know Rùnach?" she asked incredulously.

"Prince Rùnach?" he said, then he shrugged. "Personally? Nay. Of him? Of course."

Aisling found that particularly unsatisfying, so she turned to Rùnach. "What did you call him?" she demanded.

Rùnach nodded at the other man. "I called him by his proper name, though you would have had no means of knowing that. Perhaps I should have allowed him to introduce himself, if he dared."

The peddler sighed, then looked at Aisling. He inclined his head. "Ochadius of Riamh, at your service, my lady."

"I am not your lady and you are a walloping liar," she said, glaring at him. "You sold me your own book!"

Ochadius shrugged. "Had to have some of my own back, didn't I?"

"I suggest you not go anywhere near Gobhann," she said shortly, "or Weger will give you more of your own than you'll care for."

"No doubt," Ochadius agreed with a brief laugh. "Let's just say I have a finely honed sense of humor, re-term all that went between us as hedging not lying, and move on, shall we? I did what was needful, as did you. And whilst we're about introductions, allow me to present you to our hosts tonight. You may leave your gear over here, if you like. It will be safe enough."

Aisling shot Rùnach a look he only lifted an eyebrow at before she shrugged out of her pack and left it next to Rùnach's by the door. She walked with him over to the people standing in front of the fire. Aisling had no idea who they were or why they would be hosting anything, but being plunged into things she wasn't prepared for seemed to be her lot at present. Ochadius made the couple a low bow just as he'd done to Rùnach, then turned from them. He gestured expansively to the pair.

"If I might present Their Majesties, Frèam and Leaghra of Bruadair," he said formally. "Your Majesties, Prince Rùnach of Tòrr Dòrainn and our own Aisling of Bruadair itself."

Aisling wondered if she should curtsey or bolt, but Rùnach

was bowing, so she chose a curtsey instead. The king held up his hand.

"Of course we will dispense with the formalities," he said kindly. "Prince Rùnach, we know of your doings, of course, from various sources. We are leaving tomorrow for a visit to your brother Ruithneadh and our niece Sarah."

"Ruithneadh made mention of his delight over your impending arrival when last I saw him." Rùnach said with a smile. "I recommend sampling the wine my grandmother Eulasaid makes, but perhaps not indulging overmuch in anything from Prince Sgath's cellars."

Frèam laughed a little. "I'll be sure to remember that. And now we must greet our own Mistress Aisling."

Aisling found herself being studied by both the king and queen. Given her experience with royalty over the past pair of months, she knew she shouldn't have been unnerved, but these were the ousted king and queen of her country. She took a deep breath, then made them another curtsey.

"Your Majesties," she said quietly.

To her utter surprise, the king and queen made her a similar courtesy. She tried not to gape at them, but she had to admit she was perhaps too tired to trot out her best manners. The king gestured to chairs.

"Sit, friends, and take your ease for as long as we're able to provide peace for it. Unfortunately, there is much to discuss and perhaps less time than we might hope in which to do so."

Aisling found herself sitting in a chair next to the woman who should have been her queen. She hardly dared venture a glance, but found she couldn't help herself.

Leaghra was watching her gravely.

"Your Majesty?" Aisling asked carefully. "Is there something amiss?"

"You are so young," Leaghra murmured. "And so beautiful for such a burden."

"Oh," Aisling said uneasily, "I am not beautiful."

"Aye, you are," Rùnach said, then went back to discussions of swords and replacement arrows.

Aisling looked at the queen. "He has trouble with his eyes."

"Rather he is an excellent judge of many things," Leaghra said with a smile, "now, as he was in his youth. And somehow I am not at all surprised to find him here."

"I can't help but wish he weren't," Aisling said before she thought better of it. She supposed it was too late now to call the words back. "I don't want to have to tell his grandfather that I'm the reason he is dead."

Assuming, of course, that Sìle was still alive after he'd gone off to divert attention from their flight, which, again, had been because of her quest.

"Oh, my dear girl," Leaghra said gently, "don't take that on yourself. I knew his mother—and his father, it must be said—and if Prince Rùnach inherited even a fraction of her determination, there is little you can do to sway him when his course is set. And I don't think you need worry about his safety. He has faced things you and I never would save perhaps in our worst nightmares. He will be well." She glanced down at Aisling's hand. "His chivalry speaks loudly."

Aisling realized Rùnach was holding her hand. She knew she should have likely pulled away, but found she couldn't. He squeezed her hand briefly and continued his discussion with the others.

Leaghra smiled. "I believe his mother would be pleased with him. And you, if I could venture an opinion. I will tell you what I know of her when I have the chance. For now, you should rest whilst I go fetch wine—"

"Oh, nay," Aisling said quickly. "You shouldn't be doing that. I'll see to it."

"We'll go together, then." The queen rose. "Where have you been keeping yourself all these years, my dear?"

Aisling could scarce believe the queen could be interested in her whereabouts, but she wasn't going to insult her monarch by not responding.

"I was working in a weaver's guild," she said. "In Beul."

"In my day, the Guild was a good place," the queen mused as they walked to a sideboard. "Weavers are highly prized."

"Of course," Aisling said, trying not to choke on the words. "Highly prized."

"You must know Muinear, then."

Aisling almost dropped the cups she was holding. It was only the queen's quick hands that rescued them. She nodded her thanks, then set them back safely on a tray. "I did, Your Majesty. She was very kind to me for all the years I knew her."

"You speak of her as if she is gone—" The queen went suddenly still. "What happened?"

Aisling looked at the queen gravely. "She was slain helping me across the border."

"Those are grievous tidings indeed," the queen said quietly. She stood there for a moment or two, unmoving, then shook her head. "I can't think about that now. Later, when I can grieve properly." She picked up the tray with hands that weren't all that steady. "Can you manage the other things, Aisling? Let's see that you're properly fed, then you'll have a safe place to sleep for the night. Morning will come soon enough."

Aisling followed the queen back toward the fire and wondered a little at her words. She had the feeling that putting off grief had become a habit for Leaghra of Bruadair. Doing what had to be done in spite of the cost, then thinking about it later. She knew that thought shouldn't have chilled her as it did, but it occurred to her that up until that point, she'd always had something else in front of her that wasn't the accomplishment of her quest. Now, there was nothing standing between her and stepping back over the border into the country of her birth.

She set her tray down on her chair, had help moving a table in front of the fire, then assisted the queen in laying out a decent supper in spite of the lateness of the hour. She supposed she ate, but she didn't taste it. She finally simply sat in her chair and watched Rùnach, Ochadius of Riamh, and King Frèam discussing things she didn't particularly want to know.

In time, she gave up listening and settled for watching. The peddler, who was Lothar of Wychweald's grandson however many accursed generations there were between the two of them, glanced at her a time or two, smiled, then went back to his business. He didn't seem at all surprised to see Rùnach there, which surprised her. It wasn't possible that he could have known she would encounter Rùnach at Gobhann, much less anything else of a more romantic nature, surely.

She shifted a little in her seat so she could look at that object of her unfaced romantic intentions. She supposed she could wear herself out thinking about the fairness of his face, so she decided to accept it and move on. What she noticed at present were other things, things she supposed she hadn't had the luxury of seeing before.

She had always had the impression that elves were all painful beauty and nothing else, but she could see that that wasn't giving them credit where it was due. Rùnach conversed easily about centuries of history she'd never heard of, discussed the current climate of various realms without so much as a pucker of concentration on his perfect brow, and argued strategies in a way that wasn't argumentative but was certainly respected by the other two.

Losing himself in an obscure garrison would have been a terrible waste.

"I don't think you'll enter from Beul," Ochadius said doubtfully. "Too many guards there."

"But Gairn is too far," Frèam said, shaking his head. "It will have to be Cothromaiche, though I don't know how you'll beg passage there, no matter your connections with them."

"I'll think on it," Rùnach said slowly. "But what of when we enter? Who is this Sglaimir and where did he come from?"

"His father is forgettable," Frèam said in distaste, "but his grandfather was Carach of Mùig."

"Are you sure?" Rùnach asked, clearly surprised.

"Aye, I am," Frèam said. "Do you know of him? I only ask because not many have heard of that line. 'Tis very obscure."

"I recently had occasion to discuss him with Uachdaran of Léige," Rùnach said. "Not a pleasant lot, are they?"

"Not at all," Ochadius said grimly.

Rùnach looked at him. "And what is your interest in all this, Your Highness? If I might ask."

"His interest is my niece Alexandra," Frèam said dryly. "She has been inside the palace all this time, trying to win the war from within."

Aisling caught the look Rùnach threw her, then found her hand taken by him. He held it in both his own, then looked at the king.

"And she's alive still? I hate to ask it, Your Majesty, but . . ."

"She lives still," Frèam said. "Which Ochadius well knows."

"In that hellhole," Ochadius said, "which begs the question: why is Sglaimir there? I can understand Weger choosing Gobhann; he's always had a streak of austerity running through him. Sglaimir, however, is a far different story. He has the entirety of Bruadair at his fingertips, yet he strips the place of all magic." He shook his head. "Baffling."

Rùnach frowned. "How is that possible? Has he taken it all into himself?"

"Not that you'd know it," Ochadius said. "He's as colorless as the rest of us and the palace is shabby." He shot the king an apologetic look. "If you'll forgive my saying so, Your Majesty."

Aisling watched the king wave away Ochadius's words. Rùnach, however, seemed much less inclined to do so.

"No displays of magic?" he asked Ochadius carefully.

"Not a one. I've seen no displays of anything save him strutting
about the city without so much as a lad to hold open doors for him,
as if he dared anyone to lay a finger on him."

"You've shown admirable control, lad," Frèam said quietly. "I
don't think I could have managed it. Not that I have the power any
longer to do anything but sit here and rage."

Ochadius shook his head. "You were greatly weakened by the
last battle with him, Your Majesty. It is left to us to see your throne
restored to you, which we will do. I feel sure that when you cross
the border, your power will return in full force to you."

Aisling listened with only half an ear to the rest of the conversation, which seemed destined to last most of the night. She didn't
argue when the queen drew her across the chamber and showed
her where she might lie down on a comfortable cot. She did take
her boots off, but that was the extent of it. She closed her eyes and
attempted sleep.

Rùnach's words came back to her as if they'd been a whisper.
No displays of magic? She had to admit, she wondered the same
thing. If Sglaimir had taken all the magic for himself, why didn't
he march endlessly about the country with it on display, making
sure all knew what he had taken from them?

It was curious, to be sure.

S he woke sometime during the night with a gasp only to realize
that she hadn't been drowning. She sat up and looked around
her. Everyone else was asleep. Well, save that shape sitting in front
of the fire with his head bowed and his elbows on his knees, his
hands clasped loosely. She put on her boots, then walked over to
the fire. She dragged up a stool and sat down in front of him.

"Did you sleep?" she asked.

Rùnach shook his head with a weary smile. "Too much to think about."

"I'll hold you in the saddle tomorrow."

"Ah, now you see how my plan comes to fruition already."

She smiled gravely. "It seems the least I can do."

He smiled, took her hands, then bent and kissed the backs of them one by one. He straightened but didn't release her.

"I'm wondering something."

She imagined he was, which was no doubt why he was still sitting in front of the fire long after everyone had likely gone to their rests. "What?"

"What color was Beul?"

She frowned. "Color?"

"Aye. Do you remember that painting my grandmother did of the city? It was drenched in colors, wasn't it?"

She nodded slowly. "Aye, but that isn't how it is now." She paused. "I don't remember how it was when I first went to the Guild. Less grey than it is now, perhaps. Why?"

"I'm thinking."

She liberated one of her hands and reached up to smooth it over his brow. "It shows. What are you thinking?"

"I'm just wondering where all the color went."

"Perhaps it left with the magic—" She froze, then met his gaze. "Is that what you're thinking?"

He shrugged, though it was none-too-casually done. "I wonder."

"But if Sglaimir has no color in the palace as well, wouldn't that say that he didn't have the magic himself?"

"It's possible," Rùnach said slowly, "though if he'd taken all the magic to himself, I'm not sure it would show. Then again, I'm not sure it *wouldn't* show. I've never seen it done—well, let me rephrase that. I watched my father take power from several souls over the years, one by one, but I never noticed any change in him. I honestly don't remember what he looked like after he took mine and that of my younger brothers."

"But a whole country's worth would show, is that what you're saying?"

"I'm not sure what I'm saying." He looked at her carefully. "I'm just thinking."

"But where would you hide an entire country's worth of magic?" she asked. "It would have to be somewhere substantial, wouldn't it? Perhaps a lake, or a cistern of some sort?"

"I should think so, but Ochadius has been all over the country in his guise as a peddler and hasn't seen anything. But you're right about the size. It would have to be an enormous place. The magic would run like a river into . . . it . . ."

He stopped.

She understood.

"A river?" she said, finally.

He took a ragged breath. "I've heard that word too many times in the past two months for my comfort."

"Have you? Where?"

"Where haven't I?" he said, looking slightly unsettled. "First from Captain Burke, who said he was having dreams of magic running through his belowdecks, then Weger and Nicholas, both of whom said their dreams had been troubled by the same sort of thing. Miach was too busy slobbering over my sister to say anything useful, and I was too distracted at Seanagarra to ask my grandfather anything. But then there is what you heard at Léige."

"A river running beneath the king's palace," she said carefully. "But surely they're not all related."

"Aren't they?" he mused. "I wonder."

"But you would think that if anyone would know what was running beneath his land, it would be King Uachdaran, wouldn't you?"

"You would think so." He shrugged helplessly. "I suppose it's possible to siphon off a kingdom's worth of magic and send it as a river somewhere else, but I can't imagine why you would want to—especially if you had set yourself up as king of the country you were ravaging."

"You mean, he would be looking for ways to bring magic in, not send it out?"

He nodded. "Unless, of course, that's what he's doing and we're just not seeing it. It definitely seems to be a desire that runs in the family. Uachdaran told me Sglaimir's grandfather Carach had tried to steal Durial's magic several centuries ago."

"Well, that is what black mages do, isn't it?"

He lifted his eyebrows briefly. "So it is, but I've never encountered one who had aspirations for more than just the power of the lad down the way." He shook his head. "The magic of an entire country? How do you possibly take that and what would you do with it once you had it?"

She shrugged. "Rule the world?"

"And what world would be left to rule? It's been my experience that those with the desire to enslave those around them generally want those around them to live through the experience. Who else will they play to otherwise?"

"Even your father?" she asked gingerly.

"Especially my father," he said without hesitation. "I firmly believe the reason he took my younger brothers' power was that he realized immediately that he didn't have enough himself to control the well, not because he wanted the magic itself. He was sloppy about it, though, and slew them in the bargain. I also believe that he intended to use his spell of Diminishing on the well itself, to take that power to himself. Perhaps Sglaimir is no different. But you would think he would have done something with all that power if he'd had it to hand, wouldn't you?"

"For all I know about it," she said, "aye."

He squeezed her hands briefly. "I think we had best find the answers sooner rather than later."

"I never unpacked."

"I'll leave them a note—"

"I'm coming with you," a deep voice interrupted.

Aisling looked up to find Ochadius standing there just outside the light from the fire. He stepped forward, obviously dressed for travel.

"You'll need me," he said quietly.

Rùnach looked up at him. "Does your magic work there?"

Ochadius raised his eyebrows briefly. "If it had, don't you think I would have used it by now?"

Rùnach pursed his lips. "I don't think I want to hear this."

"I imagine you don't, but perhaps you'll unlock secrets with a key I don't have. I'll come along and guard your back, if nothing else. And I have that all-important trader's license on the off chance you want to simply walk through the front gates."

Rùnach nodded. "Very well. We'll be glad of the aid."

Aisling supposed there was nothing else to do but watch Rùnach write the king and queen a note in a very lovely hand, then slip silently out the door. There were a dozen questions she should have asked beginning and ending perhaps with why the exiled king and queen of Bruadair were staying in a rather rustic hunting lodge, but perhaps she would have answers from Ochadius later. He certainly owed her a few.

Within minutes they were walking out the back door and around the edge of the hall. Aisling heard the rush of wings and assumed it was Iteach. But it wasn't.

It was Gàrlach of Ceangail.

She found herself pulled behind Rùnach and a spell of Fadairian glamour and protection cast over her before she could catch her breath.

"Go," Ochadius spat. "I'll take care of this one."

"You'll need to," Gàrlach laughed, "given that Rùnach has no power."

Rùnach stepped forward. Aisling saw something come out of his mouth that was dark, as dark as what Lothar of Wychweald had spewed at them. It was a spell of death, though there was something about it that wasn't right—

"Rùnach," she said in surprise, "what are you doing?"

He paused, then apparently realized what he was saying. He stepped back, away from the spell. It fell to the ground in black, jagged shards. "Call Iteach," he said hoarsely.

"Do more than that," Ochadius said urgently. "Run, for there are more coming." He looked at Rùnach quickly. "Find Soilléir."

"Soilléir," Rùnach said, sounding stunned. "What does he have to do with any of this?"

"More than he wanted to. He'll be at—damn it, Rùnach, go!"

Aisling watched Rùnach cast an impenetrable spell of Fadaire over Ochadius—who cursed him thoroughly in thanks—then turn.

"Let's go."

"Will he live?" she asked quickly.

"They don't want him."

She supposed he had a point. She ran with him to where Iteach had appeared, pawing impatiently at the ground. Rùnach flung himself up into the saddle, then pulled her up behind him. Iteach leapt up into the sky in something that was part dragonshape and part wind.

"Don't faint," Rùnach commanded.

"I think I'm going to vomit, rather," she managed.

"I think it's your turn, so feel free."

She wrapped her arms around his waist and held on tightly, trying to keep her gorge down where it belonged. She looked over her shoulder and saw a battle of spells going on behind them. She would have suggested perhaps that they return and offer aid, but she had the feeling Ochadius would have objected quite strenuously.

There was no turning back now.

Twenty

Rùnach pressed his father's ring into the lock, such as it was, on the front door of his sire's retreat and watched with no small bit of amazement as the invisible door became first outlined, then separate from the rock around it. He put his hand on it and suppressed the urge to swear in disgust. The things he and his brother hadn't known about his father were legion. He seriously doubted his mother had known the extent of her husband's duplicities.

He had Ruith to thank for providing him with the location of what he hoped would be a temporary refuge. His brother had been looking at their grandmother's paintings and remarked casually that one of them was a very fine likeness of their father's northern-most property. That had led to a brief discussion of locks and rings that were actually keys to several things and their opinions of their sire, none of which had been particularly complimentary.

"Rùnach, look," Aisling said, tugging on his sleeve.

He looked over his shoulder and saw standing thirty paces away a sight that didn't surprise him in the slightest. And why should it have? Those lads had been following them for several hours. He just hadn't expected them to catch up so quickly.

He pushed the door open, assuming Aisling would rush inside, but she didn't. Neither did Iteach, who slipped into dragonshape and spat out terrible fire.

One of his six bastard brothers—Díolain, he thought—deflected it, but it was done with something of an effort. They were all left perspiring rather heavily.

Yet they didn't react.

He felt Aisling standing just behind his shoulder. She put her hand on his back. He supposed she wouldn't have admitted it, but her hand was shaking badly.

"They're not doing anything," she whispered.

"Aye," he murmured, because he could say nothing else. He was tensed and ready for an attack and that took all his powers of concentration.

Yet still the attack didn't come.

"Go inside, Aisling," he said, speaking behind the hand he'd pretended to use to rub his mouth.

"Nay."

He didn't dare look away from the six mages standing in front of him. "You can do nothing here," was what he said, but what he meant was that she didn't dare do anything. Her spinning would no longer surprise them because it simply wasn't possible that Gàrlach hadn't told them about her abilities, no doubt altering the tale to make himself look as if he'd had the upper hand. Rùnach honestly wasn't sure how they might entrap her if she attempted anything.

Nay, it was best that he see to it.

Acair stepped suddenly out of nothing and all hell broke loose.

He supposed the only thing that he might look back on with

any amusement at all would be the look on his bastard brother's
face when he realized that Rùnach had more magic than previously supposed. Acair staggered back a step, then shot Gàrlach a
murderous look.

"You said he had no magic left," he snarled.

Gàrlach threw up his hands. "He *has* no magic. Unless—" He
frowned. "Unless he had it hidden."

"Of course he had it hidden, you fool!"

"I am your elder brother—"

"And I will treat you with respect," Acair said coolly, "or what?
You'll use a spell on me? I suppose you might try." He turned to
look at Rùnach. "Or will you make the attempt, little one?"

The term was so ridiculous, Rùnach smiled before he could
stop himself, which he supposed, in hindsight, had been a somewhat unwise thing to do.

"I think he's insulting you, Acair," someone pointed out.

Rùnach supposed, by the look of his rather scarred face, that
that helpful soul had been Amitàn. Then again, that one had never
been particularly adept at keeping his mouth shut. He winced a
little in sympathy at the scars on his bastard brother's face, then
dismissed him and turned his attentions back to Acair.

"I'm not insulting you," he said mildly, ignoring his first instinct,
which was to keep his own mouth shut. Perhaps he'd been cooped
up in Buidseachd for too long and the fresh air was turning his
head. "I wouldn't waste the breath for it."

Acair didn't move, didn't curse, didn't so much as shrug. He
simply held up his hand, and his older brothers, grumbling a bit,
began to speak in unison what Rùnach recognized as a very crude
spell of Diminishing.

How fortunate he knew the proper spell for that sort of thing.

It was half out in the air in front of him before he realized Aisling was shouting at him and understood what it was he was doing.
He drew his hand over his eyes. Uachdaran had told him to be

careful, hadn't he? He supposed it might be wise to take that coun-
sel a bit more seriously.

And then things took a turn Rùnach hadn't expected.

It took him a heartbeat to realize what that was coming toward
him and another heartbeat to shove Aisling inside behind him,
pray Iteach had gotten inside as well, then leap inside the house
and slam the door shut. The force of the spell crushed the door and
sent him flying down what he sincerely hoped was a hallway and
not something more sinister. He pulled himself together enough to
make werelight, then reached for Aisling who was sprawled on the
marble floor next to him.

"Are you all right?" he asked hoarsely.

She sat up and looked at him blearily. There was a thin trail of
blood running down the side of her head. "I'm not sure, actually."

Iteach hopped up onto her lap and rubbed his feline self against
her, purring loudly. Rùnach felt her head gingerly, then healed her
with a spell of Fadaire that didn't seem to care for their surroundings and was rather unwieldy in his hands, truth be told. He
wished he had the time to simply spend a fortnight doing nothing
but testing his magic and its limits. Perhaps later, when he was
sure they would manage to escape their current predicament.

He put his hand out and touched Aisling's cheek. "How are
you?" he asked.

"Better," she said breathlessly. "You?"

"I'll let you know in a minute or two."

He left Aisling holding their, ah, *cat* as he pushed himself to his
feet and went to see what was left of the front door. He was unsurprised by the strength of the spell of protection still intact on the
inside there, but he supposed he couldn't have expected anything
else. His father had been nothing if not fastidious about his own
personal safety. That of others in his care, perhaps not so much,
but Rùnach wasn't unhappy to be the beneficiary of that selfish-
ness at the moment.

He turned around in a circle, marveling at the opulence of his surroundings. He sent werelight bouncing down what turned out to be a very long passageway. A score of chandeliers caught that light and threw the shadows back against the walls. The sheer luxury he was seeing just in that passageway was dizzying. He had no idea how long ago his father had created the place where he stood, though perhaps it had been even before he had wed with Sarait. The one thing he was certain of was that his mother hadn't known of its existence.

"Rùnach?"

He turned and looked at Aisling who was standing behind him. "Aye?"

"There's something pulling at the spell guarding the door."

He realized that what was making him dizzy wasn't his astonishment over his father's luxurious hideout, it was that the spell guarding the front door was somehow being undermined as he stood there, as if a rushing river were pulling at its banks and continually washing them away.

Rùnach swore and dragged his hand through his hair. He was fairly sure their escape didn't lay through the front door, which left him with very few options. He didn't care for being trapped, though perhaps that was understating it. There was never a time, even in his long years of haunting Soilléir's chambers, that he hadn't had an exit strategy ready. He wasn't sure why the thought of having nowhere to run seemed so suffocating. He supposed it was that it had been drummed into his wee head by Keir for so many years that he should never find himself trapped by their father. Perhaps they had watched Gair drain too many mages of their power whilst those mages had cowered in corners like terrified rabbits.

He wove a spell of imperviousness, but that was unsteady and unruly beneath his hands. He cursed under his breath. It would have to do. He had nothing else to try.

He turned and hastily pulled Aisling to her feet. He held her briefly.

"We'll have to try the back way."

"Is there a back way?"

Her teeth were chattering. He couldn't say he blamed her.

"I can't imagine my father wouldn't have had one," he said grimly. "We'll just have to find it."

Quickly was what he didn't say, but she apparently heard it anyway.

He took her hand and walked swiftly down the passageway, pausing only to open doors and peer into rooms, though he honestly wasn't sure what he hoped to find. A window obscured by foliage? A door cut into the side of the mountain as the main entrance had been?

Aisling gasped suddenly, and it took no special powers of observation to understand why. It sounded as though the entire mountain was fair to coming down around their ears. He looked behind them and realized that hadn't been just his imagination. He could see the werelight being extinguished and the hallway collapsing.

"They're bringing the whole damned mountain down on us," he growled. He stopped, turned, and threw the first spell that came to his tongue toward the darkness, but it fell onto the floor, useless. He froze, then looked at Aisling. "We're in trouble."

"Why?" There was almost no sound to the word.

"Because this has become a magic sink."

"Magic sink?"

"Nothing will work here."

She drew her finger through the air, but it did nothing save send dust motes dancing—what he could see of them from the werelight that he realized had been growing progressively fainter the farther along the passageway they'd come.

"What now?" she breathed.

"There has to be a back way out," he said firmly. "My sire never would have built even a hut without one."

"Maybe he never intended to be found here."

"Perhaps not, but he still wouldn't have left himself without an escape."

Much like his own wont, something he supposed he would think about and shudder over later, when he was at his leisure. He took Aisling's hand, laced his fingers with hers, then nodded toward the darkness.

"Trust me."

"I do."

He supposed she might regret that, but he had no choice but to continue on. Turning back was now impossible. Even if he'd been able to claw through the rock—something he most certainly couldn't do—seven mages with his death on their minds would have been waiting for him there.

He walked swiftly with Aisling, keeping his hand skimming along walls. He ignored things that had once been on those walls but he had knocked off, spared the effort to wonder how his father had lit this part of his house without any magic to hand, and hoped he wasn't missing something in the dark.

It was slightly unnerving when he realized that the passageway was becoming narrower until they could no longer travel side by side. He pulled Aisling behind him and continued hurrying down the way until . . .

Until he realized there was nowhere else to go.

He pushed against the wall in front of him, but it was as solid as it was no doubt meant to be. He started to turn back, but he realized that wasn't possible either. What was behind them wasn't spell; it was rubble. He and Aisling were trapped in a space that hardly allowed them to turn about. He had no doubt they would run out of air to breathe sooner rather than later and then they would die.

He put his arms around her and pulled her close. He wasn't sure if he was the one shaking or if it was her. Perhaps at that point, it didn't matter. He took as deep a breath as he dared.

"I fear I've led us into a trap," he admitted slowly. "I am so sorry."

She shook her head; he could feel her do it. "You couldn't have done anything else."

He closed his eyes and tried to memorize the feeling of her in his arms. The memory of it might be the only thing he carried with him into that undiscovered place in the east where there was reportedly no more sorrow and no more pain.

"Would this be an inappropriate time," he said finally, "to ask you for your hand?"

She shivered. "Ridiculous."

He smiled against her hair. "It isn't."

"You're just saying that because we're going to die."

"Aisling, we could be standing in the midst of the very roomy and quite endless plains of Ailean and I would be asking the same thing."

"You could have anyone," she said with a sigh.

"As could you," he countered, "but I want you. You'll have to decide for yourself. Or are there lads I must needs push out of my way before you look at me twice?"

He could feel her reach up and touch his cheek. "I can't see you—oh, wait." She lifted her head from his shoulder and apparently looked up at him. "I can see the runes on your brow. You know, Rùnach, I believe Weger's mark did take. Twice."

"No wonder my brow hu—" He froze. "What did you say?"

"I said something about your runes."

Her voice had begun to sound rather far away. He supposed he understood that, because he was becoming lightheaded. He held up his right hand and saw a very faint outline of the rune Còir had given him.

The rune of Opening.

"Your cousin's rune?" she whispered.

"Can you see it?" he asked in surprise.

"Aye, but I hadn't noticed it until you said that's what it was. Don't you remember?"

Rùnach promised himself a long rest when their task was done. That he was starting to talk to himself without realizing it was rather alarming. "Nay, I don't remember saying anything about it. But I can see it as well."

"Will it work?"

"I don't know how to use it," he said frankly. "They're gifts, not weapons."

"Is this one like the runes your grandfather gave you?"

"Nay," he said slowly. "Còir said it would work all on its own. He wouldn't have said that if it weren't true, given that he'd gouged it out of his own flesh."

"Perhaps you must do the same."

"I think my ears are failing me," he said grimly, "for I'm almost sure you just said the word *gouge* when speaking about my flesh."

She laughed a little. "I believe your choices are to help me pull Còir's handkerchief out of my pocket and have him rescue us, or you use your grandfather's knife on your hand."

Well, the first was definitely something he wasn't quite ready to resort to yet. As for the other, she had certainly used his grandfather's knife on his hand already. Or, rather, Uachdaran had. Rùnach supposed of all the things he could entertain as his last thoughts, that morning in Uachdaran's solar was at the end of his list.

"I can't reach it—ouch, damn you, Iteach—"

He had no idea what shape his horse had taken, but he had the feeling it was serpentine in nature. He took the haft of his knife from something with fangs, ignored the feeling of that serpent slithering back down his leg, then shifted so he could try to use the knife.

"Here, let me," Aisling said.

It hurt less than he expected, but he was absolutely dumbfounded to see the rune impaled through the middle on the tip of an enspelled knife. It glowed softly in the gloom.

"Perhaps they do come with power of their own," Aisling whispered.

"So the tales go," Rùnach said, "though I've never seen it done."

"Something to write down for future generations, then."

"Our children will appreciate it, I'm sure."

"Children?"

"Didn't you say me aye?"

She laughed a little, though it sounded a rather sick laugh. "I don't remember."

"I'm sure of it."

She coughed. "Use the rune, Rùnach, before we perish."

He wasn't at all sure it would work as promised, but he had no choice but to try. He took a careful breath, then flung the rune off the knife against the solid rock wall in front of him.

The wall gave way with a mighty explosion of silver and gold. Rùnach felt the floor disappear from beneath his feet and barely managed to make a grab for Aisling before they both fell into icy cold water.

It was very deep, something he realized as he resurfaced, coughing and gasping for air. He assumed Iteach would manage to keep himself afloat and concentrated on getting himself and Aisling out of the middle of the rushing waters and over to the side, if that sort of getting was possible. The hillside sounded as if it were still coming down above their head, which added greatly to his haste. He pulled Aisling's arm around his neck and struggled to keep them both from drowning.

"Upstream," he gasped.

She was too busy coughing to talk, but she did nod vigorously. He winced at the feeling of needles going into his back, then realized it was just his horse, clinging to him as if he were a raft. Why Iteach couldn't have chosen the shape of a fish, he didn't know. If they survived, he would be having a stern talk with the beast about what shapes were and were not appropriate when death was looming. He let Aisling take his knife out of his hand at about the same time he realized that the knife was glowing.

As was a thin stream of magic he could see running along the wall to his right. He didn't imagine the current was any weaker there, but perhaps it was. It was worth a try. He worked his way over, fighting against the drag, until he managed to get his fingers into a crack in the rock.

The magic—and aye, he could see that was what it was—found Aisling and swirled around her, spinning in a way that seemed vaguely familiar. It considered him for a moment or two, sentient bit of business that it was, then it encircled him as well. He realized with a start it was the magic of Bruadair.

"I want light," Aisling gasped.

The magic smiled, then the entire tunnel exploded into a riot of colors so bright, they almost blinded him.

Aisling shoved the knife into his hand before she gasped once more, then fainted.

He caught her before she washed away, then decided he should make a list of people he intended to speak badly of and at great length. First on the list would be Acair, for walling them into the side of the mountain, but coming a close second was Uachdaran of Léige, for being right, as usual. He held on to his knife and Aisling both, struggling to keep her head above water as he clawed his way upstream.

Rocks continued to fall into the water behind him, filling in the tunnel that had obviously been a much larger waterway at some point. He didn't spare the breath to curse, but he certainly thought vile thoughts. It was his father's bloody bolt-hole all over again, only this time Aisling was a dead weight in his arms and he was going to drown if something didn't change very soon.

He fought his way the only direction he could go, which was forward. He had to ignore the collapsing of the tunnel on his heels because thinking about it robbed him of breath.

So close to another chance at the life he'd given up, only now perhaps with a woman he had grown to love.

Taken again by his father's magic personified by his bastard brother—

He pushed aside the thoughts that didn't particularly feel as if they had come from inside his own heart and gritted his teeth. He would not give in, would not give up. Not when there was a possibility of escape.

Aisling came to with a jerk, almost causing him to lose his hold on her.

"Where—oh."

"Aye," he gasped. "That's where we are."

He ran into a bit of protruding rock with his hand, which felt about as if he'd slammed his hand into, of all things, solid rock. A little investigating revealed it to be a slight shelf, but dragging himself and Aisling both onto it was simply beyond him. He settled for clinging to it in an effort to very briefly catch his breath.

"Up ahead," Aisling said, spitting out water that seemed determined to splash them both in the face. "Just a bit farther."

"What do you see?" he managed.

"I don't see anything." She was silent for several very long minutes. "The magic is telling me there is a way out."

"Then, by all means, let's listen," he said frankly. It was for damned sure he had no solutions and a serious lack of energy.

"I'll use the wall as well. Let me get ahead of you."

He didn't want her to, but he wasn't sure they had a choice. He waited for her to move in front of him, then took a moment to shove his knife down the side of his boot. He clung with her to whatever bits of wall protruded enough to be useful. Their progress was agonizingly slow, made worse by the relentless chill of the water. Rùnach continued on until he realized he simply couldn't go any farther. He wedged his fingers into another crack in the wall and looked at Aisling.

The magic swirled up and around her. Ethereal wasn't quite the word he would have used to describe her at the moment. Terrifying was perhaps closer to the mark.

"Who *are* you?" he managed.

She smiled and the magic smiled as well. Rùnach thought he might want to lie down very soon before he simply fell over from shock.

"I'm someone who is very fond of you," she said loudly over the rushing of the water.

"Good thing, since you're going to wed me."

She rolled her eyes, the heartless wench, then put her hand over his that was wedged into the rock.

"We can open this here," she said.

"I'm not going to ask how you know that," he said, finding that he was too cold even to shiver. "Pray it leads somewhere warm." He spoke the spell to make werelight, but the ball that sprang to life above his head only spluttered feebly. He looked at Aisling. "You try."

She blinked. "I have no magic."

"Try it anyway."

She opened her mouth, then shut it with a snap. "I have no idea how." She looked at him seriously. "You'll have to help me."

He put his arm around her, pulled her close, and kissed her.

"I love you," he said simply.

She put her arms around his neck and held on so tightly, he almost asked her to stop. But the return sentiment she whispered in his ear was enough to convince him that he was most certainly not going to do anything but hold her close and not say anything about her squeezing the very breath out of him.

"Very well," he said hoarsely as she released him just far enough to look at him. "It's easy. You take the words and just say them."

"But how do they become a spell?"

He shrugged. "They draw on the power of the magic in your blood."

She looked at him in alarm. "But I don't have any magic in my blood."

"I believe there's magic here that disagrees." He paused, then looked at her. "I can't believe we're this close to death and this is the conversation we're having."

"And I can't believe you can talk so much."

He laughed, because he couldn't help it. "So said my dam on more than one occasion."

She kissed him, artlessly and with a joy that almost was his undoing.

"Be quiet and tell me what to do."

He took a deep breath, turned away to cough out the water that had come with it, then nodded. "If the magic is not yours by bloodright, then you use the words but command them to pull their power from themselves. Less simple, but doable."

She shook her head. "I can hardly believe I'm asking this—"

"But what is the spell?"

She nodded.

He gave her the simplest spell of werelight he could think of, one of Croxteth, not Fadaire. He supposed Fadaire would have done just as well, but he wanted fast and to the point. Aisling looked at him, as terrified as he'd ever seen her, then lifted her chin and nodded. Rùnach smiled. Weger would have been proud. Aisling repeated the words faithfully, though her teeth were chattering almost too fiercely for her words to be understandable.

He watched the words come out of her mouth, watched the magic in the river leap up and catch them, then continued to watch in absolute astonishment as the magic took her words and translated them into whatever Bruadairian magic it seemed to be. Aisling paused, then repeated the spell the magic itself had given her. It was Deuraich, he supposed, or perhaps a more magical version of it—

Suddenly a soft, almost painfully beautiful light sprang to life above them. He gaped at it in astonishment. He supposed he could have written quite a thick scholarly paper on the various properties of different magic and how they took shape in light alone. Goodness knows the headmaster of Buidseachd had done it and Rùnach had had to continually pinch himself to stay awake through the reading of it. If he were to compare what he was seeing at present with his own magic, he would have said that whilst Fadaire produced a light that was aggressively beautiful, the light that Aisling had called was . . .

Like something from a dream.

"So," he said casually, as casually as a man could whilst clinging to a rock wall to keep from washing away to his death, "you said the magic told you there was a way out?"

"Aye," she said uneasily.

"Here?"

She nodded.

"Well, then let's try something else, shall we?" he suggested cheerfully.

"Wait," she said. She listened, then she looked at him. "It wants us to do it together."

"Does it?" he asked in surprise. "Why?"

"It likes you."

"Well, there's a mercy," he said with feeling, though the feeling he had most strongly was one of not being able to catch his breath. It might have been from the icy water, or it might have been from his surprise. He sincerely hoped he would have the time to decide. "Very well, we'll do it together. Let's hope it doesn't blow a hole through the entire mountain, though I wouldn't mind seeing some sunshine."

"Rùnach, I don't know how I feel about this."

"Magic, or wielding it with me?"

"Oh, it isn't you I mind," she said. She paused. "I'm just not sure what to think."

He wasn't either, but he wasn't about to say as much. He put his arm around her and pulled her close, under his hand that was wedged into the rock. He nodded at the wall.

"Let's get through that, then we'll talk. We'll try Croxteth again, because I have absolutely no idea what your magic would consider a proper spell. That, and Croxteth generally comes most easily to hand. Here is the spell."

He gave the spell, then listened to her repeat it back. Her words were barely audible, but he felt the river take note—and not just the part from Bruadair. It occurred to him at that moment that whilst the bulk of the river might have had its start as a modest stream, that wasn't what had turned it into the bone-chilling flow that it was at present. It was magic, and not of a pleasant sort. Why the Bruadairian magic—and he would have asked it what it called itself if he'd had the presence of mind to do so—endured its company, he couldn't have said. He supposed it didn't have much choice.

"Let's try," he said. "Ready?"

She nodded. He took a deep breath, felt Aisling put her hand over his, then they spoke the words together.

And the world exploded.

The stream of magic from Bruadair diverted immediately into the new course, carrying them along with it. Rùnach would have been relieved, but it was too powerful and almost suffocating. He managed to keep hold of Aisling, but only just. He went under more times than he cared to count and he was fairly sure Aisling had done the same.

He had no idea how long that continued, though he suspected it was measured in hours, not minutes. There came a point when he could no longer demarcate the boundary between dreaming and consciousness. He could only clutch Aisling by the hand and try to keep his head above water. The only thing that saved them, perhaps, was the fact that the water had lost most of its chill. That hardly made up, though, for the endless rushing that carried him too quickly past anything he might have wanted to hold on to.

At the moment when he was convinced he would drown and take Aisling down with him, he found himself running up hard against what turned out to be a ledge. Iteach crawled off his shoulder onto it, shaking and complaining. Rùnach realized only then that his damned horse had been clinging to him the entire time. He left his pony-turned-tabby to his immediate ablutions and struggled to get Aisling up onto the rock outcropping. She made a valiant effort to pull him up after her, but he knew he was too heavy for her. He rested his head against the rock and closed his eyes until he realized Aisling was shouting at him and he had almost consigned himself to a watery grave.

He pulled himself up onto the ledge with the last of his strength, pulled Aisling to him, and put his arm around her. He managed to make sure her feet were out of the water, couldn't find the energy to think about his own, then laid his head down and closed his eyes.

"We'll try . . . again . . . later," he gasped, his chest burning with the effort of breathing. "Don't let go."

She shook her head, coughed, then fell silent. Rùnach would have used a spell to give them dry clothes, but given how his magic had behaved recently, he was afraid he would only make matters worse.

"Aisling."

"Aye?"

"Make . . . werelight."

She spoke his spell of Fadaire as if the words were priceless treasures she didn't dare get too close to. The light sprang to life and glowed softly above them. Rùnach looked at her and felt a strange lassitude come over him. It wasn't mere weariness, of that he was certain. Aisling was already senseless. He didn't want to join her, but he realized he had no choice. He sent Iteach a useful thought about guarding them, then succumbed to something he couldn't name.

He could only hope it wasn't the curse Aisling had been certain would take her life. There was too much left to do. He had to return her country to her king. He wanted to find a dreamspinner and ask them about their art. He had to find out what Acair was doing and why he wanted so badly the book Rùnach had in his pack, the one he was rather glad he'd wrapped in a spell or two to keep it dry and un-noticed.

He also wanted to find out just what in the hell Soilléir of Cothromaiche was doing right in the middle of everything.

"Rùnach, there's something above us."

He could hardly muster the energy to look up. He thought he might have seen light, but he wasn't sure. He actually was convinced he was dreaming. He wrapped his arms around Aisling and held on tightly.

"There's someone peering down at us from above," she said suddenly.

"Is it Acair?"

"Nay, I don't think so."

"Then if you aren't dreaming, perhaps they'll haul us up to safety and I can go have a nap."

A nap he supposed he might be taking sooner rather than later. He realized then that he truly wasn't going to be able to fight the weariness any longer.

He closed his eyes and felt consciousness slip away.

Twenty-one

Aisling woke with a gasp.

That was becoming a bad habit she decided as she had to sit up, coughing, in order to regain her breath. She clutched the bedclothes beneath her fingers and was very grateful to find those there instead of the bottom of a rushing river. She looked around her quickly, not daring to hope she was in a place of safety.

The chamber gave nothing away, though it was very lovely. The bed had a carved, wooden canopy and the bedcurtains were fashioned from a very lovely brocade that said nothing to her past a soft *good morning*. She appreciated that, gave what of them she could reach a pat as she swung her legs to the floor, then parted the curtains to see what lay beyond.

There was a fireplace, a pair of comfortable chairs, and a dressing table with a mirror. An armoire stood guard against one wall and there was water set aside on a small table for her pleasure. The fire was polite but non-committal. It seemed to prefer that she toss another piece of wood onto its burning center rather than simply leap to life on its own. She found that somewhat refreshing, actually, given the fires she had been faced with over the past several days.

She had a wash, put on clothes that seemed to have been left for her on a chair, then opened the door and peeked out into the passageway. It was empty, which made her slightly nervous. She was in her proper form, so she had to assume she wasn't dead, but the lack of fellow-travelers along her road was a bit disconcerting.

Or, more particularly, the lack of a particular fellow-traveler.

She walked down the hallway carefully, keeping her ears attuned to any hint of anything useful. She was forced to admit that it was rather more difficult than not to negotiate a hall when the walls were simply walls and the floor gave no indication of who might have walked on it recently.

She continued on, though, because she had to believe at some point she would either run into Rùnach or someone who had seen him.

Unfortunately, all that wandering was accomplishing was to give her far too much time to think. She wasn't at all sure how she felt about her journey from Gair of Ceangail's lair to wherever she currently found herself. Seeing Rùnach's brothers standing there in a cluster had been unsettling, no doubt because she had sensed all too clearly their unpleasant magic. Being trapped in Gair's house, falling into that river, almost drowning before the magic had wrapped itself around her—

Speaking a spell and feeling the words leap forward to act according to their assigned responsibilities.

Perhaps more devastating still had been speaking that particular spell of opening *with* Rùnach.

It had been nothing like having the king of the dwarves send his power through her hands. Then, she had felt as if she'd been flung against an unyielding rock wall. With Rùnach, the power that had come through his hands over hers had been immense, true, but not nearly so unforgiving. She hadn't looked too closely at the glamour that covered King Sìle's land, but she had the feeling it was akin to the power Rùnach had put behind the last word of her spell: beautiful, but full of an unrelenting elven magic that stretched back into times that had faded into dreams. She had wanted to weep for the beauty of it.

She wanted to weep from other things as well, namely that she had actually used magic and had it do as she'd asked, but perhaps she would do that later. For now, she wanted to find Rùnach and make sure he was unharmed.

She continued on until she found a set of doors that looked fairly substantial, though no guards stood before them. When she put her hand on the bar to open them, she was informed in stately tones that she was preparing to enter King Seannair's audience hall and would she be so good as to refrain from turning cartwheels down the approach to the dais, filching tassels from the tapestries, or taking a turn on the king's chair. She pulled her hand back, thought about what she'd heard, then smiled.

She liked where she was.

She considered the doors. "I don't suppose," she said slowly, "that you know where Prince Rùnach is, do you?" *Or if he's alive* was what she wanted to add, but she couldn't bring herself to.

"I do."

Aisling whirled around and found a tall, handsome man standing there. He wasn't an elf, though he didn't seem to be very ordinary either. He was, she had to admit, extremely handsome. He was also looking at her as if he'd seen something he hadn't expected.

"Oh, I see," he said.

Aisling patted herself surreptitiously, grateful beyond measure that she was covered in all the proper places instead of having left her borrowed chamber in her nightclothes.

"I'm sorry," she said. "I'm lost."

"Consider yourself found." The man made her a low bow. "I am Astar, at your service." He smiled. "Too far away from the throne to be a bother but close enough to have my grandfather the king glare at me on occasion."

"Is that a comfortable place?" she asked.

"Very. Now, if I might be so bold, I would guess that you are Aisling of Bruadair."

She considered him. "Did you read that on my soul?"

"Good heavens, nay. Rùnach told me. Actually, I believe his exact words were, 'Astar, you obnoxious bit of lichen on the family tree, go stand guard outside my lady Aisling's door and lead her this way when she wakes." He smiled. "Or words to that effect. Or that might have been my uncle Soilléir. Honestly, I can't remember, but I will take you to the kitchens just the same."

Aisling smiled. "I would like that."

"Perhaps I'll manage another breakfast whilst we're there, though I suppose it's coming up against luncheon." He shrugged. "I win either way."

She supposed he did. For all she knew, she might benefit as well, so she took his arm and found it was a very odd sensation to be escorted anywhere by anyone besides Rùnach.

The kitchen seemed very large, though she supposed she might not be the best judge of that sort of thing. It was a comfortable place, though, with a pair of large hearths for cooking and many tables for the preparation of meals. Rùnach was sitting in front of one of those hearths, chatting amicably with a blond man who seemed to be telling him some amusing anecdote or other.

Rùnach glanced over his shoulder, saw her, then stood immediately. Aisling supposed she shouldn't have been so relieved to see him, but the journey had been difficult and the possibility of never seeing him again . . .

"Thank you, Astar, for safely delivering my lady to me," he said, starting toward her. "You may let go of her now."

Astar rolled his eyes. "Possessive, aren't we?"

"Very. Go find your own woman." Rùnach took her hand, looked at her for a moment or two, then opened his arms.

Aisling walked into his embrace because she had the feeling her escort wouldn't mind. The kitchen was empty save the man near the fire, and perhaps he wouldn't think her indiscreet either.

"So that's how it is?" Astar said, sighing.

"That's how it is," Rùnach said. "I believe this is the moment at which I bid you farewell and watch you trot off to look for greener pastures."

"Rùnach, old thing, you've been sending me off to other pastures for as long as I've known you."

"Let's not discuss the reasons why, shall we?"

"If you insist. A good morning to you all."

Aisling heard footsteps going off to points unknown. She remained in Rùnach's embrace for several minutes in silence, then she pulled back and looked at him.

"How are you?"

"How are *you*?" he asked, smiling.

"I think I was dreaming in that river," she said promptly. "If not, I'm going to pretend I was."

"You can cling to that for a bit, I suppose," he said. He nodded toward the fire. "Why don't you come take your ease by the fire? There's someone I want you to meet."

Aisling let him take her hand and lead her over to the fire. The man who had been sitting there rose, turned, and smiled at her. She looked at him, blinked, then felt her mouth fall open.

It was the fop who had saved her from encountering her parents on the day she'd fled Bruadair.

She took a step backward before she thought about it, then when she thought about it, she took a step forward. She pointed at him with a hand that wasn't at all steady. "You," she accused.

The man lifted an eyebrow. "Me?"

Aisling looked at Rùnach. "Who is that?"

Rùnach looked at her, then at the man standing there. "I think there is a tale here I might like to hear."

"Introductions first," Aisling said. "I continue to encounter people from my past who aided me in leaving Beul."

The blond man inclined his head. "I am Soilléir," he said. "Just Soilléir."

Rùnach pursed his lips as he drew her over to sit in his chair. "Don't listen to him. He is the youngest son of the crown prince of Cothromaiche and grandson of the king. He is a master at the schools of wizardry, all on his own substantial merits." He fetched a chair of his own, then sat down next to her. "Prince Soilléir, this is Aisling of Bruadair."

Aisling looked at Rùnach in surprise. "This was the master you knew at the schools of wizardry."

Rùnach nodded, though he was watching her with a thoughtful frown. "I owe him my life, I'll admit it freely." He studied her a bit longer. "I'm not sure how this is possible, but you seem to know him."

Aisling gestured at Soilléir. "He was the fop."

Rùnach blinked, then smiled. "The fop? What do you mean?"

"The man who stood in front of me in Beul and blocked my view of my parents as they left their restaurant." She looked at Soilléir. "Or, actually, perhaps you blocked their view of me."

Soilléir smiled faintly. "That seems more likely."

"Wait a moment," Rùnach said, shaking his head as if he couldn't quite believe what he was hearing. "You were in Beul?"

"Well—"

"He most definitely was," Aisling said. "Not only did he hide me from my parents, he helped me during part of my flight to the border crossing." She looked at Rùnach. "I'm sure of it."

Rùnach sat back and looked at Soilléir as if he'd never seen him before. "You interfered."

Soilléir only smiled faintly. "I thought a bit of aid wouldn't go amiss."

"You thought a bit of aid wouldn't go amiss," Rùnach repeated incredulously. "You? *You* interfered in the events of the world?"

Aisling leaned closer to Rùnach. "Does he not usually?"

"Never," Rùnach said. "I have never in the entirety of my life that I've known him seen him interfere in the course of events."

"I did once," Soilléir said mildly.

Rùnach snorted. "When?"

"Several fortnights ago when your lady was about to be discovered by souls who didn't have her best interests at heart."

Aisling wasn't sure who she should have been looking at more closely. Prince Soilléir looked as if he were torn between being slightly amused and slightly unsettled. Rùnach looked as if he'd just eaten something that disagreed with him quite violently. He looked at her.

"He saved you."

"For which I'm very grateful," she said. "Does he not save very many?"

"None," Rùnach said, "though it isn't from a lack of mercy. It goes against his—" He looked at Soilléir. "What would you call it, my lord?"

"My code," Soilléir said gravely. "Which has cost many perhaps more pain than was necessary."

She felt a little faint. "Then why me?"

"Ah, well, that is a mystery I believe you two will have to solve for yourselves." Soilléir rose gracefully. "I've provided you with a safe haven. The rest is up to you."

Aisling felt her mouth fall open. Rùnach was in a similar state.

"That's it?" he asked incredulously. "That is all you're going to say? You *interfered*."

Soilléir shrugged. "I'll leave you to discovering why. My

grandfather has a library. You can find your way around in it, don't you think?"

"What I think isn't fit for a lady's ears," Rùnach said with a snort, "which is why I'll keep it to myself. And out of gratitude for our many years of friendship, I'll refrain from swearing at you. Somehow, though, I don't think we're going to find the answers we're looking for in the library, not even your grandfather's."

"What you mean is you don't want to spend the time looking for them," Soilléir said dryly. "Why should I do your research for you?"

"Penance," Rùnach said. "There's a word you can chew on for a bit, if you like."

Soilléir hesitated, then resumed his seat with a sigh. "Very well. I'll give you one question a piece."

"Three," Aisling said, then realized Rùnach had said the same thing. She smiled at him. "We've traveled together for too long."

"Imagine our conversation after we've been wed for a decade," he said with a smile, then he turned a stern look on their host. "Three each."

"If I can," Soilléir said carefully. "Ladies first, as always."

Aisling looked at him seriously. "Will you answer with absolute honesty?"

Soilléir closed his eyes briefly, then looked at her. "I'm sorry, Aisling," he said quietly. "I know your life to this point has been difficult. And aye, I will answer anything you ask me now with absolute honesty."

"Why was I able to spin Rùnach's power out from under his scars that were covered by the rune his mother put there, why can I spin air, and why was I lied to for the whole of my life?"

Soilléir didn't look terribly surprised by the questions, though he did hesitate. "Those are difficult questions indeed. Because I'm a coward, why don't I answer Rùnach's questions first?"

"Coward," Rùnach said with a snort. "You've never had a cowardly moment in your life."

"You might be surprised," Soilléir said. "Aisling, does that suit?"

"Do you know what Rùnach will ask?" she asked suspiciously.

"I have known your friend there for many years," Soilléir said with a smile. "I think I could hazard a guess." He looked at Rùnach. "What do dreamweavers weave?"

"And who spins it," Rùnach said bluntly. "Also, who is Sglaimir and why does his acquisition of Bruadair's magic not show? And where has he hidden it?"

"That was five questions in total, which you know very well, but out of gratitude for your having poured wine for my guests for so long, I will humor you." Soilléir leaned forward with his elbows on his knees and looked at them seriously. "There are many weavers in Bruadair, as you might imagine. Tailors must have cloth and customers must have clothing. But that weaving happens on ordinary looms, as our Aisling could readily attest."

Aisling supposed it might be best to refrain from commenting on that.

"As for anything else—oh, what?"

Aisling realized Soilléir had stopped speaking. Well, to them, at least. He had risen and walked over to the door of the kitchens to confer with someone who apparently required his full attention.

"I'm going to kill him," Rùnach muttered under his breath.

Aisling looked at him in surprise. "Why?"

"Just wait."

Soilléir hastened back over to them and smiled apologetically. "I'm afraid I've been called away."

"Of course you have," Rùnach said sourly.

"Duty requires it. You see, Grandfather recently dug his crown out from the barrel of dried beans where he keeps it and my father and brothers trotted out their finery to accompany him to the

Council of Kings a handful of days ago, leaving me to see to things." He smiled. "We'll chat later, I'm sure."

Aisling watched him walk toward the door, then looked at Rùnach. "Is there a meeting of this council?"

"Of course not," Rùnach said shortly. "More than likely what's happened is the aforementioned lads have gone fishing and Soilléir heard tell of some sort of dessert laid out in his grandfather's fanciest audience chamber. I would hazard a guess he wants to have at it whilst he doesn't need to fight his way through the press at table."

She would have chided him for not being serious, but perhaps in Cothromaiche dessert was serious business, indeed. She thought to chide Soilléir about it, but realized he had stopped at the door to the kitchen. She watched for a moment or two as he seemingly wrestled with himself before he turned and looked at them.

She felt a hush descend. She'd felt that sort of thing before and it had always boded ill for her peace of mind. She groped for Rùnach's hand only to realize he was doing the same thing. His hand was warm and secure around hers, which she supposed hid the fact that her hand was trembling.

Soilléir walked over to them, then sat back down in his chair. He looked at them gravely. "There are, from what I understand, seven dreamspinners who provide what the weavers then use in their art."

"Ordinary weavers, or dreamweavers?" Runach asked.

Soilléir only smiled. Aisling supposed that was answer enough.

"And these dreamspinners," Rùnach said slowly. "What do they spin?"

"From what I understand," Soilléir continued, "the seventh and most powerful of them all was slain several years ago."

Aisling looked at Rùnach. "He's not answering our questions."

"He does that," Rùnach said. He turned to Soilléir. "How many is several? Years, that is."

Soilléir considered for much longer than Aisling thought he might have needed to, but perhaps he had terrible tidings to give them. He sighed.

"A score and six, to be exact. Her successor, again from what I understand, was far too young to take her rightful place in that most exclusive of Guilds, so she was sent to foster in the most unlikely and, it must be said, not ideal of places."

"And where was that?" Rùnach asked.

"A family where the father suspected her heritage, but was forbidden to speak of it. The mother was told nothing and she was— well, let's just say she was inspired to have a lack of curiosity."

"Twenty-six years ago," Rùnach said, frowning thoughtfully. He looked at Soilléir. "How long ago were Frèam and Leaghra deposed?"

"Close to that," Soilléir conceded. "Give or take a year or two."

"What happened to that dreamspinner?" Rùnach asked. "Is she still alive?"

"As for that dreamspinner," Soilléir said quietly, "hiding her was the only way to save her life and, as it happens, the balance of the world."

And with that, he rose and walked from the kitchen.

Aisling was half out of her chair before she realized there was no point. Soilléir had slipped out the door and was no doubt trotting briskly to wherever he'd been intending to go. She sank back down onto the wooden seat, then looked at Rùnach.

He was watching her closely. In fact, his scrutiny was making her a little nervous.

"What?" she asked faintly.

He smiled, then leaned over and kissed her. "You did agree to wed me, didn't you?"

"Before or after our last encounter with death?"

He laughed a little. "I believe, my dearest Aisling, that it was in the middle of that encounter." He kissed her hand, then rose, pull-ing her up with him. "Let's go walk."

"You're thinking."

"And you aren't?"

She took a deep breath. "I'm not sure I want to."

He only smiled, then hummed pleasantly as he led her from the kitchens and walked with her through passageways. The keep was lovely, she had to admit, but there was nothing particularly magi-cal about it. Perhaps Soilléir and his kin preferred it that way. It certainly made for a quieter existence.

She walked with Rùnach through passageways that told no tales, past chambers that didn't reveal their secrets, and out into a garden where the trees didn't wave their branches and clamor for her attention. They simply grew, as if they were happy with their lot in life and felt no need to discuss it further. She realized at that moment just how . . . well, how truly magnificent Seanagarra had been. It wasn't that wherever they were—the palace of Cothromaiche, she supposed—wasn't lovely, for it was. The gar-den stretched out for quite a distance, followed by pastures, then mountains that rose up majestically. There was at the very least ample room for pacing.

When she realized she could walk no farther, she stopped and looked at Rùnach.

"Do you think he knows more than he's telling us?"

Rùnach pulled her over to sit next to him on a bench beneath a tree laden with quite lovely small white flowers. "Soilléir always knows far more than he tells."

"If we were to sneak up from behind, clout him over the head, then bind him to a chair where he couldn't escape, could we tor-ture answers out of him?"

Rùnach smiled. "I'm not sure I've mentioned the spells he holds."

"Are they worse than your father's?" she asked, then she winced. "I mean—"

"Just that, and rightly so." He shrugged lightly. "My father would have cut off his own right arm to have had even a single spell of essence changing. Soilléir knows them all."

"Do you know them all?"

He laughed a little, uneasily. "Actually, I do. He gave them to me when I had no magic, out of pity no doubt."

"I do doubt that. So what do these spells do?"

"Change things," he said. "But permanently, not just for the moment or the duration of the spell."

She shivered in spite of herself. "That sounds very dangerous."

"They are terribly dangerous, which is why he rarely gives them out. The tests a mage must pass before Soilléir trusts him with any of them are unrelentingly terrible." He sighed. "I watched him reduce Miach of Neroche to the point where he had no more tears to shed, though he didn't know I was standing in the shadows, watching."

"And you didn't tell him," she guessed.

"There would never be a point in that," Rùnach said. "He might realize as much, if he were to actually think about it. But nay, Soilléir doesn't share his spells very often and he uses them less often still. He prefers to simply stand and watch, if possible. Unless there is a compelling need at which point he generally simply offers a word or two and leaves it at that."

She looked at her hand in his for a moment or two, then met his eyes. "He didn't offer a word or two to me."

"Nay, love," Rùnach said, "he certainly didn't, did he?"

"I wonder why."

"You know, Aisling, I wonder why as well."

She looked at him quickly because there was something in his tone that told her he wasn't wondering much at all. She tried to swallow, but found it almost impossible.

"I was in the wrong place—"

Rùnach shook his head. "I don't believe that."

She licked her lips, uselessly. "Then what do you believe?"

He considered for a bit, then looked at her. "I think when it comes to Soilléir of Cothromaiche, there are no coincidences. If he helped you in Beul, which we know he did, he did so for a very good reason."

"To send me off on a quest?" she asked. "For a mercenary?"

"On a quest," he said, "but not for a mercenary."

She jumped up because she had to pace or she was going to make noises she was very sure would frighten them both. She pulled Rùnach up with her and towed him along behind her as she walked the paths that seemed to present themselves to her as she required. She walked until she found herself quite out of breath, only then realizing that she had been running. She put her hand over her chest and struggled to catch her breath, but couldn't seem to.

"What are you talking about?" she said finally.

He looked at her seriously. "I think we can safely say that in Bruadair there are dreamweavers. Thanks to Soilléir, we now know there are dreamspinners."

"Six of them, at least."

He nodded. "Six of them. It would be interesting to know what happened to the seventh, the most powerful of them all, wouldn't it?"

"Fascinating," she agreed.

"We know that she—or he, perhaps—had been slain because Soilléir said as much, didn't he?"

She nodded uneasily.

"And if that most powerful of dreamspinners had had a successor who was a babe when the chief dreamspinner was slain—how many years ago did Soilléir say?"

She looked at him and knew very well that he knew exactly the count. "A score and six years," she whispered.

"Aye, a score and six years," he said. "The wee one was placed with a family, then hidden away elsewhere, if I'm understanding Soilléir aright."

"Let's go run some more."

He didn't move. "If you wanted to hide a spinner, Aisling, where is the one place in Bruadair you would put her?"

"I don't know," she said miserably. She pulled her hand away from his. "I have to run."

"I'll come with you."

She would have asked him to come with her, of course, but she had no more breath for it. It was all she could do to stumble farther away from the palace, trying to outrun things she didn't want to know.

In time, Rùnach reached for her hand and pulled her back first to a walk, then into his arms. She was grateful for his aid in remaining on her feet, for she was certain she wouldn't have managed it on her own. She held on to him for as long as she could before she knew she had to speak. She pulled back and looked up at him.

"I am no one."

"Well, I disagree with that because you are definitely someone to me," he said easily, "but apparently it isn't just my opinion that matters."

She took a deep breath. "What are we going to do?"

"First, we're going to go find something to eat. Then we'll ransack Seannair's library for the sport of it. After that, we'll find Soilléir and see what details we can pry from him. Though I suspect," he said, smoothing her hair back from her face, "that we know all we need to know."

She shook her head. "I don't know anything."

"You know the seventh and most powerful dreamspinner has been dead for over a score of years," he said quietly. "I suspect that the lack of her presence has created a void that many unpleasant mages have tried to use for their own ends."

"And just what are we to do about that?" she asked, pulling out of his arms.

He clasped his hands behind his back. "Why don't we go to Bruadair, find the remaining six dreamspinners, and ask them a few questions? They might have a suggestion or two for us."

She dragged her sleeve across her eyes. "What has any of this to do with me?"

He lifted one shoulder in a half shrug. "You spin air. Fire, too. Oh, and water." He looked at her seriously. "In my grandmother's garden, whilst I slept, you took the dreams of the trees and flowers and—"

"Don't," she pled. "Please don't."

He simply looked at her, silently, for so long that she wondered if he would ever move again. She took a deep breath, then walked forward until she walked into his embrace. He wrapped his arms around her and rested his cheek against her hair. His cheek that had been scarred but was almost scarless thanks to the fact that she had taken his power and spun it out of him.

"If you wanted to hide a dreamspinner," he murmured, "where would you put her?"

Aisling felt a shudder start at the back of her neck, travel through her, then finish at her feet. It took her quite a long time before she thought she could answer.

"In a weaver's guild," she said finally.

"Any weaver's guild?"

A half sob escaped her before she could catch it. "The most horrific of them all."

"Where?"

"In Beul."

"Hmmm," he said. "I think you have something there."

She wanted to weep, but she was too terrified to weep. "It can't be . . . it's just not possible . . ." She held on to him tightly. "I can't do this."

"I understand, my love," he said very quietly. "I understand that perfectly."

She pulled back to look at him, then. "What did you do?" she asked, though she already knew the answer.

"I did what was needful."

"Alone?"

He shook his head. "I had my family."

"I have no family."

"You have me," he said simply. "Shall we wed today?"

She smiled, because she had the feeling he was utterly serious. "Your grandfather would be unhappy."

He returned her smile. "He might be, but only because he would want to escort you to the priest."

"I don't think he was slain," she said quietly, "on the plains of Ailean."

He paused, then shook his head. "I don't think so either. He's far too canny for that. Besides, he has a wedding to attend to when I can get you into a chapel somewhere. For all we know, there is a family somewhere in Bruadair who frets every day over your welfare." He froze. "I might have to ask your sire—who I seriously doubt will find himself slaving in a mine—for your hand."

"Ha," she said. "It would serve you right to be the one worrying for a change."

He took her face in his hands, kissed her softly, then put his arm around her. "Let's rest here for a bit, pry a few more details from our taciturn host, then we'll find our way across the border and see what answers lie there. Besides, you know how I love a good mystery."

"I don't want to solve any mysteries before breakfast," she said firmly. "Do you think if we hurry back to the palace now, there might be anything edible left in the king's audience chamber?"

He smiled. "Let's go see."

Aisling supposed they might not manage to arrive before Soilléir had done his duty to the tea tray, but perhaps they would find him half asleep on a sofa somewhere, too overcome from his desserts to properly fend off their questions.

Because she had several of those.

She wanted to know why he had been in Beul at precisely the right moment, not once but twice during her escape—the entire truth, not what he seemed to want to tell them. She wanted to know why Rùnach had found his book of spells that didn't contain his spells at Eòlas where he might not have looked otherwise. Had they been driven in that direction, or had it been happenstance?

She wanted to know if Sglaimir had any idea that all Bruadair's magic was being siphoned off by rivers that ran away from her country, in all likelihood under dwarvish palaces, and terminating in a place she couldn't yet name. And if he knew, why did he allow it? In return for more power or was there another reason?

But most of all, she wanted to know with absolute certainty why she had been lied to, the asking of which seemed to bring her full circle to almost where she'd begun. She was a simple weaver, parentless, friendless. Who would have gone to such lengths to have her out of her home country . . .

And why.

There were seven dreamspinners in Bruadair and the last one was missing, the one who had been but a wee babe twenty-six years ago, a wee babe who had been first fostered, then hidden away where no one could find her.

How coincidental that she should be exactly that age, have come from exactly those circumstances, and been helped out of her country into obscurity by a prince of Cothromaiche who never did such things normally after which she'd had the very great fortune to meet a magicless elven prince who had turned out to be so much more than could have been suspected at first.

So much more than could have been suspected at first.

She wondered how many other things that could apply to.

"There are always answers."

She looked up at Rùnach. "But do I want to ask the questions?"

He laughed a little. "That is a question only you can answer, I'm afraid."

"Are you going to stay with me whilst we find the answers?"

"Be a bit difficult to wed you if I'm off somewhere else, don't you think?"

"I suppose so."

He smiled. "You know, that almost sounds like an aye."

"It does almost, doesn't it?"

He looked at her in surprise, then laughed. "You are a heartless lass, Aisling of Bruadair." He stopped, pulled her into his arms, then held her close for a moment or two. "Let's go take our ease in peace and safety for a day or two, then we'll see about those answers perhaps neither of us particularly wants but definitely must have. At least this time, we won't be walking into darkness alone."

She nodded, then put her hand in his and walked with him back to the hall. She had thought that the bulk of her life had been spent alone, but now she was beginning to suspect there had been those watching over her unseen and unmarked. That was a great comfort, made perhaps even more dear thanks to the man walking alongside her, humming snatches of things she was quite certain she'd learned from the trees in his grandmother's garden.

She was going to have a few questions for those unmarked souls.

Aye, she was going to have several questions, indeed.